"This is ⋯ **children** ⋯ **so we'll do what we must. You'll marry me."**

"No⋯" Ciania said in a husk of a voice, her lips white.

Hen⋯ ⋯ a tested breath, frustration retu⋯ ⋯ flood of heat. "Did you hear wha⋯ ⋯ aid?"

"Ye⋯ ⋯ you. Fine. I'll live behind your iron ⋯ t—" She swallowed. "But I won⋯ ⋯ u."

He⋯ ⋯ up in what he knew was her stan⋯ ⋯ round face. His ears buzzed as he s⋯ ⋯ h her words. "What do you mea⋯

"I ⋯ ⋯ with you, but I won't *live* with you⋯ ⋯ ed and pulled her shoulders up defe⋯ ⋯ und her ears.

"Yo⋯ ⋯ t to sleep with me?" His heart bot⋯ ⋯ he couldn't mean that.

She ⋯ ⋯ looked away, blinking hard. "No⋯

"Lia⋯ ⋯ out of him as a breath of absolut⋯ ⋯ n.

The Sauveterre Siblings

Meet the world's most renowned family…

Angelique, Henri, Ramon and Trella—two sets of twins born to a wealthy French tycoon and his Spanish aristocrat wife. Fame, notoriety and an excess of bodyguards is the price of being part of their illustrious dynasty. And wherever the Sauveterre twins go, scandal is sure to follow!

They're protected by the best security money can buy—no one can break through their barriers… But what happens when each of these Sauveterre siblings meets the one person who can breach their heart…?

Meet the heirs to the Sauveterre fortune in Dani Collins's fabulous new quartet:

Pursued by the Desert Prince
March 2017

His Mistress with Two Secrets
April 2017

Ramon and Isadora's story
Coming soon!

Trella and Prince Xavier's story
Coming soon!

HIS MISTRESS WITH TWO SECRETS

BY
DANI COLLINS

First Published in Great Britain 2017
By Mills & Boon, an imprint of HarperCollins*Publishers*
1 London Bridge Street, London, SE1 9GF

© 2017 Dani Collins

ISBN: 978-0-263-92518-0

Our policy is to use papers that are natural, renewable and recyclable
products and made from wood grown in sustainable forests. The logging
and manufacturing processes conform to the legal environmental
regulations of the country of origin.

Printed and bound in Spain
by CPI, Barcelona

Canadian **Dani Collins** knew in high school that she wanted to write romance for a living. Twenty-five years later—after marrying her high school sweetheart, having two kids with him, working at several generic office jobs and submitting countless manuscripts—she got 'The Call'. Her first Mills & Boon novel won the Reviewers' Choice Award for Best First in Series from *RT Book Reviews*. She now works in her own office, writing romance.

Books by Dani Collins

Mills & Boon Modern Romance

The Secret Beneath the Veil
Bought by Her Italian Boss
Vows of Revenge
Seduced into the Greek's World
The Russian's Acquisition
An Heir to Bind Them
A Debt Paid in Passion
More than a Convenient Marriage?
No Longer Forbidden?

The Sauveterre Siblings

Pursued by the Desert Prince

The Wrong Heirs

The Marriage He Must Keep
The Consequence He Must Claim

Seven Sexy Sins

The Sheikh's Sinful Seduction

The 21st Century Gentleman's Club

The Ultimate Seduction

One Night With Consequences

Proof of Their Sin

Visit the Author Profile page
at millsandboon.co.uk for more titles.

Dear Reader,

Henri is the oldest of the Sauveterre twins. After his sister was kidnapped he decided never to marry and have children, fearing they would become targets. He doesn't resent being a twin, but he knows who he is beyond that label. He's very singular…likes control and routine. Life is unpredictable enough without improvising your way through it—that's his attitude.

Cinnia is also very practical, and independent to a fault. As far as mistresses go, she was the perfect match for Henri, demanding little from him. That was why he was so blindsided when she left him.

I adore it when this happens to our alpha males—when they are über-confident and think they have their lives well in hand and then…*wham!* The heroine straightens her spine and slams the door behind her.

Cinnia is pregnant, and she knows exactly how Henri will react. *Badly!* But if they can make the jump from defensive and aloof to realizing they are perfect for one another, they have a chance at real happiness. I'll let you turn the page and discover for yourself how they make out.

Enjoy!

Dani

Dedication

For my parents,
who are celebrating their 50th wedding anniversary
as I write this. Much love always from #1.

PROLOGUE

As she entered the clinic from the stairwell, Cinnia Whitley almost knocked the door into a woman standing inside. Cinnia murmured a distracted apology, thinking she might have seen her before, but not here. She would remember someone so tall and stiff and alert standing in that particular place.

Wait. Was she a guard? It was an odd place to hover. Maybe that's why she seemed so familiar. After spending two years with sober-faced watchmen dogging her movements, perhaps it wasn't the face she recognized so much as the attitude.

Because, if the woman was merely a relative waiting on a patient, there was a very comfortable lounge at the front of the clinic. The back entrance was for people like Cinnia, the paranoid ones who crept in through the building's underground car park in hopes of keeping her visit to this prenatal specialist strictly confidential.

Cinnia didn't bother speculating who the celebrity patient could be. She had bigger fish to fry. She was here for a scan to confirm suspicions on why she was expanding so quickly.

No, she kept thinking, absolutely refusing to entertain the most likely reason. She had a lot of work to get through in the next twenty-two weeks and had struggled to find time for another morning off for this test. If the doctor's suspicions were correct, her entire future would have to be recalibrated.

Twins? Really? *No.* Multiple births weren't even hereditary when they were identical and she thought only mothers passed along the fraternal trait. A father with an identical brother and two younger, identical twin sisters couldn't pass that to his offspring.

Could he?

Henri did whatever he wanted. She knew that much.

She did not miss that arrogance, or him, or the life he led with guards like that one dogging his every step, she assured herself with another flick of a glance at the woman by the door.

So why did she spend her mornings combing through online gossip pages, reading every scrap she could find about him? Reading that Henri was back to his old ways of dating and dropping was pure self-destruction, but at least there wasn't much written about that. His twin, Ramon, was stealing all the thunder, still racing and winning while doubling down with his own passionate exploits through a rotation of women who were loved and left.

The Sauveterres were a private lot, despite their domination of the media. But in her time with Henri, Cinnia had noticed that Ramon always seemed to make a splash in the papers when something was going on with the family, like he was deliberately pulling the attention.

Her breakup with Henri was two months ago. Old news by now. It must be Angelique he was trying to cover for.

The brothers were insanely protective of their younger sisters, which was understandable given Trella's kidnapping when she was a child. Angelique was the only one seen in public these days and was becoming quite notorious, what with her affair with the Prince of Zhamair—or rather both him *and* the Prince of Elazar, if the online rags were to be believed.

Cinnia frowned, still thinking there was something about the photo of Angelique with the Prince of Elazar that wasn't right. Impossibly, she had thought it was actually Trella in that photo, but Trella was a recluse. Cinnia had only met her in person a couple of times.

The nurse was on the phone and finally noticed her. Cinnia waved a greeting and tried to smile past her jumbled thoughts. Tried not to think of Henri and twins. It was too big and scary to absorb unless she was forced to.

The nurse indicated to a clerk that Cinnia was here. The clerk nodded and turned to the cabinet to pick out her file.

Cinnia loosened her scarf and started to unbutton her coat, pleased to be warm and dry when it was such a tremendously miserable day, even by London's late-February standards.

Behind her, a door to an exam room opened, startling her into stepping out of the way and turning.

"Oh. Excuse me," the woman said.

"My fault—" Cinnia began, then blurted, "Oh, my God!" as she recognized that model-like physique and those aristocratic features. "I was just thinking about you!"

"Cinnia!" Angelique beamed and they went in for a hug like long-lost sisters, affection squeezing Cinnia's arms tight around the other woman, her excitement completely overriding what should have been *way* more caution on her part.

The reality of Cinnia's situation hit belatedly and continued to strike in successive slaps over the next few seconds.

Cinnia felt Henri's sister stiffen as she came up against Cinnia's baby bump beneath the layers of her clothes.

Don't tell him, Cinnia thought with panic.

They drew back. Cinnia knew she wore a look of horror, which was awful when she was actually happy about the baby, happy to see—

"Oh, my *God*," Cinnia whispered. "I thought you were your sister."

Cinnia had always been able to tell the twins apart quite easily. It had been surprise and a quick glance and an even quicker assumption that had made her mistake Trella for Angelique. Trella never left the compound in Spain without one of her siblings accompanying her.

Did that mean Henri was here? Cinnia looked around with alarm, only seeing the guard.

Of course—that's why the guard seemed familiar. She'd seen her at Sus Brazos, the Sauveterre family home in Spain. This was Trella, even though there was nothing distinct to tell the women apart, Cinnia just knew by something in their demeanor. Angelique had that hint of reserve that Henri wore, while Trella had the radiance of warmth that Ramon projected.

Then it hit that not only was it odd for Trella to be out in public, with no family in sight, but *she was also in a prenatal clinic.*

"Oh. My. *God.*"

What was the normally cloistered Sauveterre twin doing in London? Holding a bottle of prenatal vitamins and looking guilty as hell? How did a woman who lived like a nun and had female guards get herself pregnant? Henri was going to lose his mind!

Trella tucked the bottle behind her back and opened her mouth, but only a weak *um* came out.

Cinnia's eyes were widening to the point they stung. She was pretty sure they were going to fall right out of her head.

She watched Trella's gaze narrow as the full scope of

where they were and why penetrated her side. Cinnia's blood pressure had been stable so far, but her limbs began to tingle and her head went so hot she felt like her hair was on fire. She was pretty sure whatever breaths she was managing to draw lost all their oxygen before hitting her lungs.

"Are you...okay?" Cinnia asked hesitantly. She didn't know exactly what Trella had been through when she had been kidnapped, but she knew it had left her afraid of men for a long time. Afraid of a lot of things.

Trella, being an enormously resilient and self-deprecating person, let out a choke of hysterical laughter and rolled her eyes. It was a "look where I am," and her shrug conveyed that she was dealing with an unplanned pregnancy, but not one caused by something traumatic.

"How about you?" she challenged with wry cheer, then sobered. She frowned at Cinnia's middle. "Is it...?" She glanced around.

Henri's. That's what she was asking.

Cinnia's eyes teared up. *Please don't tell him*, she silently pleaded.

This was part sitcom, part Greek tragedy. Her own hysterical laugh pressed for escape, but her tight throat wouldn't release it.

Trella straightened her spine so she was that little bit taller than Cinnia. She gave her wavy dark hair a toss.

"We'll pretend this didn't happen." She was a stunning woman in her midtwenties, but she looked nine years old, hiding stolen candy and bravely pretending it wasn't in her red-hot hand.

This was the sister Henri had told Cinnia had existed in his childhood, the brat who had driven him crazy getting herself into trouble, always needing her big brother to step in and fix it.

Cinnia wanted to hug her again. She was so proud of

Trella, even if conquering her past had led to a complicated future.

And she desperately wanted to share this moment with Henri, instinctively knowing that after the shock, this sign of healing in Trella would be a much-needed bright spot.

Or not. Worrying about any Sauveterre would sit heavily on him. Taking care of his mother and sisters was as much responsibility as he was willing to shoulder. That's why he'd drawn such a hard line against marrying and procreating.

A wistful sigh filled her, but she held it in. Ironic that she wanted to be there for him as he dealt with his sister's news knowing full well he would lose his mind once he learned Cinnia was carrying *his* child.

I told you from the beginning I would never marry you.

Her heart clenched afresh, abraded and stung. *Scorned.*

"Ms. Whitley," the nurse said behind her. "I can take you now."

"It's really good to see you," Cinnia said to Trella, holding out her arms for another quick hug. "I've missed all of you."

Most of Cinnia's interactions with Henri's family had been over the tablet, but she felt the loss of connection to the Sauveterre clan quite deeply.

"I would ask you to give my regards to everyone, but…" Cinnia trailed off.

Trella's arms were firm and strong around her. She pulled away slowly, tilting her head so they were eye-to-eye. Would her baby have those Sauveterre eyes, Cinnia wondered with a pang? *Babies?*

"You and I can stay in touch now," Trella said with a conspiratorial twitch at the corners of her mouth. Her expression sobered to concern. "*Can* I call you? I'd like to know why…"

Cinnia knew that keeping the pregnancy from Henri was a losing battle. She just wanted a plan in place before he found out so he wouldn't feel trapped. Trella was far too close to her siblings to keep her own pregnancy a secret from them for long. Once she spilled those beans, Cinnia's condition would be quick to follow.

But if she could buy a little time to get her ducks in a row, maybe find out exactly how many babies she was actually having…

She nodded. "If you're still in London at the end of the week, why don't we have dinner?"

CHAPTER ONE

Two years ago...

CINNIA WAS NOT a social climber, but her roommate, Vera, was. Cheerfully and without apology. Thus, when Vera wangled opening-night tickets from the owner of *the* hottest new nightclub in London, she demanded Cinnia accompany her.

"I told him about your title," Vera said. "That's how I got him to say yes to our coming."

"The title that belongs to my great-uncle a million times removed whom I've never met and who wouldn't know me from Eve?"

"I might have exaggerated how close you are. But I told him about your granny's vintage tiara and since his theme is 'flappers and gangsters,' and he wants window dressing, he said we could come as staff. No swag," Vera said with a dismayed wrinkle of her nose. "Just mingle with the guests. Be first on the dance floor, that sort of thing."

Cinnia was reluctant. Her weekends were her only time away from her job at a wealth management firm to put the pieces in place for striking out on her own. She had set September as her goal and had a mile-long list of to-dos to make it happen.

"You work too hard," Vera groaned. "Look at it as a

chance to rub elbows with potential clients. This will be wall-to-wall, top-tier, A-list celebs."

"That's not how it works."

Cinnia's mother saw a different opportunity when Cinnia spoke to her over the tablet. "Tell me I can't wear the tiara so I can tell Vera there's no point."

"Nonsense. We'll get my dress out of storage, too. It's time they both saw some use. You, too, for that matter." Her mother had purposely held a Roaring Twenties party on her tenth anniversary so she could wear her grandmother's modest, heirloom tiara. She had had a beaded dress made special for the occasion.

"You wouldn't get the tiara from the safe-deposit box when we were broke and I wanted to sell it, but you'll let me wear it to a nightclub?" Cinnia asked, askance.

"This is why I kept it, for you girls to wear on special occasions. Go. Have fun. There's bound to be some nice men there."

"Rich husbands, you mean? They don't sell them at the bar, Mum."

"Of course not. It will be an open bar for something like this, won't it?" her mother returned tartly.

There was a reason she and her sisters called their mum Mrs. Bennet. She was forever trying to find their golden ticket of a husband. There was also a reason she was so determined to do so. The Whitleys had descended from aristocracy. The blue blood cells had been significantly diluted by bright, peasant red, but Milly Whitley was determined that her daughters *would* make good matches and the Whitleys *would* return to the lofty position they'd all enjoyed before Mr. Whitley had died and his fragile financial house of cards had toppled around them.

Until then, they would dress the part and hang on to a

house that was a money pit and they would attend the sorts of occasions that told the world they hadn't gone anywhere.

"I daresay you'll find a better class of suitor than your usual struggling students and apron clingers," her mother added snobbishly.

All they needed was one man with deep pockets.

Or, as Cinnia had said countless times, they could all get proper jobs like normal people.

Her two middle sisters decried that as blasphemy.

Priscilla, her first younger sister, was a *model*. Genuinely pretty, but not in high demand. Two years out of school and she had barely worked at all. She just needed a better head shot or a new outfit or a change of hairstyle and her career would take off, she kept assuring them. Completing a course in hairstyling or something useful like that would only hold her back.

Nell, their stunning little party girl, didn't need a job. Boys already bought her things and *she* was the one who would land them the Big Fish when the time came. If Cinnia could somehow keep her in school long enough to complete her A levels without getting pregnant, she'd be thrilled.

Thankfully Dorry had a brain and ten times anyone's ambition to use it. Their youngest sister had been babysitting from the moment she was old enough to wipe a nose and currently had a job in a fish-and-chip truck, much to their mother's repulsion. Dorry squirreled her money before anyone saw it and kept her head down, usually bent over a book. If something happened to Cinnia, she had every confidence her baby sister would keep the rest of them fed and sheltered.

She was trying not to put that on poor Dorry. After trying to help her mother win a fight against owing back taxes and other debts associated with her father's estate,

Cinnia had taken an interest in wills and estate planning. As careers went, it paid well enough, was stable and flexible and she found it intellectually challenging.

Her mother said she might as well be an undertaker.

Vera said, "No matter what, do not tell any men we chat up what you do for a living. Not unless we're trying to get away from them."

Cinnia didn't have Vera's interest in meeting men. Her mother's lack of a career to fall back on had been their downfall. All Milly was qualified to do was take in university students as boarders because she had a big house, which was how she paid the bills, much to her everlasting embarrassment. She spun it as a lark when people asked about it. She liked to be surrounded by young people, she said, playing eccentric.

Cinnia was determined never to have her back against the wall like that. She was already self-supporting and, even though she knew running her own agency came with risk, she had hit the ceiling where she was. The next step was to become her own boss.

Thus, she was thinking about how to build her client list as she stood with Vera, chatting to an unassuming musician and a nerdy social-media magnate. The men were ridiculously wealthy and equally shy, which was why bubbly women like Vera had been called in, Cinnia supposed, letting her gaze stray to take in an evening beyond any she would experience again in this lifetime.

The nightclub was in a reclaimed industrial building, tricked out with steel and glass and modern art. Top-shelf liquor was served in cut-crystal glasses by uniformed bartenders. The main room was open to the upper floor, making the place feel airy despite the crush of people in the low-slung chairs and standing in groups around the full dance floor.

Tonight, the tables had been covered with velvet table-cloths and the place was littered with feather boas and faux furs. The typical nightclub black light had been replaced with a sultry red. It threw sexy shadows into every corner and gave faces a warm glow. The DJ was mashing old jazz and modern hits with delightful results while a bouncer guarded stairs that rose to a walk-around gallery on the upper level. When they'd arrived, they'd been given a peek into the ultraposh, private entertainment rooms reserved for the most exclusive guests.

Judging by the movie stars and the other celebrities *not* gaining access, those rooms would be used by a very rich and exalted personality indeed.

Cinnia wasn't impressed with money and fame, but she would love to take on any of these pocketbooks as clients. Sadly, people with this much money to throw around were not interested in a boutique agency still smelling of builder's dust. She had known from the outset that nothing would come of this evening beyond a few lost hours and a cute entry in the logbook of appearances made by her great-granny's tiara. *C'est la vie.*

Then she saw *him*.

Them, really. The Sauveterre twins. The male pair. The same gorgeous man in duplicate arrived at the top of the short flight of entrance stairs, where they overlooked the sunken area of the main lounge.

Her pulse stumbled.

She was startled to see them in person. And curious, of course. She'd been eleven when their sister had been kidnapped, old enough to follow the story as intently as the rest of the world. It had had a profound impact on her. To this day it made her heart feel stretched and tense just thinking about it.

The family name had turned up in a million news stories and gossip magazines and online hits since then. That's how she knew, despite the distance across the dimly lit room, that they were as handsome as they seemed from afar.

They had identical dark hair cut close under matching black fedoras tilted slyly to the left. While every other man had turned up in a baggy, striped suit with a red tie and carried a violin case, these two wore crisp black shirts with the cuffs rolled back, high-waisted, tailored black pants held up with white suspenders and smart white ties.

The sharp look accentuated their muscled shoulders and neat hips, while the narrow cut of the pants drew her eye to their matching black-and-white wing tips. They *looked* like gangsters of old, but the really dangerous ones. The ones so powerful and commanding, they didn't have to swagger. They killed with a blink.

They wore exactly the same expression of bored tolerance as they pushed their hands in their pockets and scanned the room.

It was funny to see them move in unison, which held her attention until one stopped. He turned his head from the direction of the stairs, barely moving, but it was as if he sensed her attention and met her gaze all the way from across the club.

Cinnia's heart took a funny bounce. She told herself it was the embarrassment of being caught gawking coupled with the shock of recognizing a celebrity. Catching a glimpse of the Sauveterre twins, even in a place filled with faux royals and rock stars, was a big deal. She knew they were regular people underneath the reputation, not something to get fluttery over, but she was rather giddy holding this man's gaze.

There's my rich husband, Mum. The thought made her smile at herself.

His head tilted just a little and he gave a slight nod. It was a very understated acknowledgement. *Hello.*

"Who do you see?" Vera asked, and followed Cinnia's gaze, whispering under her breath, "Oh, my *gawd.*"

The men moved down the stairs onto the dance floor, leaving Cinnia swallowing and trying to recover from something that had been nothing. Why did her blood feel as though it was stinging her veins?

"We have to meet them," Vera insisted.

"Shh." Cinnia protested, forcing her gaze back to the crooner. She and Vera were supposed to be circulating and making small talk. "Who needs another Gin Rickey?" she asked the men.

She absolutely refused to look around and see if *he* looked at her again. Why would he? Still, she remained attuned to him, feeling prickly and hypersensitive, like she was in grade school and her first crush had entered the room. She knew exactly where he was as they both moved around the room for the next half hour.

Vera leaned into her. "They're by the bar. Let's get into their line of sight."

"Vera."

"We'll just see if we can say hi. Besides, there will be a stampede for drinks when it's time to toast. We should freshen ours now, so we can take them outside for the fireworks."

She and Vera quickly realized they'd be swimming upstream trying to get nearer the twins *or* the bar. They moved to safer ground near the bottom of the stairs and stood with attentive expressions as the club owner quieted the room and thanked everyone for coming.

Or rather, Cinnia gave their host her polite attention while Vera visually cruised for fresh prospects.

Vera would flirt with anyone. She was fun loving, pretty

and had a knockout figure that reeled men in from across a pub or wherever she dragged Cinnia for a night out. They'd met at university and Vera was not only loyal, funny and caring, but also the absolute best at keeping Cinnia from becoming the stick-in-the-mud that Vera always called her.

Cinnia wasn't as curvy as Vera, but she drew her share of male attention. She might not try to get by on her looks the way her mother thought she could, but she knew her wavy blond hair and patrician features gave her certain advantages. They were also a perfect foil for Vera's darker looks, which *Vera* used to her advantage.

Cinnia didn't date so much as play Vera's wingwoman. She had come out tonight knowing they would very likely wind up departing the club with whomever Vera had set her sights on. But, while Vera often went home with men she barely knew, Cinnia fully expected to find her way back to their flat alone.

As the speeches finished up and the fireworks were promised to start soon, there was a minor lull in noise.

"It'd be nice if we could find some men to buy us a drink."

It was classic Vera, spoken mostly in jest because she knew it got under Cinnia's skin. She knew Cinnia believed women should be self-reliant and not look to men for anything.

Cinnia bit back her knee-jerk lecture on feminism, refusing to let her friend get a rise out of her.

Behind them, a male voice said, "Ladies? Are you going up?"

Henri recognized the blonde as they made their way toward the stairs. She had a serene profile and a graceful figure draped in a vintage-style dress that he imagined his sisters would coo over. They were the fashion aficionados, but he knew quality when he saw it.

Everything about this woman was understated elegance. In a sea of heavy makeup and over-the-top flapper gear, she wore a short black number that shimmered with fringe. Her hair was pressed into the pinched waves of old and a simple line of diamonds banded it. One side of her delicate tiara was bedecked with a leafy filigree and a single feather.

She looked smart and feminine without even trying.

She had smiled at him earlier, which was nothing new. People stared and acted like they knew him all the time. Heads in the crowd were turning to do it now. He usually ignored it, but he had looked back at her for a full thirty seconds because, why not? She was beautiful. It hadn't been a chore.

Neither was this side of her. The dress didn't need to hug her figure to show off her pert ass and slender thighs. It was rather erotic in the way it only suggested at the curves it disguised.

"Company?" he suggested.

Possessing exactly as healthy a libido as Henri, Ramon followed his gaze, saw the stacked brunette beside her and commented, "Good eye."

They easily operated as one unit without preplanning. Henri paused beside the women in time to hear them wish for a man to buy them drinks.

Ramon stepped past them to open the chain on the bottom of the stairs himself, not bothering to identify himself to the bouncer. Everyone knew them on sight.

"Ladies? Are you going up?" Ramon's gaze flicked back to Henri. He'd heard their lament and Henri very subtly signaled he didn't care.

They were targets of gold diggers all the time. They had

both learned to take care of themselves. It didn't mean a good time couldn't be had by all.

The brunette blushed and smiled, standing taller, shoulders going back. She was dazzled and very receptive. "Yes. We are." She nodded confidently despite the fact they all knew who moved freely up these upstairs and who did not. She nudged the blonde.

The blonde pursed her mouth with dismay. Embarrassed at being overheard as a mercenary? No need. Henri found that to be the easiest and most convenient of traits to manage in a woman.

The music started up again, increasing his desire to leave the noise and crowd behind.

The blonde looked warily between him and his brother, giving Henri the sense she was trying to work out which one of them had met her gaze earlier.

He and Ramon didn't fight over women. There was no point since neither of them wanted long-term relationships. Women seemed to view them as interchangeable anyway. But Henri found himself annoyed by the idea she might decide to go with Ramon.

What had been a generic restlessness responding to the gaze of a beautiful female ticked up into a desire to have this one in particular.

"Watch the fireworks from our suite," Ramon said with easy command, waving an invitation. "Save me from staring at my own face."

"Why would you stare at your brother when you'll be watching the fireworks?" the brunette asked with a cheeky bat of her lashes. "Maybe if you didn't dress alike you wouldn't feel like you were talking into a mirror?"

"We don't do it intentionally." Ramon offered his arm to escort her up the stairs. "It happens even when we're half the world away from each other. We've stopped fighting it."

"Really!"

The pair was quickly lost in the shadows of the gallery.

The blonde gazed after her friend, biting her lip, then relaxed her mouth and licked her lips as she glanced at Henri. It almost seemed a nervous response, but the action flooded color into a mouth that now looked dewy and soft as rose petals, shiny and kissable. A very enticing move.

His gaze lingered on the sight, as his mind slid naturally into the pleasant fantasy of crushing her mouth with his.

"Shall we?"

She fell into step beside him.

This was not his first time picking up women with his brother. He and Ramon had long ago concluded that if they were saddled with being *the Sauveterre twins* they were damned well going to take advantage of the one outstanding benefit. Startlingly good looks, times two, along with buckets of money and celebrity status meant that the sweetest companions were in endless supply.

"Was that true?" the blonde asked, leaning in to be heard. "That you dress alike at other times, not just tonight?"

"Yes." Henri hated talking about himself and loathed even more talking about his family, but this was one of those innocuous tidbits that strangers loved to hear. The mystery of being a twin was infinitely fascinating to those who weren't. He accepted it and had stopped fighting it, as well.

At least tonight it gave him an excuse to hold her arm as he leaned down to speak in her ear, liking the silken brush of her hair against his nose as he inhaled a scent that was cool English roses and warm woman.

"In fact, when one of us changes out of what the other is wearing, we inevitably spill something and have to go back to the first outfit."

"You're joking."

He shrugged off her skepticism. His sisters were connected on an emotional level. He and his brother were more outwardly aligned. They had very different personalities, were competitive as hell with each other, but often spoke in unison or followed a similar thought process, inevitably arriving at the same end result. As Henri had been calling his brother to suggest they host this year's planning sessions in London instead of their usual Paris or Madrid, Ramon had been accepting the invite to this club opening.

"I'm, um, Cinnia. Whitley." She offered her hand as they arrived on the upper floor.

"Henri." Her skin felt as soft as it looked and was warmer than the pale tone suggested. She had a firm grip for a woman. He didn't want to let her go, but she pulled her hand free to glance behind him at Guy, who had followed them, then frowned at Oscar ahead of them, already stepping through the door to the suite where Ramon waited with her friend.

"Do you have bodyguards?"

"It's just a precaution." They followed into them the suite.

While Oscar inspected the room, Guy brought out his phone and sent a brief text—a request for a background check on both women no doubt. Helping Guy along, Henri introduced himself to the brunette, learning her name was Vera Phipps.

Aside from relying on men's wallets rather than their own, Henri judged both women to be harmless. Vera sent a "jackpot" look to Cinnia when a butler arrived to take their order, then she followed Oscar's path through the room, trailing fingers on the low-slung sofa and chairs as she circled, glancing to the flat screen hung on the wall, and stepped onto the balcony for a quick sniff of the air off the Thames.

She came back just as quickly to fetch one of the swag bags from the coffee table. "Oh! A gold one! Everyone below got silver. And yours is bigger."

"I hear that a lot," Ramon said with a smirk, making Vera laugh throatily.

"I bet you do. May I look?" She batted her lashes suggestively.

Cinnia did not flirt so blatantly. She offered a demure thank-you as the butler poured their champagne and moved outside to glance at the colored lights swirling on the water. In the middle of the river, the technicians on the float set off a test flare.

It was a warm evening without a breeze. Her gaze lifted to the sparkle of lights across the water and up to the stars.

"I'm surprised you stayed below as long as you did when you had this to retreat to," she said as Henri padded out to join her. He was compelled. Drawn. It was strange and not something he would typically indulge. The strength of his attraction made him a little uncomfortable.

Below them, people began filing out to the outdoor lounge while the music followed them.

Ramon was the one who liked crowds. Henri preferred a quieter atmosphere, but he said smoothly, "Good thing we did or I wouldn't have met you."

Her snort was delicate, if disparaging. Most blondes with blue eyes played up the suggestion of vulnerable innocence in their coloring. Not Cinnia. Her vintage hairstyle framed her face in a waifish way, but her brows had a sharp, intelligent angle. Her lashes stayed low and her gaze watchful, not cynical, but not goggling or overly impressed by any of this.

He liked that sign of inner confidence and strength. It

was compelling, sparking his curiosity. "You feel differ-ently?"

"I feel this is a well-oiled machine you two are oper-ating." She flicked her glance to the plate of canapés that appeared like magic on the glass table next to them.

"I would call that distrustful," he said, waiting until the server had gone to swing his gaze back to hers. "If I didn't think you two were running a similar routine. I'll call it hypocritical instead."

Her blue gaze flashed to his, but inside the suite, Vera was laughing at something Ramon had said. The two were meshing like cogs rolling against one another to turn out a foregone conclusion. Cinnia's mouth tightened.

"Unable to deny it?" he taunted gently.

"You approached us," she reminded with enough pique to amuse him.

"I was invited."

"I didn't mean to stare." Her gaze returned to the view, chin coming up.

It had been more than a stare. She had smiled at him.

He watched with fascination as the fringe across her breasts quivered under an indignant breath. He would bet her cheeks were pink if the light was high enough to tell.

"I doubt I'm the first to be curious about the pair of you. You make a fetching couple." Her smile was pure aspartame.

Her eyes, however, were a spun sugar blue. That was unmistakable as a huge white light swirled down from a helicopter, rousing the crowd below into cheering.

Her beauty gave him a sudden kick in the chest. It wasn't a trick of makeup because she wore very little. The requisite eyeliner made her eyes stand out, but she'd only darkened her lashes a little. They weren't lengthened with false ones like so many women wore these days. A shimmery blue streaked across her lids, but otherwise her features were clean and her skin fine and creamy.

"Did you really know it was me who looked back at you, or is that an assumption? Because it usually takes people months, even years to tell us apart." It was easy once a person realized Henri was left-handed and Ramon right, or that Henri tended to speak French as his default while Ramon preferred Spanish, but few noticed those details.

"You are remarkably alike, but…" She glanced into the suite, to where Ramon was holding open the designer bag, listening politely to Vera wax in delight over the contents. They usually let their mother pick over the contents of those bags, then handed the rest to their PAs, but Henri was just as happy to let these women take them home.

He took advantage of Cinnia's distraction to glance at his phone. The bullet points backed up what he'd already assumed. Her mother was wellborn, but the family was broke. Cinnia worked for a wealth management firm and was listed on their website as an intern. Filing and fetching coffee, he assumed. The only risk Cinnia Whitley posed was financial and he was quite sure he could afford her.

He tucked his phone away, irritated to note she was still eyeing his brother, brows pulled together in consternation.

"But?" he prompted, having to stand close to be heard over the music below.

"I don't know. I don't read auras or anything like that, but… Never mind." She flashed him another look, this one self-conscious.

Sexually aware?

"That's interesting." His annoyance evaporated, replaced by intensified attraction. He leaned his elbow on the rail so he was even closer to her, edging into her space, liking the way she tried to quell a little shiver. She smelled like roses and tropics and something earthy that further turned him on.

"Wh-what is?" She was trying to look blasé, but he knew the signs of physical magnetism. There was a pulse beating fast in her throat, but it wasn't fear. She wasn't moving away. She was skimming her gaze across his shoulders and down his chest.

Chemistry was such a wonderful thing. He didn't move, allowing the primal signals to bounce between them, stimulating him and heightening his senses. Sex was the cheapest and best high in the world as far as he was concerned.

"You react to me, but not to him."

"I didn't say that!"

"Didn't you? My mistake."

"You *are* mistaken," she assured him hotly. "Whatever you're thinking about me—*us*—and why we came up here, forget it."

She wasn't used to being so attracted to the men she exploited, he surmised. Poor thing. This must be very disconcerting for her. With that reserved personality, he bet she usually did quite well at stringing a man along. Was she afraid she wouldn't be able to hold out with him until she had squeezed all she could from him?

"I'm thinking you're here to watch the fireworks. What did you think I was thinking?"

She spun back to the view, setting her chin.

He smiled. "Listen." He very lightly stroked the back of his bent finger down her bare arm, entranced when goose pimples chased the same path.

She shot him a look that was startled and uncertain, quickly rubbing the bumps away.

"I don't have to work this hard to get a woman to sleep with me. This is how I live." He waved his champagne glass at the opulence around them. "Enjoy it without feeling obligated."

"You won't expect anything after?" she scoffed.

"By *anything*, do you mean that?" He thumbed to where Vera was on tiptoe inside the suite, painting herself against Ramon, lips firmly locked over his.

Cinnia made a pained noise and looked out across the river again. As strategies went, her friend was overplaying her hand.

"I shall remain hopeful," Henri drawled.

"Yes, you will remain that way," Cinnia assured him.

He hid a silent laugh behind the glass he lifted to his lips, deciding he wanted her quite badly and was willing to pay whatever it cost. He respected people who knew what they were worth.

But he only said, "Don't make promises unless you can keep them, *chérie*."

CHAPTER TWO

VERA, THE *TRAITOR*, left with Ramon before the fireworks started.

"That's what you two were talking about in Spanish?" Cinnia hissed as she had three seconds alone on the balcony to react.

"I told you a language degree opened doors," Vera joked, then rolled her eyes at the face Cinnia was making. "Come *on*. Look at them! Surely you're tempted? It's long past time you worked Avery out of your system, you know."

She knew. And, of course, she was tempted. She wasn't in Vera's league when it came to sexual gymnastics, but she'd had a couple of long-term relationships that had been nice until they'd gone bad. The first had been an immature thing that should have ended before they went off to separate universities, but she'd clung to what they'd had and he'd wound up cheating. Her heart had been battered at the time, but looking back she knew they'd been far too young for the level of commitment she had expected.

Avery, however, had broken her heart in two, professing love for her while they'd both been struggling through a heavy course load and then trying to make ends meet when they moved to London together. Then he had come into some money and cut her off cold, stating bluntly that

her family was too much of a handful and he didn't need
the dead weight. Thankfully Vera had been there for her
when he'd kicked her out.

Since then, Cinnia had stayed out of the relationship
arena, thinking it wiser to concentrate on getting her career off the ground.

Not that Henri would offer a relationship. She knew *that*
without asking. But she couldn't deny she was intrigued
by him. Every time he glanced at her with male appre-
ciation oozing out of his pores, her hormones swayed in
an erotic dance of come-hither. Like the extravagance of
the night itself, she kept trying to rationalize indulging in
whatever he was offering.

She didn't do one-time hookups, though. And even if
she did sleep with him purely for the fun of it, he would
believe she'd done it in exchange for being wined and dined
here in this heavenly suite. She hated the idea of him thinking she could be bought. It went right to the core of the
insecurities Avery had instilled in her.

"It's quite a signature for the autograph book," Vera
murmured with a self-satisfied grin. "You know your
mother would approve. There's a first-class trip to Aus-
tralia in that bag, you know. And a smartwatch and a year's
lease on a sports car. Get what you can out of it!"

Henri came back from taking a call, probably overhear-
ing Vera's vulgar suggestion—like he needed any more
ammunition to believe they were a pair of opportunists.

Seconds later, Ramon came out and said, "The car is
waiting. Lovely to meet you, Cinnia."

He and Vera disappeared like a snuffed flame leaving
a wisp of burned friendship hanging in the air.

Henri sat down across from Cinnia at the high-top table,
mouth relaxed, but she had the sense he was laughing at

her ill-disguised panic. He signaled to the butler to freshen their drinks.

"Where do you think he's taking her?" she asked as the butler left.

"The nearest hotel with a vacant room, I imagine."

She shouldn't have asked.

"Why does it bother you?"

"It doesn't."

"You're judging," he accused. "Why?"

She wanted to deny it. She considered herself open-minded and forward thinking. She didn't slut-shame. Women had needs and Vera was no one's victim.

"Vera can do whatever she wants. I don't like the idea that you're judging me by her choices, though." She hated it. Avery's awful accusations came back to her and she felt raw all over again. Worse even, as she thought of this man who *lived like this* thinking she wanted a shortcut to the same lifestyle. "I don't sleep with men for a swag bag. I have a job. I buy what I need and if I can't afford something, I live without it."

"What do you do?" He looked like he was asking out of politeness, not like he really believed her speech on self-sufficiency.

She almost blurted "funeral arrangements" just to put him off.

"I have a business degree and I'm a qualified financial advisor, but my focus is estate planning and trust management."

His stall of surprise was painful in how loudly it spoke of his having underestimated her.

"I'm a very boring person," she said, wishing she could be more smug at defying his assumptions about her, but she only felt the difference in their stations more keenly. He had obviously written her off as trifling. And yes, she was trying to climb higher than where she'd wound up, but through honest hard work. Still, she would never reach his level and that put *him* well beyond her reach.

Not that she wanted him.

Did she?

With an uncomfortable sting in her blood, she picked up her champagne then remembered she had decided to stop drinking now that Vera was gone. She took a sip of water instead.

"I wasn't expecting that," he admitted.

"You thought I was a secretary? Airline hostess? Model? Even if I was, those are all honest careers in their own right."

"They are. And you could model. You're very beautiful."

"So could you. You have a face so nice, God made it twice."

He snorted. "Point to you," he conceded with a grimace. "I absolutely hate to be reduced to 'one of the Sauveterre twins.' We are all more than we appear on the surface, aren't we?"

Oh, the bastard, now she couldn't hate him unequivocally.

"Is it bad?" she asked, feeling compelled to do so. "I mean, I see things online all the time that I know have to be pure rubbish. The same nonsense that shows up about all celebrities, saying you're having an alien's baby or whatever. Does it bother you, though? Do you resent being famous because of an accident of birth?"

He took a moment to answer.

"I don't resent being who I am. I don't talk about my family—" his gaze shot to hers in warning to stay well back "—but I wouldn't trade them for anything. The attention is a pain in the ass and not something we invite. It annoys me, but I've learned to pick my battles." He said it flatly, but the nail beds of his fingers were white where he gripped his glass.

"Well, I—" She stopped herself, holding out a hand. "Message received about your family," she assured him. "You've earned the right to privacy. But I hope she's well. Your sister, I mean."

She was tempted to say more, weirdly yearning to explain that his family's pain had rippled out to her in the strangest way. She'd been as taken as anyone with the Sauveterre twins. The girls were a little younger than her, but they had seemed like an ideal worth emulating, living much larger than Cinnia even though her family had been doing quite well in those days.

Then Trella had been kidnapped and she'd been terrified for the girl. Of course, she had been compelled to follow the rest of the family's exploits forevermore. She was as curious as anyone about why his youngest sister had dropped out of the public eye in her teens. Had she gone into rehab? A madhouse? A nunnery? Theories abounded, but Cinnia kept her lips sealed against asking for the truth.

Against asking him if he was still dealing with the fallout.

The butler brought another plate of hors d'oeuvres, this one with tiny deviled quail eggs, caviar and stuffed olives and a whipped salmon mousse with narrow fingers of toasted bread. It was exquisite and she kept her gaze on it to hide how thinking of his past had altered her perception of him. She wanted to dismiss him as a womanizer who should be avoided, but he was human. He'd been hurt. Scarred.

"Why estate planning?"

She dragged her gaze off the plate, heart taking a skip as she met his gaze.

"Many reasons. I started looking into it after my father died. There was a lot to untangle and as I learned what he could have done, I kept wondering why he hadn't set it up this way or that. My mother would have had it easier if he'd shown some foresight. Looking at it as a career, I saw it was flexible, something you could do without a lot of overhead. You can even work from home if you have to. Everyone needs a will, whether they know it or not. And it's one of those things that if you're good and fast, you can make a decent living. I didn't see a downside beyond its lack of sex appeal."

"Which you more than make up for in being yourself."

He said it with gentle mockery. She knew he meant it as over-the-top flattery, but her cheeks still warmed. She tried to hide how affected she was with a dry "I try."

The fireworks started and they turned to watch.

She was more aware of him than the performance. He was very charismatic with his air of aloof charm and hint of a French accent. He was also subtly demonstrative, lightly caressing her wrist as he drew her attention to the flotilla of boats coming in to watch.

Everything he did made her very aware of herself. Her breaths felt deliberate, her skin sensitized, her movements a dance of grace. She was being seduced and he wasn't even making an effort to do it. Her mind drifted to thoughts of kissing him. Feeling his weight against her.

Her skin warmed, her nipples tingled and she pressed her knees together to ease the ache in the fork of her thighs.

She was sorry when the fireworks ended and her excuse for being here was over.

"Oh, no," she said quickly, declining the butler's offer to bring strawberries and cream with a fresh bottle of champagne as he removed their plate of finger foods.

"Do *not* worry about your figure," Henri said, nodding to the butler.

"I'm worried about my *survival*. I'm allergic. I have a pen for emergencies and everything." She nodded at her clutch.

"It's that bad?" He held up a hand to halt the butler.

"I nearly died at a sleepover once, because my friend didn't want to fess up that she'd stolen a bottle of her dad's best wine for homemade sangria." She rolled her eyes, making light of what a frightening near miss she'd had.

He refused the strawberries and told the butler he would press the call button when they were ready for more champagne.

"Have them if you want them," Cinnia protested. "It's not so bad I can't watch someone else eat them."

He tucked his chin, leaning forward as the butler closed the door behind himself. "But I can't kiss you if I've eaten them. Can I?"

His words made her ears ring. She stole a long, subtle inhale, holding his gaze while she tried not to let him see how easily he sent her blood pressure into the stratosphere.

"Remaining hopeful?" Her gaze dropped to his mouth.

"Very much so."

She forced herself to slide off her tall chair, excusing herself to the attached powder room. *Time to go*, she told her reflection. The woman in the mirror was entirely too heavy lidded, her defenses against Henri thinning by the second.

When she returned, Henri was inside the suite. The lighting fell in subdued angles off the wall sconces and from the patio lanterns below the balcony, setting an intimate tone while the music inside the club pulsed in muted rhythm through the walls.

Henri had raided his swag bag for a box of chocolate

truffles with a Belgian label and was opening one wrapped in gold foil. A ball of discarded foil was already on the table next to the box.

"I have a sweet tooth," he admitted ruefully, offering the truffle.

"No, thanks. I'll, um, go. This was nice. Thank you." She stuck out her hand, feeling like an idiot the moment she did it.

He set aside the chocolate and brought out his phone. "I'll order the car and take you."

"I can manage."

He gave her a pithy look. "I meant it about not feeling obligated. I can drive you home without attacking you. I've made my appearance here. I don't plan to stay."

It wasn't him she was worried about. She was half-tempted to ask him to find the nearest vacant hotel room. Vera's voice was playing in her head, extolling the virtues of being a modern woman who owned her sexuality. *You eat if you're hungry, don't you?*

Cinnia was sexually hungry. She put it down to the excitement of dressing up for an extravagant evening, the soft breeze caressing her skin and champagne relaxing her. Henri was very attractive and she would bet any money he easily satisfied the most exotic of appetites.

"I think it's best if we end it here." She felt like a coward and couldn't help looking at his mouth again. She wanted him to kiss her. She really did. Her blood thickened in her arteries, throbbing with anticipation.

He quirked his lips. "If you tell me you have an allergy to chocolate, I'm going to be disappointed."

"I'll survive," she murmured, recognizing that she was consenting to a kiss. "My affairs are in order if I don't. And what a story to tell my grandchildren if I do." She said it to be cheeky, to keep this light and disguise that she was intrigued by him.

His breath rushed out in an incredulous *ha*, but he wasn't deterred. He crowded close, hands opening on her waist and drawing her forward into him.

"I'd best make it memorable then."

She wore low kitten heels and he was very tall, well over six feet and overwhelming as he bent his head to brush his mouth against hers.

She clutched his shoulders for balance, shivering lightly, head instantly swimming. Was that it? She swallowed and wet her lips then parted them, inviting a more thorough goodbye than that.

He started to smile and she knew his move had been a deliberate tease to make her want more. He moved in like a damned marauder then covered her mouth fully, angling to plunder. *Claiming.*

She curled her fingers against his shoulders, feeling them tense as he drew her closer. She moaned as she kissed him back, quickly over her head and suddenly drowning. He buffeted her senses, filling her brain with the faint scent of aftershave and masculinity, enfolding her as she melted under a flood of arousal. His tongue came into her mouth and she tasted dark chocolate and darker intention.

He wanted her. She could feel how hard he was against her stomach. Her own body grew hot and achy in seconds. Longing struck her loins and she looped her arms fully around his neck to mash her breasts against his chest.

Too much, she thought as she did it, knowing it was a signal of receptiveness, but it was pure instinct. Wanton need.

She drew back, gasped once for air, then found herself kissing him again. Just once more. Okay twice. The third time she might have found her willpower, but the solidness of a wall arrived at her back. He ran his lips down her throat and slid his hand to cradle her breast.

"Oh," she breathed, loving the gentle way he massaged, then found her nipple through the fringe, circling and teasing. Her knee came up to his thigh of its own accord, making space for him to settle against her aching mons.

He growled his approval and ran his hand up her thigh, taking the hem of her dress up to her waist, hooking his forearm behind her knee and caressing her bottom as she picked her hips up off the wall and met his suggestive thrust.

He kissed her deeply, tongue delving into her mouth as he fondled her breast and the skin of her bottom exposed by her thong. They rocked in mock lovemaking, their sighs too low to be heard over the noise of the crowd and music drifting in from the open doors of the balcony.

This was so not her. She liked sex, but she had never behaved like this. It had never *felt* like this. She might actually climax fooling around fully clothed, grinding herself against him if he kept up that perfectly delicious rhythm. The hard length of him was right where it needed to be, rubbing against her most sensitized flesh. She was *so* turned on and really tempted to let it happen. It was like they were dancing. The song's beat was picking up, growing more intense. Tension was gathering in her abdomen and lower, in the flesh he was stimulating so erotically.

Dropping her head back against the wall, she bit her bottom lip, one hand bracing on his shoulder. They had to stop. They were practically in public and she was *so* close!

He whispered something in French that sounded like encouragement and reached one hand to lock the door. "It's okay. Come."

"I'm not—"

"*Oui, chérie*, you are. Very close. I can feel you trembling. It's exciting. Come."

She wanted to tell him he didn't know how she felt, but he kissed her like he had the first time, barely grazing her mouth so she turned her head, seeking further contact and clinging to his lips with her own.

"Let me give you this," he whispered as he broke away and shifted to bring his hand between them, gently tracing her tender flesh through the damp layer of black silk.

She stopped breathing. Anticipation held her very still as he drew light patterns over the silk of her thong. Her entire being narrowed to the touch of his fingertip, which was so light, yet made her throb with need. She waited in agony for his caress to steal beneath the elastic and…

"Mmm," she moaned when he finally did it.

"You like?" He stroked her *exactly* the way she needed, unhurried, kissing and drawing away, stoking her arousal, kissing her more deeply, gently penetrating, then whispering praise, promising to make it so good for her. "Come. I want you to."

She was going out of her mind, but his control was equally crazy making. She wanted to let go but she couldn't stand that he was doing this *to* her.

"Do you have a condom?" she gasped when he let her breathe again.

He stilled, eyes a silvery glimmer in the low light, gaze burning into hers.

"You want to make love?" he asked on a rasp.

Oh, please. His hand was in her knickers. He knew what she *wanted*. She was dying. But she wanted climaxing to be something they did together.

She slid her hands down to his fly, hands shaking so much with anticipation she was clumsy as she tried to open his pants.

He removed his hand and hooked her thong to peel it down, letting her leg drop so the silk slid to her ankles. Then he shrugged out of his suspenders and finished opening his pants, bringing a condom from his pocket before he hitched his pants low on his hips and revealed himself.

It ought to have been the moment she woke up and realized this was way beyond where it was supposed to go. Across the suite, the doors were open to a crowd of famous faces, hidden just below the rail.

Her world became a narrow, shadowed one where her blood was on fire. Every breath she drew was filled with his spicy, masculine scent. She admired the shape of him in the low light as she watched him roll the condom down his length. She was so filled with anticipation her loins clenched in pangs of yearning.

He nudged his feet between hers, stepping the thong off her ankle as he settled against her again, the heat of his body a type of deliverance. She gathered her skirt and lifted her leg, hooking her calf against his buttocks, offering herself. He bent his knees and glided to caress, teasing her a moment, wetting the tip before he nudged for entry. He pressed, finding no resistance, and thrust smoothly into her slick channel, so she dug her nails into the back of his neck and made a keening noise at the intensity of his thickness filling her.

"Hurt?" he grunted with surprise, pulling back a little.

"Oh, no," she breathed. "So good." She tightened her foot into the back of his thigh, urging him deeper.

He growled a noise of agreement and pressed all the way in, giving her a moment to greet his intrusion with little rippling hugs of her inner muscles, joyous at the invasion of that hot, hard length. So rock hard. They kissed like that, joined, barely moving as they stood against the wall, tongues laving against each other, bodies quaking with holding back, hot, so hot.

She had never been so overcome by desire that she stood against a damned wall with a stranger. She had never felt so desperate for *more*. She nudged to signal him that he was making her wait too long. Her arousal was a screaming pitch of need.

He breathed a soft laugh against her mouth and began to move with heavy purpose, not rough, but thorough, drawing out each movement so the pleasure went to its furthest degree each time, dragging tingles to the tips of her extremities. It was so sweet it made her teeth ache. She kept thinking it couldn't possibly get better, then he thrust heavily, landing deep, and it was fantastic.

She ceased thinking about where she was or who he was. Their lovemaking became her entire focus. Nothing mattered except that he was moving within her in that exquisitely perfect way. It was earthy and uncivilized, yet so finely tuned it was art. She wanted him with her in this place where he'd propelled her, where nothing existed except this pleasure.

She ran her tongue up his neck and sucked his earlobe and angled to take him as deeply as she could. She kissed him back with abandon and brought his hand up under her dress to her breast, then slid her own under his shirt to caress his tense stomach. She whispered, "I can't believe we're doing this."

He said something in French, his whole body shaking, as though he was in the same state of straining to hold back because this was too good to release.

"You're killing me, *chérie*. I can't hold on. Are you ready?"

"I don't want it to end," she gasped, turning her open

mouth against his neck and gently biting as the crisis threatened.

"Neither do I, but—ah!"

"Yes. Oh, Henri."

"Oui. Ensemble. Maintenant." He thrust harder. Faster.

Glory rose up in a gathering wave, locking them together in ecstatic culmination.

CHAPTER THREE

IT WAS WEEKS after the nightclub before Henri found himself in London again. He hadn't stopped thinking about Cinnia Whitley and he didn't know why. Their evening together had followed exactly the pattern he'd assumed it would and it wasn't a new one.

Well, he usually closed an encounter with more grace, but she was the one who had disappeared when he'd stepped away to take what he thought might be an emergency call from his sister.

Regardless, it wasn't as if Ramon was giving a second thought to her friend Vera, so he didn't know why he couldn't stop thinking about Cinnia. Maybe it was because she hadn't behaved as predictably as her friend.

Vera had posted the selfie she'd taken with the four of them when they'd first entered the hospitality suite. She was using her rub with a Sauveterre to gain some celebrity status of her own. Absolutely nothing new and he didn't even bother feeling disgusted by it.

Cinnia hadn't shared the selfie to her own account, though. The one online quote he'd found attributed to her about him was "I met him briefly. There's nothing else to say."

Not one to kiss and tell, obviously.

Neither was he, so he appreciated her discretion.

Of course, what could one say about their lovemaking without sounding like a blatant liar or an overly romantic poet? He liked an involved partner and always did what he could to ensure the woman got as much from their lovemaking as he did. But to say he and Cinnia had had sex, or had given each other an orgasm, was to completely understate the act.

He kept rationalizing what had made it seem so powerful. She'd been resisting their attraction in a slow burn that had made her capitulation all the sweeter. The partially public location had held a titillating appeal. Their chemistry was very compatible.

As he'd leaned against the soft cushion of her body, barely able to keep his knees from buckling, he'd been... He wanted to call it empty, but even though he'd felt drained, he'd also felt utterly satisfied.

At peace.

All the responsibilities that weighed on him were still there. He hadn't stopped caring about them, but in that moment of euphoria, he'd accepted it all. If that was what had made him into the man who could be there with that woman, forehead tilted against the wall, cheek pressed to hers, inhaling her scent and twitching with reaction long after the pulses of orgasm had faded, feeling the very light stroke of her fingertips at his spine...

So be it.

Then he had heard Trella's ringtone and his demanding life had rushed back in to consume him. He had stepped away from Cinnia and straightened himself, snatching up the phone and answering it without visuals, stepping outside in case Trella was in crisis and he needed to talk her down.

Looking back, he knew he had reacted almost like a shock victim, rushing to get on with his life after a collision that had nearly taken his life. His head had been spinning, his body firing with adrenaline.

Since then, he had been telling himself he was wrong. Their lovemaking hadn't been anywhere near so profound as he recollected. Even if it had been the best sex of his life with a woman who possessed an ounce of discretion, so what? He wasn't in the market for a relationship and given the life he led, never would be.

At best, he might have stretched their association into the rest of the weekend, if she hadn't disappeared like the fire bell had rung. When he had realized she hadn't just ducked into the ladies' room, he had told himself it was for the best and asked for his order of strawberries.

The berries had been both sweet and tart, imprinting on his memory a little deeper with each bite. He suspected he would think of her every time he glimpsed a strawberry for a very long time and would wonder if she was managing to stay away from them.

Why? Such a ridiculous question to clog up his brain.

And yet, weeks later, as he entered a party he had no desire to attend and spotted her, his first thought was *so far so good*. She was alive and well, not having succumbed to fruit poisoning.

Her blond hair was gathered in a knot and held in place with a couple of sticks, but a few delicate spirals fell around her face. Her shoulders were bared by her white summer dress, her heels an attractive spike that showed off her legs. She wore only a pair of silver hoop earrings for jewelry.

She was as casually beautiful as he remembered, her expression serene as she listened to a man who wasn't her date, but looked like he wanted to be.

As was his habit, Henri had insisted his security be given the finalized guest list before he accepted the invitation. If people wanted him to show up to their affairs, they complied. That's how he had known Cinnia would be here and he'd made himself take a full ten minutes of sober second thought before he'd accepted the invite himself—without a plus one, as she had also done.

His heart started to thud with male need as he looked at her. He knew what lurked beneath that air of containment and he'd be damned if that gangly pontificator would discover it, as well.

Cinnia had convinced herself this engagement party for her friend from uni was yet another good "networking opportunity," even though she knew why she'd been invited. Once Vera's photo of the two of them with the twins had made the rounds, Cinnia had been inundated by old acquaintances eager to reach out. She was part of the "it" crowd now and her mother couldn't be happier.

If only she was in a position to decline, but she was too practical to be proud. Her friend was marrying into a very wealthy family from New York and their circle of friends included the types of fortunes that were just complex enough to need a qualified manager.

Unfortunately, you couldn't reply to casual questions about your career with "I'm drumming up biz for the agency I'm opening." Evenings like this were about making introductions and impressions, keeping the talk light yet memorable, then somehow finding an excuse at a point down the road to contact the same people and ask, "Do you have a plan for your eventual death?"

Since she didn't have a man in her life who was eager to put on a tie and show up to a stranger's engagement party, she had come alone and was now a target for the stags in rut. Gerald, here, was a perfect example, shadowing her through her last two attempts to ditch him. She swore if he asked for her number, she would give him her business

card and tell him to call when he was ready to discuss his
final wishes.

"Don't look now, but guess who just walked in," the
woman across from her said with a sparkle in her eye. "I
think you know him, Cinnia."

Of course Cinnia looked.

And promptly felt stretched thin as a strand of glass,
so brittle she would break if a wrong word was breathed
in her direction. Her throat closed and her chest stung
from the inside. It took everything in her to keep a look
of nonchalance on her face while her heart bolted for the
nearest exit.

He was looking right at her, gorgeous in tailored grey
pants and a black shirt *sans* tie, hat or suspenders. His for-
est green linen jacket should have looked affected, but, of
course, it was a simple statement that he was gorgeous *and*
stylish in modern garb as well as vintage.

"Not really," she said, turning back to her group, *begging* her cheeks not to go hot with betrayal. "I only met
them briefly," she lied. For the millionth time.

It was an open secret that Vera had slept with Ramon.
She hadn't just notched her bedpost, but had engraved the
words *A Sauveterre Slept Here* on her headboard. *Everyone* assumed Cinnia had put out as well and it had taken
her weeks to convince the world at large she hadn't.

Because, when a man could walk into a room and cre-
ate a stir without doing a damned thing, what red-blooded
woman *wouldn't* sleep with him the first chance she got?

Guilty as charged, obviously, but Cinnia was far too
mortified to admit it. Why, why, why had he affected her
so strongly she'd gone against her basic principles? She
could already feel him creating the same wicked stir in
her—which was unconscionable now she understood he
hadn't just been availing himself but *cheating*.

"Friends with the groom, I guess?" Gerald murmured. "Looks like it. Not your date then, Cinnia?"

"No," she asserted, refusing to look at Henri again. *Refusing.* Burning inside with rejection. "I'm not even sure which one that is," she said, utterly bald-faced.

But she knew that was Henri. It didn't make sense to her that her body recognized him at a basic level while regarding his brother like any other man, but there it was. She was attuned and susceptible to *this* twin.

Please, God, don't let him know how susceptible. Would it be too obvious if she excused herself to the ladies' room and caught a cab away from here?

"What did you get for the happy couple?" she asked, trying to steer the conversation off Henri. "I saw they'd registered for one of those bullets to make smoothies, but someone beat me to it. I got them the yogurt maker instead."

"He's coming," the woman said, barely moving her lips, then pasting on a big smile. "Mr. Sauveterre. It's so nice to meet you."

"Bonjour." He nodded and set his wide hand on Cinnia's lower back as he leaned in to shake the offered hand. She stiffened, burned by the imprint of his touch through the satin of her dress. "Cinnia. Nice to see you again. Will you introduce me to your friends?"

She could hardly breathe with his palm sending waves of sensual excitement through her.

"Of course, um—" she squinted at him, making a show of guessing "—Henri?"

His gaze flashed and his thumb and finger dug into her waist in a suggestion of a pinch, promising retribution. *"Oui."*

He was a master at the small talk game, asking people how they knew the betrothed couple, discovering occupations and commenting on places of travel without offering a single detail about himself.

She stood dumbly paralyzed by his hand resting against her spine, telling herself to walk away, but unable to. Her entire body was reacting with the tingling memory of his muscled body moving against hers. Within her. It was all she could do not to betray that she was growing aroused by standing next to him. If she walked away, she'd only draw attention to how gripped she was by her reaction.

"Oh, Cinnia, there's someone you should meet. Let me introduce you."

Henri smoothly snagged her hand and drew her away while Gerald stammered, "Nice chatting with you, Cinnia..." in their wake.

Enough. She had to get away. She tugged at her hand. "I'm leaving," she told him.

"Excellent. Me, too."

Oh, nice one. She had walked blindly into *that.*

"But I do have to say hello to this couple." Apparently he knew them from New York. He drew her across the room.

She followed to avoid making a scene and they chatted for a few minutes. Cinnia quietly fumed, hating him and herself for still reacting. She was just about to make her escape by excusing herself to the powder room and crawling out a window when Henri tightened his grip on the hand she was subtly working free of his.

"I'm afraid we have to run. We should say good night to our hosts," he added to Cinnia, exactly as if they were a couple who had arrived together.

"They" were not a couple. He had demonstrated that clearly enough at the nightclub. Growing hot with fresh outrage, she waited until they'd left the prospective bride and groom and their roomful of friends with a meaty chunk of gossip to chew over before saying, "Why are you doing this? You're ruining my reputation."

"Untrue. Nothing a Sauveterre touches turns to anything but gold. You can thank me later."

"How?" she demanded with undisguised bitterness.

"Don't be crass." He steadied her with a hand under her elbow as he walked her down the stairs and out through the lobby of the hotel. A car glided to the curb before them. His guard reached around them to open the back door. "Where can I take you?"

"I think you know where I want you to go. I prefer you go alone."

"So hostile. You can't possibly be upset about how we left things since it was your choice to leave. Let's have this conversation away from our audience."

Flashes started going off and she realized paparazzi were swarming like mosquitos scenting fresh blood.

She slid into the car and he followed, reaching forward to close the privacy screen before the door had been slammed behind him.

His guard moved into the passenger seat and the car pulled away.

"I didn't expect such a cold greeting."

She made a choked noise. "I can imagine how you thought I'd greet you, given the way I behaved, but forget it. That was me getting over an old boyfriend. *That's all.*"

That's what she kept telling herself and she believed it about as well as anyone else believed she hadn't slept with Henri Sauveterre.

"Vraiment?" His tone chilled by several thousand degrees.

"Oh, I'm sorry, do you find that insulting?" She flicked her head around to send him a haughty look. "At least he and I were completely over. I didn't take his call while you and I were still—"

She wouldn't say it. It was too humiliating. Her cheeks hurt with a painful blush.

Giving in to the urge to make love with him on such short acquaintance was a tolerable mistake. Yes, she'd been weak enough to succumb to a player's best moves, but from a purely physical standpoint—pun intended—it had been great. She hadn't had any regrets as he'd leaned against her, both of them damp and still breathing hard.

Then the ring of his mobile had galvanized him into withdrawing and straightening himself, as he grabbed the phone and said, "Bella." He had gone outside, seeking privacy.

He might as well have smacked her. *Of course* he had other women in his life. Maybe their lovemaking had been profound and unique for her, but it was routine for him. She was no more than the stick of gum he chewed for fifteen minutes to freshen his breath!

Cinnia had tugged on her knickers and got the hell out of there.

"Are you serious?" he muttered now. "The call was from my sister."

"Not any less offensive," she declared, turning her disconcerted frown to the window, cautioning herself not to believe him. *Fool me twice...*

"*D'accord.* You're right. It was rude," he said begrudgingly. "But there are circumstances. I don't ignore her calls."

"That's nice. Tell your driver I'm on the other side of London. He's going the wrong way."

"Cinnia," Henri growled. "Have some compassion. There are *reasons*."

The kidnapping? The isolation? She glanced at him,

desperately wanting to throw his words back in his face, but he didn't look manipulative or even like he was trying to cajole. He looked frustrated and, beneath it, troubled.

She recalled him saying he never spoke about his family and sighed. Perhaps she would have to take him at his word, but it was still insulting as hell.

"Fine," she muttered.

"Do you mean that? Or is it a passive-aggressive *fine*?"

"Does it matter? I could ask you to tell me what those circumstances are, but you're not going to, are you?"

"No." His expression darkened.

She shrugged, hiding that his reticence struck her as lack of trust, which hurt far more deeply than it had a right to.

"So what do you care if I'm fine or not? Even if we'd ended things on a warmer note that night, you were never going to call me after. We both know that, so who cares how we end things now?"

"I care, obviously."

"No, you don't!" she cried on a scoffing laugh. "You walked into that party and saw the easiest girl in the room." If she could take back her capitulation… Would she? Oh, it was lowering to admit it, but probably not. Regardless, she'd be a fool to repeat it.

"You're looking for a do-over," she accused. Her voice cracked and she forced out a tight *no, thanks*.

"Au contraire," he said, his voice so sharp and hard it stabbed through the thick plate she was trying to hold over her chest. "At least three women in that room were far easier. Trust me. I've met them in the past. Not slept with them," he quickly clarified. "But I've been invited to on very short acquaintance. I came tonight because you were on the guest list."

Her emotions were taking a bumpy ride despite the

smoothness of the car's suspension. He'd come to see *her*? She didn't want to believe that. It would make her soften toward him and she was already struggling to keep him at arm's length.

"I wish you hadn't. My supervisor already suggested it would be a good career move if I sent you a letter of introduction for the firm." She turned her face to the window again. "Now he'll be even more of a pain about it. *Thanks*."

"You want me to come into his office and let him give me his spiel? Fine."

"No, Henri, I don't!" She swung her head around, barely able to keep a civil tone. "What message does that send? Next he'll *tell* me who to sleep with in order to land a client. Men! Are you really that obtuse? Your notoriety is not 'gold' for me. It's a scarlet letter. Don't do me any favors."

He sat back, a ring of white appearing around his tight mouth.

"I can't help who I am, Cinnia. I can't help that people want to use me, or use anyone who comes close to me to get to me. If I could change it, I would, but I *can't*!" His voice rang through the small space like a thunderclap, rife with incensed frustration.

His outburst was so shocking, she sat in silence a moment, absorbing what he'd revealed—reluctantly, judging by the way he shut down immediately after.

Empathy rolled into the spaces he'd blown open in her. She couldn't help feeling bad for him then, especially as a motor scooter buzzed up alongside the car and the passenger on the back aimed a camera at the darkened window. It flashed, perhaps catching her frown of dismay.

He pinched the bridge of his nose, making a visible effort to maintain his strained control.

"Trella—Trella Bella as we call her, or Bella—has a particular struggle. Partly it's due to the attention we draw.

I make myself available to her when she needs it. We all do. If she had called Ramon, your friend Vera would be the one feeling slighted. Trella's situation is a fact of my life. That's all I'm saying on the topic and you can believe it or not or post it to your damned news feed if that will make you feel better."

"Of course I wouldn't," she said crossly. "Why would I deliberately hurt someone I don't even know?"

Now she would dwell forever on the struggles of that poor girl who had surely been through enough just from being kidnapped. No public statements had ever been made about what had really happened to her during the five days she was missing. Terrible things had been theorized, though. Cinnia dearly hoped none of them were true, but judging by Henri's grim expression, his sister had a lot to deal with.

She had such an urge to reach out to him in that moment, she had to clench her fingers together in her lap.

"Has the attention been bad?" he asked. "Are you being harassed by cameras outside your home? It's so rare I meet anyone who feels like I do, I didn't imagine it would be a burden for you."

She shrugged. "Mostly just friends and family are asking about it. I didn't say much and that's not out of character because I keep a low profile as a rule."

He glanced inquiringly, so she explained further.

"My kind of work is like banking or the law. Clients expect confidentiality and no one wants to give their portfolio to a woman who's posting party photos or running with a sketchy crowd, so I live quietly and don't put much online. But as you say, people put a lot of stock in the Sauveterre name. I realize it's not really a detriment to be associated with it. It would shatter my ego completely, however, to have people say I only succeeded because of who I know. And to have my boss pressure me like that? I was really annoyed."

"Did you report him to your HR?"

"There's no point."

"There is. Speaking as the president of a huge company, I can't fix what I don't know is broken. I need reports of that sort of thing so I can take action or it will keep happening."

She hadn't thought of it that way, only that she was leaving soon. "Fine. I will."

"Good."

Great. Annoying-boss issue resolved. "Can you take me home now, please?"

"I would like to have dinner with you."

"You don't want dinner, Henri." That damned crack was back in her voice, betraying that she was still feeling slighted because even if he hadn't been cheating when he'd made love to her, it had been nothing more than a casual hookup. "You want to go to bed with me."

"I do," he said baldly, face tightening at her tone. "Tell me you're not interested and I'll take you home. *Be honest.*"

She wanted to look away, but his intense gaze held hers, peeling back her layers of defensiveness as the streetlights flashed by. She knew she was flushing with guilty anticipation. She had managed to hate him for weeks because he had taken his girlfriend's call after their lovemaking, but that's not what he'd done. Her best reason for resisting him was nullified.

She jerked her head around, staring blindly at the passage of headlights and darkened shop windows.

"*Ça va?*"

"You could have called," she muttered. "You're not going to call tomorrow if I sleep with you tonight."

"Since you'll be with me at breakfast, there will be no need."

She snorted at his arrogance.

"You were not planning to sleep with me that night." Something in his quiet tone made her listen. It was as if he was reflecting fondly and it gave her a small shiver of pleasure because she was part of a memory he was recollecting warmly. "At first I thought it was your game to resist, but you really were intending to leave. You didn't. You were carried away by a kiss and didn't even take one of those silly gift bags on your way out. Yes, I took note of that detail," he said as she swung a scowl at him.

As if she would have sex for a BPA-free water bottle and the latest reality star's brand of lip gloss!

"You went away feeling ill used and I regret that," he continued. "But I am used by women *all the time*. Put yourself in my shoes and imagine how singular and exciting it is for me to have met a woman who not only responds so strongly to me she lost her willpower against *herself*, but doesn't want to write a damned online diary about it. Yes, I want to experience that again. You're damned right I do."

"I don't *like* that I was carried away like that. It makes me feel cheap."

"Cheap! *Why?*"

"Because you expected it. You expected me to behave that badly and I did."

"I *wanted* you to make love with me. I didn't *expect* it. And there was nothing bad about it. You have a real hang-up about when it's permissible to have sex, don't you?"

"Yes, all right? I do! I've had two lovers and I thought I loved both of them. I don't have sex with random strangers for whom I feel mostly annoyance."

He blinked once, taking a moment to pick apart her

words. She expected him to take issue with her calling him annoying, but he only repeated, "*Thought* you loved."

She looked away, aware of tension in the hands that had become fists on her thighs, and said nothing.

"Tell me about this boyfriend you were exorcising."

"No." She craned her neck to look past him. They were pulling up in front of a posh hotel. "What are we doing here?"

"We have dinner reservations."

She had eaten exactly one stuffed mushroom cap at the engagement party. She was starving. Nevertheless, she glared at him.

To hide the fact she was scared.

And shamefully thrilled they weren't parting ways yet. This man utterly fascinated her and it was so dangerous. Like swimming in petrol under a rainstorm of flaming comets.

"Why?" she asked, stalling.

"It's a *date*, Cinnia. Surely that doesn't go too harshly against your precious rules for how to behave with a man?"

She looked at her nails. "No, but I have one about providing the lion's share of sarcasm in a relationship. I suggest you take it down a notch or things could become quite scathing."

He tsk-tsked and started to open his door. His guard finished the job, but Henri held out his hand himself to help her out.

Then he kept his fingers firmly entwined with hers as he walked her through the glittering gold-and-glass entrance of the hotel, across the marble tiles and around the lobby fountain, up the red-carpeted staircase and into a restaurant where a harpist played. The maître d' exclaimed delight that she could join them when Henri introduced her.

The moment they were alone, she said drily, "And I

won't feel obligated after this to go upstairs to the room you've booked."

"No," he assured her. "You won't feel *obligated*." He gathered her hands across the white tablecloth and gave her a slow and anticipatory smile. "But I hope very much you'll feel inclined."

CHAPTER FOUR

CINNIA WOKE TO a room that was nearly pitch-black, Henri's arm heavy across her waist. They were naked, front to front, legs entwined. She wanted to press her lips into the smoothness of his shoulder and kiss his skin.

What the hell was she *doing*?

Succumbing to hormones. And charm. Henri was very engaging when he wanted to be. He smoothly deflected from anything too personal, but he was keenly intelligent and had exchanged lively opinions with her on everything from world politics to pop music. He had asked her advice about a point of estate law, which she had thought was pure pandering, but she soon realized he was serious and had to tell him he was better off consulting someone who specialized in international trusts.

Then the evening's trio had arrived and he had taken her to the dance floor and *seduced* her, right there in front of the world. Not that he was obvious about it. Henri was far too subtle for that. No, it had been a light brush of his chest against her breasts, a whisper that she smelled delicious, a brief contact with his hips so she knew he was aroused.

"I can't help it, *chérie*. You have that effect on me," he had said without embarrassment.

Dessert had arrived, a caramel flan they'd shared, but

they hadn't even finished when he said, "Will you come upstairs? I'm dying to kiss you."

They both knew how she reacted to his kiss.

They might have made love in the elevator if his guard hadn't been with them, standing discreetly at the front of the car with his back to them so Henri could steal a first kiss, then a second, longer, more passionate one.

Inside the suite, they'd barely made it to the bed.

How had she been so aroused? Until that moment, he'd barely touched her.

But even as she lay here next to him, thinking about the way he'd hurriedly skimmed away her knickers and covered himself with a shaking hand, she was growing wet and achy. She had been pure butter beneath him, locking her legs around his waist and lifting into his heavy thrusts.

She should go home. She didn't want to do the walk of shame in the morning, not when she already knew the paparazzi were on to them.

But she found herself slithering closer, sliding her legs against his and giving in to the temptation to taste his skin. He smelled sharp and masculine against his neck. His stubble abraded her nose and lips, but in a sexy way that turned her on because it accented how different they were. Female and male, meant to come together like pieces of a puzzle.

"Encore?" he murmured, moving against her, hardening at her first touch.

"What's wrong with me?"

"Not a damned thing, *chérie*. Ah, this," he growled with satisfaction as he trailed his hand between her legs and found her juicy and plump. "I'm addicted. I have to taste you again." He slid down, pressing her legs open.

She moaned at the sheer indulgence of being pleasured by him like this. He made her feel like she was giving him something when she allowed this, which maybe she was because he pretty much took ownership of her. This act lowered her defenses completely so she was without inhibition, ready to beg when he drew back before she'd climaxed.

"I need to be inside you, *chérie.* I can't wait." He rolled her over and brought her onto her hands and knees.

He covered her like a male animal dominating his mate, filling her with a possessive thrust, so deliciously hard where she was soft and needy. One wide hand slid over her breasts, teased her nipples, rubbed her stomach, then fondled where they were joined as he moved in lusty thrusts.

She received him with cries of encouragement and abandon, so caught up in the raw excitement of it, she didn't care who might hear or what he thought of her behavior. When she climaxed, the paroxysm locked a scream in her throat while he shuddered over and around her, his noises guttural and final. She was *his.* Neither of them could deny it.

That was in the dark.

When she woke in the light of day, and recalled all they'd done, she wanted to *die.*

Why, oh, *why* couldn't she resist him?

Henri had been tempted to join Cinnia in the shower when he woke and heard her starting the water, but he forced himself to put a small distance between them while he contemplated a decision that had been rooting a little deeper into his mind with each hour of lovemaking that had ticked by.

He had never had a mistress, had never wanted anything long-term at all. Not since…

The wrenching memory struck like a kick in the stomach, ambushing him as that dark day sometimes did.

Do you love me?

She had been a pretty thing with caramel eyes and a mouth he'd been trying to kiss for weeks. They were cornered in a stairwell and he was flushed with more attraction than he'd ever felt. Suddenly there was Trella, telling him it was time to *go*.

Go, then, he told her. *Little sisters are such a pain*, he had told the object of his affection, as Trella ran off to be stolen by Gili's—their affectionate name for Angelique— math tutor. *I do*, he had assured the caramel eyes as they were given privacy again. At least, he supposed it was love. He grew excited seeing this girl in the distance. He wanted to hold her hand, touch her all the time. He could hardly take his eyes off her when she was anywhere near him.

And then their friend Sadiq had shouted his name, telling him, "Trella's been taken."

He had seen that girl again, after Trella was home and he and Ramon returned to school. She'd tried to talk to him, but he'd avoided her.

After that, if girls and women came on to him, if they wanted to give up their bodies for mutual physical pleasure, fine. But he was never going to make the mistake of letting a female mean something to him. It put him off his game, exposed a flank.

It could cost the life of someone near and dear.

Romantic love, he had determined, was a weakness he couldn't afford.

Taking a mistress, however, was a slightly less dangerous risk.

He presumed, wondering if he was rationalizing.

Dressing in his pants and shrugging on his open shirt, he moved into the lounge, where he called in an order for breakfast, put in a request for the boutiques to send a selection for them and picked up the paper left outside his door.

"Bon matin," he said to Pierre, who had relieved Guy overnight. "Anything I should know about?"

"All the coverage seems run-of-the-mill, but fresh posts are still coming out. We're keeping an eye out."

Henri nodded, thoughtful, as he closed the door.

He'd never taken a mistress for the same reason he refused to marry and have children: the threat of kidnapping. Women who were only briefly linked to his name were not likely to be targeted or used against him. Precautions would have to be extended to Cinnia if he went through with this.

He scanned the headlines, then picked up his phone to see a text from Ramon. A question mark. Obviously he'd seen the headlines and wondered why Henri was seeing that woman from the nightclub again.

Henri ignored it and returned a text from Angelique with a video call.

"Problème?" he asked, continuing in French. "That was a cryptic message. Why are you worried about something you said to Trella about Sadiq? Are they having a romance I don't know about?"

"What? No! Of course not. No, I think he's falling for someone back in Zhamair. Do you know if that's true?"

"He didn't say anything when I spoke to him last." Sadiq might be the best friend he and his brother had, but they did not discuss their love lives. They talked about important things like stock prices and politics.

"Why does that affect Trella?" he prompted.

"I don't know." She frowned in her introspective way and he knew to give her a moment to gather her thoughts. Angelique was a quieter personality, more like him, preferring solitude, while Trella and Ramon were the extroverts. Everything Trella did was full bore, including a nervous breakdown. She had been making him mad with worry since her birth, when she had turned blue in his arms the first time he held her.

He often thought that if it *had* been Angelique outside the day of the kidnapping, and her tutor had called her over, planning to stuff her in his van, she would have waited for Ramon and insisted he hold her hand and come with her. Shyness had been a hurdle for her, but it was a type of self-protection that served her well.

Trella had possessed none of that. She had run headlong over to the tutor, eager to be helpful and say she wasn't Angelique.

They had stolen her despite her kicks and screams, because how effective was a nine-year-old girl against two strong men?

The trauma affected his sister to this day, which made him blind with fury if he didn't carefully drip-feed himself those memories. It made him want to hurry Angelique to tell him how she imagined Sadiq, their friend who had actually helped save Trella, could be a threat to their sister now.

"I was just talking to her about him," Angelique continued as though still gathering her thoughts. "And saying it was bound to happen that he would marry someday, even if he's not in love now. She got really quiet. Now I feel…" She shrugged. "You know. Like she's upset."

"Deeply upset?"

"No." She said the word on a rush of relief. "Normal upset. But I think she's worried that if he did get married, she wouldn't be able to go to his wedding."

"We can cross that bridge when we come to it," he said. "But thank you for telling me."

Trella had been stable for half a year. They were all holding their collective breath that this time she was actually conquering her panic attacks.

He heard Cinnia and glanced up to see her with dry, windswept hair, wearing one of the hotel robes. "I, um, just want my phone." She scurried to where he had set her handbag on a table after finding it on the floor, where she'd dropped it last night.

"Who's that?" Angelique asked.

"A friend." A very beautiful goddess who had done wicked, devilish things with him in the night. He had not misremembered the power of their chemistry. He kept reminding himself he wasn't a man to be led by his organ, but as many times as they'd made love last night, it wasn't enough. That's what he kept coming back to. He wasn't prepared to go another few weeks, let alone a lifetime, without making love to her again.

"Don't run away," he ordered Cinnia before she could lock herself in the bedroom. "I'm finishing up here." To his sister, he said, "I'll touch base with her later. Let me know if anything changes."

He ended the call and stood, still conflicted now his sister had reminded him of the threats they faced daily and their far-reaching effects.

At the same time, his hands rolled of their own accord, silently inviting Cinnia to come to him.

She didn't move, only hugged herself and flicked her glance to his phone. "Who was that?"

"Gili. Angelique. My other sister."

"You're very close to your siblings."

"They're the only people I trust completely."

She looked at her bare toes. "I speak French. I wasn't trying to eavesdrop, but I heard a little."

"And?"

"And nothing." She shrugged. "I feel bad for your sister. I don't imagine something like that is anything you get over. I mean, I still cry about losing my dad and it's been over a decade, but it sounds like she's quite haunted and I'm sorry she's still affected." She glanced up, expression so soft with compassion it cracked things inside him. "I know you lost your father, as well. I'm sorry for that, too."

"You're sorry for a lot of things." Deepening their relationship would come with many types of risk, he realized. Long-term relationships demanded more of this sort of thing. He was not eager to open up to her, but he hated the distance she was keeping between them right now. The physical distance, at least.

"Are you sorry about last night?" he asked, trying to understand why she wasn't rushing into his arms.

"A little," she mumbled.

"Why?" he demanded, not pleased to hear it.

She kept her head down, but he could see her growing red. With embarrassment?

He swore and went to her, tugging her close with gentle roughness so they knocked together and she threw back her head to scowl at him.

The vulnerability in her eyes made his heart swerve. He was not the only one disturbed by the level of intimacy between them. He found himself rubbing his thumbs against her upper arms where he gripped her, trying to offer reassurance.

"We gave each other a great deal of pleasure. That's not something to be ashamed of."

She swallowed and hid her thoughts with a lowered gaze. Her mouth pouted, maybe even showed a hint of bruising from their thousand rapacious kisses.

Oddly, that hint of injury was the turning point, allowing him to make his decision. They needed time so they could pace themselves. Otherwise, they were liable to kill each other.

"I *like* that you held nothing back," he told her. "Quit being shy about it or I'll do all those same things to you right here on the floor in the lounge. In *daylight*."

Cinnia was tempted to scoff and say, "You can try," but she had a feeling he *would*.

And she'd let him.

He started to kiss her, but the knock on the door interrupted. "Breakfast," he said with a small grimace, releasing her to let in room service.

She touched fingertips to her tingling lips, scolding herself for being disappointed. She was achy and exhausted, very tender in delicate places, and all she could think about was how much she wanted to feel his touch on all those sensitized places again.

Other staff came in with the wheeled table of covered dishes. A woman brought an assortment of outfits and held up each in turn for approval.

"Not that one. It's hideous," Henri said as the woman showed them a green dress. "Why does it even exist? That one, the blue. To match your eyes," he told Cinnia.

He accepted a striped button shirt and the boutique owner left clean underthings for both of them. Cinnia waited until everyone was gone to check the price tags.

"You're not paying for those," Henri said, barely glancing up from the plates he uncovered.

"Neither are you. I guess I'm going home in last night's dress."

"You're my guest. I will provide everything you need while you're with me."

Something in her midsection did a little curl and twist, anchoring and panging inside her. *Get what you can.*

"Are you going to join me? Surely you're as hungry as I am."

"Are you going to keep teasing me about it?" she demanded.

"Last night? Did that sound like teasing? I mean it as praise and gratitude." He looked at her and his shoulders relaxed as he gave her a perplexed look. "*Vraiment*, why does it bother you that we spent a night making love?"

He had stripped her bare, not just physically, but down to her soul. She was never going to be the same. He would always be the man who had done those things and made her feel that way and he would always *know* it. *She* would always know it and compare future lovers and feel wistful. Cheated, even.

"I told you," she muttered, moving to sit across from him, absolutely starving from her expenditure of calories, but feeling defenseless and needy. Tired, she assured herself. She was just tired. And filled with impossible yearning. "I don't do this."

"If you think last night was common for me, you're overestimating my libido."

"Oh, I have a healthy respect for that animal, believe me." *Coffee*. She poured a cup for each of them with shaking hands and quickly doctored hers, sighing with her first sip even though it burned her tongue.

When she glanced at him, he was watching her with an enigmatic look.

"You're also underestimating your effect on me. We have a unique connection." He seemed to choose his words very carefully. "We could leave things here and go on with our lives. I would probably call you the next time I was in London. I will optimistically believe you would be available and want to see me."

That was what was killing her right now. She had been able to put him mostly out of her mind after the first time because she'd been angry and genuinely hadn't thought she would see him again. For him to show up and pursue her so blatantly, however, set her up for believing he would do it again in the future.

She would counsel any girlfriend or sister to *never* wait on a man or give him so much power over her personal happiness, but here she sat, looking into her coffee because she didn't want Henri to see that he already held her on the end of a leash and all he had to do was tug for her to come to heel.

That's where her shame was coming from. Her eyes stung and she made herself blink to stem the tears of humility at being his sexual pet.

"What do I assume by your lack of response, Cinnia? That you would be agreeable to that arrangement?"

"I'm not going to hold a reservation for you," she lied, setting her cup into its saucer with a hard clink and a little slosh of coffee over the rim.

"Exactly what I thought you'd say." He braced his elbows on the table, hands loosely linked above his plate. "Much of your appeal for me is that you expect so little of me. You're very independent. But I do not care to take my chances with your accessibility. I would like to propose a different arrangement."

When she glanced up, his gaze was waiting to snare hers. The hazel-green tone was very, very green. Avid in a possessive, masculine way. *Mine.*

Her stomach swooped and she scented danger, yet it was the lofty danger of swinging out on a rope over a cliff on a bottomless lake. Life threatening, but exhilarating.

"A retainer?" she mocked.

"Of a sort. I've never had a mistress, but I begin to see the benefits."

She was knocked speechless. For a few painful heartbeats, she could only stare, then pointed out, "So. Not a proposal. A *proposition*."

Her pulse raced in panic and she looked across the room at the pretty clothes he was already trying to purchase for her.

Get what you can.

"I believe there are websites where women advertise for sponsors. Perhaps start *there*," she suggested thinly.

"I don't want *a* mistress. I want *you*. Look." He waved at the plates they hadn't yet touched. "I can eat plain scrambled eggs and there's nothing wrong with that, especially when I'm hungry, but if I have the option to eat one poached to perfection, delicately spiced and accompanied by a tempting banquet of other flavors, one that not only sates the appetite but is a joy with every bite, why the hell wouldn't I want the quality ones?"

"And since you're used to buying the best, I'm sure you think you can afford the eggs you see in front of you today. In this case, you can't."

"I'm very rich."

"I'd rather go hungry than sell myself."

He made a noise that was decidedly French. "Forget the metaphors and eat the damned eggs before they go cold."

After they'd both taken a couple of bites, he said, "I'm never going to marry. Long-term dating, in the traditional sense, is a false promise I won't make. Women come to me, come *on to* me, at a steady enough rate that I've never lacked for company."

"I kind of prefer the not calling over this turn of conversation." She flashed a humorless smile. "Just saying."

"But if I expect a woman to make herself exclusive to me, I ought to provide something in return."

"Your charm isn't enough?" She blinked in fake shock.

"Have you heard of erotic spanking, Cinnia? Some

women find it pleasurable and deliberately test a man's patience with backchat, looking for a hot bottom." He showed his teeth. "Just saying."

Wicked, evil man. For one second, she thought about that. Started to blush, and told herself to smarten up.

"You want it straight, Henri?" she challenged, stomach twisting. "Not shaken nor stirred? Fine."

She seemed to have no pride where he was concerned anyway. She dropped back in her chair and gave him a hate-filled glare for forcing her to bring up the pathetic mistakes of her past.

"I told you my father left his estate in a mess. We were in dire straits, actually. Really dire. Mum and my sisters have a hard time seeing it, especially Mum. She has this throwback notion that if one of us marries well, all our problems will be solved. You asked me last night what happened with my ex-boyfriend. That's what happened."

"He was rich and didn't want to marry you?"

"Exactly. Except that we'd been poor together, struggling through school and scrambling for rent every month for a year when we moved here to the city. I was actually the one making more money for the first while. I thought we were in love and that we would get married. Then his folks sold a piece of property and said they were going to split the money between their children. It was a few hundred thousand each, enough to make a nice down payment on a good home. I honestly thought he was being cagey for the weeks following the sale because he was shopping for an engagement ring and planning how to propose."

"Non?" He was holding on to a very neutral tone, betraying nothing of what he might be thinking.

"Hell, no! He was telling his parents to hold off doling out his portion so I couldn't put a claim on it, then he siphoned off half of what was in our shared accounts and kicked me out of our flat the day we were supposed to renew the lease."

She looked at her eggs and knew Avery had been dry, white toast at best while Henri was a mouthwatering croissant.

"I know my family is a handful. I know Mum came on strong when she learned his news. She was on the phone calling local churches that *day*. She flat out told him he should sink his money into her house and said we should move in with her. I never would have let that happen, though. I'll never live with her again if I can help it. She makes me bananas."

She crossed her legs and adjusted the fall of the robe, noting her hand was trembling. She was trying hard to keep a grip, but she still felt so *stupid*. She had thought Avery loved her and it had shaken her confidence in herself, in her belief that she could judge a character and even in her belief that she was lovable. Her voice quavered with old emotion and she couldn't seem to steady it.

"Even though he had known me all that time, he wrote me off as only wanting his bank balance. He said I had always known his parents were sitting on that potential, that I had known money would come to him, and that everything I had done was a calculated investment in getting a piece of it. I did know about it. I had counseled his parents on whether it was better to sell the land before their death or leave it as part of their estate. *Because he asked me to*. And I didn't charge them, by the way. Friends-and-family discount." She picked up her fork and stabbed her egg and watched the yolk bleed out.

Henri reached for his phone and said very casually, "What is his name?"

"Jerkface McPants on Fire. Don't bother ordering a hit. He's not worth the bullet."

He set down his phone again. "This is why you're so sensitive about letting me buy you a meal or a dress?"

"Or a hotel room or a favor with my boss or a rental agreement as a mistress. I earn my keep, Henri. I refuse—I absolutely refuse—to become a kept woman. I'm aiming to start my own agency. I will not work my butt off to succeed only to have people say it's because I was sleeping with a sexy French tycoon."

"My sisters are constantly accused of succeeding with their design house because Sauveterre International underwrote it. Do you know how they respond to that accusation?"

"How?"

"By ignoring it. You do not owe explanations to anyone. You certainly don't have to justify yourself to McFacey man. Stop worrying about what he thinks of you. As for opening an agency, I encourage you to send us a business plan regardless of the terms you and I negotiate for our personal partnership. Ramon and I are investors. We invested in Maison des Jumeaux because Trella wrote a solid plan that has exceeded all of our expectations. If yours shows promise, we may extend you a start-up loan. It won't be nepotism. We do not offer friends-and-family discounts. When it comes to money, neither of us is influenced by sentiment or sexual infatuation. That's why we're rich."

He was not joking.

She was crushed by his reduction of her to a sexual infatuation, but suffered an immediate urge to knock his socks off with her business acumen, wanting to secure a loan from him simply for the achievement of it.

She murmured, "I'll think about it," and returned to eating.

He made short work of his plate and freshened their coffee.

"I like the idea of you working for yourself," he said.

"Why?"

"Because I have a very busy life. It would be hard to find time to be together if you had a strict workweek."

"I love the way you talk like I'm going to agree to be your—oh!" She leaned forward with mock delight. "Let's use the French term, shall we? *Courtisane*."

He gave her a flat look that grew into a considering one.

"An educated woman who values herself and her time? One who is not ashamed of her sex drive? *Is* that you, Cinnia?"

She sat back. "You're trying to make it sound like that's all it is. It's not."

"No, it's potentially quite complicated. But seeing as you are so smart, walk through this with me. I am based in Paris, but I travel to New York at least once a month. I have an office here in London. I could work some of my time out of it, perhaps one week a month. Ramon and I would like to expand into Asia, but we're already stretched thin. And I occasionally drop everything to fly home to Spain if my sister needs me. Tell me how much time we'll have together unless you come with me for some of that travel."

"Presuming I want to spend time with you," she said tartly.

"Look at me," he commanded in such a stern voice her heart stalled and her gaze flashed up to his. "Were you there last night? The bed is a pile of ashes, we set it so completely on fire. If you don't want to do that again, fine. Get dressed and leave. I'll never bother you again."

His words spiked through her heart and she found herself pushing to her feet in a rush of pique, catching the wild flare of something in his eyes before she turned away and—

She halted, unable to make herself take another step.

Something hooked sharp and fierce behind her breast-bone. Tears slammed into her eyes. She brought her fists up and pushed the heels of her hands into her clenched lids, catching a shattered breath. She couldn't move. Couldn't walk away from him.

"Idiot," he said behind her, chair scraping before he pulled her back against his chest, strong arms encasing her, but in a way that felt secure and reassuring.

"I don't want to feel this way," she said in a whisper, voice breaking. All of her breaking. She was self-reliant. She didn't need anything from a man.

But she needed *him. This* man. Who offered *things*, not his heart.

"How do you feel? Hmm?" One hand stole into the front of her robe and he cupped her bare breast, flicked her nipple.

She made a noise of pleasure-pain, instantly catapulted into memory and desire, but her nipples were so tender she covered his hand and stilled his caress.

"Sore?" he asked against her ear, nibbling in a way that sent shivers down her nape, all the way to the small of her back.

She arched, pushing her bottom into the hardness at his loins.

"You're going to kill me, Henri. I ache all over and I don't care. I want you anyway."

"Ah, chérie. You're hurting like this because you don't want our time to end. I feel the same." His mouth opened on the side of her neck, delicately sucking a mark into her skin. "But I will be very, very careful with you, I promise."

His free hand went in below the belt and found her naked and slippery, already responding to being close to him. "You like that?"

"You know I do," she breathed, tilting her head to the

side so his kisses could reach all down the side of her neck. "But I don't think I can."

"Come here." He backed up, bringing her with him.

She heard him unzip his pants and turned to see him putting on a condom. He sat in the chair and drew her to straddle him.

"Gently," he murmured, taking it slow as he drew her down.

Even though she was tender, she breathed a sigh of relief when she was seated on him, full of his turgid heat and completely possessed by this terribly wicked sorcerer of a man.

He opened her belt and spread the robe, looking down at her breasts. His hands moved on her thighs and buttocks, caressing without urging her to move. Then he kissed her, gently and sweetly. Slowly and languorously.

"See?" he breathed against her lips. "We don't have to be greedy if we know we have time."

She was greedy anyway, running her hands across his chest to spread his shirt, then placing kisses there, pinching his nipples and feeling his response inside her. She smiled with secretive joy.

And she began to move instinctively, riding him in an abbreviated rock. She was so tender and sensitive she was gasping in moments, squeezing him with her powerful orgasm.

"Magnifique." He stroked her hair back from her face, set light kisses on her cheekbone and brow and the tip of her nose. His eyes were bright green with arousal. "Do you want to stop? I don't want to hurt you."

"You didn't finish," she said in an urge for him to do so, nerve endings coming alive under the fresh stimulation. She was nearly in tears because it was such an intense sensation.

"I will later, when you're feeling better." He cupped her face, thumbs coming together in the center of her lips, then parting to rest in the corners.

"You're shameless, aren't you?" she said on a trembling breath, frightened by his assumption she would be there for him later today and every day from now on. Maybe she would. Right in this second, she wanted to be whatever he needed her to be. "Don't manipulate me through my body's response to yours."

"Now you won't even accept an orgasm given freely? You are a difficult woman to please."

She ducked her head out of his hands and tucked her forehead against his throat, nose to his collarbone so his scent filled her head.

"You won't ever marry me." She didn't know if it was a refusal, an accusation, or merely a statement of terms.

He tensed, but said firmly, "*Oui.* I will never marry you."

She waited for some kind of repugnance to arrive and prompt her to reject him. All she could think was that at least she would have this, him, for a little while. She closed her eyes, still swimming in the high of orgasm while tendrils of fresh arousal wound around her. He was offering a sensual, sexual contract of association, that was all, but it would be such a pleasurable one.

"I want to marry and have children. Someday. I'm not going to give you all of my best years and wonder what happened when you throw me over for a younger model."

His fingers were under the fall of her hair, working upward in a comb to the back of her skull.

"I'll let you go when you're ready for that. You're not searching for those things today, are you? Be with me until you are."

A half sob pressed out of her. Was she really going to agree to this?

"If either of us was willing to give this up, *chérie*, you would have left in the middle of the night."

"I know," she said on a sob of surrender. "Please don't be smug."

"It's not comfortable for me to be this taken by you." He massaged her scalp, holding her in compassionate, irrevocable intimacy. "I am yielding, too."

It didn't feel like it. He was still hard inside her. She moved restlessly, drawing back to nip his chin, then looked into his eyes. "I bet I'll get there before you do."

"I bet I'll make sure of it." He threw himself forward, swooping her to the floor beneath him, sending them both soaring with the masterful thrust of his hips.

CHAPTER FIVE

Present day...

"KILLIAN." HENRI STOOD and rounded his desk to greet the owner of Tec-Sec Industries as he was shown into Henri's Paris office. They shook hands and Henri asked, "How are Melodie and the baby?"

"Well. Thank you."

Henri wasn't surprised by Killian's succinct reply. Cinnia had summed it up nicely when she had first met the man who was an international security specialist and held the contract for the Sauveterre family's safety. *Did you meet at reticence school? He doesn't care for small talk, does he?*

They had met eight years ago, when Killian had come to Sauveterre International seeking investment capital to expand his global security outfit. Underwriting Killian's ambitions had been one of the first really big risks Henri and Ramon had taken with their father's money after their initial power struggles with the board. A year into watching Killian skyrocket with his business model and suite of military-grade services, they had hired him themselves.

That had been another type of gamble, a move Henri had not made without a great deal of reflection. Ramon operated on gut instinct while Henri was more fact driven. Killian had a good track record, but not a long one.

Ramon had left the final decision to Henri, after making a very good case for the change. "But we both have to believe in this. If you don't like it, we won't do it," his brother had said.

Which had left the massive responsibility for any muck-ups squarely on Henri's shoulders—where the weight still sat. Heavily.

Fortunately, Killian was a brilliant mind hidden behind an impassive face. Nothing escaped him. Aside from the occasional blip of overly exercised caution, they hadn't had one security incident since signing contracts with him.

Not that Henri planned to become complacent as a result, but he felt he and his family were in very good hands. Even marriage and the arrival of his first child hadn't thrown Killian off his focus on business.

"Coffee? Something stronger?" Henri offered.

"I won't be here long," Killian said with a wave of his hand and hitched his pants to sit.

Henri was relieved Killian was so reserved, not trying to bend Henri's ear about the wonders of fatherhood. Henri didn't need to hear what he was missing. Not when he was still stinging over Cinnia's departure for that very reason.

The recollection jabbed like a rapier into his gut, swift and unexpected. She had left him to find the man who would give her the family she craved. Thinking of it sent a reverberation of frustrated agony through him every time he thought of it, so he refused to think of it and quickly pushed aside the temptation to brood today.

He took the chair opposite, distracting himself by getting to business. "You said it wasn't an emergency. I assume it's a price increase?"

"No, although there will be one at the end of the year

to go with a system upgrade. The briefing for that will come through regular channels. No, this is something I thought was best dealt with promptly and face-to-face. One of my guards—I should say, one of the Sauveterre guards—brought me an ethical dilemma." Killian braced his elbows on the chair's arms and steepled his fingers. "In performing regular duties, this guard became aware of a situation that will be of interest to you, but the guard couldn't come to you without compromising the privacy of your sibling."

Henri frowned. "Which one?"

Killian canted his head. "I work for all of you, Henri. I won't betray the trust of one to another. You'd fire me yourself if I did. This guard was reluctant to say anything, but brought it to me because Tec-Sec is charged with protecting the *entire* Sauveterre family. We take that responsibility very seriously."

"Ramon has an illegitimate child somewhere," Henri deduced, and was struck by something he rarely felt, but it was most acute if it happened to involve his brother. Ramon had something he wanted.

He didn't want children, though. He didn't want the responsibility. He had decided that long ago.

Nevertheless, the idea of his brother becoming a father seared his bloodstream with envy so sharp it felt like pure acid.

Then he heard Killian say, "I would take that up with Ramon, wouldn't I?"

Henri's mind blanked as it tried to recalibrate.

There was no humor in Killian's face, no judgment, no emotion whatsoever. He was a master at hiding his feelings, which was one of the reasons Henri liked working with him. Their dealings were always straightforward and unsentimental.

"One of the girls?" he said, hazarding a guess. It was impossible in Trella's case. There had been that one night three months ago, when she'd slipped out in public as Angelique. She'd been photographed kissing a man—a prince, no less—but she had sworn to Henri that's all that had happened.

Gili was tangled up with a prince of her own, had even taken off into the desert overnight with Kasim while they'd all been in Zhamair for Sadiq's wedding. He'd had a message this morning to say that things were back on, but hadn't had a chance to catch up with her about it.

Even if she was back with Kasim, Gili was so cautious he couldn't imagine her failing to take steps to prevent a pregnancy. She would definitely make arrangements to protect her child if she did happen to fall pregnant. Killian wouldn't have to bring it up with Henri. Same went for Trella, for that matter.

Which had to mean…

"You can't mean me," Henri said dismissively. "Cinnia is the only woman I've been with—"

He ran straight into it like he was in one of Ramon's high-performance race cars and hadn't seen the big, red, tightly stacked, rough-edged bricks cemented into a giant wall that had arrived right in front of his nose.

I didn't ask if you wanted to marry me. I asked if you loved me.

And the reason you're asking is because you want to change things between us. I told you I'd never marry you.

He'd been taken aback that morning three months ago, not having seen that conversation coming, either. They were comfortable as they were. He'd grown quietly furious as she had put him on the spot with her "do you love me?"

He *couldn't*. Too much was at stake.

From there, the separation had unfolded like surgery

without anesthetic. He'd endured it with stoicism so he wouldn't betray how much he begrudged her not being content with what they had. That's all he could offer her. She knew that. *He* had to accept it. Why couldn't she?

I would say that things have already changed, but they really haven't. I've always wanted children. You said when I was ready to start a family, you would let me go. Are you going to keep your word?

Of course. He didn't make promises he wouldn't keep.

They had parted with as much civility as possible. Hell, he'd left the flat and come back a week after she was packed and gone. He hadn't looked her up on social media. There was no point. She rarely posted and the last thing he needed was to see whom she was dating in her quest to marry and procreate.

Now he knew she wasn't dating anyone.

Because she was having his child.

It couldn't be true. *Couldn't.* She would have told him. Unless...

The next thought that followed was a screamingly jagged "was it even his?"

Of course it was. It had to be. Killian wouldn't have brought this news to him otherwise and Henri couldn't imagine... Didn't want to imagine... No. Cinnia was highly independent, stubborn to a fault and honest. She would not sneak around having affairs behind his back. When would she have found the time? One way or another, they had shared a bed most nights and while she had been extremely passionate between the sheets, she had never been promiscuous.

No, if she was pregnant, the baby was his.

But how? She knew he didn't want children. On that point he had been blunt, so what the hell had happened?

Had she stopped taking her pill? Was this pregnancy deliberate?

Did she not realize how dangerous that was?

From the moment the responsibility of protecting his family had become his, he had felt as though a Russian roulette gun was pressed to his head. The mere suggestion he had a child on the way slid an extra bullet into one of its chambers. She wouldn't put that on him. Would she?

An excruciating twist of betrayal wrung out the muscle behind his breastbone as he took in that she had disregarded his wishes.

"I see I've given you a lot to think about," Killian said, rising.

"You have." Henri stood, brain exploding. He was coated in a cold sweat beneath his tailored suit. It was all he could do to form civil words as his mind raced to Cinnia and a demand for answers. Somehow he managed to grasp the relevant threads of this conversation and tie them off. "Ensure the guard in question receives a suitable bonus."

"Of course."

"And submit a quote for extending your services to include my growing family." There were times when he recklessly played tennis in the heat and wound up this light-headed, walking through gelatin. He could barely breathe.

"The proposal is being prepared along with a selection of suitable résumés. Are you headed to London? I have staff on standby if you need them. Let me know."

"I'll go straight to her flat, but didn't you put someone on her the minute you learned she was pregnant?" He snapped the words, straining to hold on to his temper, not wanting the pregnancy to be real, but slamming walls of protection into place with reflexive force anyway.

This would be the longest flight of his life. His palms

were clammy, he was so fixated on ensuring the safety of his child. If she was pregnant, he wouldn't breathe easy until he had Cinnia locked behind the Sauveterre vault-like doors.

"I came here the minute I learned," Killian said. "Less than two hours ago. Although I gather the guard has been aware for a few weeks. Preliminary surveillance reveals she's paying one of my competitors to keep the paparazzi at a distance. They're good enough they would notice if someone started watching her, so we're maintaining a distance. She's staying at her mother's, by the way."

Henri nodded and shook Killian's hand.

"Merci," he said distantly. "And one of my siblings knows about this?" He struggled to take in that incredulous piece of the news along with the rest.

"Yes." Killian refused to say which one.

From there, Henri operated like a robot in a sci-fi thriller. *Get to her.* Order the car, text his pilot they were flying to London, climb on the plane, blow through any obstacle without regard.

Wring Ramon's neck. It had to be Ramon. Was he still in touch with that friend of Cinnia's? Cinnia had told him Vera had married last year.

Henri couldn't imagine either of his sisters learning something of this magnitude and keeping it from him. They were far too softhearted to leave him in the dark, knowing how heavily the family's security weighed on him.

But Ramon would have taken the necessary steps to guard her. He wouldn't be satisfied with leaving Cinnia to make her own arrangements.

It was all a jumble and nothing would make sense until Henri saw her. Topmost in his mind would be… *What the hell had she been thinking?*

* * *

Cinnia was tired. Not just tired because she was building two more human bodies with her own, but because today was one thing after another. Nell had been quick to tell her it was because Mercury was in retrograde, when she'd used the phone from the pub where she worked to say that the Wi-Fi was on the blink at the flat.

Perhaps it was true, since Cinnia's new partner running her London office was having phone and network issues. She was forwarding all the office calls and emails to Cinnia today. Cinnia had asked her tech guy to check both, but he was stuck in traffic. Again, thanks to a certain planet traveling backward, *apparently*.

Dorry, bless her, had something going on at school. She was doing most of her learning online these days, accelerating to finish early. She usually sat at the desk in the parlor across the hall, answering the handful of calls Cinnia typically received, allowing Cinnia to concentrate on the piles of work in front of her.

Not today. Nope. Today Dorry was out and their mother was "pitching in." Which meant rather than screen calls and take a message, or look up a price and answer a simple question, she said things like, "Sorry to interrupt, love, but they want to set up a video chat. How do I do that again?"

When her mother knocked for the billionth time, and pushed in without waiting for an invitation, and the phone hadn't even rung this time, Cinnia snapped, "*Mum.* I'm *working*."

"Well, he wasn't going away, was he?"

Cinnia glanced up and the sight of Henri struck her like an asteroid. Like an atomic bomb that had been packed with nuclear energy bottled up by the weeks of being apart from him. Instantly she shattered into a million pieces—

and had to sit there trying not to show it. Her entire body stung with the force.

He was painfully gorgeous. Cutting-edge dark blue suit, a narrow line of ruthless red in his striped tie, clean shaven, tall and trim and larger than life, as always. His intense personality honed in on her with that piercing quality that made her insides twist with joyful reunion.

It was quickly choked off with a quake of abject fear.

She wasn't ready for this.

Because the flutters in her belly were not just the butterflies of excitement he always inspired. They were the movement of his offspring.

She said a word that was *very* unladylike.

"Lovely to see you, too." His mouth curled in something that was the furthest thing from a smile.

"You called him?" she accused her mother, because that's what one did in times of deep stress: attack the people who loved you unconditionally.

She couldn't believe it, though. She'd been so careful to hide her pregnancy, practically living like a shut-in since she had begun to show. In the most uncompromising of terms, she had bribed and cajoled and threatened her family into silence. How had he found out?

"I did not." Her mother chucked up her chin in offense, silver coif trembling. "But it's long past time you did, isn't it? Shall I hold your calls?"

"Oh, thanks, Mum. That would be great." Cinnia rolled her eyes as her mother closed the door, locking Henri into the library with her.

"Trella told you?" She lowered the angle of her laptop screen to see him better over it, but quavered behind it.

"Trella?" His sister's name came out with the weight of grim consideration. "I was wondering which one of them it was. How the hell does my sister—" He held up a hand. "We will come back to that."

"You haven't talked to her?" Oh, damn. *Sorry, Trell.*

Cinnia glanced at her phone, wanting to warn her friend that big brother was on the warpath, but she had to survive his wrath first.

She took in the way he looked like a caged lion, tail flicking and muscles bunched, ready to pounce. They had argued in the past, but he'd never been this angry. He'd never looked at her like this—as though whatever he'd felt for her was completely *gone*.

Their breakup had been agony for her, but it was nothing compared to the raw squirming torment that accosted her under that accusatory glare of his.

"How, um…" Wait. If Trella hadn't told him, did he even know she was pregnant?

She scooched her chair a little tighter to the desk and tugged her lapels over her noticeably more ample breasts, adjusting the angle of her laptop one more inch, hoping to hide what was pressing up against the edge of her desk.

"Why are you here?" she asked shakily.

"You know damned well why I'm here." He planted his hands on the two-hundred-fifty-year-old Chippendale masterpiece that her mother refused to sell. "Stand up."

"You came to school me on my manners?" She pretended she wasn't torn to shreds inside and lifted haughty brows. "Sorry I didn't rush around to greet you like a long-lost relative!"

He made a choked noise.

"Yes, *chérie.* I think there is a certain courtesy concerning relatives that you have grossly overlooked." His hazel-green eyes were stainless steel. Chop-chop, his gaze warned. Prepare to be sliced and diced.

She had known he would be angry, but this was so unfair. Her hand wanted to go protectively to the bump that had sent him away and was now bringing him back, but not with so much as a hint of pleasure at seeing her again.

She had been trying to work up the courage to call him. Her ego had held her back. Pride and ego. Pride because she was still devastated that he had let her go, obviously feeling nothing toward her despite the fact they'd essentially been living together, and ego because she looked ridiculous.

She gathered her courage and stood, bracing to take it on the chin.

He slid his gaze down and jerked, pushing off the desk, clearly taken aback by the small planet that shot straight out of her middle and arrived a full minute before she did in any room she entered.

"Thanks," she said acerbically, but couldn't blame him. While she was a little plumper in the face and chest, she really hadn't gained much weight except in her middle, where she looked like she'd stuffed a sofa cushion under her shirt. The whole sofa, actually, and she was only midway through this pregnancy!

Henri took a long inhale, cheeks hollowing as he stared at her belly with such laser focus she was compelled to block his fierce stare with her hand.

His own hand went into his hair. His nostrils flared as that cutting glance swung up to pierce hers. "Why would you do this?"

He was gray beneath his swarthy skin. Obviously he was shocked.

She had expected this accusation. It was precisely the reason why she had left him and had worked so hard to put in place a means to do this alone. It still went into her like a knife. Nearly two years, *two years* of never asking him for one damned thing except "do you love me?"

"*I* did this to *you*?" she said, barely managing to keep a level tone. Oh, she felt so discarded and misused in that moment, worse even than when he'd shrugged off their breakup. "I suggest you take a hard look at which one of us is carrying three stone of our combined DNA." It was closer to five, but shut up, bathroom scale.

"You were supposed to be taking your pill."

"And I had the flu for a week last fall."

"I used condoms after," he reminded her, stabbing the top of the desk with his finger.

"I thought we were fine, too. What am I? A reproductive scientist? I don't know how it happened! Sometimes when people have sex, they make babies. Super weird that it could happen to us, right? 'Cause we hardly ever had sex."

Every night. All the time. She wanted to have sex with him right now, the bastard, coming in here smelling all yummy with that aftershave that drove her crazy and not having gained an ounce. If anything, he was sculpted into an even harder, sharper version of the man she had lusted after without reserve.

She looked away, hating her cheeks for flushing with awareness and her body for *remembering*.

If her eyes began to tear, she would throw herself through the curtain-cloaked window behind her.

"I never wanted this responsibility!" Henri blurted, like he'd been saving that statement for miles and miles. All his life. "You *knew* that."

"Then you should have kept your pants on," she hissed back at him.

He glared at her like he was furious with her for forever tempting that beast from behind his zipper. Like he resented her and her pregnancy and everything they'd shared.

Well, she was as volatile as any pregnant woman. Probably twice as emotional as the average. Salty tears rushed up to sting her eyes. Her throat closed with emotion and her inner mercury shot up so high it bounced off the inside of her skull.

"Don't feel you have to accept any responsibility today." She rounded the desk and headed for the door. "This is all my fault. You're completely innocent and have no obligation. I am more than capable of parenting without you." She pulled the door inward and waved an arm to invite him to exit. "Fly. Be free."

He folded his arms, such a filthy glare on his face she should have been turned to stone.

"I'm serious," she said, not caring if her mother was in earshot. She'd heard it all and the rest of the house was empty. "I'm one hundred percent ready to do this on my own. As you can see, I've started working here, where Mum and Dorry have agreed to help with child care. The London office is paying for itself and turning a small profit. So is my flat. Nell and her friends are renting it, but I give what I make on that to Mum since I've kicked out all her boarders. This place has been outfitted with a security system—"

"I'm supposed to imagine that my child is safe in a house where strangers—I'm sorry, *potential clients*—are coming and going?"

"You're supposed to imagine that I did not do this on purpose and I am *not* trapping myself a wealthy husband, as you obviously thought when you came storming in here on your high horse. I knew you would think that of me. I *knew*. Why else did I send back all your stupid jewelry? I could have kept it and sold it, you know! That money would be really handy right now, and God knows I earned it, didn't I? But I never asked you for it, Henri. I never asked you for *anything*."

"Calm down," he growled.

"You calm down! I never wanted to be pregnant by accident! I wanted it to be something I did *on purpose*. With the man I *loved*!"

His head went back like she'd clawed at his cheek. Her own emotions were clawing open her chest, leaving her heart exposed, raw and vulnerable. She railed on, protecting herself the only way she could, with mean, nasty words.

"I never asked for anything until that last morning and I would have settled for you telling me you *cared*. I would have settled for you asking me not to *leave*. But you didn't give one solid damn that I wanted to end it. Bye-bye, Cin. Nice having sex with you. Take your pretty payoffs. And all you can think about right now is how hard this is for *you*? Try hiding this from paparazzi!" She pointed at her massive bump. "Congratulations on being as big an ass as I thought you would be."

"Are you finished?"

"Really?" she cried. "You're going to take that patronizing tone with me? No, I'm not finished! I'm allowed to freak out! While you've spent the last twelve weeks screwing other women and carrying on with your completely unaffected life, I've been overhauling mine. I've been working damned hard so you never have to be inconvenienced by something that *we* did *together*. Say 'Thank you, Cinnia' and get the hell out of my house."

"Well aren't you the great martyr," he scoffed. "Excuse me for not being grateful when I wasn't given a choice in the matter, was I?"

"Oh, you had choices. And you made them. I'm making the same one, which means getting on with *my* life without *you*. Ta-ta," she sang in a jagged, off-key tone. "I have to get back to work now." After bawling her eyes out over this stupid man and his complete lack of regard for her.

"That's very cute. You know I have no choice. Neither do you," he warned, chin low, brows flat and ominous.

That did it. Her heart broke along old lines and her eyes filled up with hot, fat tears.

"Right," she said in a voice that cracked. "Your only choice is to be saddled with a woman you don't want. A gold digger, obviously, who had her eye on your money all along." She couldn't do this. She started to leave the room.

"Don't put words in my mouth." He caught at her arm.

She shook him off and blinked rapidly, but her lashes were matted together and her composure was thinning to the breaking point.

"Don't put babies in my belly."

"I'll confine it to one, trust me."

"Too late!" It came out shrill and loud. She spun to leave again, but quickly found herself halted and turned back to face him.

Through her tears, he was a blur of ashen skin.

"What?"

"Oh, look at me, Henri!" she intoned. "Have you ever been satisfied with only giving me *one* orgasm? Of course, you had to give me *two* babies!" Her fists clenched and she wanted to pound them against him, against the wall of his chest, as if she could break past the invisible wall he presented to hold off everyone.

Including her.

Especially her.

Instead she found herself stumbling across the hall as he dragged her with him. He plonked himself onto the love seat in the parlor and tugged her to sit beside him.

She was shaking so badly she let it happen and sat beside him in stiff silence, trying to hold her threadbare self together.

He sat with his elbows on his thighs and his face pressed into his wide hands.

She reminded herself she'd had weeks to process her pregnancy and the fact it was twins. He'd had, well, she would guess a few hours on the first baby and about ninety seconds on the second.

Oh, she didn't want to feel sorry for him! Maybe the idea of being a father was hard for him, but it didn't change the fact he'd thought awful things about her and hadn't tried *at all* to hang on to what they'd had.

What had they had? she asked herself for the millionth time. Sex. So much sex and yes, a few good laughs and many excellent meals. But while they'd been profoundly intimate physically, on an emotional level he'd held her off in a dozen subtle ways. Two years she had spent banging her head against that reserve of his and yes, she knew things about him like his taste in music and had a handful more facts on his family than the average person did, but he had never let her into his heart.

How many times had she counseled a girlfriend not to let a man own her soul without giving back a piece of his? Dear God, it was easier to give that advice than take it.

She reached for a tissue off the side table and blew her nose, fighting to pull herself together. She hadn't realized how much poison she'd been harboring over all of this. At one point her mother had accused her of punishing Henri by keeping the pregnancy from him and Cinnia had denied it, vehemently.

Just as she had vehemently done her best to annihilate him in every possible way today, holding off on stabbing him with the fact it was twins so she could do maximum damage when his shields were down.

Because she was crushed and she wanted him to join her in her anguish. She wanted to know she *could* hurt him.

Taking a shaky breath, she started to rise.

His hand shot out and he kept her on the sofa.

"I have to use the toilet. It's nonnegotiable."

He released her and she went, then lingered after washing her hands, studying the profile of her body while avoiding her gaze in the mirror.

She had come from a loving, nuclear family. It was what she had always aspired to have for herself and had never been comfortable as Henri's mistress. He had called her his friend and his companion, sometimes even his lover, but the lack of emotional commitment had always stung.

Part of her had wanted to believe Henri did love her deep down, but she had believed Avery had loved her because he *had said the words* and he hadn't. Even her first boyfriend, who had possessed her whole heart, had let her down. So she had tried to hold off giving up too much of herself to Henri. Had tried to stay autonomous and strong.

Still, she had hoped they were moving toward *something*. When she had turned up pregnant, however, she had had to face how superficial their relationship really was. She hadn't been able to stay with him at that point, not if she had any self-respect left.

At the same time, she knew how he would react to a pregnancy. Ties. Short, cold chains and tall, barbed wire fences.

It wouldn't be easy to hold herself apart from him while he tried to do what she knew he would want to do: pull her inside his castle and shut the drawbridge. *That* was why she had held off telling him. She couldn't be dragged back into his life knowing she meant nothing to him.

That was why she had to find the strength to continue resisting him now.

CHAPTER SIX

THE RATTLE OF china made Henri lift his head.

Millicent Whitley—Milly—came in with a tea tray. She set it up on the coffee table before him. The only noise was the sound of the dishes, but she made a statement with the force with which she served him.

He knew that Cinnia had had words with her mother at different times about their relationship and his refusal to offer a ring. Milly had never said a word to him about it, though. She was too wellborn, too possessed of impeccable manners.

Today, however, she brilliantly conveyed that she would love to see him choke to death on his petit four.

"Thanks, Mum," Cinnia said in a subdued tone as she came back.

"Eat one of the sandwiches," Milly said to her, pointing at the stack of crustless triangles as she straightened with the now empty tray, adding as she passed her daughter at the door, "You're behaving like a harridan."

"Gosh, I hope I haven't ruined my chances for a proposal."

Her mother shut the door on that comment and Cinnia made a face.

"How is your health?" Henri asked her, grasping for a lifeline of fact and logic to keep from being blown into the abyss of unknowns circling in his periphery.

Cinnia blew out a breath that lifted her fringe and came to perch next to him. She reached for a sandwich. "No issues. The weight packs on fast, which is expected. I'm not watching calories, but I try to avoid the empty ones. I've started drinking my tea black and I skip things like mayonnaise and sweets."

He nodded, watching her bite into what looked like plain tuna with a slice of tomato between two dry pieces of bread. Her lips looked fuller. Plump and kissable.

"There haven't been other women." His voice came out a shade too low.

She choked, hand going to her mouth before she reached for her tea and took a cautious sip, clearing her throat and flashing him a persecuted look.

"I'm ready to be civilized, but let's agree to be honest, shall we?"

"I had to date, you know I did." If she was offended that he'd accused her of deliberately getting pregnant, he was insulted that she believed he'd slept with all those women—*any* woman—since her. "Our breakup was well documented. I couldn't appear to be carrying a torch, could I? That wouldn't be safe for you." He'd been plagued by concerns regardless, teetering on wishing she would find a man to look out for her while passionately hating the idea.

"Well, you did an excellent job of convincing *me* you weren't carrying one."

He waited for her gaze to come to his, but she kept her attention on the plate she held.

Her features were softer and, if anything, prettier for it. More feminine. She wasn't wearing makeup, her hair was clipped at her nape, but he found her casual elegance as fascinating as ever.

He wanted her, every bit as much as ever.

He pushed to his feet, restlessly moving away from temptation. He was still processing that she was pregnant. His brain was not ready to take in twins and he was still very much reeling from the anger she'd thrown at him.

"There were no other women," he repeated. "I'm not going to say it again."

It was too much of a blow to his ego. He *couldn't* screw other women. She wanted them to throw toxins at one another? Fine. He would love to tell her how much he resented her grip on him. He felt like a cheat merely allowing another woman's hand to rest on his arm. Had he realized that would be a by-product of a long-term, monogamous relationship, he never would have entered into one.

Damn. He wished that was true, but Cinnia had entranced him from the first time he'd seen her. She still did, sitting there cutting a suspicious glare at him from beneath pulled brows. This connection between them was as base as an alpha wolf imprinted by a mate.

He wasn't comfortable being ruled by anything so visceral, but even now, as he was reeling from this life-altering news, part of him was soaring with the knowledge that he now had the perfect excuse to yank her back into his bed.

"As for expecting things of me, you expected me to behave badly and set me up to do so." He pushed his hands into his pockets. "How long did you think you could hide this? I can see if you had a single baby, you might have convinced the press it was someone else's, maybe pretended your infidelity was the reason we broke up. But twins? Of course they'll assume they're mine and go stark raving mad! How did that even happen?" He tried to wrap his brain around it. "Are they identical? Do you know?"

"One placenta," she said with a bemused shrug. "I realize it's like your family has been struck by lightning three times. I'm buying lotto tickets, but I'm told that's not how it works…"

Her joke fell flat.

She had finished her sandwich and was nursing her tea, brow furrowed in contemplation. He always had an urge to kiss that little wrinkle in her brow when she looked like that. She always tsk-tsked at him when he did, complaining it broke her train of thought.

Because he invariably wound up kissing her mouth next, and that led to making love.

That's probably why he liked to kiss her brow.

Could they make love? What the hell was wrong with him that that was all he could think about as he faced such a daunting prospect? Escape, he supposed. Making love with Cinnia had always provided him with a sense of peace to balance the rapid juggling of priorities that was the rest of his life.

She rubbed between her brows with two fingers, like tension sat there.

"I knew I'd have to tell you," she mumbled in a disheartened tone. "I was putting it off because I know what you're going to say, and…" She dropped her hand and said firmly, "I don't want to marry you."

In his lifetime, there were a handful of words that had gone through him like bullets. *Trella's been taken. Your father is gone.* Now, *I don't want to marry you.*

He'd been trying to ignore what she'd said earlier about wanting children with the man she loved. He had been fairly convinced she was in love with him, even though she'd never said the words. Then she had left him.

Today, all that rage she'd aimed at him? His brain told him that came from a scorned heart. He *had* scorned her.

Bye-bye, Cinnia. Yes, he had let her go without a fight. What was he supposed to have done? Denied her the family she had told him from the beginning that she wanted? If she had been telling the truth on her way out the door, and really *had* wanted to run off and find Mr. Right, to make a family with that unknown man, Henri had been honor bound to let her.

She hadn't been telling the truth, though. She'd been *testing* him.

He'd failed, obviously.

Had his rejection killed whatever she *had* felt?

He pinched the bridge of his nose. It didn't matter.

"You still have to do it," he informed her.

"No. I—"

"Cinnia," he interrupted, unequivocal. "I will accommodate your career if you want to keep working. Dorry can be our nanny. I will give you just about anything you ask of me, but you know that you are coming with me today. Our children must be protected. *You know I won't negotiate on this.*"

"No."

Cinnia had never been a pushover, something he had always admired in her, but Henri had written the book on how to get your way. He didn't bother saying anything, only gave her a look that warned she was wasting both their time.

"Divorced people raise children apart. If you want to amp up my security, that's your prerogative, but I'm handling things just fine."

"Are you?" He scratched his cheek and glanced toward the draped window. "Shall I open those curtains and we'll see how well you're keeping the world at bay?"

"Oh, you didn't drag a swarm of those buzzards here, did you?"

He could have taken steps to lose the cameras they'd picked up at the airport, but he'd been too intent on getting here. "You know what my life is like."

"I do!" she asserted with a crack in her voice as the words burst out of her. "And I put up with your guards and all the awful trolls who post those nasty things and I never made a peep because it was my choice to be with you. I could have walked away anytime if I didn't like it. And I did! So don't ask me to sign up for a lifetime of it. Don't try to *make* me."

His fuse, the one that had slowly been burning down since Killian had set a match to it, reached powder.

"Do you honestly think either of us has a choice?" He managed to keep his voice under a roar, but it was fierce with the bitter vehemence he normally kept pent up. "Don't tell me how hard it is to live under such attention. I know, damn you."

She sat back, intimidated by his muted explosion, but he couldn't contain it. Not if she was going to throw it in his face as the reason she didn't want to marry him. Damn it, she *would* understand, if nothing else, that it wasn't just a nuisance, but a life-threatening menace.

"Trella wasn't kidnapped because we're *rich*. We were valuable because we'd been portrayed as a national treasure. *I* didn't sign up for that. None of us did! And did they have the decency to give us privacy after she was rescued? Hell, no! It was worse!"

He thought of all the ugly conjecture that had followed them for years.

"They pushed her into a breakdown and I swear they caused my father's death. He might have withstood nearly losing his child, but trying to keep us out of that microscope? There was no pity for the pressure he was under! If he showed signs of cracking, they turned it higher. *I know.*" He smacked his hand into his chest. "I stepped into his shoes. The corporation is enough for any man and then to be worried sick for the rest of your life that another attempt would be made? All because those vipers insist on making us into demigods?"

He threw an accusatory point at the closed curtain, vainly wishing, yearning, for the ability to incinerate every camera on earth.

"I hate them. I bloody well hate them. They're vile and they set us up to be victimized in every way—by trolls, by opportunists, by criminals who want to steal a child for profit."

He ran his hand down his face, trying not to think of such a thing happening to *his* child. He pointed a railing finger at her.

"You have no idea what they're really capable of. And you definitely don't have the resources to hold them at a decent distance. So, no. Do not think for a minute that I will leave it to you to 'handle' security. I can't even say I will take the babies and let you live your life away from us because you are part of this now, like it or not. So you *will* come to Paris with me and *I* will handle security."

At some point she had pulled a cushion across her chest and had drawn her knees up, buffering herself against his outburst.

He pushed his fingers through his hair, scratching at his tight scalp, feeling like a bully now that the worst of his temper was spent, but—

"This was why I didn't want children. This is how I knew it would be." He was defeated by circumstance. "But we're here now, so we'll do what we must. You'll marry me."

"No," she said in a husk of a voice, lips white.

He drew in a tested breath, frustration returning in a

flood of heat. "Did you hear what I just said? *You can't stay here.*"

"Yes, I heard you. Fine. I'll live behind your iron curtain, but—" She swallowed. "But I won't marry you." Her chin came up in what he knew was her stand-ground face.

His ears buzzed as he sifted through her words. "What do you mean?"

"I mean I'll live with you, but I won't *live* with you." She flushed and pulled her shoulders up defensively around her ears.

"You don't want to sleep with me?" His heart bottomed out. She couldn't mean that.

She flinched and looked away, blinking hard. "No. I don't."

"Liar." It came out of him as a breath of absolute truth. A dying wish.

She made a face that held shame and guilt and self-contempt, but when she brought her gaze back to his, she didn't try to convince him she was being honest. She couldn't.

The naked vulnerability in her expression caught at something inside him, though. It was out of character and gut-wrenching, making him tamp it down with resistance. Cinnia was tough. He had always liked that about her. He needed her to be resilient and as impermeable as he was. It was too much on him if she was fragile.

Despite the revelation of weakness, however, she was resolved.

"We can carry on pretty much as we did before." Her voice was a tangle of conflicted emotions. "I'll work remotely around your schedule and go into my office when I can. I'll have to see what my doctor says about travel, but I'm not up for a lot. I was planning to take a few months off work when the babies come, but I don't care where we are when that happens. We can figure that out as we go along, but I'm not going to take up with you again."

"It's not 'taking up.' It's *marriage*." Did she realize how deeply she was insulting him? "Are you trying to make some kind of point? Damn it, Cinnia, are you still trying to prove something to a man in your past who has nothing to do with me?" He wanted to physically hunt down the jerk and shake him.

Her stare flattened to a tundra wasteland of blue that chilled him to the marrow.

"Do you *want* to marry me, Henri? If I wasn't pregnant, would you even be here right now? If I had ended things purely because I wanted to marry and have children, would you have crossed a street to even say, 'Nice to see you'? No. So, no, I'm not being perverse. Yes, this has everything to do with you. If you want to marry me, you can damn well get down on one knee, ask nicely and *mean it*."

Cinnia went upstairs to pack.

Henri forced himself to sit and drink his cold tea while he ate a sandwich, determined to regain his composure after his flare-up.

He hadn't meant to ignite like that, but Ramon was the only one who really understood how dark that time had been after their father's death. Grief had crippled all of them, but a fresh round of attention had fallen on them with the funeral—the girls especially. At fifteen, they'd been long-legged fillies, striking in their youthful blossom of womanhood, hauntingly beautiful in their sorrow.

He and Ramon were used to being sexually objectified by then, but nothing had prepared any of them for the reprehensible, predatory way strange men had begun stalking the girls once the photos were published. For Trella, it had been particularly insidious, sparking panic attacks that had been debilitating.

While other young men his age were drinking themselves stupid, hooking up and partying, he and Ramon had been forced to a level of maturity that exceeded any geezer on the board.

In some ways, combating those dinosaurs for control of Sauveterre International had been a much-appreciated outlet. Ramon was the verbal one, passionately arguing their case and hotly quitting a tense meeting to let off steam by racing cars.

Henri had retreated to spreadsheets and numbers, facts and figures that fueled his ruthless pushback against attempts to sideline him.

He couldn't count the nights he'd sat in a room lit only by the screen of his laptop, angry with his father for abandoning him to this, but sorry for him. Empathizing with him while silently begging for advice on how best to protect his mother and sisters.

Things had grown easier as the girls had matured and taken more responsibility for their own safety. Hell, Trella's self-imposed seclusion had been a relief when it came to how vigilant they all had to be, not that Henri would have ever asked her to go to those lengths.

But he'd never forgotten those first years of wearing his father's mantle, wondering how he would withstand the next day or the one after that. The pressure was too much to expect of anyone. It had hardened his resolve against ever having children and being charged with their safety.

Yet here he was. With Cinnia.

Leaning on his elbows, he rested his tight lips against his linked fingers, examining the assumption he had made before he'd even confirmed her pregnancy. Of course they would marry. For all his reluctance to become a family man, he was the product of one. He and Cinnia were compatible in many ways. It was a natural conclusion.

But she didn't want to rekindle their physical relationship. If the reason was medical, she would have said, "I can't," but her words had been "I won't."

Because she wanted more than sex?

Do you love me?

He jerked to his feet as though he could escape his own ruminations by physically running from them. Now, more than ever, he couldn't afford such distractions. Look at him, dwelling on things that couldn't be changed when he should be putting wheels into motion for all that *had* changed.

He shook off his introspection, decided to tell his mother when Cinnia was with him, and video-called Ramon.

When he and his brother had been children, his mother had always spoken Spanish while their father had used his native French. They had wanted their boys to be fluent in both. Before he and Ramon went to school and learned otherwise, they had thought that if someone spoke to them in Spanish, they had to reply in French. It had amused Ramon to no end when the girls had come along and done the same thing. They were all still guilty of reverting to the habit in private conversations with each other.

"Cinnia is pregnant," Henri announced in French.

Ramon visibly flinched. "*Es lamentable.* Who is the father?"

"Me. I am the father," Henri said through his teeth, offended his brother would think otherwise. "The babies are mine." He was still assimilating that outlandish fact. Saying it aloud made it real and all the more heart-stopping.

"'Babies?' *Twins?*" Ramon choked out with disbelief. He swore. Let out a laugh, then swore and laughed again. *"Es verdad?"*

"So real." Henri wiped his hand down his face, trying to keep it from melting off. "You and I need to talk. She has four months to go, but they'll probably come early. I'll have to curtail most of my travel this year. We'll station in Paris, but you and I must discuss how we'll restructure. The press will be a nightmare." His knee-jerk response when thinking about their name in the press was to worry about how it affected Trella, which reminded him... "Trella knew. Did she say anything to you?"

"Knew that Cinnia was pregnant? *No dijo nada.*"

"She's still in Paris?"

"*España.* But go easy." Ramon held up his hand in caution. "She's doing so well. Don't give her a setback."

Henri took that with a grain of salt. His sisters often accused him of smothering, but he still tried to head off potential problems before they triggered one of Trella's attacks. Given how agonizing the episodes were for her, he would never forgive himself if he *caused* one.

He didn't bother defending himself to his brother, though. The warning was pure hypocrisy, coming from Ramon. Ramon and Trella had the most volatile relationship among the four of them. Where Angelique was so sensitive she had always cried if her sister said one cross word in her direction, and Henri was so pragmatic and coolheaded he refused to engage when Trella was in a snit, Ramon had always been more than eager to give her a fight if she wanted one.

But Ramon and only Ramon was allowed to get into a yelling match with their baby sister. Somehow it never caused an attack and sometimes, they all suspected, it had been the only way for Trella to release her pent-up frustrations in a way that didn't leave her fetal and shattered.

Nevertheless, Ramon would not stand between Henri and Trella on this.

"There is no good explanation for leaving me in ignorance." If something had happened before he'd been able to set precautions in place... He refused to even consider it. "It was cavalier and reckless."

"I'll speak to her about it," Ramon said.

Henri made a mental note to be in another country when that happened, saying only, "Meet me in Paris. I'm taking Cinnia there as soon as she packs."

He ended the call and tried Trella. After a few rings, she came on the screen shoulder-to-shoulder with Angelique, both of them wearing a look of apprehension.

"I forgot you were home, too, Gili," he said as he recognized the lounge at Sus Brazos. "Is Mama there?"

"Siesta," they said in unison.

He nodded. Seeing them side-by-side like that, he was struck by Trella's very slight weight gain. It allowed him to get a firmer grasp on the temper he was already holding on a tight leash. After the kidnapping, she'd gone through a heavy period. Comfort eating, her therapist had called it. Insulating. The press had labeled her The Fat One and that had been only the tip of the iceberg with the ugly things printed and said about her.

By the time their father had died, her eating habits had gone the other way and she'd been starving herself. They'd worried about how underweight she was and then the panic attacks had arrived, carrying on for years. After a lengthy bout of trying different medications, which had amounted to drug dependency more than once, she had removed herself from the public eye. Eventually her moods had stabilized, then her weight and overall health had, too.

Things had been going so well that, when Sadiq had announced he was marrying last year, Trella had insisted on coming out of isolation to attend his wedding a few weeks ago. The event had forced her back into the public eye and he and his siblings had been walking on eggshells since, holding their breaths in fear she'd backslide.

Henri wanted her to live as normal a life as their family was capable of, but that fullness in her cheeks and the trepidation in her eyes made him worry that she was not coping as well as they all hoped. He was angry, but forced himself to tread gently.

"I'm at Cinnia's mother's," he began.

"I know. Cin texted me."

That was a surprise. He hadn't seen Cinnia fetch her phone. "Am I to understand you knew about this, too, Gili?"

"Not about Cinnia, no. Trella just explained that bit after she got the text that you were there. Congratulations." Her smile grew to such bright warmth and sincere joy he wanted to groan. Leave it to Gili to undermine his bad mood with her soft heart and warm enthusiasm. *"Twins?"* She patted her hands together in a little clap of excitement. "We each get one! *Merci*, Henri!"

He and Ramon had thought the same thing when their mother had produced a pair of girls when they were six, one for each of them. He might have rolled his eyes, but something in what she'd said niggled.

"What do you mean, you didn't know about *Cinnia*? What *did* you know that I don't?"

Angelique looked at their sister.

"Um." Trella's mouth twisted as she bit the corner of her lip. She held Gili's gaze with a pleading one of her own.

Gili put her arm around her, bolstering her. *"Ça va,* Bella. Just tell him."

"Cinnia didn't tell you where we bumped into each other?" Trella asked, catching his gaze in the screen, then flicking hers away.

"Here in London, I presume. You've been coming to see a client the last few weeks, haven't you?"

"Sort of. Cinnia is a client, right? She couldn't buy maternity wear from anyone else without risking a tip-off to the press."

"Bella," he said in his most carefully modulated tone. "I'm trying very hard not to be angry with you, but I have every right to be. Don't make it worse. Whatever you need to tell me, spit it out."

Her eyelashes lifted and she finally looked at him, speaking swiftly and sharply. "We saw each other at the clinic. The prenatal one. I'm pregnant."

He sat back, absorbing that along with the three dependents he'd just picked up—six, actually, because Cinnia's family would be under his protection, as well. Now, his vulnerable, fragile baby sister was…

He closed his eyes, unable to take it in.

"How…?"

"I was blessed by God, *obviously*. Same as Cinnia," Trella said with a bite in her tone. Then she picked at a nail and mumbled, "It wasn't anything bad. I had a chance to be with someone—"

"The prince. The one you were photographed with a few months ago?" His sisters were even more difficult to tell apart than he and Ramon, especially in photos, but he'd known at the first glance that Trella had been the one caught kissing the Prince of Elazar. Since he'd helped her impersonate Gili himself as part of her process of moving in public again, he hadn't been too hard on her for going rogue.

Now, however…

"You didn't even know him."

"I won't confirm or deny until I've figured out what I'm going to do," Trella mumbled.

"Speaking as a man who just missed several weeks of impending fatherhood, *don't do that, Trella*. It's bad form."

"I'm the one who told her to hire guards and I offered to pay if she couldn't. And speaking as a woman facing an unplanned pregnancy, *this isn't about you*. I *will* handle this, Henri. But I have enough on my plate worrying about myself and my baby without bringing the father into the mix. So does Cinnia, by the way, except she has *two* babies to worry about. Plus, you were the idiot who didn't ask her to stay when you had the chance. *That's* why you missed those weeks, so don't throw that on me. Ugh. I have to go to the bathroom." She pushed to her feet.

As Trella stormed off, Gili gave him a sympathetic look. "Pregnant women are moody." She skipped her gaze in the direction Trella had gone. "Don't tell her I said that. But, you know, keep it in mind with Cinnia."

"How is she, really?" he asked.

Gili's brow pulled with worry, but there was a wistful, pained quality to it. "She's trying so hard not to lean on *anyone*, especially me. Obviously it's a lot to deal with, but I think that's why she's refusing to, you know, tell the father. She doesn't want to feel like a burden again. Give her some time, okay?"

"Oh, I have quite enough to keep me busy here. But you'll tell me if she needs me."

"I will," she promised.

"And how are you?" Had it really only been yesterday that she'd sent him that beaming photo of her with Kasim? She had captioned it "this time we're serious."

He expected a joyful response to his question, but she pulled a sad face.

"Kasim had to go back to Zhamair. I won't see him again until the end of the month. But we want to have a little engagement party." Now came the smile and she was incandescent. "That will take a few weeks to organize, given all our schedules, but I'd like to do it here. Now I'm wondering about Cinnia traveling?"

"We'll have to check with her doctor."

"Please do. If we have to go to London, we will, but I'd rather stay here."

"Agreed." They all relaxed at their childhood home in a way they never could anywhere else.

Besides, he anticipated making his home there with Cinnia, at least at first. His mother still lived there, but she would be thrilled to have them while they worked out exactly where they wanted to live and built their own heavily guarded accommodation. She had despaired for years at having no grandchildren and had been fond of Cinnia. She would express only delight when she heard they were reunited and expecting.

He ended his call with Gili and took the tray to the kitchen, checking in with Milly.

"Thanks, love," Cinnia's mother murmured. She was leafing through an old-fashioned telephone book, flipping through the *C* section, he noted as he set the tray on the island across from where she stood.

"If you're looking up churches, don't bother. She said she'll live with me, but refuses to marry me." He skipped the part where she'd refused to "take up" with him—it still stung.

"Mmm. Claims to be the sensible one." *Flip.* "Perverse is what she is. My husband was the same. It's his fault she's like that, too. The mess he left when he died. Same reason, too. Figured he knew better and the government could go hang with their taxes and formalities and such." *Flip.*

"She seems to be doing well for herself, helping people

navigate those regulations and avoid that kind of debt." He had to defend Cinnia. She worked hard. Surely her mother saw that.

"Oh, she does. I only mean she has that same streak of independence my husband had. And his stubborn… She calls it a failure to plan, but no, it was a kind of anarchy, his refusal to fall in with what was clearly the accepted approach. He was being a bit of an ass, trying to prove he knew better. She's the same, completely determined to show her dead father the choices he should have made. And show me that a woman should never rely on a man," she added pithily. "The exact same obstinacy channeled in a different direction. But you're quite right. I'd have been in the poor house long ago if not for Cinnia knuckling down with her career and sorting things out for all of us."

Flip.

Henri thought again about how hard life had been after his father had passed. Their situations were very different, but Cinnia's devotion to her family, her desire to look out for them, was every bit as strong as his. She must have been overwhelmed.

"How old was Cinnia when you lost your husband?"

"Fourteen."

"Fourteen," he repeated, wondering why he didn't know that already. For all the times she'd admonished him as being reticent, she wasn't terribly forthcoming about herself. "That must have been a lot on you at the time."

"On Cinnia," she amended with dismay. "Little Dorry was barely walking. I was a wreck. Well, you know. It's devastating for the whole family when the cornerstone is gone, but I was completely unprepared. I didn't know how to even pay a bill. Genuinely didn't know how to write a check or how to call a plumber if the sink backed up. All I knew was that I needed to keep my girls in this house.

It's the only home they knew. That's all you think, isn't it?" She set her hand on the open book and looked at him, old grief heavy in her expression. "Hang on to what's left so you can stay on your feet after such a terrible blow."

Henri nodded. She was stating it exactly right. His mother had been shattered, his sisters distraught, he and Ramon overwhelmed.

"Cinnia doubled up with Dorry so we could let her old room along with the rest. It wasn't worth asking the other two to share. You've met them. You know what I mean," she said with an exasperated shake of her head. "The blood wouldn't have come out of the carpets, but at least they express themselves. Not Cinnia. No, she and Dorry bottle everything up and use it like fuel to get where they're going. Heaven help you if you try to give either a leg up. Dorry is allowed to answer the phone because Cinnia pays her to do it. Quid pro quo, but if I so much as pick it up so it stops ringing? Well!"

Henri folded his arms, thinking of the way Cinnia had refused to let him glance over her business plan until after she'd secured financing elsewhere. Then there had been her reluctance to tell him what she was looking for in a flat, let alone the location she preferred or the price range she could afford. As it turned out, living above her office space had been her plan all along, and a sensible one, but he'd been in the dark on the entire thing until she'd closed the deal. It wasn't just that she hadn't wanted his help, he was seeing, but she needed every last shred of credit to be hers. She *was* independent to a fault.

"That self-sufficiency isn't just because of your husband's situation, though, is it? Tell me about that boyfriend she lived with in London."

"Avery? That is a perfect example of how obdurate she can be. She let that, well, it's not fair to call him a ne'er-do-well, but you could tell at first glance he wouldn't amount to much. I made the mistake of saying I thought she could do better and that was it." Her hand went up in surrender. "She let that boy attach to her like a lamprey. I say 'boy' deliberately. Her first suitor wasn't ready to act like a man, but you could see straight away he had some stones. You remind me of him, if you want the truth."

Henri wasn't sure how to take that, especially when Milly was taking his measure with such a shrewd eye. He didn't like talking about Cinnia's past, either. Not when it included men her mother knew so well.

Aside from Cinnia, his mother had rarely met any woman he'd slept with. Cinnia was the only woman he'd ever trusted enough. First he'd taken her to watch Ramon race a few times, then he'd included her in a dinner with Gili in Paris after she began staying with him there. They'd been seeing each other a full year before he'd taken her to Spain for his birthday, where she'd finally met Trella and his mother.

Those had been big steps for him and she hadn't pressed him to meet and mingle with her family, either, disappearing for a dozen lunches and overnights to see them before she'd started inviting him to accompany her.

He'd been relieved, but now it irritated him that other men had come and gone from this kitchen. He'd had many lovers before Cinnia. Why did he care that she'd had *two*?

"James would have been a good match for her, but they met too young. He let her down," Milly continued with a disheartened sigh. "She went to the opposite end of the spectrum with Avery. Saw him as safe, I suppose. Not so capable of breaking her heart."

That was why he hated the thought of her previous lovers. No other women had impacted him the way Cinnia had, but those other men had been fixtures in her life. They'd shaped her. They affected how she reacted to *him*.

"Avery could barely spoon his own oatmeal. It was my fault she got in so deep with him, of course. 'Mum thinks we should marry for money.' I never said that." She held up an admonishing finger, then waved it away. "But that doesn't matter. She had to prove she's a feminist who can support a man, like someone would pin her with a Victoria Cross for *that*. Oh, she wanted so desperately to make me eat my words about him. And how did that turn out? He was a complete waste of her time and stole a thick slice of her savings, didn't he? Exactly as I called it."

She lowered her nose to the book and gave another page a loud flip.

Everything she'd said had given him a fresh view of Cinnia. Not so much a new angle, as a deeper understanding of her edges and shadows. Was this why she was holding him off? He came on strong at the best of times and his children's safety was a red line for him. She *had* to live with him.

He shouldn't have lost his temper, though. That must have scared her.

At the same time, she must also know he wouldn't let her down the way those other men had. He kept his promises.

You said when I was ready to start a family, you would let me go. Are you going to keep your word?

Of course.

The pit of his belly roiled.

"I have my opinions about you, too, Henri," Milly told him without looking up. "Not *all* of you falls short so if my daughter decided to marry you, I would support her decision." Her head came up and her mouth was tight, her brows arched. "Exactly as I will if she refuses."

He was absorbing that statement as she dropped her attention to the book, adjusted her glasses and set a fingernail onto the page.

"There we are. Classifieds. If she's leaving, I can let out the rooms again, can't I?"

CHAPTER SEVEN

CINNIA DIDN'T HAVE much to pack. Her sisters had been through her wardrobe like locusts once she had grown too big to wear most of it. Trella had been incredibly generous, bringing her maternity clothes and refusing to let her pay. Cinnia had given things back as she grew out of them.

She and Trella had been meeting in secret every other week and without her, Cinnia would have fallen apart by now.

Burying herself in work had also helped her cope. She'd busied herself with bringing on her partner who was taking over the payments on her start-up loan. Then there'd been all the arrangements to set up an office here at the house. For hours, sometimes days at a time, she could forget she was sitting on a ticking time bomb.

But she had always known that Henri would have to be told.

And that he would insist on her coming back for safety reasons. She didn't blame him for that, she didn't, especially after he had pulled back the curtain on how he really felt about the press.

She was still shaken by the bitterness he had revealed. And defeated. Her firm intentions to make her own way had buckled not from his show of temper, but from his helpless anguish. She couldn't, absolutely couldn't, make things harder for him. Not in good conscience.

But her life would change irrevocably now. It would have anyway, she supposed. Twins did that to a woman. But things with Henri would be profoundly different this time. She would no longer be his equal.

Not that she'd been his equal in the past, but she had been able to pretend they were traveling in parallel lanes, living their own lives and intersecting when it suited them for the same reason: sex.

Even before she had turned up pregnant, however, she had known she was following more than pacing. She was becoming more emotionally invested than he was, wrapping her life around his. She had hid it from herself as much as him, but the pregnancy had forced her to confront it. She'd had to ask herself, and him, how deeply he was involved.

"Do you love me?" she had asked him that morning in January, making sure to wait until they'd returned to London so she had an escape strategy that didn't involve getting herself to the ferry.

In typical Henri fashion, he had dodged the question with a faintly bored "If you're looking for a proposal—"

"I didn't ask if you wanted to marry me," she had interrupted sharply, hiding that his attitude stung like a scald. "I asked if you loved me."

"And the reason you're asking is because you want to change things between us." He hadn't even looked up from whatever he was reading on his tablet, like this was a tiresome conversation. "I told you I'd never marry you."

She had sat there with her sip of orange juice eating a hole in her stomach.

Her pregnancy had already been weighing on her conscience for two weeks, earning her a few queries from him about why she was so withdrawn and distracted. He'd even set a hand on her forehead at one point, looking concerned when he asked if she was coming down sick again.

She had been heartsick, aware that he would not be happy about the pregnancy, while deep in her soul, she was *so* happy. There was no man whose baby she would want more.

But not like this. Not so he would feel manipulated and forced into marrying her. Not when she might be a little in love while he clearly didn't have any deep feelings on his side.

So, yes, she had set him up to disappoint her. Maybe if she had said "I love you" first, he might have found some tender words of his own. Perhaps they could have progressed amicably toward an arrangement from there.

She hadn't. She had locked her own heart down tight, preparing herself for rejection and yes, even engineering it so she could walk away wounded yet righteous.

"I've always wanted children," she had reminded him, nearly trembling she was holding herself so tightly together as she gave the greatest shake of dice in her life. "You said when I was ready to start a family, you would let me go. Are you going to keep your word?"

"Of course."

Two words. Bam, bam.

Why couldn't he have at least said he was fond of her in that moment? Why hadn't he said he would miss her? Or acted in some small way like he didn't want her to go? He had spent all the time they'd been together making her think he felt something, even if it was just affection. He was terribly protective of her and often expressed admiration at how hard she worked and what she accomplished. Maybe he didn't laugh outright at all her jokes, sometimes he even gave her a look that scolded her for crossing a line, but he invariably smirked. He appreciated her snark, whether it was witty or facetious.

Why else would she feel so much for him if he didn't at least appear to care for her, too? She wasn't a self-destructive idiot.

Was she?

Did he really feel nothing? From the moment he had walked in here, he hadn't betrayed one iota of pleasure in seeing her again. Just anger and resentment.

You want to change things, he had accused her that day.

She hadn't, she really hadn't. Things had changed all by themselves. Cells had split.

Then she and Henri had.

Her eyes welled as she recognized that nothing had changed between then and now. Absence hadn't made his heart grow fonder. He still felt nothing.

Despair accosted her afresh.

Don't be stupid, she told herself as the pressure built behind her eyes and in her throat. She only cried late in the night, when she lay awake in the dark, missing him, curled around their babies, freezing to death because his side of the bed was empty.

During the day, she was pragmatic and confident.

Which had been easy when she'd been convinced she would hold her position and stay right here in this room.

How would she protect her heart if she was living with him again, seeing him every day?

The pressure behind her eyes built as she contemplated how hard this was going to be. Her breaths were already coming in shaky jags of panic.

She told herself to quit being so silly, but her hand pulled a tissue from the box, then kept grabbing a string of them as she felt her world crumbling around her. The agony of not having his love rose, too much for one or two measly tissues. It was a freight train bearing down on her, filling her throat with a wail of agony that she held her breath against releasing.

She didn't want to love him. It was too big, too hard. It hurt too much.

She buried her face in the cloud of tissues, but this swell of emotion wouldn't be stemmed. Her whole body became wracked by anguish. She had tried to keep everything together and was falling apart. Everything was splitting and rending. She gasped for a breath and it was a ragged sob.

"Cinnia."

His voice, so gentle, so tender, was the last straw. How did he do that? How did he sound like he cared when he didn't?

Her heart broke open and she started to buckle forward, knees giving way under a keening moan.

Strong arms caught her, gathering her, muscles flexing as he picked her up, breath rushing out with the effort. She gave his shoulder a knock with her closed fist, hating him for being virile and powerful when she was fat and weak and falling apart.

He laid her on the bed, coming down alongside her, gathering her into his chest and pressing his lips against her brow, murmuring in French.

She tried to stop crying and listen and wound up wailing, "I don't understand you!" She didn't mean because he was speaking French, but because he was being so *nice*.

"I'm telling you not to be afraid, *chérie*. I shouldn't have scared you, saying those things about being a target. You're safe. I promise I will keep you and the babies safe."

He had it all wrong, but she was so shaken to be held by him, so relieved, she surrendered to emotion and let the pain of these weeks without him release.

He continued to stroke her hair and murmur reassurances. She knew he had probably done this with Trella. Henri had spent fifteen years trying to help his sister recover from something that never should have happened. It was no wonder he drew such a thick line around himself and his family, holding everyone else at a distance.

But even though he begrudged Cinnia for daring to get pregnant, here he was, making promises, letting her burrow into his warmth. It was sweet and right and she cried all the harder.

Bastard. How dare he keep this good, generous heart of his out of her reach?

"Shh. Calm yourself, *chérie*."

"I don't think I can do this," she said, feeling pitiful as she admitted it.

He misunderstood her again. "It's not all on you, Cinnia. You can trust me." He rubbed her back and smoothed his lips against her brow. "I'm here now."

"But you don't want to be." That was the crux of the matter.

He held his mouth against her forehead for a long moment, then sighed a warm breath against her hairline.

"You're fair to berate me for that."

She waited, but he didn't say anything else. Despair rose afresh and she started to roll away.

He tightened his arms, keeping her against his warmth.

"It was painful enough that the kidnapping happened," he said in a low voice that sounded like it barely scraped through a dry throat. "It was frightening enough to live with the knowledge that we're not impervious. But then I became the one responsible for standing watch. Of course I will always look after my mother and sisters, but I never wanted to take on a wife and child. A *child*, Cinnia. If you knew what my parents looked like when Trella was missing."

She swallowed, shocked out of her desolation. He never talked about the kidnapping.

"*I* was in agony. My mother… It was inhuman what they did to her by taking her daughter. And what they did to Trella? I have *never* wanted to bring the potential for more suffering into my life by having children. That sounds cowardly, I know, but I couldn't volunteer for it."

"I'm sorry," she said, wilting in helplessness, voice nothing but a rasp as she realized he would never forgive her.

"*Non,*" he insisted. "You are not sorry. Neither am I. I'm not." He cupped her face, tilting it up so she could see he was sincere. "I am concerned. I will worry about our children for the rest of my life. But I'm not sorry to be their father."

She could hardly see him through her swollen eyes as they filled with tears of tentative hope.

He caressed her cheek with his thumb. "Our children are not something either of us will regret." He tucked his chin to send his gaze down to her belly and very carefully set his hand on the firm, round bump. "These babies are wanted. By both of their parents. *Oui?*"

Being held by him had already warmed her through, but that touch, the reverence in his gentle, splayed hand, sent joyous light through her, so sharp and sweet she had to close her eyes to withstand it. She ducked her head against his collarbone, feeling all the sharp edges of her broken heart shifting, trying to find a way to fit back together.

"Yes." Her lips trembled as she felt his hand move, lightly exploring. It was pure magic.

"How are there two in there, Cinnia? That's unbelievable."

As if they knew it was him and wanted to say hello,

a tiny rolling sensation went through her abdomen. She choked on a little laugh.

"Did you feel that? Maybe it's not strong enough—"

"Shh." He seemed to hold his breath as they both held very still.

Pressure nudged where his hot hand rested. He let out a breath of wonder.

"Is that really them?" he whispered.

"You don't have to whisper. They're not sleeping." She tilted her face to look at him again, unable to hold back her smile. He was too devoted to his siblings to withhold his love from his children. She'd always known that, deep down, but she was still relieved to see him react with the beginning of parental love. She was overjoyed. "It's incredible, isn't it?"

"It is nothing like I imagined it could be." He shifted so her head was pillowed on his shoulder.

She relaxed, comforted by his seeming desire to get to know his babies through the wall of her belly. But she had to ask—with more than a little trepidation. "You really don't hate me for this? I swear I didn't do it on purpose."

A pause, then his voice was very grave, rumbling beneath her ear. "I know. And I could never hate you."

Not "I love you." Not even "I care." Just "I don't hate you."

Fresh despondency closed her eyes, but she had to wonder if he was withholding his heart because he was afraid of being too attached. What if something happened? As he said, he had every reason to believe bad things could happen if he wasn't vigilant.

Oddly, she found herself thinking of his young self, fifteen and worrying about his missing sister. Her arm went across his chest and she tucked her face into his neck, hugging him tight. Saying nothing, but offering belated comfort.

"Are you changing your mind, *chérie*?" he asked, snuggling her closer with hands that cruised in a familiar way. "Would you like to make love?"

She suspected if this silly belly wasn't in the way, she would feel he was aroused. She was growing warm and boneless, feeling him against her like this.

"No," she lied, shifting so her head was on the pillow, putting space between them. "No, I—" She sighed, confronted by how difficult it would be, living with him again, resisting not just him, but herself. "No." Just *no*.

She wondered how long she'd be able to keep saying that.

They didn't make it to Paris until late the next day.

Cinnia was subdued, making Henri think of those days leading up to their breakup. He'd churned through those moments of pale silence a few times since, always concluding she had been deciding whether she wanted to leave him.

He saw it differently now. She had known she was pregnant. Along with that weighty knowledge, her body had already been under a lot of demands. The Cinnia he thought of as quite tough and impervious had fallen apart in his arms last night, then crashed for almost three hours.

Her mother had cautioned him to let her sleep, implying Cinnia didn't always take as much care of herself as she should in her condition, which didn't surprise him. She was as driven by ambition as he was. But her tears and exhaustion had thrust an unpleasant sensation upon him. Humbleness.

She had been carrying more than his children. Guilt. Fear that he would hate her. He had been honest when he'd told her he could never hate her, but he couldn't give her the love she sought, either.

To counter some of that disappointment for her, he had stood in the doorway of her sister's bedroom, cutting a deal with Dorry.

"My preference is to make Spain our base," he had said. "My mother will be there, but she will be Abuela. We'll need an au pair. Since you were already planning to nanny for Cinnia, I'd like you to come with us, at least for the short term."

"Really?" Dorry's quizzical eyebrow had gone up behind the round rims of her glasses. "Wouldn't you rather, like, have someone professional? Who knows karate?"

"The babies will have their own bodyguards, *absolument*, but the guards' duties will be protection, not feeding and changing. And Cinnia may be homesick without family nearby. It would be nice to have you there." Cinnia often talked about her mother and sisters in a tone of exasperation, but she loved them to pieces. "We both trust you, and you and I get along well."

"Also, his brother won't try to hook up with you," Cinnia had called sleepily through the cracked door of the darkened room behind him.

Henri had shaken his head, secretly delighted to hear her rallying, but sometimes her remarks were in such poor taste.

Dorry hadn't flinched or laughed. She'd given him her sister's exact deadpan look and said, "Forget it then."

"I take it back," he'd told the girl. "Two sharp Whitley tongues under one roof is too many."

He hadn't meant it. They'd all convened in the dining room for a late dinner, Dorry contemplating a year in Spain. He had also negotiated with her mother to bring in staff to serve as security and run the family mansion as a B and B if she wanted to continue letting rooms, but he promised to find her a flat near them in Spain so she could come and go as it suited her, and see her grandchildren.

Those were the simple details. There were a million more complex ones still to work through, but he found himself unable to catch at any of them as they entered his penthouse, tired from a long day.

They had slept last night in the London flat, arriving very late and using separate rooms, then visited her doctor first thing this morning, ensuring she was safe to travel and transferring her file to a specialist here in Paris—whom they'd briefly met on arrival in the city.

He liked the London flat fine. He and Cinnia had made it a sort of base in the past and had been comfortable there, but family came and went from that residence.

This penthouse was his. With six bedrooms, his family each had a room here, but only stayed occasionally. His mother and sisters typically put themselves up in the secure flat atop the girls' design house, Maison des Jumeaux, while his brother made do with hotels—so he could have a guest if he desired.

Henri preferred these spacious rooms with their modern decor and plethora of conveniences. It was his retreat, a space he had purchased for himself for the private terrace overlooking the Eiffel Tower and the Seine.

Cinnia let out a sigh as they entered, exactly expressing how he felt.

She had always been a pleasant companion, providing a side commentary that made cocktail parties or gala dinners that much easier to endure, but always as relieved as he was to close the door on the world.

She took off her coat and hung it herself like she'd arrived into her own home.

He watched with a twist in his gut, realizing how much

he'd taken her place in his life for granted. He'd been impatient when she had sounded like she wasn't satisfied with their arrangement. He had been. Eminently. You didn't mess with perfection.

He'd been furious with her that morning. He'd not only resisted allowing her to stir things in a different direction, but he'd also let her go to prove to himself he would quickly get past any disappointment at her departure.

He hadn't. Her absence had been eating a hole in him, not least of which because he had no interest in other women. It was the longest stretch in his life he'd been abstinent since discovering what the opposite sex had to offer.

She had her back to him, not even looking pregnant from this angle. She was his ever-alluring Cinnia with her wavy blond hair falling down her narrow back and her lovely round bottom creating an exquisitely feminine hourglass below her wide shoulders. Her supple backside flexed as she kicked off her shoes into the closet.

He wanted her. *Craved* her. Had for months.

Hell. When had he not hungered for her? From the first moment he'd seen her, he'd been captivated.

Now, finally alone with her, the talons of lust were taking a firm hold in him—destructive lust, since the press already knew something was up, forcing a lot of trying detours today. He needed to keep his head, his mind, focused.

He ought to keep his distance, but he moved to stand beside her and toed off his own shoes.

He could smell that familiar, elusive scent of hers. Subtle. She never wore anything overpowering. He always had to get in close to catch the faint hints of rain and roses in her hair, lavender and geranium on her skin.

Her profile was stark, shadows playing deep into the contours of her face, making her look pale and shell-shocked. She stared into the closet like she was searching for a passageway to another world.

"What's wrong?" His arm went out in a reflexive need to catch and hold. He hooked it across the top of her chest, pivoting to draw her back into him.

"Nothing." His action turned her and she lifted her gaze to where they were reflected in the mirror by the door. Her hands came up to hold on to his forearm, but she didn't press him to remove his touch.

He looked at their reflection.

Her brow pleated with accusation before hurt clouded into her sky blue eyes. She lowered her lashes to hide it, but her mouth remained pouted with disappointment.

In him.

He tightened his arm on her.

"I didn't think I had to ask why you wanted to leave, *chérie*. You told me why. You're not allowed to hate me for letting you go when you said it's what you wanted. I'm not a barbarian. I wasn't going to keep you against your will."

Laughter burst out of her. "Really? Where am I now? With how much choice?"

He folded his other arm across her, splaying a hand over the babies he would protect with his life. "You could have been honest. *You* decided to make this hard by not telling me."

Her lips trembled and she tightened her mouth to steady them. "Two years is a long time to be a courtesan, Henri. I wanted to know I meant more to you than sex for hire."

"You do."

"Do I?" Her gaze flashed back to his in the mirror, filled with dejection as she nudged her bottom into his groin. Where he was hard. "That's all you ever gave me. That and jewelry, and now a pair of babies. Never *you*."

"This *is* me," he said through gritted teeth, barely containing himself as a rush of excitement went through him at the press of her soft cheek. He chucked his chin at his reflection. "This man who is obsessed enough to risk bringing you into my home, where you can see the inner workings of my life. Do you honestly think our affair was something I took on lightly? No, damn you, it wasn't. It's a weakness. A dangerous indulgence. But I wanted you. I want you all the time. Do you really expect me to apologize for giving in to that? When you want me every bit as much?"

She tried to glare him down in the mirror, challenging his claim, but he dismissed her bravado with a scoffing breath of a laugh.

"You're nipples are hard, *chérie*. Think I haven't noticed?" He slid his hand to cup her breast, full enough now to make him splay his fingers to contain the abundant flesh.

She gasped and hunched away from his touch, bumping into him to escape the pressure.

He released her with a jolt of shock. "I hurt you?"

"They're really tender." Her eyes were shiny with tears.

He turned her to face him and asked, "*Can* you make love?" The doctor had said it was safe, but if it would be painful for her—

She threw back her head and he braced for another rejection.

But as he held her gaze, unable to disguise how ferociously he ached to make love with her, the glow of outrage dimmed in her eyes.

His pulse hammered in his throat, in his chest, in his groin. He might have tightened his hands on her arms, unconsciously urging her to match his need. He couldn't be the only one affected this deeply. It was too much to bear.

Her blue irises began to swim with longing and her weight pressed into his hold. Her shoulders dropped in capitulation.

He swore, control snapping. He cupped her face and kissed her. He tried to be gentle, tried to hang on to a semblance of control, but damn it, it had been *so long*. He opened his mouth wider to take full possession of hers, finally tasting her again and feasting on what he'd been missing. He curled his fist into the silken tresses that had grazed every inch of his naked skin at one time or another, wrapped his other arm around her so his hand braced between her flexing shoulder blades, and he kissed her without restraint. He took.

Raided.

Owned.

And she gave.

She slid her fingers into his hair and pressed him to kiss her harder, opened her mouth beneath his and met his tongue with hers. She scraped her teeth against his lips and clung across his shoulders with a slender arm and let her knee crook up to his thigh.

She moaned in the way that begged him to take her to bed and find fulfillment with her. Within her.

His skin stung, feeling too tight for the heat of desire exploding in him. It was a monster that wanted to consume both of them. He scraped his teeth down her throat to where her neck joined her shoulder. That fantastic, exciting place that always made her gasp and shiver and soften her knees so she wilted in his embrace.

Mine.

"Henri," she moaned and pushed at him.

Pregnant, he reminded himself dimly, saying, "Bed," as he took a half step back.

"Damn you," she whispered in pained despair. "I need more than sex!"

CHAPTER EIGHT

CINNIA WAS SHOWERED, dressed and putting the final touches on her makeup when Henri knocked and came into her bedroom. He had knocked once, an hour ago, telling her without inflection that he'd let her sleep as long as he could, but that they had a busy day and she should get up.

"Ramon is en route. PR will be tricky. I'll want you in several of my meetings. There will be photos."

He'd been on the phone with someone when she'd slipped into the kitchen for a glass of orange juice and scrambled eggs. She'd stolen a yearning look at his back, admiring the way his white shirt clung across his shoulders and his belted pants outlined his firm butt.

Now she was forced to look him in the eye for the first time since he'd walked away from her last night, stepping onto the terrace and staying there, despite the pecking rain.

She hadn't slept well, having sat on the edge of her bed half the night, fighting the temptation to go to him and damn herself and her stubborn principles all to hell.

Was she just being pigheaded, as her mother sometimes accused? She didn't think so. Henri was an easy man to yield to. To drown in. If she started having sex with him, she would let him take over her entire life—become dependent. She couldn't allow herself to become that weak.

But she suspected he would always be stronger than

her, always, which was unnerving, especially when he strode with that easy, panther-like confidence toward her.

"Yours." He placed an open envelope on the vanity before her.

She recognized it and her heart fell into her toes. It was the courier envelope with her own handwriting. She had stuffed it full of all the jewelry he'd given her and sent it back to him right after their breakup.

His expression was implacable. Confrontational.

There'd been no reaction out of him when she'd done it, which had fed her misery. Now she saw there were very strong feelings on his side, so strong she had to look away, getting the sense he was barely holding back a blast at her that had nothing to do with being rebuffed from her bed.

She twisted her mascara back into its base and set it aside. "Is Ramon here?"

"Any minute."

Damn. Hurry up, Ramon.

She took a half step back from the mirror, gave her hair a flick so it was behind her shoulders and wondered if Henri liked what he saw, then heard her own thoughts and wanted to groan. She wore a blue wrap dress with a satin belt and a tulip cut to the hem. As with any Maison des Jumeaux creation, it was incredibly flattering. Of course, she looked her best.

She still longed for his approval. His hot stare was making her skin sizzle.

"You're not going to see if it's all there?" Henri challenged. "Perhaps accuse me of bringing that in here to persuade you into bed?"

She kept her gaze on her reflection, feeling the sting as her cheeks flooded with color, but refused to let her attention drop to the envelope or even back to what she sensed would be his hardened expression. His voice sounded like granite.

"You said last night that all I ever gave you was sex and jewelry. Jewelry *for* sex, in fact. Whereas I thought we'd settled that argument with this one." He spoke in a tone that held an undercurrent of danger. He plucked out a bracelet, the first thing he'd ever given her, and dropped it onto the vanity with an air of dismissal. Disgust even.

She gave a cry of protest and reached to catch it before it slithered off the edge and onto the floor. Then she stared at the puddled jewels in her palm, inordinately pleased to cradle them again.

She had worn this bracelet almost every day. It was a line of individually set rubies and diamonds. A tennis bracelet, some called it. "Fireworks," he had said of the color in the stones when he'd presented it. "I saw it and thought of our first night."

She had gone through the roof, accusing him of paying her for sex. They'd had a rousing big fight about it. He had been more offended than she was.

"If I wanted to pay for sex, I would have grabbed the first gaudy piece of trash that came along. *Same goes for a woman.* No, I saw something that made me think of the night we met and I wanted you to have it, because I will always remember—"

He had cut himself off and walked away.

Her? Their first time? That night?

Chastened, she had put on the bracelet and had only taken it off to bathe or if she happened to wear something else for an evening.

"Do you know how angry I was when this showed up?" he said now, the steadiness of his tone belying the latent fury within. He tipped the envelope so everything tumbled out.

She flinched and threw out her free hand, keeping everything on the vanity top.

"This—" he snatched up a bejeweled pendant in the shape of a key "—was never, ever about sex and you know it. It was something I wanted you to have."

He had given it to her a few days after she'd closed on her office and flat. They hadn't even made love there until she'd taken possession and she had had the carpets replaced so, no, it absolutely had nothing to do with sex.

"I'm proud of you," he had said as he had pushed the little velvet box across the restaurant table where they were celebrating. "You worked hard to achieve something and did it. Hell, you're walking around sparkling with such pride in yourself, I thought you should have something sparkly to commemorate it."

She'd been bemused yet touched, and had often worn the pendant when she happened to be having a rough time with a work file or even just a gray day. It never failed to pick her up and make her feel good about who she was and how far she'd come.

"This?" He held up an anklet from their first trip to New York. "What sex was I paying for with this?"

She pinched her mouth shut, knowing full well it had been a silly joke between them. She had bemoaned the fact that the Americans seemed to have a fixation with shoes, but she had no interest in which designer was which. He'd given her that cord of gold, the reticulated links heavy on her skin and always a more pleasant conversation piece when the shoe topic came up. She had threatened to get herself a charm of the Statue of Liberty to hang off it, which had earned her such a stare of revulsion, she still snickered thinking of it.

"I enjoyed having you with me in New York. That's all

I was saying when I gave this to you," he said, shaking the little snake of gold.

"Don't," she muttered, worried he would kink a link. She stole it from him and closed it in her fist against her heart.

"What do you care what happens to it? This is a pile of junk, isn't it?" He gave a solid platinum arm cuff a disdainful bat with his fingertips. "It's not like each one represents a special memory between us. It's not like I spent any time choosing these things specifically for *you*. You're right. They're meaningless and I should have thrown the works in the garbage when they came back. I'll do that now."

"Don't you dare!" she cried, knocking his hands away from sweeping everything back into the envelope. "You made me feel lousy, acting like you didn't give a damn that I was leaving, so I tried to do the same to you. All right?"

She pushed herself between him and the trove of emeralds and diamonds, gold and platinum.

"Message received. Our two years together weren't even worth remembering. When that came back, I wanted to—" In her periphery, she saw his fists clench, but his jaw pulsed. His brow flinched. "We had more than sex." His voice was raw, the words bit out between clenched teeth.

Funny thing about trying to hurt someone you cared about. It wasn't nearly as satisfying as you thought it would be.

She dared a glance up into his face, fearing she'd see anger or resentment. There was only regret. Apology, even.

"Is that why you're refusing to marry me? We're good together, Cinnia. Not just there." He pointed at the bed where she had tossed and turned. *"Everywhere."*

She waited, but he didn't profess undying love.

She looked away, blinking at the sting in her eyes. It wasn't so much disappointment as a feeling of inevitability. What would it even prove if he did say the words? She wouldn't believe him.

A painful jolt went through her, realization striking like a hard pulse of electricity, making her catch her breath. She hadn't just been testing him when she'd left. She'd been driving him away, *afraid* to want his love. Proving to herself she didn't need it.

She was still holding him off to protect herself.

"I care about you. *Ça va?*" He ground out the words like he begrudged even giving her that much.

"No," she said, voice strained, facing something she had barely peered into that day in January. She threw back her head, ignoring the dampness on her lashes as she stared into his wary expression. "It's not okay. Because even if you'd said the words that day…"

Her voice thinned and her throat strained to swallow.

"I've heard them before and it didn't matter. I still wound up hurt and on my own. So yes, I knew deep down that you meant these as signs of affection…" She waved at the jewelry. "But I expected to be left to fend for myself eventually. And was."

"That won't happen again," he vowed fiercely. "It's different."

"Is it? I won't take any chances, will I?"

He started to argue further, but they both heard the door chime.

He swore. "That's Ramon."

"I'll be out in a moment," she promised and turned away to fix her makeup.

Henri ruminated as he watched his brother greet Cinnia. Ramon genuinely liked her, probably because she expected even less from him than she had ever demanded of Henri.

Henri disguised a wince, thinking of what she'd said

moments ago. He supposed he should be relieved that she'd essentially told him she didn't want his declaration of love, since she wouldn't believe him anyway, but it was as much a slap in the face as her return of his jewelry.

He couldn't believe she had so little faith in him.

She was pale and Henri imagined that if his brother noticed, he put it down to her delicate condition.

Ramon, however, being an inveterate flirt, still went out of his way to charm her.

In a moment of shaken confidence, Henri watched closely for her reaction. Cinnia tended to respond with smiles of amused tolerance when his brother turned on the charisma, occasionally flattered, but never swayed, never tempted.

He'd seen it the first day they met, of course, but her preference for him hadn't been fully cemented in his mind until the first time he'd taken her to watch his brother race in Nürburg. It had been a good trip, the first one where he introduced her to perhaps not the family's *inner* circle, but people in their regular social circle. She had fit in well. They had all enjoyed the race day and danced the night away afterward.

The next morning, Henri had taken her down to breakfast only to receive a call as they were entering the restaurant. She had gone ahead to the table with Sadiq and some others from their group. While Henri had watched from afar, Ramon had arrived.

Of course Ramon was wearing the same shirt Henri already wore and of course Ramon had tried to trick Cinnia into believing he was Henri.

Henri's hand had tightened on his phone and he'd missed what his executive was telling him as he watched Ramon come up behind Cinnia and set a familiar hand on her shoulder *exactly* as Henri might have done. Without a doubt, Ramon had said something like "*Je m'excuse, chérie.* I'm here now."

Then his bastard brother had leaned down to kiss her in greeting, exactly as Henri would have done.

Cinnia had paused in midconversation, lifted her mouth in absent acceptance of his arrival and kiss—and had nearly leaped out of her chair before Ramon's lips touched hers. Henri had heard her scream of surprise through the window. If Ramon hadn't caught her and kept her on her feet, she would have stumbled to the floor.

Henri might have found it as funny as everyone else if he hadn't been worried she had hurt herself. He'd cut short his call and hurried into the restaurant, where Cinnia, being a good sport, was laughing at herself even as she scolded Ramon to never *ever* do that to her again.

Henri had then heard every account from every other person who had witnessed it, all ringing with great humor and awe that she could tell the brothers apart so easily. Most of them had also presumed Ramon had been Henri. Pretty much the entire party had been taken in by his joke *except* Cinnia.

Cinnia didn't react to Ramon the way she reacted to him.

He might have been reassured by that, but her heart, he was realizing, was as out of reach as his own. It made him jealous of the rapport Ramon still had with her.

"If you laugh…" Cinnia warned with a sideways look.

"I said you look stunning. As always." Ramon held Cinnia's hands out at her sides. His mouth twitched as he took in her belly.

"I look like a boa constrictor after it swallowed a goat."

"Two. Let's be honest," Ramon said, then he laughed as he dodged her attempt to slug his belly. "Small ones. Kids!" He gathered her into a gentle bear hug and kissed her hair, exactly as he would do if he'd teased one of their sisters into reacting.

"You're a brat!" She playfully shoved out of his arms.

Henri was forced to turn away as the doorman rang to announce their second guest. "*Oui*, send her up."

"Who else is coming?" Cinnia asked as Ramon dropped his hand from her arm and frowned a similar inquiry.

"Isidora Garcia." He didn't bother moving away from the door since she would be knocking momentarily. "You would have met her father, Bernardo, at my mother's birthday."

"Oh, yes! He's lovely."

"He doesn't retire until next month." Ramon's scowl held more than confusion. "We have a team of people under him. I thought we agreed to promote Etienne."

"We have a lot of sensitive information to manage. Angelique and Kasim will go public with their engagement in a few months and you spoke with Bella?"

"I did." His brother's mouth flattened and he shot a look at Cinnia. "Do *you* know who the father is? Is it that Prince of Elazar?"

"She wanted me to have plausible deniability," Cinnia told him with a rueful moue. "She refused to say."

Ramon made a noise of dismay. "Regardless, I don't see why you think we need—"

The knock on the door interrupted him.

Henri opened it and greeted Isidora.

She was a Spanish beauty with a fiery hint of auburn in her long dark hair. Her warm brown eyes were framed in thick, sooty lashes. She took after her notorious socialite mother far more than the short, barrel-chested man she called Papa. Henri privately had his doubts that Bernardo *was* her father, biologically, but had never asked. Bernardo

had always guarded the Sauveterre family secrets so dili-
gently, he allowed the man his own.

"*Bonjour*, Isidora. Thank you for coming."

"Of course. It's always lovely to see you." They exchanged cheek kisses. Hers were well-defined and aristocratic, perfumed and soft. She turned to greet Cinnia.

Her smile fell away as she saw Ramon.

"Ramon," she greeted flatly.

Isidora was a little younger than their sisters. Given
her father's close relationship with their own, and Trella's homeschooling after the kidnapping, at times Isidora
had been one of the few playmates the girls had had.
The adoring crush she had developed on Ramon through
her adolescence had been awkward, but they had never
teased her over it. She was too nice. And Ramon had
never encouraged her. She'd been too young, for starters, and he was too conscious of her father's protective-
ness of her virtue.

As she had grown into womanhood, however, and developed curves that didn't quit, Henri had thought his
brother might be tempted. Now, seeing the frost Isidora
directed toward Ramon, Henri had to wonder if his twin
had finally raced those curves and left a trail of dust.

He introduced her to Cinnia, adding, "I was just ex-
plaining to Cinnia that your father has always been a
trusted leader of our team. He's more than entitled to enjoy
his golden years, but we are very disappointed to lose him,
especially since our lives have become very complicated.
We need a delicate touch."

"So Papa said," Isidora murmured. "I don't mean he
gave me details," she clarified quickly. "Only said he
would feel better if it was me, which I took to mean sensitive information." Her gaze flicked to Cinnia's belly.

"He put the thumbscrews to you?" Henri asked, making a mental note to double Bernardo's retirement bonus for coaxing Isidora to take them on. "I've always said we would hire you when you completed your degree," he reminded her.

"I'm only finishing now. That's why I was in London. And I have never wanted to ride Papa's coattails. You know that." She flashed a glance at Ramon. Didn't want to ride with *him*, she seemed to imply.

"I've been badgering Isidora to join our team since she decided to follow her father into PR," Henri told Cinnia. "She would rather work her way up the ranks of an independent career. Does she remind you of anyone?"

"Look at that. I have a twin myself." She smiled at Isidora. "Would you like something? I was about to make tea."

"I'll help you." Isidora allowed Henri to take her coat before she disappeared into the kitchen with Cinnia. He had the impression she was distancing herself from Ramon.

He threw his brother an admonishing look. "You slept with her?"

"I was turned down," Ramon said blithely, but it didn't sound like the whole story—which surprised Henri. The two of them kept little from each other.

"That happens?" Henri asked drily, allowing his brother his privacy.

"I was shocked, too." Ramon threw off his suit jacket as if he was too warm, leaving it draped across the back of the sofa. Business shirts were all the same, especially white ones, but Ramon's wore the exact crest that embroidered the pocket of Henri's. His pants were an identical shade of gray and even his belt was the same.

Henri didn't even bother remarking on it, only asked, "Is it going to affect her work? Tell me now. We need someone in our midst for months. Not Etienne. He's good on the professional side, but with this much personal information…"

"*Sí*, I know." Ramon shook his head in exasperation. "How am I the only one not causing a stir in the press right now?"

"Meaning you won't be working directly with her. Is that your only reason for hesitating? Because she has always shown excellent potential. We saw it when she was a teenager." She'd begun coming to the office on Take Your Daughter to Work days, drafting soft press releases that had shown better composition than finished work turned out by some of their long-standing professionals. "She's as discreet as they come. Learned that at her papa's knee, I imagine."

"There are other reasons she keeps her own counsel," Ramon said cryptically. "But, *sí*, you are right. She's a good fit. She can't stand me, but she's fond of Gili and Bella. They will be far more comfortable with her than anyone else. Cinnia already likes her." He nodded at where the women's laughter drifted from the kitchen.

Henri nodded, satisfied, but caught the look of inquisition his brother sent him.

"*Qu'est-ce que c'est?*" Henri prompted, even though he knew where Ramon's thoughts had gone.

"I thought we signed a blood oath not to have children." Ramon was a master at affecting a light attitude, but he was far from as shallow as he pretended. His voice was dry, but his expression grave.

"This isn't entrapment." Henri grimaced. "It's an oldfashioned slipup. She left because she was trying to spare me."

Ramon dismissed that with a wave of his hand. "*Pah*. It doesn't matter if you didn't ask for the responsibility. We would never leave one of our own at risk. She must have known you would step up."

"Oui." But given how much he now had at stake, he wouldn't have gone after her without the pregnancy as incentive.

The knowledge caused a white light to shoot through him, jagged as lightning, rending something in him. What if she hadn't been pregnant? What if he really had spent the rest of his life without her?

Ramon slapped his shoulder, yanking him back from staring into a bleak void.

"I have your back, *hermano*. Together we'll keep *tus niños* safe. Your wife is my wife."

"A comforting sentiment," Henri said with a humorless snort. "If she was willing to marry me. She's not."

"That happens?" Ramon stepped back, astonished.

"Apparently."

Do you love me?

Did it matter?

Given all he faced, he couldn't allow himself to be preoccupied with courtship. It was better that she was holding him off.

Still, as the women came back and Cinnia's smile of good humor fell away, he found himself snaring her gaze and holding it, searching for something he couldn't name.

"I was just telling Isidora that I don't even want to *think* about a wedding dress until I've got my figure back," she said, expression neutral.

The singed edges of his ego continued to smolder, filling his throat with an acrid aftertaste.

The media circus was in full swing by the end of the month.

They had released a photograph with their statement that they were delighted to announce the upcoming birth of twins, but that wasn't enough. The paparazzi went berserk. Cinnia only went out a handful of times, once for a

checkup with her new doctor and twice to visit Henri's
sisters at the design house. She was mobbed every time.
Her guards earned their exorbitant paychecks, practically
needing a whip and a chair to keep the lions at bay.

What made her groan loudest, however, was how many
of the photographers didn't even bother capturing her face.
Shots of her belly cluttered every gossip rag as if the twins
she carried were visible if you looked hard enough. It could
have been any woman's swollen abdomen. She told Henri
she was going to start wearing T-shirts with obscene logos
and vulgar catchphrases.

He gave her his don't-you-dare look, but then suggested
something decidedly unprintable, making her snort.

Henri, who rarely spoke to the press unless it was
through a prepared statement that invariably pertained to
the business of Sauveterre International, became old news.
Why photograph any of the adult Sauveterre twins when
they could harangue the mother of the newest set? Even
Ramon's best efforts to draw fire with his racing antics
and half-naked supermodels failed.

Henri would have taken the attention off her if he could.
They were living in an armed truce, managing to be civil
and, in some ways, falling into their old routine very easily.
Most days he worked at his Paris office while she worked
out of his home office at the flat, exactly as she used to
when staying with him here in Paris. Their evenings were
filled with arrangements for their future: how they would
modify the family home in Spain to accommodate the
twins, signing up for a private birthing class, reviewing
résumés for the babies' security staff.

He took pains to include her in all of it, but she felt the
undercurrents of being one more thing he had to manage. Maybe some of that was sexual tension, since they
were still sleeping separately, but she saw how frustrated

he was with the press and precautions and the sheer volume of to-dos.

It fueled her sense that things were tenuous between them, making her all the more determined to maintain her own income and have a fallback position. Which made *him* say she was working too hard, forcing *her* to point out they had enough topics to debate without throwing her career into the mix.

He began swearing yet again as their car was swarmed when they arrived at a hotel in Milan.

Already prickly and nervous, she flinched at his tone.

"You told me the day we met that you've learned to pick your battles," she reminded him, forcing herself to bite back a reflexive apology. It wasn't her fault she was pregnant. She told herself that every day.

"You should be able to move in public without being harassed," he growled as he helped her from the car and held her arm up the red carpet.

She wore sunglasses, but was still terrified the flashes were going to blind her into stumbling. She clung to Henri's arm as she walked. At twenty-four weeks, she was already ungainly, and tonight she'd put on proper heels, wanting one thing to feel normal after so many changes.

They were attending a charity gala put on by a banking family he worked with regularly. Ramon had taken on all the long-distance travel, but Henri was still covering Europe.

She had vainly hoped this weekend would be a break from the paparazzi. She was due for a night out at the very least, even if it was only a business appearance.

It was decidedly more peaceful inside, thank goodness. The hotel was one of the most exclusive in Europe, the guest list for this ten-thousand-euro-per-plate dinner tightly vetted.

Henri guided her through a grand lobby inspired by a fourteenth century Venetian palace. Marble columns rose like massive sentries above them. The wide staircase spilled a line of royal red carpet down its center. Above, crystal chandeliers sparkled and threw glints of burnished light off the gold leaf accents.

Strangers, all dressed in tuxedos and evening gowns, turned to smile at them.

Cinnia had learned to keep a serene smile on her face and keep moving.

They arrived at the coat check and she let Henri take her sunglasses along with her light full-length jacket. It was faintly medieval in its generous cut and flared sleeves. The gray fabric was shot with threads of silver detailing by Trella's clever hand. Her gown was Angelique's finest work, a Grecian style with a halter bodice and an empire waist. The miles of gathered white silk could drape her growing form with elegance through the rest of her pregnancy.

She wanted to believe she looked attractive, but it was hard when her body was so different and the man at her side had grown even more contained as their relationship solidified behind lines of abstinence.

Maybe she should have sex with him, if only to feel close to him again. Of course, her sexual confidence was eroding as quickly as her waistline was expanding. It didn't help that he was acting like he was escorting his sister. He was solicitous, ensured she had a drink, held her chair when they sat for the dinner, but it wasn't the way it used to be. His touch on her was light and incidental, not carrying the possessive, proprietary weight of the past. No stolen caresses or tender brushes of his lips against a bare shoulder.

After dinner, they made the rounds, spoke with their

hosts, Paolo and Lauren Donatelli, along with Paolo's cousin Vito and his new wife, Gwyn. Cinnia had met them a handful of times in the past and they warmly congratulated her.

The music started and Henri asked her to dance.

In the past, she would have slid naturally into the space against his ruffled tuxedo shirt and tucked her hair beneath his chin, enjoying the light foreplay of moving against him.

Tonight they had to angle their bodies to accommodate her bump. She gave a wistful sigh.

"These events are tiresome, I know, but I'd forgotten how much more bearable they are when you're with me." His thumb caressed where his hand was splayed against her rib cage.

He found an extravagant evening like this "tiresome"? Her mouth twitched as she recalled him telling her the first night they met, *This is how I live.* At the same time, she couldn't help softening toward him, flushing with sweetness at his saying he liked having her at his side.

"I should have taken you on a proper date before this, but things have been…"

"I know." She looked up at him, rueful, startled to find his gaze on her mouth. Her foot slipped.

He caught her close with strong arms. Her hip brushed his fly.

Hard?

Her eyes widened and a flood of sensual heat went through her.

He guided them back into the waltz, but there was a flash of something dangerous in his gaze. "Don't look surprised. You know your effect on me," he said in a quiet rasp.

"It's hard to feel desirable when you're pregnant," she mumbled, blushing with self-conscious pleasure.

"Is *that* why you're still holding me off? Because you have nothing to worry about. You're sexier than ever. It's all I can do to behave like a gentleman."

She would have stumbled again if she hadn't been clinging to his shoulders. His hands firmed on her and stayed that way, deliciously possessive. The rest of the dance became as subtly erotic as any they'd ever shared.

She floated in a sea of possibility after that, deeply tempted. As she freshened her lipstick in the powder room, she gave herself a stern lecture about keeping her head and not succumbing to his charms.

But, oh, it would feel so good.

Then she made the mistake of checking her email and her heart stuttered. She had become enough of a liability to turn him off completely.

Who is Avery Benson? Isidora asked. He just sold a story claiming you went after his money in the past. We should refute his accusation that your pregnancy is a deliberate ploy to snare a piece of the Sauveterre wealth.

Suddenly the sideways looks she'd been receiving all evening were explained—and intolerable. Cinnia felt sick. Of course people would speculate, but to have it stated like that, by *Avery*…

She turned her ankle returning to the ballroom, having to catch herself on the back of a nearby chair, which only added to the humiliation as people turned their heads to stare even harder.

Yes, I'm drunk along with being a gold digger, she wanted to lash out.

Henri was watching for her and rushed to meet her. "Are you all right?"

"I have a headache." Her throat was so tight, words barely fought their way through it. "Can we go?"

"Of course." He waited until they were in the back of

the car, then said sharply, "You're white as a ghost. Should we go to the hospital?"

"No. Read your email." Isidora had sent it to both of them. There was no use trying to hide from this degradation. She stared out the side window, the darkened Milan streets a blur through her tear-filled eyes.

Henri said nothing, but she heard a couple of taps and a phone call being placed.

"Avery Benson," he requested.

She swung her head around. "How do you have his number?"

Henri covered her hand on the seat between them and squeezed a signal for quiet. "I don't care if he's having tea with the queen. Tell him it's Henri Sauveterre."

"Don't make it worse." Cinnia reached for his phone.

Henri fended her off, giving her a dark glower. "No, this is not a joke," he told his caller. "Retract your story."

"He won't," Cinnia warned.

"No, *you* listen," Henri said in a voice that made her sit back and hold very still.

She hadn't thought he could sound more deadly than he had the day he had railed about paparazzi. He could. He definitely could. Ice formed somewhere between her heart and her stomach, deep against her spine.

"You were on my watch list and have now been elevated to my red list. I take the security of my family *very* seriously—why were you on my watch list? Because you're a known opportunist who can't be trusted. I had a dossier prepared with your contact details for just this possibility. If you had remained in the background, I wouldn't have given you another thought, but now you've shown yourself willing to profit off my family. That makes you a threat so I must neutralize. No, I don't intend to kill you!"

Henri cast her an impatient look.

"I wouldn't call you to warn you, would I? You would be at the bottom of the ocean with an explanation for your disappearance concocted. No, I prefer you alive to see how I dismantle everything you've acquired after Cinnia gave you a leg up... Oh, she did. You had her convince your parents to sell and stole half her savings on your way out the door. Now if you value your house and your job, you will retract your story and never speak of us again."

Henri paused briefly, then sighed.

"Say you were drunk, on drugs, owed gambling debts. I don't care *how* you explain it, just retract it. Prove to me you are not intending harm to my family or I will push you to my blacklist and I can assure you, your prospects for a promotion, or refinancing your mortgage, or for buying that boat you're looking at, will evaporate. I will sue you into obscurity. Cinnia is not a tool you can use. Ever. Not even just this once."

Henri listened again.

"You will not do that. I've just explained what it means to be on my blacklist and that's where I'll put you if you do anything but retract your story. No, she didn't put me up to this. You poked the bear. This is the consequence. Be smart or lose everything."

Henri ended the call.

"I can fight my own battles," Cinnia muttered, mortified.

Henri kept his gaze on his phone as he tapped out a text. "I'll have Isidora help him. He really does need to be spoon-fed, doesn't he? What did you ever see in him?"

Cheeks stinging, Cinnia looked out the side window again, listening to his phone ping a few times with an exchange of messages, presumably with Isidora.

"Hmm?" Henri prompted a moment later. "I'm curious.

What drew you to such a weak man? You're far too smart to be taken advantage of. Why did you let him use you?"

She shifted, uncomfortable. "You didn't have to be such a sledgehammer. We could have talked first and I could have called him."

"You want to *protect* him?" Henri asked, astounded.

"No. But you didn't even… *I can fight my own battles,*" she repeated.

"This isn't your battle. It's ours."

"It was about me. He wasn't really intending—"

"Do not ever be naive about people's intentions, Cinnia," he interrupted, sharp and severe. "Promise me that. Trusting someone who seems harmless is a mistake."

Like a math tutor.

She swallowed and nodded. "Fine. But you could have let me do it. You didn't have to make it seem like I was…"

"What?" he prompted.

"I don't know. Not capable or something."

Henri swore under his breath. "This is about your precious independence? You know, when Trella was four, she went through an annoying phase where she wouldn't let me tie her shoes or zip her jacket. You don't have to do every single thing yourself."

"Name calling isn't any more mature than toddler level, you know."

"Did you *want* to talk to him? Because I don't understand what we're fighting about."

"Do you rely on me for anything?" she demanded as she swung around, thinking maybe, just maybe, if she thought she fulfilled some corner of his life that was more than arm candy at a banquet, they had a chance. "Beyond sex and, you know, building two babies you didn't ask for?"

"Pleasant companionship?" he suggested.

"I loved my first boyfriend, you know." She threw it

at him and should have been more pleased at the way he stiffened as it struck, but she just felt raw. "Maybe it was puppy love, but James felt the same. I knew better than to let a man hold too much sway over my life, though. Learned that from losing Dad, right? So I didn't change my plans and follow James to the school he preferred. I followed my own path, thought we could weather it, but he cheated on me and it felt *awful*."

"Your mother said she thought you picked Avery because he was safe. Is that what she meant?"

"Yes." She shrugged off how self-delusional it had been. "He was nice, but socially awkward and, yes, he was the beta in the relationship. Okay? It felt good to be the one in control. To feel adored without risking too much. *You know how great that feels*."

They held a locked stare. His jaw was granite, shadows flicking in his face as the angle of lighting changed. The car was pulling into the underground parking of the hotel where they were staying.

"Maybe I unconsciously thought if I took care of him, he wouldn't cheat or leave," Cinnia muttered, gathering her purse and straightening in preparation for the dash to the elevator. "Even if he did, it wouldn't hurt like it had with James, but Avery still found a way to make me feel horrible for believing he cared and, yes, that left me convinced I need to do things myself. I hate needing a man for *anything*. Thank you, Guy," she said as the door beside her opened and the guard offered his hand.

She even needed a man's help crawling from a car these days. It was pathetic.

Oscar already had the elevator open. Cameras flashed from between the shrubs outside the open grill windows as they scurried the short distance into the lift.

They didn't speak again until they were inside their

suite at the top of the building. The space was full of plush furniture in burnt reds and toasted golds, welcoming with fresh flowers and bowls of fruit. None of it softened her mood.

Henri took her coat to hang it and she went to the sofa, sitting to remove the stupid shoes that were killing her feet. That's when she remembered she'd had to ask him to buckle them for her earlier.

She let out a muted scream of frustration and dropped onto her side, burying her face in a tasseled pillow. It was that or break down altogether.

Warm hands gathered her ankles and he lifted her feet out of the way to sit, then set her shoes in his lap and worked on a buckle.

"I hate being weak," she said, shifting the pillow so it covered her ear and she spoke from beneath it, arm curled to hold it in place. "I hate that I can't get through a day without a nap. I hate that I can't sit long enough to get through all the work that needs to be done so I can put away the money that you keep telling me I don't need. I hate that you're taking over my bills and won't let me pay for groceries. I hate that no matter how hard I try, I'm becoming dependent on you."

He dropped her shoes away and kept her bare feet in his lap, rubbing them. It felt wonderful and tender and it was one more way she was letting him do something for her. Her breath caught, nearly becoming a sob.

"I hate that those men hurt you and you don't trust me as a result," he said gravely. "You're right that I crave control even more than you do. At your expense, even. I wasn't trying to make you feel weak when I called him, though. I was reacting." He squeezed her feet, warming them. "I would have preferred to kill him, if you want the truth. Apparently there are laws."

He was trying to make light, but she had heard his tone in the car and heard that same ruthlessness now.

"I used to find it so refreshing that you were self-sufficient. Lately, I find it insulting. You *can* entrust yourself to me, Cinnia. I know that's not easy for you, I understand why you're so reluctant, but I have already put many things in place that will ensure you never want. You'll always be comfortable and, to the extent I can manage it, safe from harm. We are a team where these babies are concerned. It's basic parenting dynamics that I do the providing and protecting so you can do the birthing and nurturing."

"If that's you trying to get out of nappy duty already..."

"And she rallies," he said with a warm stroke of his hand up her calf. "You are never weak, *chérie*. It is the last word I would use to describe you. All of those things you are trying to do before the babies come? You are doing them while building those babies. Why can you not see how much you are accomplishing? I can't help you with the pregnancy, so why can't you let me help you with the rest? Hmm?"

Because it would make her love him even more.

And then what? He wouldn't leave. She knew that much. He wouldn't let her leave, either. Not again. Not ever.

It was oddly humbling to realize that.

She flipped the pillow away and looked at him. He had loosened his bow tie and opened a couple of shirt buttons, which only made his tuxedo look sexier.

"Do you feel stuck with me?" she asked, confronting the root question.

"No." He looked affronted she would ask. "I feel privileged that I'm starting a family with someone I respect and admire. You are the one who is stuck, *chérie*. You will always be the mother of Sauveterre twins. My mother can tell you that comes with serious drawbacks." He reached higher to set his hand on the side of her belly. "*I* have placed a burden on *you*. At least let me carry what I can of it."

She considered that as she looked into his hazel-green eyes. She loved him *so much*. What was the point in keeping hostility between them when they would be together for the rest of their lives? Holding him at arm's length certainly wasn't the way to win his heart. Letting him see how much she cared might.

"Can I sleep in your bed tonight?"

Something flashed in his gaze and his body tensed. "I won't let you leave it," he warned.

Oddly, as monumental and terrifying as his implacable possessiveness was, it also reassured her that they were a unit, moving into the future *together*.

"I know," she whispered.

He rose in a fluid motion, drawing her up with him, then letting her lead him to the room he was using.

He closed the door and turned on the light.

"Don't!" She shot out an anxious hand.

He released a ragged laugh and pulled at his clothes so roughly she could hear how little care he was taking.

Despite the near blackness, she moved to the blinds and gave them an extra twist then tugged the drapes fully closed.

"You really think the dark offers you any sort of protection, *chérie*?"

He was suddenly behind her, naked. She started at the touch of his hands, not because she hadn't heard him coming, but at the zing of electricity he sent through her.

He gathered her hair out of the way and found the zipper on her dress.

As it loosened, she turned in his arms and put hers around his neck, offering her mouth to his hot, hungry kiss. She moaned, closing her eyes in the darkness, but feeling dampness against her lashes as emotion welled. She kissed him back, hard.

"You missed this, too." He slid the fabric away and pressed his lips to her neck. "But don't be frantic. We have a lifetime now. I'll take care of you, but *gently*."

She wanted to protest and tell him to go fast, but he kissed her again, languorously, smoothly skimming her dress away, then taking his time tracing the lace across her hips, slowly, slowly working it down her thighs.

She panted as she waited for it to fall away, to be bare to his touch.

He turned her and leaned to set light kisses across her upper chest, skin brushing skin in a whisper. His hand drifted to pet her mound.

"Yes. Please." She covered his hand.

"Shh. I'll make it good, I promise." He explored deeper, carefully.

She caught her breath and arched into his touch, reaching to hold on to him as she let him take control of her pleasure.

"*Oui, chérie*, you love this, don't you? I do, too."

The closest he'd ever come to telling her he loved her and she could only gasp, digging fingernails behind his neck as she responded to his touch with a rock of her hips.

"That feels so good." She rubbed her face into the spicy aftershave in his throat, purring like a cat enjoying strokes.

How had she resisted this for all these weeks? *Why?*

His free hand moved over her, shaping her hip, cupping her bottom, encouraging her to move against the hand still nestled between her thighs.

They shifted hot skin against one another, trying to get closer, angling this way and that, finding each other's lips and kissing. Kissing and kissing for eternity.

"You're so hot." She slid her hand down his front, finding where he was pulled taut with arousal and clasping him, remembering all the ways to make him groan and push into her touch.

"Say it," he commanded her. "Tell me exactly what you want, *chérie*. I won't have accusations in the morning."

"I want you inside me, Henri. This." She caressed his smooth, hard shape and ran her thumb into the point beneath the tip, feeling him pulse in her palm. *"Please."*

He pressed a groan of abject hunger into her neck, opened his mouth to suck a love bite there. The sting caused a delicious counterpoint to the sweet pleasure of his touch parting her wet folds. She clenched on his fingers and cried out, holding tight to him as climax flooded through her in a rush, so powerful her knees folded.

He held her up, one hard arm around her back, releasing a jagged laugh of triumph against her skin, soothing, caressing, keeping her pulses going and maintaining her arousal.

"Nothing excites me more than knowing I do that to you," he told her, backing her toward the bed. "Nothing makes me want you more. I want to eat you alive. Have you in a thousand ways. Tie us both to this bed and never leave it."

He pressed her onto her back at the edge, leaning on one hand, looming over her as he guided himself against her, rubbing and nudging where she was plump and slippery and welcoming. Still tingling.

"Don't tease," she protested.

"Want?"

"So much."

"How much?" He gave her just the tip.

"More." She used her heel in his buttock to urge him deeper, releasing an unfettered groan as he sank into her.

For a moment there was nothing except the pleasure of returning to this place of joy. Ecstasy.

He said, "Cinnia," like he was exactly as overcome. Then, after a long time, he said, "I don't want to hurt you. Tell me if it's too deep." He caught under her legs and offered a few shallow strokes. His whole body was trembling with strain.

"Show me you want me, Henri."

"How can you doubt it?" he growled. "I'm so hard I hurt." He moved with deliberation, carefully withdrew then pressed as deeply as he could. Tingling sensations pushed into her, so sharp they were almost too much to bear.

"There," she cried as she lifted her hips to meet his and he folded over her. They melded together, mouths, bodies, kissing deeply with abandon. Then she slapped her hands far out to her sides and nudged her hips up against his, urging him to move with more purpose. "Take me."

He ground out a few muttered imprecations, trying to hold a civilized pace, but they were on a plateau of acute, mutual pleasure. Each stroke was a delicate torture that kept her on exactly the knife's edge of wanting orgasm, but withholding it.

She caught at his shoulders and dragged her nails down his arms. "You're not going to break me," she said fiercely. "*Do* it. Harder. Faster."

"You are going to break *me*." He thrust with more power. "Stop me if—"

"Yes!" she cried. "Like that!" She moved with him, meeting his thrusts, keening under the onslaught of pleasure. And there it was. Culmination. Hovering before her, detonating around them.

"Now, Henri. Please… With me," she gasped, shuddering with climax.

He abandoned his grip on his restraint, and let out a

shout of gratification, holding himself deep inside her as they both shattered with rapture.

It was beautiful and perfect and she smiled as he shifted them into the bed and settled her to fall asleep in his arms.

But just as she began to drift, her smile faded. She opened her eyes to the dark. He hadn't answered her question. In fact, as her pregnancy continued to take a toll and she leaned on him more and more, the answer became obvious.

Henri didn't *need* her for one single thing.

CHAPTER NINE

CINNIA WAS ENTERING her thirty-first week, feeling big as a house, but healthy enough that her doctor agreed she could travel to Spain for a few days. Angelique and Kasim were hosting a very small, private engagement party of immediate relatives in the Sauveterre compound. The formal announcement wouldn't be made for a few more months, due to Kasim's situation in Zhamair, but they were eager for their siblings to get to know one another.

The gathering was relaxing and lovely, giving Cinnia something she had longed for the first time with Henri: a sense of being a real part of his family. She and Trella had grown closer since their pregnancies, and Angelique had always been warm and welcoming. Now the twins felt like real sisters, calling her into their rooms to try on this draped top or one-size skirt, sharing little confidences along with a sample of hand cream or asking an opinion on a color of lipstick. His mother trimmed her hair when Cinnia bemoaned that going to the stylist was too much trouble when it was such a horrid crush of cameras.

Then there was Hasna, Sadiq's new wife and Kasim's sister.

Angelique had met Kasim when she and Trella had been designing Hasna's wedding gown. Cinnia already knew Sadiq. He was the most trusted friend Henri and Ramon had. She had actually been invited to the wedding in Zhamair, but she and Henri had broken up right before it.

Hasna made her feel like an integral part of the inner circle when she told her in private that Sadiq was very happy to see her again. "He was *so* upset when he heard that you and Henri had split. It bothered him for weeks."

"Sadiq and Hasna seem really happy," Cinnia said to Henri later, as they were preparing for bed. "I've missed him."

"Me, too," Henri said drily. "This is the first time I've seen him since the wedding. But yes, they do seem happy. I'm pleased for him."

"I don't think I've ever asked how he became such a fixture in your lives. I mean he's not—" She took off her earrings, recalling how often Henri had switched plans to accommodate his friend coming into town or making a point of catching up with him if they had an opportunity. "I'm trying to figure out how to say this nicely. He's not like most of the people I've met through you. He always came out to Ramon's races, but he didn't care about cars. I guess you do business together, but he seems more passionate about computers and software. I'm trying to figure out what you and Ramon have in common with him."

Sadiq was soft-spoken and quick to laugh, but didn't make jokes or put forth strong opinions. He was the male version of a wallflower when he was around the Sauveterre men.

"I see so many people trying to *gain* your attention," she pointed out. "He isn't like that at all. Which answers my question about why you like him, but I'm still wondering how you ever got to know him well enough in the first place, to know that he would make such a good friend."

Henri was silent as he removed his shirt and unbuckled his pants.

"We met at school." He stripped to his snug navy blue underwear. "The day Trella was taken." He folded his pants on a hanger and placed them on the rung. "He was on the steps next to Ramon. Saw it happen and ran in to find me."

"Oh." She was already in her nightgown and paused in pulling back the sheets. "I had no idea."

"I don't talk about it," he said flatly. "But he was instrumental in our locating her. He *is* passionate about his computers and was able to help the police by hacking into the math tutor's computer. Afterward, he was one of the few men Trella could tolerate being around other than family. Maybe because he saved her, maybe because his personality is, as you say, low-key. Either way, we didn't care. He was a hero in our eyes and has always been a true friend."

He turned off the closet light and moved into the bathroom to brush his teeth.

Cinnia crawled into bed, stunned by Henri being so open, but thinking, *be careful what you wish for*. It was so disturbing. She hurt terribly for him.

But she was oddly encouraged that he'd chosen to share this with her. Their relationship wasn't perfect, but she was back to believing he cared for her to some degree. Perhaps he was coming to entrust her with his heart if he was willing to entrust her with his most painful memory.

When he came to bed a few minutes later, she snuggled close, wanting to offer comfort even though he was stiff and unreceptive.

"I didn't mean to bring up bad memories," she said, fitting herself under his arm and kissing his shoulder. "Every time I think of it, I wish that I could take away how scared you must have been."

"I wasn't scared, I was *guilty*," Henri acknowledged in a soft hiss.

Cinnia drew back a fraction, trying to see him in the filtered light. "How?" She knew the whole family had had therapy at different times in their efforts to heal from the incident. He must know he wasn't at fault. "You were fifteen. Victims are never to blame for the hurt done to them."

"I was talking to a girl."

His tone reminded her of the day he'd let his hatred of the press burst out of him, like he had kept it pent up too long. There was also a quality of confessing the worst crime in history, as if he'd never told anyone what he was saying to her now.

"Trella came by and said she was going outside. I told her to *go*. I wanted privacy, but Trella was *my* responsibility. That's how it always was with the four of us. Ramon kept an eye on Gili, I watched out for Bella. I might as well have handed her to them."

Her heart stalled. This poor man.

"Henri, if you had been outside to stop Trella, they would have gone for Angelique," she argued, lifting on an elbow. "That's not a better outcome."

"If they'd called out to Angelique, she would have made Ramon go with her. She was shy. We might have had a fighting chance at stopping it before it happened. I should have told Trella to wait for me, but I didn't." He pinched the bridge of his nose.

"Because you were talking to a girl."

She was trying to make him see how insignificant that was, but a chill moved into her heart. A realization was dawning, but it was a dark one. More like a shadow dimming the landscape inside her.

"Who was she?" Her ears rang, making it nearly impossible to hear his response.

"Just a girl."

Cinnia pulled all the way back onto her own pillow, no longer touching him. She wanted to ease his conscience, she really did, but said, "No, she wasn't." She didn't know how she knew it, she just did. "There were lots of girls after that. She wasn't *just* a girl."

"I don't want to talk about this. Go to sleep."

"You cared about her," she said in realization. It hurt. Oh, it hurt like acid and corrosive and nuclear waste, all being poured over her heart.

"*Mon Dieu.* It was puppy love, Cinnia. You had that yourself and know it means nothing."

"No, it doesn't. Not when it means… This is why you won't let yourself care for me. You're worried it will impact your ability to take care of the rest of your family."

"I *care* for you, damn it."

"But you don't *love* me. You're never going to love me, are you? You will never let yourself feel anything like it because you think it takes too much of your attention. Do you know how hard this is, Henri?" She gave the mattress a smack with her fist. "I've fought and fought falling in love with you. I've let myself rely on you. I sleep with you and I'm having children with you. And you can't even love me back? You won't even *try*."

"You love me?" He rolled toward her.

"Yes, and I'm *sorry*. I know it's one more burden you don't want!"

"That's not true." He reached for her.

"I keep telling myself to give you time, that you'll come around, but you are never going to relent, are you? It's not because I'm not lovable. You're just that stubborn!"

"Cinnia." He tried to gather her into his front.

"No." She rolled so her back was toward him. "I want to go to sleep."

"Cin," he cajoled, pressing his lips to her shoulder as he fit himself behind her.

"Don't touch me." She pushed at his leg with her foot and brushed his hand off her hip. "It's one thing to put something in a cage because you love it and want to protect it, but when you don't actually care, it just makes me a prisoner. So forget it. No conjugal visit."

"Stop it. You're blowing this out of proportion." His hand settled on her waist.

"I'm *tired*." Her voice broke. She was *so* tired of wishing and yearning and winding up empty. She pushed his hand off her, wriggling so she was on the very edge of the bed. "Leave me alone."

He swore and threw off the covers, leaving the bed and their room.

Cinnia woke late, alone, eyes like sandpaper. She held a cold compress on them, somehow pulled herself together with a comb and a toothbrush, put on a sundress that wasn't too much like a circus tent and went downstairs, raw as an exposed nerve.

Everyone was outside, seeming in good spirits, which made her depression all the harder to disguise. She pretended she was merely tired when she joined Hasna at the table under the umbrella. Trella was on a nearby lounger, showing something to her mother on her tablet. Kasim and Sadiq stood with Angelique at the rail, laying bets on the tennis match below.

Henri and Ramon were on the court, trying to kill one another. She'd seen them play before and they were hideously competitive, equally strong and skilled, and they knew each other's weaknesses. Their games could go on for ages.

"They're so well matched," Hasna said, craning her

neck. "I suppose loyalty demands you put your money on Henri."

In the mood he was in, yes, he would likely prevail. In the mood she was in? She'd love to see him lose abysmally, especially to Ramon. That always annoyed the hell out of him.

"Is this the yogurt we heard so much about yesterday?" Cinnia looked over the tubs set in ice. "They got away okay this morning?" she asked of the guests who'd brought it.

"They did and, yes, it is," Hasna said with an absent smile. "Ooh, that's tied it up again. Goodness, this is a nail-biter. The muesli is very good, too," she added over her shoulder, then looked back to the rapid *plonk, plonk* of the ball.

Cinnia avoided the pink-tinged yogurt and went for the plain, sprinkling muesli without really looking and re-seated herself to take a bite. She started to ask Trella what she was reading and felt the first tingle streak from the roof of her mouth down the back of her throat.

She swore. "The muesli." She grabbed Hasna's wrist. "Does it have dried strawberries? Call an ambulance." Her tongue felt like it was swelling as she spoke. "Call Henri. Tell him I need my pen."

"What?" Hasna asked with incomprehension.

"I'm allergic." Her throat was growing raspy. She watched Hasna's fear turning to pain as Cinnia increased her grip, driven by terror to impress how bad this was. She was barely able to force out the rest of her words. "To strawberries."

"Henri!" Hasna screamed at the top of her lungs, standing to wave at him. "Cinnia ate a strawberry!"

Distantly she heard Trella say something, maybe that she would call an ambulance. Cinnia wasn't tracking, just closed her eyes and gripped the edge of the table, concentrating on breathing, managing long, slow, strained wheezes. Rapid footsteps ran toward her and hard hands grasped her, moving her to a lounger. She kept her eyes closed, feeling like she was sipping tiny drinks of air through a narrow straw. A tiny, hollow piece of dry grass. Her throat strained, trying to pull her breaths through the constriction.

Henri's voice was hard as he shouted for her purse. She opened her eyes. He looked gray. Angry.

Scared.

There was a spare pen behind the mirror in their bathroom. Did he remember that? She wanted to reach out to him, grab him, but her limbs felt heavy and her hands were on fire. Her ears itched inside her head and her brain had gone swimming.

A sting went into her thigh, like a bite or the snap of a rubber band.

"That's one," Henri said, cupping the side of her face very forcefully. "Stay with me, *chérie*. Breathe."

She tried. *The babies*, she tried to say, but her lips were fat and numb. Tears filled her eyes. She was scared. Her entire body felt as though it was glowing with fire, her skin cooking, too tight to contain all this heat. What if her carelessness hurt the twins?

Henri took his hand away from her cheek as he accepted something. Another stab went into her thigh and he rubbed it hard.

She closed her eyes, begging the medicine to work, trying to listen for the ambulance, but her heart was pounding so loud she couldn't hear anything. It took everything in her to draw a breath, then to focus on pulling in one more.

Her hand hurt. Henri was holding it and his voice was *furious*. "Cinnia. *Breathe*."

She was *trying*.

* * *

Cinnia had been right last night, but he'd refused to admit it. He was being stubborn. He had shut her down. Shut her out.

But even as he had left her, fully aware she was beginning to cry, he had told himself this was for her own good. He was keeping her *safe* by keeping a clear head and withholding his heart.

Her safety meant everything.

Then he'd heard Hasna scream, *"Cinnia ate a strawberry!"*

He added it to the list of worst phrases he'd ever heard.

"We're here." Ramon appeared at his side and clamped a hard arm across his shoulders.

Henri staggered, only then realizing he was swaying on his feet.

On his other side, Trella took his arm. "Where is she? What did they say?"

Henri realized he was standing in the middle of the hospital hallway, staring at the doors where Cinnia had been whisked away from him. Of course Ramon was here on the heels of the ambulance. Of course their pregnant sister had climbed into the passenger seat for that hair-raising ride.

"Her blood pressure dropped," Henri said, repeating all the terrible, terrible words. They detonated fresh explosions of despair as they left his lips and hit on fresh ears. "They said the babies might not be getting enough oxygen. They're taking them."

"Taking—" Trella gasped. Ramon swore.

"I should call her mother," Henri said, dreading it. He had failed. *I'm so sorry.*

He didn't think he could manage it.

"Mama is calling her. Kasim said he would arrange a flight to bring her." Trella pulled out her phone while

Ramon physically helped Henri to sit. "I'll relay that she's gone into surgery. Was she conscious in the ambulance? They gave her something, right? Medicine? She was breathing? She'll be okay?"

"She was trying," Henri said, throat raw from shouting at her, as if that would help. "They put a tube in her throat. Then she had a seizure. She wasn't conscious after that."

Ramon was crushing him with that hard arm across his shoulders, but Henri crumpled forward, elbows on his knees, stomach churning. Putting his hands over his eyes didn't help. He still saw her blue lips, still felt the strength go out of her grip.

"Oh, Henri." He could hear the plea for reassurance in his sister's voice, but he had none to offer. He was terrified.

"I saw the yogurt this morning. I saw it had strawberries and I made a mental note she shouldn't have any." He had been restless, hadn't slept properly. He'd been feeling guilty and angry and small. Defensive.

When Ramon had asked if he wanted to play tennis, he'd let the activity consume him, working out his frustrations in a hail of powerful volleys.

"I shouldn't have been playing tennis. I should have been there, at the table, waiting for her, ready to warn her."

"We all knew she was allergic. You told us last year when she came for your birthday. We just weren't thinking," Trella soothed. "Cinnia is always careful, too. She always asks. I don't know why she didn't today."

"We'd had a fight. She wasn't thinking."

"This is not your fault, Henri." Trella's small hand dug into his arm, trying to press the words into him.

It *was* his fault.

If he had said the words that Cinnia had asked for last night, the ones that had burst out of him in the ambulance, everything would be different right now.

I know it's one more burden you don't want...

She loved him. He'd been touched, elated, filled with such tenderness he had reached to gather her in, wanting to hold her against his heart.

Then she had said something about feeling like a prisoner and kicked him out of bed.

He had walked out on a sense of righteousness, telling himself he would not let her make him feel obligated, but when had Cinnia ever done that to him? She had begun to lean on him lately, literally holding his arm out of physical exhaustion, but she had been carrying her love for him like a dogged little soldier, refusing to *burden* him with it.

He had always expected to feel hampered by love, but *Cinnia's* love? Her sunny smiles and cheeky asides, her passion and even that streak of pigheadedness had kept him going for two years, not that he'd realized it at the time. It was only as he looked back on their separation, recalled how short-tempered he'd been after Cinnia had left, picking fights with Gili, of all people, that he recognized how badly he'd been missing Cinnia.

Since she'd been back with him, it had been one adjustment after another, but he'd attacked all of the changes with determined energy, eager to carve out her permanent place in his life. He hadn't just accommodated her. He'd made her part of his foundation. He wanted to *marry* her.

Because he couldn't live without her. There was no point.

Why hadn't he told her all of that last night?

"I tried to tell her I loved her. In the ambulance. I don't think she heard me."

"She knows," Trella said, brushing the tickling wetness from his cheek. "She knows, Henri. I promise you."

"No. She doesn't." Because he had refused to say it. Refused to admit it even to himself until it was too late. "I do all these things, go to such great lengths, to try to keep us all safe. I told her she could trust me and what happens? *A goddamned strawberry.* What am I going to do if I lose her? What if I lose all of them?"

CHAPTER TEN

CINNIA OPENED HER eyes to such bright light, she immediately shut them again. Where was she? She peeked again at the tiled ceiling, the stainless-steel contraption beside her with an IV bag hanging off it.

Hospital?

Oh, right. She winced and tried to touch her belly, apprehensive because it didn't feel nearly so heavy as it should.

Someone had hold of her hand.

"Chérie." Henri's whisper had grit in it. He carried the back of her hand to his closed mouth as he stood to loom over her.

She peered from one eye. He looked gorgeous even when he looked horrible. His eyes were sunk into dark sockets, his jaw coated in stubble, his clothes wrinkled.

Her eyes welled with fear.

She tried to say *the babies?* but her throat was a desert that caught fire as she tried to speak.

"Les filles sont très bien. Our daughters are beautiful," Henri said with quiet urgency, setting his hand on the side of her face. "They're very small, but they're little fighters." He stroked her cheek. "Just like their mama. And so alike, Cinnia." He gave his head a bemused shake. "They are the most magical thing I have ever seen."

She started to smile, but her mouth trembled with emotion. "Can I—" She cut herself off with a wince and a moan, touching her throat. Talking really hurt, but she glanced toward the door. She wanted to see them. *Bring them to me.*

"You had a tube in your throat. That's why it hurts." He leaned to press the call button. "The nurse was just in here, said your vitals are good, but the doctor will want to come now you're awake. I'll get the girls."

First he lowered to set his mouth on her forehead, holding the kiss for a long moment, slowly drawing back with such a look in his eyes it made her throat ache in a different way.

"Do not ever do that to me again. Not ever," he said gravely.

"Deliver twins?" she joked in a dry whisper.

"Not funny." His eyes winced shut, lashes appearing matted with wetness when he opened them. They were practically nose to nose. The emotion in his eyes made her catch her breath. He stroked the backs of his fingers against her cheek and started to say something.

The nurse bustled in, forcing him to straighten in a jerk and cast a scowl at the poor woman.

Minutes later, Cinnia met her daughters, tearing up all over again as Henri and a nurse set their tiny swaddled forms into her shaking arms.

"You're sure they're okay?" She wanted to squish them tight, but held them like fragile eggshells. She couldn't take her eyes off their identical little faces with their rosebud mouths and button noses, one sleeping soundly, the other blinking blue eyes at her.

"Colette needed a little oxygen at first and they're both still working on regulating their body temperatures, but they're taking a bottle and squawking when they want more." Henri's hand looked ridiculously huge, overwhelming the tiny form as he splayed his fingers ever so gently on the infant in her right arm.

"Colette?" That was not a name she had had on her mental list, but it suited the inquisitive gaze that met hers.

"And Rosalina," he said with a rueful smile, moving to use one fingertip to adjust the edge of the blanket away from Rosalina's cheek. "We are under no obligation to keep those names, but my sisters refused to call them Twin One and Twin Two. Given the custody battle going on in the nursery between them and the grandmothers, we'll be lucky to have our *own* names on the birth certificates."

"They're perfect. *Hola*, Rosalina. *Bonjour*, Colette," she whispered, pressing a kiss to each girl's warm, soft forehead. "Wait. Grandmothers? Mum is here?"

"*Oui*. And she's as anxious to see you as you were to see *your* daughters. Let's let the doctor do his thing so we can reassure her you're recovering."

Cinnia allowed the babies to be whisked back to the nursery and thirty minutes of playing snakes and ladders with her dignity followed. She suffered exams and questions and prodding. On the plus side, she was allowed a drink of water, a facecloth, a hairbrush and, best of all, a *toothbrush*.

She learned they were well into the afternoon of the day *after* she had taken her near-fatal taste of strawberry-tainted muesli.

"I'm going to devote my life to eradicating that particular fruit from the planet," Henri muttered as the doctor finished up his own riot act about the dangers of anaphylactic shock while pregnant.

"I'm *sorry*," Cinnia said, wincing at the trouble she'd caused.

The doctor pronounced her well enough to be wheeled down the hall to try nursing the twins and the nurse left to fetch a chair.

As they were left alone, Henri hitched his hip on the bed beside her. At least she was sitting up now, beginning to feel human again.

"I am sorry," she said with genuine remorse, unnerved by the way he looked at her with such deep emotion in his eyes. It made her feel compressed. Breathless. "I saw the pink yogurt and thought the plain would be fine. I didn't even look properly at the muesli."

"*I* am sorry, *chérie*," Henri took her hand and handled it very gently, turning it over as though examining it. "I keep expecting to see bruises. Your bones could have broken, I was holding on to you so tightly. I was so afraid it wouldn't be tight enough."

"Mum is going to ground me for sure," she said, trying to make light because his shaken tone made her insides tremble. "Has anyone told my sisters? They won't let me hear the end of it."

"Ramon is at the airport, collecting them."

"Oh, no, seriously? I'm *so* sorry."

"I'm not trying to make you feel guilty. I'm telling you we were worried. We all love you very much. We didn't want to lose you."

Her heart caught and she tried to pull her hand from his.

He made a noise of refusal and held on. "You didn't hear me in the ambulance. I *love* you, Cinnia."

"You don't have to say that just because—"

"I *do* need to say it. I should have said it when you asked back in January. Before that even." He scowled in self-recrimination. "Hospitals are excellent places for confronting your failings. Cowardice. Wrongful thinking. Time wasted that could have been spent with someone who brings joy into your life. I can spell out all my mistakes, but I don't have to because you know all of them. You know *me*. You say I'm a closed book, but you know me, Cinnia. In ways no one else does."

He pressed her hand to his thigh, looked into her eyes with so much openness it was like standing over the Grand Canyon, her mind incapable of taking in the vastness before her.

"I took you for granted. I expected you to just *be* there," he continued. "But that *is* all I need from you, *mon amour*. I know you want to help me pay the bills or make my dental appointments. You want to play a role so you feel you are pulling your weight, but what I need most from you is *you*. I need you to *be* with me. *Alive*."

The corners of her mouth pulled, lips trembling, chastised, but deeply touched. "It's hard to feel like I'm enough," she confessed, stroking his thigh. "When you're…you."

"Who else can I trust with my heart? Hmm?" He cupped the side of her face. "I didn't ask you to carry it, but you picked it up and took such care with it all this time."

She had, and all the while she had felt like it was turned away from her. Now, suddenly, love was shining back at her, gleaming from his eyes and his heart and his soul, bathing her in a light so blinding her eyes watered.

"I want yours, *chérie*," he said tenderly. "Will you give it to me?"

Her throat closed and her chest felt tight. "It's always been yours."

He shifted, rising to stand, then set his knee on the mattress beside her hip. "You told me to get down on one knee, but I'll be damned if I'll do that on a hospital floor."

She caught back a laugh even as she caught her breath.

"I mean this, *chérie*."

She knew what was coming, but was still unprepared.

"I love you, Cinnia. Will you marry me?"

The words expanded the air around them so everything disappeared except this beautiful man holding her hand, holding her gaze. Her heart grew so big, pounded so hard, she thought it would burst with happiness. Her eyes flooded and such love filled her, she could only lift her arms and say, "Yes. Of course. I love you. Yes."

He gathered her close and they kissed, first briefly, tenderly, then with deeper feeling. Passion, but something else that was healing and unifying, solemn and binding.

"Enough of that," the nurse said as she interrupted. "The babies you've already made are still fresh. And hungry, Mama. Let's take you to them."

Henri wheeled her, impulsively kissing the top of her hair as they went into the warm nursery. Her mother was cradling a sleeping Rosalina while Elisa Sauveterre was fending off her daughters from Colette, who was fussing and rooting with hunger.

"Oh, love," Milly said, letting Henri take Rosalina so she could hug Cinnia. "This is the last time you do this, do you hear me?"

"Get engaged?" Cinnia teased, sending a cheeky wink to Henri. "Agreed."

The women erupted in excitement, kissing and congratulating Henri.

"Have you set a date?" Angelique demanded, clasping her hands with excitement. "Have a double ceremony with me and Kasim!"

"I don't want to wait that long." Henri was still holding Rosalina, but he grazed the backs of his fingers against Cinnia's cheek in a tender caress. "We can wait until you're discharged if we have to, but right after. *Oui?*"

"Why wait until I'm discharged?" Cinnia held his gaze

in a small dare. "What do you think, Mum? Could you arrange something for tomorrow? Since everyone is here?"

"What?"

"Are you serious?" A smile grew on Henri's lips.

"Are you?"

"Never more." There wasn't a shred of hesitation in his expression. "I love you with everything in me. I can't wait to call you my wife."

"Then yes, let's do it." She lifted her lips for a quick, sweet kiss, then gave her attention to the women. "Ladies, your assignment, if you choose to accept it, is to plan a wedding for tomorrow."

"Way to clear a room," Henri said drily a moment later, as she latched the hungry Colette.

"Do you want something more formal?" she asked with sudden concern. "A longer engagement?"

"Hell, no. Once you see what's going on outside these walls, you won't want anything to do with being a Sauveterre. No, I am perfectly happy to keep the wedding small and fast and do it while we have a semblance of privacy."

For a ceremony thrown together at the last minute in the hospital chapel, it was touching and beautiful. Cinnia wore an ivory sundress altered by the twin designers into an elegant afternoon wedding creation. Her sister Priscilla brought all her modeling skills to bear as she did Cinnia's makeup and hair. Nell handled the music, the grandmothers took care of the bouquet and flowers, Ramon stood up for Henri and Dorry witnessed for Cinnia.

The rings were tied to ribbons around their swaddled daughters, who were held tenderly by the aunties who had named them. Fortunately the aisle was short since Cinnia could only manage a few steps.

Her husband put a possessive, bolstering arm around her

as she arrived next to him. He was rested, clean shaven, wore a tailored gray suit and had a fresh haircut. The pride and contentment in his expression as he gazed down on her made her tuck her face into his shoulder, too moved to withstand how much she loved him.

But as they spoke their vows and exchanged their rings, she knew he loved her just as much. In this, the most important way, they were equal.

EPILOGUE

Four years later...

CINNIA MADE THE mistake of thinking that if the girls weren't with her, she could walk the few blocks from the clinic to her mother's flat without being noticed.

It was a nice day. She was wearing a sun hat and sunglasses. She was in a good mood and wanted to feel the early summer sun beaming down on her. The city wasn't yet overrun with tourists. Surely she could get away with it?

Not.

A Swedish couple noticed her and the selfies started. Her guards helped her navigate the handful of pedestrians who then accosted her. Everyone was very polite, but very quickly there were too many of them. She skipped with a sigh of relief into the quiet of the lobby, where she waved at the doorman and headed to the lift.

Henri was waiting for her when she entered. "I thought you'd be here ahead of me."

"I walked. Big mistake. Now the paparazzi will be waiting when we leave. Sorry."

"Such a scandal, to be caught meeting my wife for an afternoon tryst in her mother's empty apartment," he said, scooping her into his arms and kissing her with enough enthusiasm to make her heart race as quickly as it had the first time he'd kissed her. He drew back. "How was the appointment?"

"We can go." She smiled with anticipation. They occasionally managed a weekend away, leaving the girls with family, but most of their alone time was stolen here in an afternoon. Which was lovely, but with another baby coming, they'd decided to book a week on an island so long as she was cleared to travel.

"And?" he prompted.

"One." She set aside her sunglasses and handbag, then linked her arms around his neck. Her tennis bracelet slid down from her left wrist and her stylish and subtle, beautifully engraved, gold allergy bracelet skimmed down her right. It didn't do a thing to protect her really, except to remind her daily to be very careful what she ate, but Henri liked her to wear it, so she did.

"Are you disappointed?"

"Never." He closed one eye, considering. "But I think you will get an earful from other quarters."

"I know, right?" She wrinkled her nose in amusement.

Their daughters had recently reached an age of enough understanding to ask where Mama's twin was. Papa had a twin. *They* had a twin. Where was Mama's twin?

Cinnia had explained about singles and twins. They had cousins who were singles, remember? Not everyone had a twin.

Colette, being her father's daughter, had taken the explanation with equanimity. She had snuggled into Cinnia's lap with a despondent little sigh and said, "That's sad." A hug and a kiss later, she'd been off to other more important things, like learning to write her name.

Rosy had been beside herself. That was *not* right, she insisted crossly. Mama *must* have a twin. Where was she? *Go get her.* She had cried on and off for days.

"Merci, chérie."

"For?" she asked, smiling up at him.

"Our children. The joy you give me, every day."

"We're not even in bed yet." She nudged her hips into his, feeling him harden against her as she gave him a smoky look. "Take me there. I'll show you joy."

"I *love* your libido when you're pregnant. Do you know that? I love *you*." He backed her toward the wall.

"Ooh. Look who's feeling sentimental. Shall we open the windows? Have you arranged fireworks?"

"You deliver joy, I deliver fireworks," he vowed, catching at her mouth with a brief kiss. "I think about our first time often. Don't you? It's one of my favorite memories."

"It *was* a good night," she acknowledged.

"It was very good. Let me remind you *how* good."

Lucky her, he had an excellent talent for recall.

* * * * *

If you enjoyed
HIS MISTRESS WITH TWO SECRETS,
don't forget to read the first instalment of
THE SAUVETERRE SIBLINGS *quartet*
PURSUED BY THE DESERT PRINCE
Available now!

And why not explore these other
great Dani Collins reads?
THE SECRET BENEATH THE VEIL
BOUGHT BY HER ITALIAN BOSS
THE MARRIAGE HE MUST KEEP
THE CONSEQUENCE HE MUST CLAIM
Available now!

'Dante, there is nothing I want to do more right now than this.'

And Lucie held his eyes, then leaned forward to cup his face. Still Dante held back. Until her tongue eased his lips apart and slid into his mouth.

'Please don't stop,' she breathed, tightening her legs and tilting her hips. She reached her arms up and pulled him down into a kiss he could no more resist than resist taking his next breath. She defined *irresistible*.

Her eyes, when she opened them to see why he had stopped, were anxious.

'Lucie, are you sure you've done this before?' he asked, not even knowing himself that those words were going to come out of his mouth. It seemed ridiculous—but he had to know…

She glanced away.

'Sweetheart?'

'I never said I had or I hadn't—but I want to… so badly. Please, Dante.'

He looked bewildered. 'Are you telling me you're a *virgin*?' He shook his head at his own stupidity. She was so adamant. So resolute. And she just *did* it for him. Completely.

When she didn't answer he rolled that fact around for a bewildered second even as she moved under him, used the legs hooked around his back to pull him nearer.

'Oh, angel, you're killing me…'

Claimed by a Billionaire

Commanding and charismatic,
these men take what they want—and who they want!

Dante Hermida, polo player and playboy
extraordinaire, meets the only woman to tame him in

The Argentinian's Virgin Conquest
April 2017

Billionaire tycoon Marco Borsatto has never forgiven
Stacey Jackson's betrayal, but he's never forgotten
their chemistry… Meeting her again, he's determined
that this time she will never forget him!

The Italian's Vengeful Seduction
May 2017

You won't want to miss this dramatically intense,
scorchingly sexy duet
from Bella Frances!

THE ARGENTINIAN'S VIRGIN CONQUEST

BY
BELLA FRANCES

First Published in Great Britain 2017
By Mills & Boon, an imprint of HarperCollins*Publishers*
1 London Bridge Street, London, SE1 9GF

© 2017 Bella Frances

ISBN: 978-0-263-92518-0

Unable to sit still without reading, **Bella Frances** first found romantic fiction at the age of twelve, in between deadly dull knitting patterns and recipes in the pages of her grandmother's magazines. An obsession was born! But it wasn't until one long, hot summer, after completing her first degree in English Literature, that she fell upon the legends that are Mills & Boon books. She has occasionally lifted her head out of them since to do a range of jobs, including barmaid, financial adviser and teacher, as well as to practice (but never perfect) the art of motherhood to two (almost grown-up) cherubs.

Bella lives a very energetic life in the UK, but tries desperately to travel for pleasure at least once a month—strictly in the interests of research!

Catch up with her on her website at bellafrances.co.uk.

Books by Bella Frances

Mills & Boon Modern Romance

The Playboy of Argentina

Mills & Boon Modern Tempted

The Scandal Behind the Wedding
Dressed to Thrill

Visit the author profile page
at millsandboon.co.uk for more titles

To my daughter Katie,
filling the world with love everywhere she goes.
I couldn't be more proud. X

CHAPTER ONE

IT WAS ONE thing to plan the perfect party—it was another thing entirely to pull it off. The Honourable Lucinda Bond of Strathdee knew that better than anyone. Oh, yes. Sipping a scalding mouthful of a really rather bitter Americano, she made yet another mental note of how she would improve things next time.

Next time! As if there would ever be a next time…

Down in the galley kitchen of her infamous father's infamous yacht she could hear voices rise and explode between the chef and the caterers.

Lucinda—Lucie to her very few friends—stepped out onto the nearest sleekly polished deck to get a moment to herself, but there was no escape. The fierce Caribbean sun was already causing the air to throb, and the flotilla of little boats and giant yachts that were moored off Petit Pierre reminded her more of a flock of killer seagulls than a flutter of happy butterflies.

Honestly. What on earth had possessed her to have this charity auction, the biggest bash of the season, in aid of her beloved Caribbean Conservation Centre, here in the Bahamas, on the *Marengo*, with a guest list to die for and a crippling lack of confidence as deep as the Caribbean Sea?

Money. Dollars—Bahamian or American. Pounds. Euros. It didn't really matter at the end of the day. As long as her sanctuary—her pride, her joy, her reason for being in this hot, bright heaven—got every last cent from the people who would soon be treading all over her father's floating emporium.

Her stomach lurched again, but the calm, flat sea definitely wasn't to blame. The thought of this party tonight was.

As long as *she* came—Lady Viv, her mother.

As long as she came to call the auction and schmooze the crowd everything would be fine. No one would give a damn about Lucie and her crippling social anxiety if her glamorous, glorious mother dropped from the sky in her helicopter and beamed her brilliant smile all around. She was adored by public and press alike. Loved for her golden hair, her sparkling eyes and her utterly perfect figure.

The fact that she had an utterly imperfect style of parenting was neither here nor there. The world had no idea that the custody battle that had raged between her mother and father had been more about each having *less* time with her than more. All they knew was that she'd had enough of her husband's affairs and had decided to have one herself—with James Haston-Black, or 'Bad-ass Black', as he was known. Glamorous divorcees sold many more newspapers than neglected children, after all.

Lucie swilled the final inch of bitter dark liquid around the cup, then tossed it back. She screwed up her face and shuddered, wishing desperately that she could drink full-fat lattes instead of these vile brews. Soon. As soon as tonight was over she would unhook the un-forgiving satin frock, screw it in a ball and head to the fridge without a care in the world. She would eat what she wanted and drink what she wanted. She would slob about in shorts and T-shirts and wash her hair when she felt like it. She would exercise by lifting food to her mouth. She would pack her make-up bag away in a drawer and smash her bathroom scales with a sledge-hammer. End of.

Well, she might…

Her mother's 'conditions' for flying halfway across the world to host this party were fierce, but she had met them. Three months of abject misery—lose ten pounds, drop two dress sizes, style her hair, tone those 'thun-der thighs'. Each and every obstacle—or 'betterment', as her mother described them—she had overcome. But this was the end. In ten hours' time she would be wear-ing the dress and smiling at the rich and the beautiful and counting all those lovely pennies.

And five hours after that she would be counting her blessings. If she pulled this off without having a panic at-tack or throwing herself overboard then a miracle would indeed have happened.

Lucie looked up at the place she had felt most happy in her whole life. The verdant green island, with its dor-mant volcano and swathe of blue ocean, truly was one of the prettiest islands in the Bahamas. And the fact that she had spent so much of her childhood there, especially in the years after her mother had left, made it doubly im-portant. No one here cared that she was minor aristoc-racy, with a father who was more interested in dogs and horses than anything that had two legs—unless the legs belonged to a pretty young woman. No one here really cared about her mother either. Each second of life was just too succulent for them to bother about what Lady

Vivienne Bond—as she would be known for ever, despite the divorce—was wearing to someone's party on the other side of the Atlantic.

Life here, in every stolen moment, was simple, happy, and as beautiful as the calypso music played all over the island. Lucie wasn't 'hiding', as Lady Viv claimed. *She* simply didn't understand that anyone could find pleasure working with smelly animals in a conservation centre, whereas Lucie couldn't understand how anyone could find pleasure wading through all those air-kisses at parties.

Much like what was going to happen tonight.

Yeuch.

She looked back over her shoulder at the ballroom—one of the many rooms on this three-hundred-foot yacht that would be used for the auction tonight, and was already being decorated by a silent swarm of staff who were transforming the darkly elegant interiors into something from a thirties musical film set.

She had taken care of promotion and ticket sales, passing on the growing list of familiar and unfamiliar names to her mother, Some of them had caused a seismic shift when she'd heard them.

'Urgh! Dante Hermida! He's a polo player and an utter Lothario. You'd best stay well away—though, having said that, you're probably not his type. Really, darling, you should put more effort into knowing who's who,' she'd added, when Lucie had reeled from yet another spray of her mother's vitriol.

A lull in the rapid exchanges from the galley allowed her to hear that her phone was ringing. Lucie looked at where it lay, face down on top of a pile of crisp napkins. It couldn't be Lady Viv—she was supposed to be halfway across the Atlantic by now. But even as she took the four paces across the deck she knew just whose image would be flashing.

God, no. She couldn't… Not this time…

Sure enough, her mother's iridescent smile flashed up at her. Lucie lifted the phone and stabbed the green call symbol like a crazy person.

'Why are you phoning? Where *are* you? Why aren't you on your way?'

She waited, clearly imagining the slight roll of her mother's artfully lined eyes and the slight twitch of her perfectly painted lips.

'Darling, *must* you answer your telephone in such a belligerent manner?'

Lucie clenched her eyes closed and prayed for composure.

'We'll overlook it for now and begin again. Good morning, Lucinda. I trust you slept well?'

Lucie was in no mood to play her games.

'Where are you, Mother?'

There was a slight pause—long enough for her to know that she was right. Her gut had told her that she would be left high and dry with this, that her mother would let her down yet again, but she had refused to believe it—refused to believe she could be so cruel. She *knew* just how much Lucie hated social situations, but one in which *she* would have to host was inconceivable.

Her mother was babbling on in her ear, but what did it matter? It was just one more example of where she featured in her mother's list—Badass Black at the top, then her beautiful boy Simon, then her friends, her charities, her houses, clothes and jewellery—and the thing lolling about at the bottom was Lucie.

'I'm calling to say I might be a little late.'

She sounded clipped, defensive. Or was that just wishful thinking?

'I'm almost sure I will still manage to make it—some of it—but things are really rather difficult at the moment...I'm sure Simon has got himself into a little trouble, and I can't just up and off until I know he's all right!'

Simon and trouble were like strawberries and cream. For twenty years her half-brother had been getting himself into trouble. He was quite the expert.

'I know your little party is important to you, but clearly I have to look after Simon—and, really, it was a bit selfish to expect that I could drop everything and fly over the Atlantic for something as trivial as a *tortoise*, or whatever it is, when I've got all these other commitments...'

Lucie didn't hear the end of the sentence. She stood in a daze, hearing the crystal clipped vowels and imagining the perfect nails drumming. James Haston-Black would be pouring a Scotch and Simon Haston-Black would be lying in someone's bed, lining up his next party.

And Lucie? She would be getting on with it. Herself.

She wondered if she would ever, *ever* feature to her mother as anything other than the irritating, overweight, unattractive daughter of her first husband.

'I have to go,' she said woodenly into the air, and then stood. Her shoulders sank and her head dipped and a sigh as heavy and wide as the gunmetal skies of home poured from her soul.

'Go where?' her mother whined, her voice like claws on thin wood. 'Look, Lucie, you'll be absolutely fine. You've watched me a thousand times. You simply speak into the microphone, pick a face in the crowd. And *smile*!'

'I have to get some—air. I have to go. For a swim.'

Lucie's mouth almost formed her *Love to Simon, love to James* standard response, but this time it choked her. She swallowed it back.

'Love you, Mother,' she said, and she clicked off the call, powered off the phone and walked, one flat sole after another, to her cabin. She'd clear her head. She'd work this out. She had to. Because, once again, she had no other option.

It was the morning after the night before—and the night before that—and if he could focus enough he knew that he might be able to recall exactly when this party had started. Because for Dante Salvatore Vidal Hermida— Dante to his several thousand friends, acquaintances and fans—this was turning into one hell of a hangover. Not that he had been drinking too much—he'd long since outgrown *that* particular route to oblivion. But the whole effort involved in happily hosting was catching up with him.

What he needed now was a clear run of mindless athleticism before getting back on a horse and leading the team to the glory of the Middle Eastern circuit.

There were noises behind him—a slurred squeal, a crash, a muffled laugh—and there was only so much more he could stomach. It was already nearly eleven a.m., and the day surely held a lot more than getting back 'on it' with Vasquez and Raoul and whoever else was left.

He scanned the bay. He was glad they had come here. Such a beautiful part of the world. He normally never ventured farther than the mid-Caribbean islands of Dominica and Costa Rica—he didn't have the time. But they were heading out to a full-on schedule that would last weeks, and he'd planned to squeeze every last drop of fun from the run-up to finally sealing the deal on the new polo club with Marco in the Hamptons.

All that before the big sober-up in New York with his family.

Five days until New York. The clock was ticking and his mother had been remarkably patient—for her. He'd sort that out later today—his date for the awards ceremony. There had to be *someone* he could take. Someone who would know that attending with his family didn't mean she was next on the list to join it. And that 'white tie' didn't mean turning up like a gift-wrapped Playmate. He smiled to himself. Though admittedly that held a certain appeal.

Five days. He could achieve a lot in five days. Starting with a trip on board Lord Louis's infamous *Marengo*.

He looked at it where it was berthed in the bay, dwarfing everything—like an iceberg in an ice floe of dinghies. He braced his arms on the balcony and really scanned it. He'd never been on it, but according to Raoul it was the Playboy Mansion of the seas. Well, he'd judge that for himself. Maybe. He had at least three offers tonight—and they were in the middle of nowhere.

His reputation was getting out of hand. But the oblivion of hedonism was sometimes exactly what he needed.

Tonight…? He might make an appearance and then call it a day. Though how many times had he said that? And how many times had he woken up buried underneath another blanket of limbs and loving, with another mindless, numbing headache and people wanting more than he was ever prepared to give.

He dropped his head, stared at his braced hands, white knuckles, and tensed his jaw. *Happy-go-lucky Dante.* What a sham. Like the happy family they'd show the world at the Woman of the Year Awards. A united front of high-achievers, with perfect lives and perfect partners, the Argentinian Hermidas would be honouring their American-born mother as she collected a Lifetime Award for services to charity. Charities that *didn't* begin at home, of course.

Yes, his mother would be back on the case at any moment—asking who his 'mystery date' was. The mystery was why everyone. including the press, thought he had one. He hadn't! Not yet, anyway. But he would—all he had to do was call up one of the endless stream of women they were speculating he'd bring. As long as she had an IQ above eighty and dug her own gold.

He chuckled as he recalled the list of minimum assets his mother had rattled off when she'd first told him about tonight.

He would figure it out. He always did.

Right after he figured out what was going on over there on the *Marengo*…

He frowned, lifted his binoculars. A woman was climbing up and along the very edge of the bottom deck. A woman in a bikini. Even from this distance she was uniquely, outstandingly female. Nothing unusual in that on the *Marengo*, he supposed, but there was something strange about her.

She made her way to the side and stood completely

upright on the railing. as if on the ledge of a skyscraper. waiting to jump. Tall, proud, dignified. Seconds passed. Minutes, even—and still he stared. And then, with an almost regal shake of her head, she stepped into mid-air and plunged.

God! He dropped his binoculars. She'd disappeared. Straight down into the water. No elegant dive…no playful jump. Just down like a lead pipe.

He grabbed the binoculars, paced forward. 'What the hell?'

He waited a moment, scanned the water round the yacht, but it was a shimmer of brilliant white and blue. He forced his focus as the sun needled his eyes. There was no sign of life—just the glitter and glare of heat and light. He pulled his binoculars away, rubbed at his eyes. Put them back. Nothing. Not. One. Single. Thing.

Dante paused. Surely there was nothing wrong? Surely the people on the yacht would be on hand if something *had* happened? Surely he should mind his own business?

But he had no option. Hand on the rail, he vaulted—right over into the speedboat that was tied up as a tender. Music blasted behind him, and Raoul called his name, but he landed in front of the wheel, turned the key and was off.

The party could wait.

The boat bumped, soared and crashed over the water but he kept his gaze still and steady. What the hell had he just seen? It could just have been a daredevil jump, but it wouldn't be the first time he had known someone try to hurt themselves…

Closer, he slowed. The last thing he should do was make the situation worse by ploughing into her.

He looked up at the *Marengo*, at its infamous majestic outline—there were people milling about, but nobody seemed to be shouting, *Man overboard!*

And then he saw her. A single pale arm like a white reed rose above the water, then lowered in a circle as she stroked the surface and moved back effortlessly.

He waited—watched, mesmerised. Each arm was raised high above her then down in a slow, graceful arc. He smiled. Put the binoculars that hung round his neck up to get a better view—he had to make sure she really was okay. She was swimming out past the safety buoys—and only a really experienced swimmer or a complete lunatic would be doing what she was doing. This was speedboat turf. Anything could go wrong.

He saw her tread water and watched for her arms to rise and circle again. For a second there was immense calm. As if time had stopped. As if all the air had been sucked from the whole wide expanse of sea and sky. And then the surface of the water churned as white limbs thrashed.

He narrowed his eyes—what had happened? She'd been gliding like a pro one minute, then thrashing like a novice the next. He powered up the boat immediately and went to her, eyes trained like a tractor beam on her. Her head sprang up and he almost felt her gaze, wide and frightened. He had to help her. There was nothing else in that moment but her safety.

He cut the engine and nosed the boat away, and then in one move dived into the water and swam with bursting lungs towards her. She was still on the surface and he reached out, grabbed her light, silky limbs and clutched them to his chest, flipping backwards and powering them on.

The frail limbs in his grasp suddenly took on a fe-
rocious strength, and he had to dig a bit deeper to keep
them afloat and moving.

'Let me go—*let me go!*' she yelled.

Shock. It had to be. But it was really not helping.

'You're fine—you're going to be okay. Relax!'

He loosened his hold and then gripped her again,
tucked his arm around her and propelled them back to
his boat. She was still thrashing and yelling, and even as
he reached round her waist, his hands meeting on warm
wet skin, he could feel her strength and hear her rage.

A part of him fired up.

Like breaking in a new pony, he needed to overcome this flailing, furious female—pin her down and
soothe her. But he had nothing to push back against,
no purchase to propel her up and onto the boat. With
one huge effort he raised her up and over the edge. His
face caught curves and clefts, firm, soft wet skin, tiny
triangles of bright green fabric and string and all sorts
going on.

She landed, and leaped out of his hands as he hauled
himself up and over the edge, his breath steadying into
pants as he stared at this bundle of nervous energy.

She was even more beautiful up close. Her skin was
pale, glistening satin, barely covered by the bikini that
lay askew over lush curves. Her hair hung in soaked
blonde tresses around her shoulders. Her arm… She was
rubbing it up and down, up and down. He frowned as he
realised just how mesmerised he was by her.

Shaking it off, he stepped towards her. 'Are you hurt?'

The look on her face…

'Am I *hurt*? You tore across the sea in this stupid boat!

You nearly carved me up. *And* the marine life that actually *does* belong here—it's a miracle that I'm *not* hurt!'

Dante stared. This was beyond shock.

'I got *stung*, you stupid great idiot! That's all—there was no need for all—this.'

She stared at him, ran glinting green eyes all over him, and he felt his jaw tense, his hands flex. He found himself standing taller, puffing out his chest, staring down at her.

'No need for all what?'

He could not get this framed right in his head. She'd been struggling in the water—he was sure she had! If he hadn't seen her God knew what would have happened to her. What sort of person was ungrateful for that?

'So you didn't need any help? Well, my mistake, but you certainly didn't look like you were in control out there.'

Her head came up and she gave him that haughty look he'd clocked just before she'd vanished into the sea.

'You didn't *rescue* me! I didn't need *rescuing*! I was fine—it was only a jellyfish! And if I hadn't had to swim away from you and your stupid speedboat I would have seen it!'

Dante opened his mouth and then bit down. What a foul-tempered witch! He should have left her there. She was screaming at him when all he'd tried to do was help her.

'You might want to learn some manners, Princess. Before I toss you back overboard.'

That was exactly what he wanted to do. He could feel his shoulders tensing further and his fists bunch—he had to get himself in check. What was going on? He was easy, slow—even lazy when it came to women. He never, *ever* got fired up. Never acted without brain and body being in total harmony. Hadn't he learned anything all those years ago?

So what the hell nerve was she touching that had him flexing and puffing and grinding his jaw when he looked at her?

He looked at her now as her green eyes widened. Her rosy mouth fell open slightly, and maybe that was a moment of vulnerability stealing across her face like a cloud across the sun. Likely she was just another one of Lord Louis's cast-offs, dramatically throwing herself overboard because she'd just realised her shelf life had expired.

Who knew? Women were all games and drama. He had the T-shirt to prove it. And the only sure thing was that he was never going to be taken in by a woman again.

'Do *not* call me Princess. I do not hold that title. And you might want to *ask* people if they want to be man-handled before you chuck them onto your boat.'

'Plenty do.' Dante smiled then, and watched her eyes widen all over again. He nodded his head back to the *Sea Devil*, where the gang would be getting well back on track now. 'There's a party over there, waiting for its host to return. So if you'll excuse me…?'

He gestured to the water—jerked his thumb. She could get on with her own rescue.

'Off.'

'What?' She frowned as if he was speaking a different language—and not very clearly at that. 'Who do you think you're talking to?'

He looked round at the *Sea Devil*. Another boat was

making its way towards it and now berthed alongside. He put the binoculars back up to his eyes. Looked like the Cotier sisters climbing out. He'd know those legs anywhere…

He turned back to her.

'Sorry—what?'

'You know, people like you—you *disgust* me! You're just tourists, intent on destroying this place—it's all parties and speedboats and you don't give a damn about the island, or the people, or the animals, or—'

'Maybe you didn't hear me. I said, *off*.'

Her eyes widened in shock and up went her chin even further.

'Honestly! You think you can order me around now? Really? Do you know who I am?'

'Know who you are? Apart from being the biggest pain in my ass, I couldn't care less if you were the Queen of England. Which you're not. So now I think—'

He cocked his head, relishing the pink tinge to her neck, which seemed to be spreading to her chest. *Her chest.* She certainly had one—and it was well worth a lingering stare. But he wouldn't give her the satisfaction—even though the swell of her left breast, set almost completely free by her bikini, was quite a test.

'I think you and I have nothing left to say to one another. So I'm *ordering* you now to get off my boat.'

She stared right at him, and he knew that a lesser man would flinch. But not he. Not Dante Hermida. He might not have a doctorate from Harvard Law School, or a *Fortune 500* business like his brother—yet. But he could fight and he could ride and he could charm every woman within a hundred-mile radius.

So why was this one being so difficult?

'You've got twenty seconds. *Damn!*' he said, suddenly catching sight of the misted face of his grandfather's treasured watch.

He shook his head, held his annoyance in check. He'd nearly lost it once before over a stupid woman, but he'd managed to keep it intact for all these years—a gift from the one person on this earth who'd had time for him. Damn this woman. Standing on his boat, spraying her poison and leaving him soaked to the skin. She might look like a goddess—like some kind of deity in female form—but life was far too short to waste another second with a woman who made his hackles rise this high.

'Ten,' he said.

Biting down on the urge to throw her off himself, he ripped his T-shirt over his head and grabbed up a towel. Out of the corner of his eye he saw her watching him through narrowed eyes, seething and ungrateful. *Yeah, but there was no mistaking her hunger.* He could feel it—emanating out of every selfish pore. She might sound as if she wanted to fight, but she was eying him like a late lunch.

He patted the towel down each arm and over his pecs. 'Five.'

She was still gawping, still showing no signs of going anywhere. Slowly he grabbed each end of the towel and rubbed it across his back, then down over his abs. Finally he smoothed it over his face and dragged it roughly through his hair. Then he stood right in front of her. His shorts were soaked too. Her eyes landed there and her mouth opened on a coy, 'Oh...'

Her skin glistened in the bright late-morning light as stray droplets of water continued to course their way down all those curves. Idly he wondered if her waist-to-hip ratio was the best he'd ever seen, because it had started a reaction in his body that seemed to pay no heed at all to the fact that he really didn't like her.

It looked as if she was planning to play hardball. Okay. He was open to the idea.

Feeling more than a little turned on himself, he lifted the towel again and swiped down each leg. He had great legs—or so he was told, he thought laughingly. 'Great legs' were legs that could grip a horse, make it twist or stop with a squeeze of the thighs. But she didn't look as if riding a polo pony was what she had in mind for him.

'You don't seem to be moving, Princess. Were you hoping for some more body contact before you go?'

He was. He let his gaze travel all over her now. The twisted bikini provided *such* a generous view of her left breast. The hard bud of her nipple peeped out invitingly and he felt another hard kick of lust. For all she was annoying, she was also an incredibly attractive woman—and he could think of many ways she could redeem herself.

He cupped himself and dropped his hands to his waistband, tugged at the string and raised his eyebrows in invitation. Just how far would she let him go?

'Zero,' he said.

In one move he loosened the shorts, slid them down over his jutting erection to the wet floor of the boat and stepped out. She stood for a split second, a look of utter shock on her face, and then she spun, bolted to the side and dived off into the sea.

'Man overboard!' he called after her. 'Again.'

He felt the splash of water on his sun-warmed skin

and walked to the side to see limbs and white foam as she thrashed her way back to the *Marengo*.

'Pleasure, Princess,' he said, sending her on her way with a mock salute.

Then he pulled his shorts back on and with his hand on the wheel and his foot on the floor, he powered back through the waves. If he never saw her again it would be far too soon.

CHAPTER TWO

LUCIE HEAVED HERSELF back onto the *Marengo*, wheezing and gasping and incandescent with rage. Staff appeared from every possible corner, staring at her bedraggled form, complete with purple rash. She stomped through them, flapping her arms to get them out of her way. After what she'd just been through the last thing she needed was a crowd of strangers babbling on about jellyfish stings!

Back in her quarters, she went straight into the bathroom—and it was only then that she noticed that what had started out as a hastily thrown on bikini that she'd grabbed to do a quick circuit of the yacht had now turned itself into three postage stamps of ill-positioned fabric.

She turned herself this way and that in the mirror, looking to see what he had seen. And it wasn't good— the ten pounds she had lost certainly hadn't gone from her boobs or her bottom.

She pulled the skimpy thing off and tossed it in the laundry basket, wondering if she would ever have the nerve to wear it again. Then she stepped into the shower and let the hot water course down over her. What on earth would happen next on this disastrous day?

All she'd wanted when she'd jumped in was a relaxing, calming swim to clear her head, and then she'd planned a bath and an hour or so with the hairstylist and the beauty therapist to help her prepare for tonight. But instead of an aromatherapy massage and pampering to within an inch of her life she'd been nearly ploughed to death by a speedboat and stung by a jellyfish—not to mention that whole encounter on the boat.

She shuddered and reached for the shampoo. So much for being relaxed. She'd have to deal with her social anxiety on top of all the other anxieties she'd developed so far today. One thing was sure—she was in for hours of deep breathing until she finally put her head on her pillow tonight.

Damn that stupid man and his stupid boat!

And his *outrageous* behaviour.

She let the soap run free and stared down at her body, cringing because he had seen so much of it. But, even though she might not have been exactly dressed for an audience with Her Majesty, that didn't excuse his unashamedly egotistical actions! Standing there in those red swim-shorts, with his manhood outlined so clearly…

She shook her head and scrubbed at the jellyfish sting like Lady Macbeth, as if by trying to get rid of the mark she would get rid of the image of him. The look that he'd speared her with—that supercilious grin and those twin dimples, those bright blue eyes that had mocked her. Those shoulders and those impossibly firm, smooth pectorals. An actual six-pack that one could imagine—*touching*…

What an arrogant, egotistical, boneheaded…

Urgh!

At least this was one thing that she and her mother agreed on. Men who were so *obvious* about sex were normally more to be pitied than despised. And he was definitely obvious! And she *totally* despised him.

Who was she kidding? She knew absolutely zero about men and even less about sex. One didn't really fall over them at home with the governess or at an all-girls boarding school. Thankfully.

The last thing she wanted was a life like her mother's—diets and dresses, reporters and snappers. With every last move scrutinised and analysed and published for the world to see. And having to wear that *everything's fabulous, darling* face everywhere she went—even if she'd just caught her husband cheating or her weight had ricocheted to above eight stone.

It wasn't that she was vehemently opposed to men—but they had very little to recommend them.

Take this yacht, for example. It was such a drain on the family finances when they could be funding more eco projects, out here or at home. But her father simply *had* to have it so that he could 'entertain'.

She flipped the taps off and stepped out of the shower, twisting her hair up into a turban and grabbing a towel as she went.

Her father's answer to everything was to throw money at it. He'd paid for the food, the drink, the staff, her dress, the harbour fees and the biggest auction item—the use of his yacht for a month.

But his most generous gift, as far as she was concerned, was that he had stayed away—as instructed. It would be a disaster to end all if he suddenly turned up. She'd seen first-hand what happened to women under the age of ninety whenever he was near—and it wasn't a pretty sight. No wonder she'd found that man today so irritating. He was just a young, blond version of her father. All ego, all sex appeal—and disaster written all over him.

She began searching for something to cool her skin, but really there wasn't enough coconut oil in the whole of the Caribbean to smooth away the vicious red marks from the jellyfish sting—or the mental scarring from her encounter with that—that lunatic on a speedboat!

She checked her phone, registering that the blank screen meant her mother was now even less likely to put in an appearance.

She put it down with a sigh and lifted a pot of her most expensive unguent. She dropped a thick, gloopy dollop onto her palm, spreading it across her arm and chest where the jellyfish sting now bloomed like a cheap tattoo. But it still didn't look any better. And she had less than an hour now until she had to squeeze herself into that hideously revealing frock and face those hideously overbearing crowds—completely alone.

Another wave of nausea announced itself and she swallowed quickly, lest any more acid land in her mouth.

Its lid screwed back on, she replaced the little pot on the dressing table and stared at herself in the mirror, suddenly noticing that lights were starting to appear in the harbour, announcing the evening ahead. And here was she—stressed, not dressed, and with no mother in sight to take over the horrific task of hostessing.

Maybe she could 'have a migraine'. She'd always thought it such a convenient ailment. How could anyone prove it one way or another? She could feign some sort of illness and let the whole thing look after itself. The conservation centre staff would be there. Somebody was bound to be willing to host...

She wanted to scream into a pillow, but this was her

mess and there was nothing else to do but to get on with it. It was bad enough that the guests thought they were going to be schmoozing with Lady Viv—who now only just might be persuaded to put in an appearance on camera—so Lucie certainly couldn't leave the whole thing to anyone else.

She ran to the bathroom. This nausea was overwhelming. She had to get it under control—one way or another.

CHAPTER THREE

LUCIE CLUTCHED A glass of fortifying champagne between white-knuckled fingers and stood like one of the pillars on the mid-deck. Any minute now someone might drape a piece of muslin over her and tie a balloon round her neck.

Her first glass had been half emptied in a single gulp in her room, which had led to a choking fit and a grave look from the hairstylist, who had been packing up her stuff. She'd better not start throwing alcohol down her neck—even though she'd run out of ideas for a quick and painless death. A little deadly nightshade—how did that work?—or something one could simply inhale or swallow. And then she'd fold like a chimney struck by a wrecking ball, while all these strangers continued to sip obliviously on their champagne.

They were arriving all the time. She could hear them, smell them, see them—one big, sensory blur. Her face felt tight—was she even smiling? She had no idea—couldn't feel anything other than the hammer of her heart and the flush of burning red that still bloomed across her chest and neck. She tried to open her mouth to say hello, but the word stuck in her throat, died there.

All she could do was stand there—shoulders back,

stomach in, chest out—with her glass clutched in her hand and her face stretched into what she hoped was a smile. All she could do was breathe deeply and wait for it to be over.

'I haven't seen Lady Vivienne yet—is she here?'

The Mexican Wave of those words washed over her every few minutes. If she heard it one more time she might actually throw herself overboard. That would be quite dramatic. Lucie ran a mental image as another crowd of people who, like her mother, probably couldn't tell the difference between a turtle and a tortoise, came trundling onto the yacht, making too much noise.

Suddenly the Mexican Wave turned back on itself. Bodies seemed to wheel around and preen and pose and Lucie's heart began to pound even more loudly.

Someone interesting was arriving. Someone very interesting.

Could it be…? Could it *possibly* be…? Had her mother actually dropped everything back home and got on a jet to get here? Maybe she had heard the hurt and felt some kind of empathy or love or even just motherly duty towards her. Was that possible?

She turned with the crowd and strained her head to see. Everybody was thronging towards the steps. It *had* to be her. Who else would get this level of interest in a crowd that was already chock-full of the so-called 'it-list'?

Maybe she had been too harsh? Too quick to judge? She hadn't really given her a proper chance to explain. She had said she would come for part of it—hadn't she? And *she* had been the one to plan most of the party—who'd laid down all those rules. And they'd really, really made Lucie focus. She did like the fact that she could

see past her stomach to her feet now. And it felt good—
it really did—that she could tolerate the heat so much
more easily and not worry about her thighs rubbing together when she walked.

Yes, she had her mother to thank for all that—and she
would. That *was* her, wasn't it? Coming aboard? Strange
that she hadn't come in on the helipad, but maybe she'd
found a different way to get here. Maybe that was what
she'd been about to say on the phone before she'd cut
her off so abruptly.

Lucie finally found a space in the crowd and got ready
to greet her. But…where was she? There was no sign
of Lady Vivienne. No gleaming perfect smile or cou-
ture-perfect outfit. No. There, strolling towards her, was
another version of perfection. The male version. Dark
blond hair flopped over an eye, golden skin, bluest, tru-
est gaze and the laziest, most indolent grin.

The idiot from the boat.

What on earth was everyone doing, staring at him?
Lucie looked to her left and right. And what on earth
was he doing *here*?

Suddenly her dry voice formed words and actually
delivered them.

'Who invited you?'

He was strolling towards her as if he could barely
find the energy, but her words had an effect. Oh, yes.

He straightened and his shoulders went back—rigid
just for a moment, but no mistaking it. Exactly the same
way he'd looked on his boat earlier, when she'd had the
temerity to question his intelligence. When he'd seemed
made of steel and stone.

And then he slipped back into that easy, breezy, noth-
ing-is-a-problem attitude.

'Invited? You mean begged, don't you?'

Lucie fumed. The big idiot was standing right in front of her now. On either side of him stood two pull-up banners—sea turtles swimming, with white lettering clearly displaying the name of her foundation: Caribbean Conservation Centre.

'Not if you were the last man alive! This is for people who're trying to do something to save endangered animals. You probably can't even *spell* endangered!'

He looked at her, tucked one hand on his hip—and her eye slid *there* again! Despite herself. His perfect wide shoulders, broad, strong chest and narrow waist were all tucked up inside a soft blue shirt the colour of his eyes. Not that she particularly cared about his eyes. Or how arresting they were. Or how hard it was to look away.

'Maybe you can find someone to play schools with later, Princess.' He was looking down at her as if he had some other kind of game in mind. 'But you don't have a monopoly on helping save the planet. I'm sure my friends' money is quite as good as everybody else's.'

Lucie slid her eyes around to see the party he'd come with all disappearing into the crowd. She knew she should get over her disappointment towards her mother and her anger towards him and find someone out there who could run the auction. But his very presence riled her.

'You have *friends*? How did you get them—kidnapping them? Throwing them onto your boat?'

'Trust me, kidnapping you couldn't be further from my mind.'

He slipped her a self-important smile, bared a flash of teeth between two proud dimples.

She could sense the crowd getting fuller, the time

coming closer. Suddenly the realisation of where she was and who she was and what she was supposed to be doing overwhelmed her.

An anxious voice to her right told her there were only twenty minutes until the auction. Followed by yet another question about her mother. Followed by a third question about who exactly was going to announce the items if not Lady Vivienne… Were they to assume that Lady Lucinda would be doing it in her stead?

She hadn't sorted anything out. She had buried her head, hoping the problem would just solve itself. That a miracle would happen. But it hadn't.

The faces around her were all staring. People began to crush in. Her personal space was disappearing, and with it the air to breathe. And still he stood, right in front of her, with that dimpled smile plastered all over his face, that supercilious look dripping contempt.

'Lady Lucinda…? We need to get started now. Will you…?'

She turned, and a sickening grey mist swept down over her vision. A hand moved, sweeping out to show her where she should proceed. Blindly she moved ahead, her eyes focused on the little podium that had been built up at the head of the ballroom.

To its left and right were the various objects and arte-facts that had been gifted by her mother and her coterie of high society friends who had been persuaded to be part of this. A couture gown here…a handbag there… Jewellery, silk scarves, cosmetics and more. A week on someone's island in the Indian Ocean…a fortnight at an English country house in the shooting season. A signed polo shirt and tickets to a match in Dubai…

Dazedly she realised that *that* was who he was—the

polo player. The one her mother had practically passed out over when she'd heard he'd be coming. The one who was an *'utter Lothario'*.

But what did any of that matter now? Her mother wasn't here and she was—and she had to step up, get on with this auction. She *had* to.

She stared again at the tables set up with all the goodies. She could list each and every one. She had typed them into the programme that she'd sent out, into the advertising copy she'd placed in various local and international publications—she knew every single thing and who had donated it.

But there was no way she would be able to say that. Say anything at all. Her voice was buried under a rock of anxiety.

There was nothing she could do—*nothing* she could do. The suffocating fear built, the tightness returned, and the terror of being right here, right now, became excruciating. She looked for one of the staff from the conservation centre. She scanned the room, but all she could see was the crushing crowd of people, hovering and staring. They were all around her, gawping as if she were some kind of crazy. Which she was.

She had to get out—had to get out or she'd pass out.

'Hey, what's going on?'

She could see jewel-bright colours, dresses,, jewellery, glasses… She could hear voices, feel the daggers of their derision.

'Hey.'

A warm, strong hand wrapped around her arm. She jumped at the sudden contact and tried to jerk away, but the sickness was overwhelming.

'Get your hands off me,' she whispered.

'Slow down, Princess. You trying to take someone's eye out?'

Lucie slowed…stopped. He was right behind her, his hand still on her arm. Her skin, clammy now, felt the chill of the night breeze and the warmth of his touch. She reached out, tried to lay her hand on the railing—missed. She stepped forward, unseeing, stumbled…

'Steady on. Stand still.'

She grasped the rail and stood staring down at the black sea. Her stomach still heaved, but the spinning had stopped and the whirling grey settled as the world became centred around a solid warm wall behind her, stabilising her. A large male body. He laid one hand beside hers on the rail and placed the other at her neck, weighted and heavy, and for once she didn't flinch.

'This is the last thing I want to be doing, but you look as if you're about to pass out.'

She felt the warmth seep through her. Her freezing skin was suddenly soothed, enveloped and wrapped up in another human's body. How many times had she been held like this? Ever? Never?

Could she remember a time when the touch of another had been accepted, never mind encouraged? No. She wasn't the type. The Bonds did not hug each other—never mind strangers.

She pushed away from him—put her hands against the solidity and shoved hard as she could.

'Get off me—go away.' Her voice came out like a hiss.

He stepped back, hands up in mock surrender. Her eyes flashed to his face and she caught a look of surprise.

'No problem.'

'Ladies and gentlemen, the auction is about to begin. Can you please take your places in the salon?'

'No problem at all—and believe me when I tell you this: there won't be a third time.'

'Can Lady Lucinda please make her way to the podium for the start of tonight's charity auction? So many wonderful items for such a wonderful cause.'

The voice, like a call to the gates of hell, boomed out across the Tannoy.

'I can't...' she breathed to the wind. 'I simply can't...'

He turned. The blue shirt, broad back, warmth and strength moved away, and she knew that there really was no way out.

'Me either,' he said, and he was stepping away, leaving her in the grip of the suffocating black velvet night and the sickening dread of the sea of upturned, staring faces.

'Please...' she said, reaching him, grabbing for his arm.

He turned immediately, glancing down at the hand that gripped his elbow.

'What?'

She opened her mouth, looked over his shoulder.

The tinny voice boomed out again, calling people forward, making some kind of apology about her mother's lack of appearance. Her fingers gripped his arm. Pressed into his flesh.

'I've got to say, Princess, you're sending out some *very* conflicting signals. So allow me to be clear...'

He put his hand over hers and slowly began to prise her fingers up.

The voice sounded again. Everyone was in position. She *had* to do this. She had to locate her breath, count in and out slowly, and then she'd be fine. She would be absolutely fine.

Her fingers, now free of his arm, hung in mid-air like a wizened claw.

'I can't go in there. I can't be in front of all those people.'

He stepped back into her space, blotting out the view. 'You can't be in front of all those people? Hang on—is this *your* party? Are *you* Lady Lucinda?'

She clenched her eyes and nodded.

He looked behind him, as if expecting to see something horrifying, then turned back to face her. 'What's going on? Is this some kind of emotional blackmail?'

She could barely breathe now, the panic had gripped her so fiercely.

'It's the auction,' she gasped.

'You're telling me *that's* what's got you like this? Is that what this is all about? Really? The auction?'

He was staring at her as if she was deranged. Which was exactly how she felt.

'You might have thought of that *before* you organised it, then, wouldn't you say?'

She nodded, swallowed, put her hand on her chest and tried hard to slow her furious heartbeat.

'Just another example of your consideration for others? Impressive. Awesome. You really *are* something else, Princess.'

And he turned on his heel.

'No—no, you can't. Please!' Lucie heard herself begging and saw herself reach out, grab his arm, pull him back. She really pulled him back.

He turned. Looked down at her, hands on hips.

'Please? Please, what? What do you expect me to do? Help you? Are you serious? After the way you've acted?'

'I can't go in there.' Her voice was little more than a whisper. 'I simply can't.'

She didn't know herself what she expected him to do. All she knew was that for some reason his presence, his body—whatever it was—she felt warmed by it. And when she felt warm she was less likely to run away—or in this case swim away.

He turned to look at the room full of people. Restless people.

'All these good people here are waiting patiently for you to go in there and start this off, aren't they?'

Lucie nodded, held her head in her hands.

'And you're in no fit state to deliver. Are you?'

Her shoulders drooped as she shook her head. What an idiot she was. A gauche idiot with social anxiety as an extra talent.

Suddenly she felt her chin being lifted up.

'Is it nerves? Is that it? You're stressed out because your mother hasn't turned up and suddenly the spotlight's on you?'

She heard him murmur the words. Someone understood. Someone genuinely understood. How many times had she tried to explain to the people close to her that she simply couldn't do the things they could? How many times had she heard the word 'nonsense' fired at her? And how many times had she seen her mother sweep past her, shaking her head and rolling her eyes, making her feel such an abject, worthless piece of garbage just because she wasn't like her?

'God only knows why I'd do anything other than get as far away from you as possible, but I don't suppose it would kill me to help you out. And I can't really stand back and watch you let all those people down...'

She stared up into that face. It was suddenly serious, the dimples subsumed into all that beautiful golden skin. His eyes were grave. And she felt again that strange sense of caring, of kindness, of being anchored.

Lucie nodded. She stood in the shelter of his warm, strong body and nodded.

He looked at her for a long second, then stepped away, shaking his head.

'God only knows…'

She watched his back as he walked into the crowd, her breaths lengthening and her heart gradually steadying. Easy and lazy—no problem at all for him to go and stand before a crowd, all eyes trained on him.

Lucie's gaze fixed on the breadth of his shoulders, the slight swing of his backside, so fabulously formed inside those trousers, the angle of each leg as he stepped so damn nonchalantly onto the podium, before the crowd of women who clearly thought exactly the same as she did closed over his path like waves of hungry harpies.

She might have solved one problem, but she had the feeling she had launched herself head-first into another.

CHAPTER FOUR

SHE WAS OUT there on the deck, watching. He could feel her stare from time to time. He searched for that shimmer of green satin, or the glint of her golden hair. But there were far too many people in the room, pledging their money for things they really didn't need, and he was working them as if his life depended on getting them to bid for each and every one of these glamorous trinkets.

When his own prize came up—the holiday in Dubai and tickets to the race day his team would be riding in—the air was electric. Of course it helped that he was there, and flirting with every one of those women, some of whom he was pretty sure he might have flirted with before. Maybe he'd even done more than flirt, but tonight, for sure, he only had eyes for Lady Lucinda Bond—'Princess' to him.

He saw her pass along the back of the salon, deckside. She looked as if she was back in the game—her shoulders were down and her chin was high. Her face was side-lit, but only flashes of those proud features appeared through the rows of women who waved their paddles at him. He knew he should leave well alone, but he was going to track her down as soon as the last item was sold—if only to give her the chance to apologise and to thank him.

He was feeling pretty good, to be fair. It wasn't every day you got the chance to help raise two and a half million US dollars for charity. She should be stoked. So her glamorous mother hadn't turned up? No bad thing as far as Dante could see. She came across as a bit self-obsessed anyway.

He exited the salon to a round of applause and several slaps on the back and kisses on the cheek. That was all he was offering.

Night on deck was thick and black, but the trail of the moon across the water that separated the *Marengo* from the *Sea Devil* was a silvery carpet of light topped with a veil of blinking stars. Even *he* couldn't help but be struck by the prettiness of the scene, by the twinkling and bobbing of buoys and lights and the fairytale island of Petit Pierre in the background.

He rounded the deck, staring in at the other rooms that held the usual party suspects. Drink was flowing and chat was getting easier. On he moved, pausing at a tiny sweep of steps that led to a dance floor and a pulsating beat where bodies moved in time to the music. He scanned it. A few people waved him over. Friends. Raoul, for one. He'd join them shortly—as soon as he'd tracked down Her Ladyship.

They looked to be having a great time—there were some new faces, new bodies, and Raoul looked as if he was already predating on them. Normally that alone would have been enough to spur him on—the competition, the hunt. He glanced back, held up his hand—five minutes. Raoul grinned.

Someone in front of him turned. A blonde, about five seven, slim and sure, her long hair in a knot on top of her head.

Dante froze.

It couldn't be.

A familiar sickening chill seeped through his body. It had been so long since he had felt that—*so* long. The cast of that jawline, the angle of that cheekbone…

But of course it couldn't be. There were no such things as ghosts.

Still, he was rooted to the spot. A body bumped his, someone else spoke, yet another person touched his arm. He jerked it away angrily as he stared at the profile, waiting for her to turn, waiting for his eyes to tell him what his rational brain knew were the facts. The dead didn't come back to life. And Celine di Rosso was well and truly dead. Hadn't she made sure *he* would be the one to find her, after all?

Raoul was frowning. Tipping his chin up in question. The conversation stopped. The woman turned herself right around. Right around to face Dante.

The face of a stranger. The same angle of the jaw, hollow of those cheekbones, the same long neck and knot of blonde hair—but at least twenty years younger than Celine. Even thinking those words was like succumbing to the sickness again.

He blinked and the woman smiled. Raoul waved him over. And then he felt pressure on his arm again.

'Señor Hermida?'

He turned and there she was. Lady Lucie. He came to as if he'd been out cold—as if she were standing there with smelling salts instead of a rigid arm held out in front for some kind of ceremonial handshake.

Her outline formed in the haze of long-ago horror that had descended all around him. He felt his smile slide back into place—more easily than he would ever have imagined, having just seen that doppelgänger. He could see her features. He scanned her. She looked questioningly at him and he knew he must look as if he'd been bludgeoned, or worse.

She was tight-mouthed, but she looked a damn sight better than when he'd last spoken to her. She hadn't been pretending, that was for sure—that had been a panic attack if ever he'd seen one. And, hell, he'd seen more than a few. What on earth her own demons were was anyone's guess, but he knew better than anyone that all was rarely as it seemed.

'Princess?' he replied, watching her eyes drifting to the smile that he knew warmed even the hardest of hearts.

She flashed her eyes right up into his and scowled. 'I know you're doing that simply to annoy me, but for the last time may I ask that when you use a title you use the correct one?'

He bowed, Walter Raleigh–style. 'Yes. Whatever Your Ladyship says.'

He would have sworn she almost stamped her feet underneath the satin shimmer of the dress that skimmed down her body and even now had his hands twisting out of the bunched fists and flexing with the unspent touch of her. She had spirit. In spades. And it was back in abundance.

'What I said was thank you,' she delivered in clipped, sharp tones, and she tilted her nose up, as if he had come to the main entrance when he really should be using the servants' door.

'Thank you?'

She looked flustered now. But she was back to acting the princess and he'd be damned if he was going to let her wriggle away that easily.

'Yes, thank you. For…you know…stepping up…'

Dante took a step back, let his smile do the work, let his eyes trail all over her the way he wanted to trail his hands. The glorious spill of her breasts, scooped and positioned for a man just to release into his hands, to tease with his mouth. The shoulders curved gently, the hips swelled from that tiny waist. She was a feast, a banquet, an image of woman he had rarely, if ever, seen before.

But she was trying to pull rank with him, and he for one was not going to play ball in that particular game of ego.

'So, yes. Thank you. It…er…seems to have been a success.'

He watched a fan of colour seep all over her creamy chest and this time he didn't move his eyes. She was too tempting, on so many different levels. And, yes, maybe seeing that image of Celine had aroused his passion, raised his ire, but he was going to make her apologise over and over again—and thank him in ways she'd never even dreamed of.

'Lots of happy people back there, Princess, yes.'

She scowled.

'And it was for them that I did it. I hate to see people getting short-changed when their expectations have been raised. You know, in a way it was a bit of a rescue situation…I saw someone in trouble and I dropped everything—and I mean *everything*—put my foot to the floor, put myself out there. I mean, what do I know about auctions?'

He lanced her with a stare and watched as her eyes widened like saucers. Then he gave her a little wink and a smile. She was thinking. She knew exactly what he meant and she was reliving those moments. The pretty pink bloom shifted further from her glorious cleavage to the column of her neck.

'Is that where the jellyfish got you?' he asked, nodding to the scattering of the rash all over her beautiful chest.

She looked down, then up. Opened her mouth. Looked even more embarrassed. He could let her off the hook now, but she really *had* been incredibly rude. And he really *was* incredibly angry.

'I...I...'

He leaned in to her space, and her eyes widened even further as she leaned back. Then he placed a finger on her lips.

'Shh, Princess. It's okay. Apology accepted. I was happy to help out.'

He lifted his finger from the moist, soft pillow of her lips before he gave in to the temptation to slide it right inside and have her suck it. He tilted her chin up instead and leaned forward—just a tiny inch, just close enough to scent the luxury and the class that oozed from her pores. He lingered there, savouring in equal measure her surprise and her femininity. Letting her get caught up in the moment of thinking that he just might kiss her.

His hand slid out, all by itself, and lightly skimmed her waist. And just like that he felt her melt—felt all those thorns wilt and fall like petals to his feet. He nodded to her, telling her with a wink that he knew she was moments away from giving in completely.

And then he stepped back. 'Really, I was happy to help—it was no problem at all.'

He slipped her a smile and let his hand slide off the side of her hip. She was hot. For him. *Oh, yes.*

He walked away.

'Wait! I mean...' She was literally pulling on his sleeve now.

He stopped. Raoul was watching closely, raising a shot glass with the others in his little circle of new blood, and downing it to a chorus of cheers.

Dante waited, then turned as slowly as he could, savouring every last moment.

'You mean *what*, Princess?'

He glanced at her, one eyebrow raised in a jaunty, light-hearted way that belied every last emotion that coursed through his veins like trails of lit gasoline.

'Okay, I'm sorry for the things I said earlier. I realise now that you were only trying to help. And thanks— thank you for then, and for now. You really...got me out of a hole.'

'Forget it,' he said, and moved away.

She moved with him. He felt the hand on his arm.

'Look, let me make it up to you.'

Perfect, thought Dante, silently high-fiving himself, aware of the scrutiny from Raoul.

'Okay,' he said slowly. 'Did you have something in mind?'

He turned right around now—slowly—moved ever so slightly back into her space, watched the telltale signs spill across her face.

'Would you care to join me for a drink?'

She turned hopeful green eyes on him and he smiled softly. She was like a moist, plump peach, ripened on a tree and just about to fall into his hands. But sometimes the fruits that looked the sweetest were the ones that tasted toxic. He knew that better than anyone.

There was something about Lady Lucie that made him pause. He could so easily take her to bed...give her a night she'd never forget. And then what? Another night? There were only a few days before he had to head east. He didn't want anything lasting with anyone. Even if their chemistry *was* good—and, yes, there was every indication that it would be—even if they stayed in bed for the next four days it would all end as it always did. With his *Hey, it's been great* chat.

The last thing he wanted was any drama whatsoever. And this one had 'starring role' in lights all around her. He needed release, yes—but not with someone as emotional as she. That was one script he didn't want to read ever again.

He cupped her shoulder, gave it a soft rub.

'Thanks, Princess. Another time, maybe.'

He didn't wait to see how she took that—he just moved on. He was going to split...head into town and sort out his head. Ghosts required exorcism, and he was itching to start.

CHAPTER FIVE

LUCIE WATCHED HIM lope off with that overtly sexual athleticism she found so fascinating.

What on earth…? Talk about reading someone wrong. She'd been sure he was interested in her—much more than she was in him. In fact less than twelve hours ago she hadn't even known his name, far less given him this amount of headspace. She actually shook her head to see if she could clear him out of it. But since the nausea and breathlessness had dissipated as she'd watched him own the auction, she'd found him creeping inside it—images of him and his golden smile and sinful body. He'd wowed the crowd…in fact she was sure he'd done a much better job than her mother could ever have done. And part of her longed for her to know that.

Right on cue, one of the staff indicated to her across the room. *Phone. Lady Vivienne.* Lucie felt her shoulders tense again and her fists fill with handfuls of the satin of her dress. But she had no option.

She made her way across the room, smiling stiffly at those who greeted her.

'Hello, Mother.'

'Lucie, what on earth is going on?'

'How's Simon? Much recovered? All trouble sorted?'

'You know it's rude to answer a question with a question. I can only assume you've been drinking, Lucie, because I can't for the life of me think of any other reason why you'd be acting like this.'

'I'm sorry, Mother. Shall we start again? You were asking what on earth is going on. We've just made over two and a half a million dollars for the charity. That's what's going on.'

'You know perfectly well what I'm talking about. This was the ideal opportunity for you to sort out those silly panic attacks and you didn't even try.'

Lucie was stunned. 'You surely don't mean to tell me that you set me up like this on *purpose*?'

'I didn't say that,' her mother answered stiffly, 'but it was a perfect opportunity wasted.'

'Sorry, Mother, but I had to make a decision to prevent five hundred guests being bitterly disappointed. Dante Hermida—the polo player—offered, and I think we—*he*—actually did a really good job!'

She wouldn't rub her mother's nose in it. Of course not. But she was desperately keen for her to hear just how well they'd done.

'"A really good job"? Let me be clear, Lucinda. First of all I learn that you stood in the middle of that classless great boat like a gibbering jelly, and then—worse—you actually passed the gavel to *Dante Hermida*, of all people! That utter Lothario? Didn't I warn you to stay well away from men like that? This very afternoon? And then you substitute him for me and are seen hanging all over him. Have you no shame? I thought I'd brought you up to be better than that. I absolutely forbid you to have any more to do with him—do you hear me? Lucinda?'

Lucie stared at the patterns she was drawing on the mink velvet carpet with the pointed toe of her shoe. Then she examined her nails. They were flawless—lovely, actually—and she thought she might keep the polish on past tomorrow morning. Perhaps. She pressed her lips together to see if the stickiness from the gloss was still there, but of course the last thing that had been there had been Dante's finger.

She dropped her head back and let the phone slide to her neck, where she cradled it in against her skin—anything to drown out the sound of her mother's unstinting whingeing. Brought her up? If it weren't so sad it would be funny. The house mistress and the nanny had brought her up. Her mother and father had been far too busy living their own lives to bother with anything as inconvenient as a child.

A tray of champagne passed by at just the right moment and she snagged a glass. Her second of the night. She was learning to enjoy it—and it slid down easily. More easily than usual, since she knew her mother would disapprove so heartily.

'I have to go, Mother. Thank you so much for calling, but my guests need me.'

'Guests? I hope you don't mean that polo player? I'm warning you, Lucinda—do you hear me? Stay away…'

'Actually, Mother—that's exactly who I mean. And this time I'm going to make a proper job of it.'

She didn't wait to say goodbye. She stared at the phone heard the whining, appalling voice of her mother—her *own* mother—still screeching at her. She clicked it off and dropped it in an ice bucket.

She was too far gone for tears—too wrung out, too exhausted. If she ever had a daughter she would never,

ever say or do the hurtful, horrid things her mother did. She would nurture her child, love her and care for her. She would protect her from harm, but make her strong enough to stand up on her own two feet.

She'd had enough. Totally had enough. All those weeks and months of diet, of exercise, of listening to her mother's 'rules' and her stress about her 'real' family. She didn't give a damn about the success of the night, or the money they raised. She didn't give a damn about anything other than herself!

Well, she might think she could lay down the law from three thousand miles away, and tell her who she could see and what she could do, but there was no way she was going to let herself be dictated to like that. The hypocrisy was outrageous. All these years of listening to her rant about men suddenly crystallised into one clear thought—*why?* What was so bad about them? Why was her mother so animated when it came to her rules about men?

For the second time Lucie made her way through rooms full of people laughing and drinking, but this time she held her head up. Rage was her engine, and she knew it. She didn't glance left or right, just focused on moving swiftly through the crowd. She'd get off the yacht, so that the staff didn't have to be put on the spot the next time her mother called. Someone had been grilled by her mother before she'd called her. Someone had told her all about her moments with Dante.

Dante!

The one man she had been warned to stay away from. And the one man she felt incredibly compelled to seek out right now.

He was interested in her—she knew he was. All she

had to do was act a little less like a blubbering idiot and a little more like the sophisticates he was used to.

She owed it to herself to try…

The *Marengo* was moored on the busiest stretch of the harbour, directly opposite the chicest nightclub on the island. Dante stood a moment on the jetty, watching the lines of partygoers queuing along the front. He could feel the 'good times' tension in the air—could feel it in his own body. He knew exactly how this evening was going to roll. It was like a drug to him—a few beers, a few laughs, women flirting, he taking his time, then the after-party, then the aftermath of that.

Pure. Unadulterated. Oblivion.

He reassured himself every time that everyone else was praying to the same gods in this particular church. That way there was no guilt. No need for confession.

He couldn't remember ever caring about the motivations of any romantic partner before, but he was pretty sure that Lady Lucinda didn't shake what her mama gave her every weekend, like some of the rest of that set. Good-time girls were just that. And he wasn't fool enough to ignore the fact that for many of them it was all a big act. A big hook with which they landed their catch.

But he had never bitten yet. Never would. Lose his unlimited pass to oblivion? Get mired in a relationship? Smoke and mirrors—that was all happy relationships were. He didn't begrudge anyone their 'lifetime partner', if that was what they wanted to call it, but he didn't believe the hype.

Seeing that Celine body double tonight had shaken him up—he had to admit it. But there had been a time when it would have taken him a lot longer to calm down. Back in his late teens, when it had still been a raw wound. Back then he would have been laid out for days on a self-destructive path. Now he was fine. He had more important things to worry about than something that had happened all those years ago. He'd learned to switch off, to deal with it.

He just hoped tonight would be one of those nights where he found the switch easily.

He looked along the front of the black glass building at the outdoor lounge area. Tall white tables and bar stools. Parasols and potted palms. Ice buckets and cocktails. Women wearing very little. Some of them beautiful, some of them hot. But as his gaze skimmed back and forth he found it hovering even longer on the jetty. He felt strangely underwhelmed by the whole thing. There really was nothing he was remotely interested in pursuing—nothing enticing him to step into that particular haven.

He wanted fire. He wanted passion. He wanted beauty.

Class.

And he was beginning to think that there was only woman who was going to do it for him. If he got the chance a second time he doubted he would be able to say no.

'Hello, there! I thought it was you.'

Dante heard the perfectly pronounced vowels and knew his deal was sealed.

He turned away from the crowd. 'Party over?'

She was truly lovely. He let his eyes slide and savour. Her hair fell in long waves, skimming over those shoulders, lying in inviting silken folds over her cleavage. He took his time. He had no wish to hurry as he re-learned every soft curve, felt himself become aroused, welcomed it.

'Only I thought it was good etiquette for the hostess to stay until the last guest had left?'

She blushed in that haughty, *how-dare-you?* manner and he felt a grin spread out across his face. The corner of her mouth twitched up and her eyes danced in answer, but still she held herself aloft and aloof.

She was here, she'd come after him, but she was going to make him work. He got that.

Wind skimmed around them, causing the hem of her dress to rise. The fabric clung to her long legs, outlining slim calves and the flare of incredibly feminine hips. His eyes dropped to the soft V between her legs and his arousal kicked up another gear as the shimmery satin outlined her mound. A long slow breath of approval escaped through his lips and he raised his eyes to hers in approbation.

She accepted it.

'As far as I am concerned, you *are* the party.'

She spoke quietly, but he didn't miss the shiver of hesitation.

'You've really thought this through?'

He owed her one more lifeline. Because something told him that when she fell—as they all did—she was going to fall headfirst.

'Because you don't want to wake up with your head on the wrong pillow.'

'I want to wake up with my head on *your* pillow,' she said.

'Is that so?' he asked, stepping a little closer. He watched, becoming more and more aware that her regal act was just that—she was not quite so in command as

she liked to portray. 'That's some honour you're be-
stowing—and with that honour comes responsibility,
should I accept it...'

He took another step, and she leaned back ever so
slightly before straightening herself up. He watched her
perfect throat as she swallowed, the movement in her
skin drawing his eye, inflaming his blood. *Oh, yes.*

'Well…' she breathed, and the sound disappeared into
the slap of water on the sides of the jetty and the bustle
and buzz of the night all around them. 'Do you accept?'

'What exactly are you offering, Princess?'

'As soon as you drop that stupid moniker I might
tell you.'

Dante laughed as he closed the gap. They stood almost toe to toe. And this time she leaned back only to
look up at him. She was getting into her stride now and
he was loving it.

'You don't need to tell me anything. I can see it written all over you. In giant neon letters.'

Her eyes flashed and darted over his face.

'Is that so?' she asked, repeating his words, mocking
him. 'We have our little spelling test after all.'

And then he grinned, and she grinned, and he put his
hands on her waist, exactly where he had wanted to rest
them all evening. They fitted nicely in the soft curves.
He tugged her to him. Her hands jerked up in a defensive movement but they landed gently on his chest. He
looked down as she spread her fingers wide.

'What exactly is it,' she began, lifting her eyes in a
coy little move as old as time, 'that I'm spelling out for
you?'

Dante stepped a little closer. He took his hands from
her waist and skimmed them up over her ribs with im-

mense restraint, feather-light. He slowly brushed the sides of her breasts, her shoulders, and then gently cupped her jaw. He trailed his fingers over her cheeks and gently drew a circle round each eye.

'With these bewitching eyes, you're showing me every single thought that's going on in here.' He tapped her brow. 'And those thoughts are...' He leaned in, took a breath beside her ear, and whispered, 'Dirty.'

She shivered. He heard it and he saw it. Then she closed her eyes, and he knew that he was as hard as he'd ever been. She was going to be delicious.

He moved to her other ear. She flinched but he held her steady.

'You have a very filthy mind, Lucie,' he whispered, and she shuddered right there in his arms.

It was all he could do not to grind himself against her. One or two people had passed by and they were just in sight of the queue of partygoers. He was going to have to exercise huge restraint. *Huge.*

'You're bluffing,' she breathed back. 'You think everyone thinks like you.'

'Is that right?'

He kept his mouth right beside her ear, an inch above it. A warm, sweet smell—*her* warm, sweet smell—wound up and he breathed it in. She melted against him, stretched her neck out for him, and he let his lips graze the satiny skin all the way down to her collar.

'Mmm, Lucie... What do you think I'm thinking right now?'

Her hands were still lying across his chest, getting in the way of what he wanted. He lifted first one hand, then the other, and she wound them round the back of his neck. He looked down at her upturned face. She was undone, but she was pulling herself together. He had to hand it to her.

'What *you're* thinking?' she said. 'Oh, I don't quite think we were finished with your amazing assessment of what *I* was offering. It was apparently "written all over me"—remember?'

He smiled. 'Good call. Now, where was I…? Ah, yes.'

And he cupped her jaw again, brushed his thumb over her bottom lip, tugging it.

'This mouth… These lips… They are quite clearly promising what you plan to do with them.'

'And that is…?'

He could hardly hear her. Was it the blood rushing in his ears or her sexy breathlessness—he had no idea. But he held her right where he wanted her, slid his hands further into her hair and positioned her at the slight angle he preferred. And then he waited. This was too divine to rush. She was easily the most tempting morsel he'd ever had—the last thing he was going to do was gorge on her out here, in full view of everyone.

But that didn't mean he couldn't have just a little taste.

He moved them together, so close only a sliver of air was between their mouths.

'You were saying…?' she whispered.

And as she spoke her lips brushed his and his resolve evaporated. He covered her mouth with his own in a hungry, passionate kiss and it was all he had known it would be. Soft, sweet and pure hot heaven.

Her lips were the perfect fit, the perfect pout. He made her deliver up kiss after kiss as he bit down on his resolve to keep them both decent. But with her breasts pressed fully against his body and his erection straining against her stomach it took all of his will to stay in a low gear.

'I was saying—before you interrupted—that these lips…' He slid his tongue over them. She whimpered. 'These lips have been telegraphing to me…'

He used his tongue to flick from the centre of her open pout to the upper edge of her top lip. And back. All the way along.

'That they're going to kiss every last part of me. Every. Part. Isn't that right, Princess?'

He felt her tongue dart out to meet his and the need to grind into her almost felled him. This game was overplayed. The public version, anyway. He grabbed her hand, looked up and down the jetty.

'We'll finish this back on the *Sea Devil*. Come on.'

He took her hand and almost marched her further along the runway to where a row of silently bobbing motorboats waited. He spotted his launch, stepped down and held out his hand, anxious to get this precious cargo aboard quickly.

His heart was hammering as he reached for her, and in one movement he'd tucked her close and taken his place behind the wheel. She leaned right in tight as he nosed the boat carefully around and out past the other launches. They came alongside the *Marengo*, its huge gleaming sides bearing down on them as he passed it and moved out into the bay.

In less than ten minutes he'd have her across the water, and five after that he'd have her across his bed.

The throb of the motor and the crash of the waves joined a crescendo of sensations with more to come. Dante loved this part of the chase—the anticipation, the build-up. The arc of tension gathering height until he could let his mind empty and his body just feel. And this felt *right*. This felt as if the particular symphony they were co-composing was going to have all the depth and drama he needed.

So she hated crowds...had social anxiety. So what? She was well in command of herself where her libido was concerned—that was for sure. And he could handle those emotions once they started to show.

But wasn't that the part that was dangerous? Wasn't that why you gave her the big brush-off earlier?

Like a mallet to a polo ball, he struck those thoughts out of his mind. He felt Lucie leaning against the crescent of his arm and shut out anything that was set to interrupt his mood. Wasn't that what he was best at?

No words passed between them as he cut the engine and tossed the speedboat's rope onto the yacht. He stepped out deftly, tied her up, and then held out his hand and guided her aboard the *Sea Devil*.

A third of the size of the *Marengo*, it was fast, sleek, and reflected the only aspect of his personality he was prepared to go public with—he gathered no moss. He was no apologist for liking things the way he liked them. Another benefit of the single life—no compromise in pretty much anything. Of course he'd had girlfriends who had tried to soften things up, the way women did, and that was fine. As far as it went. But it did no one any favours if you let them think they were going to gain permanency rights.

Permanency was the last thing he wanted to think about as he led Her Ladyship by the hand up the three steps to the sundeck. Darkness swathed the night, backlit by the pinpricks of deck lights. There was nobody else on board, his staff having taken him at his word and gone off for the weekend. Good for them—they worked hard. And good for him too, as it now turned out.

'I half expected there would be some party in full swing,' she said aloud, her cut-glass tones slicing through the night.

'*I'm* the party—remember?' he said as he moved them further along and down into a sunken area.

Plump banquettes skirted the space, and were scattered with an array of cushions—and that was as feminine as it got. A black glass table sat between three sides, and on the other side lay loungers in various positions. A small plunge pool to the left sank down even further, and more seats and beds were arranged there. It was comfortable. He liked it.

He switched on the side lights and quickly selected a muted melody underscored with the low throb of African drums. He poured them both champagne and walked to where Lucie had stalled in the middle of the space and was gently swaying her hips. He paused. Watched her.

She didn't ooze sexuality, the way some women did but, regarding her now, he saw that what she lacked in overt, in-your-face eroticism she more than made up for in sensuality—it ran through her like the bass line in the tune that was pulsing around them right now.

'Perfect…thank you,' she said as she took the glass from him and took a sip. Nervously?

'You know, I heard the staff call this boat "Dante's Lair" earlier today?

Had she, indeed? He shrugged it off.

'People like to speculate, I suppose. They imagine they know all about me and my business.'

And they knew nothing. Why should they? His own parents had no idea of half the things he'd done. He wasn't the type to bleat about his woes. He and his brother, Rocco, had been brought up to be independent, to stand tall. The last thing he'd ever do was feel sorry for himself. Or, worse, let his guard down.

He had a great life. Gloss and glamour and good times. He knew how lucky he was—how much of a good start he'd had compared to his adopted brother. He'd never had to run in the streets to survive. He'd had everything he'd ever wanted. His mother hadn't been the most demonstrative with her affection, but he'd wanted for nothing. So when a bit of a trauma like Celine had come along he'd been able to deal with it. Of course he had. He hadn't told a living soul—hadn't needed to. He could handle life.

The Hermidas were proud—every last one of them. Proud and silent. And that was what made them so interesting to the press.

'"Lair" suggests something of a predator though.'

'Do you think that about me, Princess? That I'm predating on you? Right now?'

'Hardly,' she answered wryly, touching her hair. 'As far as I recall it was me that suggested this…this…'

He walked to her. 'This…private party?'

'Exactly,' she said, looking very much as if that was the only type of party she would consider attending. The long swish of her blonde hair obscured one eye, starlet style, and she completed the look with another coy smile.

He almost shook his head at her. Who would believe this confident, in command woman was the same one who had literally begged him to help her out at the charity auction earlier.

'Maybe, but you must know that despite what's said

about me I'm very choosy about who I allow into my…
lair.'

He lifted the glass from her hand and set them both
down on the table.

'I take it I am supposed to consider that a compli-
ment?'

'All I'm saying is that being a princess doesn't give
you any special rights.'

She smiled through the eyes she narrowed at him.

'You're not going to give up with that, are you?'

He winked slightly. 'I might. Depends…'

'On what, exactly?'

'On whether you're going to follow through with all
those signals you've been telegraphing since the first
moment I saw you.'

'Oh, that's right. Something about my filthy mind
and my suggestive mouth. Was that it?'

The bubbling of the hot tub suddenly seemed to fill
the night air. Dante nodded to it. Lucie's eyes drifted
over, and then flipped right back to his.

'Not forgetting your body—which I recall was a lot
less covered up then. And. Completely. Soaking. Wet.'

She seemed to take that like a sucker punch, and her
hand slid to her chest. Her mouth formed a silent 'oh'
and for a second he thought he had genuinely shocked
her. Then she slipped him another smile. Oh, yes, she
was feeling it as much as he was.

'What are you suggesting, Dante?'

He started to unbutton his shirt. 'Princess, I'm well
past the point of suggestion.'

The hand at her chest went to her mouth now. Oh, she
was very, *very* good. Coy and cute and causing him all
sorts of constriction issues. He tossed away his shirt and

laid his hand on his belt, ran the leather through the loops and pulled it free. His erection strained uncomfortably as he tugged down the zip and yanked off his trousers.

Still she stood there, in her Little Miss Innocent pose. He had to laugh.

He gripped the sides of his boxers, raised his eyebrows and gave her a full-beam grin.

'Seems like we're right back where we started, Princess.'

She was still standing as if she'd been struck by lightning. Just as she had when he'd scared her off the boat earlier. Only this time the last thing he wanted her to do was disappear overboard.

But she didn't move a muscle and the glimmer of a red flag suddenly waved in his mind. Surely this was an act? Surely she wasn't *really* freaked out by his nudity?

'I hope you're not going to abandon ship this time?'

There was nothing else for it—he tugged down his boxers, releasing himself. Then he stood up and faced her head-on—fully hard, fully erect and fully loaded.

Lucie stood utterly still, but her eyes zoned straight in on him. Seconds ticked by as she gorged on the sight of him, and he felt so damn turned on that he put his hand around himself and stroked. This was getting out of hand before it had even begun.

'You'd better make your mind up, because soon I might not be in any fit state to rescue you.'

Another long beat as he continued to stroke, and she continued to stand, and then suddenly she began to walk towards him, her eyes trained directly on his. For some bizarre reason he felt as if he were guiding her across a rope bridge, willing her to take the next step. But that was just ridiculous.

'Nice to see you,' he said as she stepped into his space.

He placed his hands on either side of her jaw and closed the last inches between them. And then he pressed his lips to hers and kissed her.

Some kisses were sweet. Some kisses were hot.

Dante felt as if sunspots were bursting in front of his eyes and all through his body as his tongue slid into Lucie's warm, wet mouth and found hers. He thought he could hear moans and sighs escaping her, but that might just as easily be him. Her lips and his lips and her face and his face had become one.

He grabbed her and plunged and plundered and savoured. His hands were in her hair, on her neck, her shoulders, her beautiful cleavage. He was unstoppable.

'Lucie, if you want to wear that dress ever again you'd better take it off now, before I rip—'

But the control he normally had in spades had evaporated before he could even finish the sentence and he spun her round and pulled.

Harnessed by her sleeves, she stood before him, her hair wild, her eyes wilder. Her mouth was wet and open and her breasts were almost completely bare. She looked more feral than regal, but he knew then that he had never seen a more beautiful woman in his life.

'Too late, I guess,' he said, reaching for her jaw and then latching his mouth onto the nipple he'd released from the veil of strained fabric.

She screamed, he thought, but it was as much as he could do not to throw her to the ground as he kept up the pressure on her nipple. Round and round he moved his tongue, sucking and tugging, and moulding with his other hand. Such full, beautiful breasts. He palmed and weighed and shaped them as he moved his mouth from one to the other, as each bud hardened to a point he knew would be bringing her intolerable, exquisite pleasure.

And, yes, he knew she was breathlessly begging him to stop, but that only drove him on. Until he felt her hands on his shoulders and realised he was bearing her weight. He straightened, scooped her up then spun her round and tugged the dress down further.

'This has got to go,' he said as he found the buttons that were hidden and ripped at them.

Her dress came apart in his hands. He looked at the shards of silk and then at the pale-skinned goddess before him. Her face was flushed and her breasts were soaked where his mouth had sucked and teased them. Her waist, flaring out to the perfect balance of feminine hips, was scored with tiny marks.

'Hey...' he said, smoothing his fingers over them. 'Sweetheart, was that me? Did I hurt you?'

She looked at him, and then down at herself, frowning for a brief moment. 'What?' she breathed. 'Hurt me...? No.'

He stepped up to her, his erection immediately pressing down against her stomach. He so badly needed to be deep inside her.

He lifted her. He couldn't stop himself. He placed himself neatly in between her legs. Immediately she hooked her legs round his waist and threw back her head.

A loud, low groan escaped from his mouth.

'Oh, yes, you're quite the princess for everyone else... but you're one very dirty girl for me.'

He glanced around—a wall, a floor, a sofa—he had to lay her down somewhere. But nothing was right. She deserved better.

'Let's do this properly,' he said.

And he stepped past the hot tub, past the cushion-strewn banquettes and discarded scraps of fabric and clothes. And then he walked with her, naked but for the last scrap of silk and the teetering heels that pierced his flesh with each step. Down three stairs and on through the salon. Along the passageway that led to his suite. The lamps were low, sending soft Vs of light over the slices of dark polished wood that were used throughout the yacht. It wasn't cold—far from it—but Dante hugged her body close to his, protecting her.

Opening up the door of his suite, he saw the panoramic windows displaying a view of the whole of the bay. Of course the *Marengo*—stupendous—presided over the whole space, even at this distance. But she was the last thing Dante wanted to look at right now, and he quickly pressed the button that slid the curtains closed, closing off the twinkling night and any nosy paparazzi that might be circling like the sharks they were.

The *Sea Devil* might have already appeared on every piece of trashy, glossy paper and online feature, but Dante was always well aware of what was going to be published before it happened. *He* was in control of what the world saw. And he had a sixth sense that he really *didn't* want the world to have even a glimpse of this particular assignation. Oh, no. This was indeed a strictly private party.

He stepped fully into the room, feet landing on soft, plush carpet. The door closed behind them.

Immediately he felt her hands on his head, cupping his cheeks. She was kissing him deeply, passionately, and with a wantonness he was finding harder and harder to resist.

Blindly he stepped forward, past the four club chairs

and the walnut coffee table, his thigh dragging against the skirt of one of the cabinets that arced from one end of the room to the other.

The bed.

He felt his leg bump against it and grabbed Lucie's wrists, pulling them back from his head and her mouth from his face. He held her and looked at her make-up-smudged eyes and hot pink cheeks.

'You beautiful girl,' he said.

And he set her down on his bed.

She blinked at him as she kneeled up, and for a moment a sad little smile graced her face. 'Well, we both know that's stretching it a bit, Dante. Nice of you, though.'

He frowned at her. What on earth was going through her mind?

'Sweetheart, you're beautiful—believe me.'

'Anyone can be beautiful with a stylist and a bucket of make-up. I hardly think I still qualify all these hours later.'

She had no idea.

'I'm no fantasist—I know my limitations.'

'Is that a fact?' he said, bending towards her and letting his breath seep in through the fine silk of her panties. 'Why don't you lie back here and I'll show you how lovely you are.'

And he kneeled before her and put his hands on her hips, then round to the curve of her bottom, moulding and kneading, urging her legs a little more open.

'Dante, please!' she said.

'I want to kiss you here,' he said, ignoring her gasp as he bent to press a kiss between her legs. 'Take these off.'

With one hand he held her by the waist and with the

other he tugged down her panties, again feeling that growing realisation that she was...*shy*?

But he knew women, and he knew what they loved.

She lay back now, as he gripped her ankles and tugged her legs open, ignoring her little squeal. She was outstanding. Completely. Never shifting his gaze, he took a single finger and gently stroked his way slowly between the swollen lips, slicking the wet flesh until he came upon the tiny hard nub. With a harder rub he pressed, until he heard her cry out in pleasure.

He placed one hand on each of her thighs and started to dip his head forward. There was nothing he wanted to do more than feel his mouth at her core, taste her. He tried to hook her legs over his shoulders, but as he looked up at her lush body, saw her eyes wide and watchful, suddenly she jerked up and slipped out from under him.

He made another deep, throaty sound and then he dipped his head. He so badly wanted to lap her with his tongue.

'Dante, please. I really don't want you to do that.'

'Honey, you'll love it,' he said, barely pausing.

'No, honestly,' she said, struggling away from him.

He stopped. Instantly. Leaned up. Backed off.

'Hey, if you're not comfortable this stops now.'

There was no way on this earth he would ever force himself on a woman, no matter how his sanity depended on it. But this one was outdoing herself with the conflicting signals.

Sudden silence fell between them. He waited a moment, then made to stand up. He'd known this was a bad idea. She was a whole bag full of issues—and none of them easy to solve.

'Time out,' he said.

'Please, don't— I really want to— I want you...'

She reached for him—lunged.

'I'm sorry. I want you so much. Please, Dante.'

And she kneeled up, wound her arms around his neck and slid her beautiful lush body against him.

He took her wrists, held her back even as his body reacted.

'We're mature adults. Mature, *consenting* adults. This is not about coercion. Ever.'

'I know,' she breathed, staring up with big bruised eyes. She was all vixen again. God, she killed him. But there was no way he was going to do anything with a woman who wasn't as into it as he.

'Dante, there is nothing I want to do more right now than this.'

She held his eye, then leaned forward to cup his face. His eyes fell to her full breasts, swinging towards him. Still he held back. Until her tongue eased his lips apart and slid into his mouth. He felt the very tips of her nipples graze his chest. And then the rest of her.

She pulled him down as she lay back and he let her. He let go. Her legs slid round his back. He was big, and he really didn't want to hurt her, but when he stalled after only an inch the need to fill her battled with the need to answer the nagging doubt that was creeping into his head again.

'Please don't stop,' she breathed, tightening her legs and tilting her hips.

She reached her arms up and pulled him down into a kiss he could no more resist than resist taking his next breath. She defined *irresistible*.

He tried again. So sweet and so tight...but something was just not right.

Her eyes, when she opened them to see why he had stopped, were anxious.

'Lucie, are you sure you've done this before?' he asked, not even knowing himself that those words had been going to come out of his mouth. It seemed ridiculous—but he had to know...

She glanced away.

'Sweetheart?'

'I never said I had or I hadn't—but I want to—so badly. Please, Dante.'

He looked bewildered. 'Are you telling me you're a *virgin*?'

He shook his head at his own stupidity. She was so adamant. So resolute. And she just *did* it for him. Completely.

When she didn't answer he rolled that around in his mind for a bewildered second even as she moved under him, used the legs hooked round his back to pull him nearer. He groaned as he felt himself slide in deeper. And then deeper still. And then he could only follow the urges of his body until he was buried in her to the hilt.

'Oh, angel, you're killing me.'

She moaned, deep and long, and he'd never felt such a perfect fit—it was visceral. He bent down and kissed her, drinking in the sounds of her satisfaction and starting to pulse to the tempo of his own.

'You feel amazing,' she whispered against his neck.

She whispered his name. He whispered hers back, asked her if she was okay. Because *he* was. More than okay. And the sensation of being inside her, so hot and deep and primal, was absolutely right. That was it—he felt absolutely *right*.

He looked down at her—at her face, her breasts,

where he was sliding in and out. Then back to her face. She was with him all the way. And then she began to cry with her own pleasure and he knew he was stroking that special place.

'You're okay?'

She opened eyes that had been closed and smiled at him. She didn't look remotely virginal.

'Oh, yes. Never better.'

'Oh, I think we can do better.'

And he tilted her hips up higher and drove in deeper. He felt his climax coming like a freight train—unstoppable and thunderous—and he called his release out to the night, unguarded and unedited.

Dante rolled to one side and lay on his back, his arms above his head. He could feel Lucie turning onto her side and moving to close the distance between them.

Had that really just happened?

The best sex of his life with a…?

He couldn't get this straight in his head. Had to process it. He sat on the edge of the bed, heard her shift behind him. Then the heavy fog of silence.

'Was that your first time?'

He tilted his head—didn't look but waited to hear the truth.

Nothing. Except the wispy strains of music that emanated from the salon and the unravelling of the moments they had just shared. Then her hand…burning on his back—only her fingertips, but still he felt as if he had been scalded and jerked away.

He stood up. 'I'm going to hit the shower.'

He should have listened to his gut. Should have let his eyes see the red flag that had fluttered in the corner of his mind. Should have stopped when he'd first had that inkling. What an idiot! Lose himself in a woman? An evening of no-strings sex? With English aristocracy who turned out to be a virgin. A virgin who had decided to relinquish that status with *him*. Tonight. *Now.*

You couldn't make this stuff up.

He turned on the shower and stepped in, caught a glimpse of himself in the mirror as the steam crept across it like an embarrassed flush. He looked haunted—grim. His eyes had been dulled by the effort of holding it together and then letting it all out in—*that woman.*

What a woman.

Damn her. What on earth had just happened? *Why* him? Why *now*? Women were such devious, scheming creatures. There was *always* an ulterior motive. Every time!

He racked his brains, trying to think of what she might hope to get out of it, what emotional ransom she was going to hold him to. She didn't need money, she certainly didn't need fame. He didn't think she'd been bluffing when she'd told him of her shyness. And she was so beautiful she could have her pick of men.

Yet she'd waited until tonight to have sex.

With a man she'd made no secret of hating from the first moment they'd met…

Was it payback for something he'd done? It was the best payback he could imagine if that was the case!

It was incomprehensible—but when it came to women nothing would surprise him. Who knew what was going on in those pretty little heads? Those months with Celine had taught him that, at least. She had been a woman who would stop at nothing to get what she wanted. The care-

fully executed seduction…the lies and then the venom…
And then the final act.

Dante felt the water streaming down his face. He
rubbed the back of his neck with both hands and shook
his head.

Images of Celine—or Miss di Rosso, as she'd been
then—seeped into his brain. The first time he'd seen
her, in that tight, bright skirt, walking through a vale of
sunbeams in the cloisters with the school principal. He'd
fallen in love with her then—everyone had. The only
sexy young female teacher in a boys' boarding school.
It had been inevitable that she would become the pin-
up girl.

But of all the men and boys there she'd targeted *him*—
leaning over him, her blouse artfully undone, while he
sat powerless with an erection under his desk. Then the
'extra lessons' she'd felt he should have. Slowly, carefully, she had seduced him into a secret world. A world
where he'd felt like a king compared to his classmates.
He was screwing the object of their wet dreams and she
was screwing his mind.

He'd felt like that right up until the moment when
it had all become so obvious. When the lust he'd been
feeling hadn't turned into the love she'd demanded. That
was when he'd drawn back. Right at that moment. And
then the tables had turned. Spectacularly.

But that had been fifteen years ago. And he'd been
on his guard ever since. Nothing had got past his impenetrable shield. No one could see through the smiling, charming, engaging young man he'd become since
those dark months.

Dante squeezed some shower gel onto his hand and
the lemon scent of it burst through his senses—just as

the image of Lucie's trusting eyes burst into his mind. He frowned at the memory of that moment. It had felt as if he'd—*let her in*. There was no other way of saying it.

Well, that was definitely not going to happen again.

Lucie could hardly bear to look at the perfect picture of his backside, walking away. She drew her eyes quickly to the small slice of window that was not covered over by curtains. It was still terribly dark outside. The faintest trace of lilac laced the horizon but it would be hours until sunrise. Her strappy shoes lay on the pearl carpet. Her dress was back in that salon. Lying like a puddle of satin where he had as good as ripped it off.

So *that* was what it was all about.

She squeezed her eyes shut and let the feelings flow over her again. She'd never have believed anyone could make her feel like that. It had been beyond fantastic. *Way* beyond. Her body was liquid, melting after his touch. And she'd almost, *almost* let him kiss between her legs.

Almost—but, no, she couldn't. Not *there*. She didn't want to think about it.

She opened her eyes and stared at the wall. The shower was running, the sound muted through the veneer walls of the bedroom. She lay back and stared up at the ceiling. What should she do? Leave? Join him in the shower? Lie here and wait for the second course? Was this normal behaviour for a man? If so it was terribly disappointing.

She sighed and shook her head. She certainly wasn't going to wait around to find out.

She wrapped herself up in a sheet and went over to the panoramic window. Framed there, between the slightly open curtains, was the bay. The *Marengo* was in pride of place at the jetty. Lights still twinkled, but the great big thing was always lit up—in perpetual readiness for the next port, the next party, which her father had let slip was to be in Florida.

The crew had two weeks to sail her there. She had planned on staying on overnight and then heading back to the villa later today. Now she was stuck on the other side of the dratted bay, and she'd be damned if she was going to swim back a second time.

The door of the en-suite bathroom opened.

She saw his reflection in the window. A puff of steam and then the man himself, in a shaft of light, a black towel wrapped around his hips. He glanced at her. Just for a second. Then he moved across his room, every step emphasising that this was *his* place. His *lair*.

'You're welcome to use the shower,' he said.

She processed his tone. She was good at that, having learned from a very early age to work out which of her mother's moods was in operation at any given time. That had helped her to modify her own responses and behaviour, to work out when to melt into the background—which had almost always been the best thing to do.

This tone from Dante...?

She barely knew him, but one thing she'd picked up was that there was a storm behind all that sunshine. He could turn it on and off. On and off. Stepping up to take charge of the auction he'd been at his sunniest. Standing like a statue in the middle of the dance floor he'd been at his most thunderous. He'd looked then as if he'd like to rip someone's head off. And then he'd slipped back into laconic, lazy lover mode. But there was something dark, something lurking behind that dimpled grin and sexy walk. She could feel it.

But that was no reason to be so hideously inconsiderate. None.

'Thank you,' she said, 'but I'd rather get going.'

He pulled the towel off. Uninhibited. Totally. Dried himself and then tossed it onto the bed.

'Look. If I'm angry with you it's because you didn't tell me about your sexual past—or lack of one.'

Lucie was stunned. That was the last thing she'd expected to hear. He couldn't possibly be bothered about her inexperience. Deflowering virgins was something that men boasted about. Stupid men, admittedly.

'Well, gosh, I'm sorry. If I'd known it was such a big deal I would have had a T-shirt made.'

He was walking to one of the cherrywood cabinets when he stopped and cast her a look down the side of his face.

'Sarcasm doesn't suit you, Lucie.'

'No more than contempt suits *you*.'

'If that's how you interpret it, then I'm sorry. But I'm serious—you should have told me about being a virgin.'

'You would have stopped.'

He started moving again. Reached into a drawer and pulled on a pair of super-tight, super-sexy black boxers. She tried so hard not to stare—but how on earth did he expect her to keep the drool in her mouth when he was standing in front of her looking as if he'd just stepped from the pages of a magazine?

'I would have stopped for good reason, Lucie.' He straightened and then reached into another drawer. He pulled out a T-shirt and slid it over his head. The shock of damp blond hair fell into place perfectly.

'You're not a silly little girl—you're a mature woman. And you've chosen to sleep with your first ever sexual partner *tonight*? What am I supposed to think? It was clearly important for you to keep yourself chaste all these years—how old are you, anyway?'

He was frowning. There was no trace whatsoever of Mr Sunshine.

'I am twenty-five, since you ask. So charmingly.'

She sounded awful, she knew—like some kind of snobbish harpy. And she was beginning to see his point of view. But for heaven's sake...

'My point exactly. *Twenty-five-year-old princess beds Argentinian polo player in Get Rid of Virginity Quick game.* Yeah? See how those headlines would read? Some people might say you used me.'

'I did not use you!'

He was now pulling on a pair of jeans, sliding a belt through the loops and buckling it. He eyed her sceptically.

'Don't be ridiculous,' she said, puffing herself up as much as she could while draped in a sheet. 'Everyone knows that women don't have equal rights in the bedroom. Men are sexual predators who take what they want, and the more that they do, the more they're admired. What a stud! What a hero! The minute a woman goes after what she wants she's a tart.'

Suddenly the storm broke. Thunder spread across his brow.

'You think so? You think that's *always* how it works? Well, take it from me: there are a lot more female predators out there than you might imagine.'

He blasted out the words. Fury laced every syllable. It was like being in the eye of a typhoon that had come right out of nowhere. She stood, stunned, waiting to be sure that the storm had passed before she spoke.

'And your actions tonight could be interpreted as predatory…'

Now he was barely audible, moving about, running his hands through his hair, avoiding any eye contact.

'Even *you* don't believe that I'm a sexual predator! How ridiculous! Listen to yourself. You know perfectly well that all that happened was that we were both in the right place at the right time. You wanted it as much as I did.'

'You really expect me to believe that it was just a question of "tonight's the night"? After twenty-five years?'

'Look, I don't expect you to believe anything.'

'But you still owe me an explanation.'

He kept his back to her, sat on the edge of the bed pulling on deck shoes.

'How about this, then? Yes, I used you. I used you for sex. But you can be sure there won't be a repeat of it.' She sounded shrill. She sounded waspish.

He stood up. Faced her. Hands on hips. Raised eyebrows.

'Yeah, well, that was always a cert.'

Lucie stared. 'You really are just another insensitive pig.'

And she walked in the column of her sheet, with as much grace as she could muster, to the door. She heaved it open and made her way back along the corridor. She passed the hot tub, bubbling away under dawn's canopy, and stepped up into the salon, spotting her dress immediately in its shards of shame. She grabbed up her underwear and tried to wriggle into it.

How the heck was she going to get ashore? She'd rather die than ask him for a lift in the speedboat. Could she swim? Call a water taxi?

She was desperately fastening the legions of buttons when she heard him come close. Suddenly protecting her own space became the most critical thing she could do. She dropped the dress and gathered up the sheet.

'Even an insensitive pig like me knows a liar when he sees one.'

She turned to face him. He was leaning casually, one arm on the doorframe, head cocked to one side—but he looked as relaxed as a starched shirt.

'What's that supposed to mean?'

'You really need me to spell it out? Okay. I've known you less than twenty-four hours. But in that time I think I've seen every one of your princess-cut diamond faces. You went from the rudest, most ungrateful bitch I've ever met to a—a wreck.'

Lucie stood her ground as he straightened up and began to pace towards her.

'That panic attack? It nearly drew the curtains on your big night. And it was the only reason you even gave me entry to your father's yacht. If I hadn't stepped up you would have had me clapped in irons and thrown in the— the tower, or whatever you aristocrats do. And then something happened. Because the next thing I know you're hunting me down and offering yourself to me on a plate.'

He paused and stared at her with that penetrating gaze. She was determined to hold his eye—to stare right back while she fired a retort. But it was useless. He was right. She *had* used him. And she'd lied to him. How awful. How utterly, disgracefully awful.

She stepped away, bowed her head.

'When I rescued you the last thing you had on your mind was losing your virginity. Isn't that right?' he asked.

She opened her mouth but he put up his hand to stop her.

'Yes, I *know* you didn't need to be rescued. And I know that I probably upset the whole of the marine biodiversity of the Caribbean—but that's not the point. Here,' he said, holding out her shoes. 'Tell me I'm wrong.'

Lucie reached for her shoes but he held them just out of reach and eyed her carefully. Through the haze of guilt she cast him a quick look and grabbed for them again. This time he shook his head and released them.

She clutched them and moved away.

'Lucie?'

'Yes—okay,' she said. 'I hated you from the minute I saw you.' She turned round to face him. 'And when you came on the yacht I hated you even more.'

She had. All that arrogance. While she'd been feeling so wretched! Thinking he might be her *mother*, of all people.

Her mother—who had let her down. Who didn't have time to fulfil her promise but had all the time in the world to order Lucie about, demand that she do this or that. To tell her to stay away from the very person who had stepped up and actually helped her.

She turned to him. 'But I was genuinely grateful for what you did. You did more for me than anyone has ever done before—helping me out like that.'

He looked at her curiously. Suddenly she felt she'd gone too far. Given too much away. She tossed her head back.

'I wanted to taste forbidden fruit, if you like. I didn't intend that we would go as far as we did. I didn't think for a minute that I would sleep with you. But then I thought, *Why not?* That's all. There's no big mystery.'

She knew she sounded self-righteous. But wasn't that always the way?

She started furiously to pull the dress on. It was ripped at the shoulders and it was still a monster to get on, sticking at her hips and causing her to heave at it in an ungainly way. Her hands fumbled with the dratted buttons, missing the silk loops over and over, and suddenly it was too much.

Fiery tears formed in her eyes. She'd held herself together all night and now some stupid buttons were going to be her undoing? No way. *No.* She tried again. Bent her head and tried to manoeuvre her fingers while he stood utterly silent behind her. Damn him. *Damn.*

'You wait twenty-five years and then you think, *Why not?* I've had better compliments in my life.'

Her mind flashed with images of him worshipping her, mounting her, leaning down on her, glorying in her femininity and making her feel proud of her body for the first time she could remember.

'I'm sure you have.'

'So I was right the first time. You used me. I was just some kind of problem-solver—first with the auction and then with the virginity.'

How horrid. How utterly cold and calculating. Was that what he really thought of her? She could barely see her fingers through the thick, wobbling veil of unspilled tears in her eyes.

'If that's how you want to put it.' Her voice was choked and thin but she wouldn't turn her head, wouldn't let a single tear fall as the buttons—finally done—held the two torn sides of her dress together.

'I can't think of a better way.'

The hot tub bubbled back into life. Like some Greek chorus filling in every awkward pause.

'And the reason you had to lose your virginity tonight was…? Because, believe me, this is the part that really interests me.'

He really had her like a worm on a stick, turning it and making her squirm.

'Because of my mother,' she blurted, shocking herself with the words that had actually poured from her mouth.

'Your *mother*?'

Saying more would make her sound absolutely ridiculous. Saying less would be crazy. 'Yes. My mother has warned me my whole life to stay away from men like my father. Men like you.'

'Like me? You think I am like your father?'

'Yes—and when she found out you had replaced her at the auction she was furious.'

He narrowed one eye. 'Your mother was furious because she thinks I am like your father and that I replaced her. And *that's* why you slept with me?'

Lucie sat down heavily on a sofa and tried to stuff her toes under the narrow straps across her evening shoes.

'My mother is a bitch. That's why I slept with you.'

'Oh, that makes *so* much more sense.'

Lucie looked around for some kind of distraction. Her shoes were tied, her dress was on—she needed something to occupy her hands. There was nothing—except this great hunk of man in front of her, demanding answers.

'Okay. You really want to know? My mother was supposed to do this whole event with me. It's why the CCC approached me in the first place. I might raise two quid on my own, but Lady Viv could easily raise two million. I asked her. She knows how bad my social anxiety is, and she promised she would do it. I would never in a million years have got involved in any of this if she hadn't agreed. She said she would do it if I accepted her conditions— Oh, good grief. I don't even know why I'm telling you any of this.'

Suddenly his hands were round her upper arms, warm and steady. And his eyes were trained on hers.

'What conditions?'

Lucie pulled away—but he strengthened his grip.

'What conditions?'

'Look, none of that matters. She wants me to be more like her—and I'm nothing like her—and she doesn't care for the things I care for. That's all.'

'Like turtles?'

She turned on him.

'Hey! I'm serious—I'm not mocking! But you said "conditions". What conditions?'

How did she explain?

'Lose weight. Other things too, but mostly the weight.'

She couldn't look at him. Saying the words out loud made her feel ashamed.

She heard two things then—the beginning of a long whistle and the ringing pulse of a phone. She looked round for hers, then remembered she didn't have so much as a pocket handkerchief with her—and that her phone was drowning in an ice bucket somewhere.

Lucie followed Dante's gaze to where a phone was lighting up.

'It's fine. It's my mother. No one else would phone this early.'

Its ringing filled the air.

'Aren't you going to get it?'

He half-smiled, shook his head. 'No, I'm going to listen to the end of your story.'

'My story?'

He nodded his head. 'Everyone has their story. And it sounds like yours is quite a complicated one.'

'I'm really not in the habit of telling people my "story" or anything about me. So let's leave it at that.'

'Fine—except that your story now involves me. And it will for ever.'

She felt that stick poke her a little more keenly, and the worm squirmed a little more painfully. Normally when people got this interested she had no difficulty whatsoever in putting them in their place—or exiting. It was part of who she was—her essence. Nobody must know anything—ever.

And, yes, although that came more from her father than her mother, even Lady Viv 'managed' things. She only put out what she wanted. And she certainly wouldn't want anything like this. Wash dirty linen in public? *Never.* Though wasn't that exactly what she'd done to Lucie last night? She didn't care one iota about Lucie's public image, or rather public humiliation.

Yes, she had totally stepped over the line yesterday. Leaped over it. Way over.

'My mother courts attention. Craves attention. Needs it. I abhor it. She likes to look pretty. I don't. Look pretty. So I don't try.'

'Yes, you said that already. I have to say I'm not sure where all that ugly duckling delusion comes from.'

'Dante...' She sighed, almost exasperated. 'I'm what you'd call "the outdoors type". In England that means I'm at home in muddy fields—well, you have horses... you know what I mean. And over here it means that I swim, I tag animals, I run on the beach. I like what I like. And I don't try to be anyone else or please anyone else.'

'That's obvious.'

'Lady Viv is all about things being pretty.'

'And she finds it hard to accept that you're more than just pretty? You have depth.'

Lucie's eyes widened.

'And she's jealous of you.'

At that she laughed out loud. 'Don't be ridiculous. She's not jealous! She's *embarrassed* by me!'

The words hung in the air. Unsaid for all these years. Yet there they were—bold and ugly. But resonating with truth.

'I doubt that.'

'Do you?'

Lucie turned away from his gaze. It was too humiliating. She realised she must sound as if she wanted reassurance.

'Look, I don't care. I don't need anyone to tell me what I've spent my life witnessing. It's fine. It is what it is.'

'You've really no idea.' He seemed to say it almost to himself. 'I really *do* have to spell it out to you.'

'No, you really don't. Trust me—the last thing I want is anyone's pity.'

'The last thing I'd *give* you is pity. But it seems to me that you're living under some grave misapprehensions. Anyway...' He smiled and rubbed his hands up and down her arms. 'You used me. For sex. The least you can do is indulge me.'

'Indulge you in what?'

Why did the smile that slid across his handsome face make her feel so warm and woozy? It was just a smile…a parting of the lips. Okay, his eyes crinkled and twinkled, but so what if the teeth he flashed were heart-stoppingly perfect? And, oh, those dimples—it was like being shot at close range, she would imagine, hit with both barrels.

His hands cupped her jaw. He pulled her closer.

'You are beautiful. You are sexy. And you care. Not just about what you're wearing. You care about important things. And you'll fight for them. Even if it means putting yourself out there.'

He kissed her, and she felt that something open and deep and raw was suddenly a little more exposed. And it frightened her. Who did he think he was, analysing her? She pulled away.

'That's very kind of you, but let's not start making stuff up to gild this particular lily. As I said, I really don't need it.'

'No—you need this.'

And as quickly as she'd pulled out of his grasp he'd pulled her back, turned her round and kissed her. Hard. And deep. And long.

She could fight or she could go with the flow. But after a single moment she knew that there was no real choice. A sigh as wild as the ocean breeze slid from mouth as she realised she could do nothing but answer his demands. He paced backwards, kissing her all the while, his mouth mastering her, his body hard and uncompromising and exactly what she'd never even known she needed.

'Don't you, Princess?'

He didn't wait for a reply. He slid his hand over her breast and then hoisted up her skirt. She groaned into his mouth.

'Payback begins now.'

With frenzied hands they ripped at each other's clothes. Her mouth covered every inch of his body, greedily grabbing and kissing and licking, and then she was lying down on one of the banquettes, and he was inside her, thrusting with all his might as he brought her with him to the very edge of passion and beyond.

This time when he rolled over she rolled with him. Her head lay on his chest and he wrapped her in his arms. Neither spoke. Through the windows the lilac dawn turned pink and then blue and the day awoke properly.

'What time do you think it is?' she asked, drawing patterns over his smooth bronze skin, marvelling at his male beauty.

When he didn't answer she cocked her head to look at him. He was staring straight up, unseeing.

'Oh, I'd say about ten. Listen, I've been thinking…'

At that the pulsing beat of his phone sounded again.

Dante loosened his arm from under her and reached over.

'Yep, right on cue,' he said, looking at the screen before pressing the button to answer.

'Good morning, Mother. It's still early. Though not as early as your last call.'

Lucie lay still, acutely aware of her nakedness and of the low burr of the woman's voice on the other end of the phone.

'Yes, of course—go right ahead. I haven't forgotten. I know how important this is for you—for all of us.'

He sat up, skilfully tucking two pillows behind him in a way that suggested he'd done it a thousand times before. A sharp sense of sadness suddenly struck her as she realised that, yes, he probably had—with a thousand different women in his bed.

So she had made a wonderful grand gesture to her mother, had she? She had *shown* her! Proved that she wasn't her property—that she had a mind of her own.

Really?

Maybe all she'd done was prove that she was another statistic.

'Yes, I was just about to sort it.'

She saw his fingers drum on the sheet as he shot her a quick glance. No, she mustn't think like that—she mustn't let all that mental chatter take her down the wrong path. She must think positively. She'd made a choice—she hadn't just thrown herself at the first man available. She had decided to step out of her mother's shade and into the light. *Dante's* light. And she felt warmed by it—not ashamed.

'Not at all, Mother.'

Lucie rolled round, pulled the sheet up to her chin and stared at the utterly perfect blue sky. Her mother would have made at least a dozen calls to Lucie's drowned phone by now. The last time Lucie had been incommunicado it had almost led to the armed guard being called. Leaving one's phone behind was the ultimate offence.

Calling was her mother's way of salving her conscience. She couldn't really care less what Lucie was up to, but she liked to be able to say with some certainty exactly where she was. And of course Lucie's role, as far as her mother was concerned, was to talk her back from the ledge when her own anxiety levels soared.

Like in the early days of her parents' separation, when her father had been entertaining new lady-friends and Lucie had been expected to file a daily report to her inconsolable mother. Yes, she was always expected to be available—so goodness knew what kind of reception waited for her when Lady Viv finally did track her down.

'As soon as I know for sure I'll tell you.'

On the other hand maybe she *had* been a bit rash to throw her phone away like that. Her mother might actually be *worried* about her. It would be the first time, but then she'd never given her cause for concern before. Apart from that time when she'd sat on her phone and smashed the screen... Oh! Who could forget the barrage of abuse she'd faced for that?

If she hadn't let her bottom spread with all that horse-riding... If she'd been a bit more like Lady Viv in her day...

Lucie cringed, recalling that moment. She'd heard Badass and Simon laughing in the background after her mother's, 'You *sat* on it?' had been repeated three times with increasing volume.

'Today. Sure.' Dante whistled.

She really didn't want to be listening to his private call with his mother. She knew more than most how they could turn out. No—it was time to get off the boat, get back, and get on with the aftermath.

She sat up and reached for a second time for her clothes. The dress—minus another dozen or so buttons—lay at her feet, but she really had no other option and so began the arduous task of fastening it up again.

'Yes, you *know* I will.'

Something about his tone made Lucie pause. She was trying to fasten the stupid ankle straps on her shoes, but why bother? She could just as easily leave them hanging out of their ridiculous diamante loops.

'Give me five minutes. I'll call you right back.'

Maybe she should be giving him privacy, she thought, standing up and catching sight of herself in the mirror. How utterly ridiculous she looked. While Dante, also now standing up, walking around the bed, the purest, most male, handsomest form imaginable, was even more attractive than he looked with his clothes on. How was that possible?

He was walking round to her.

'Sorry about that—I had to take it.'

He hooked the phone against his neck as he smoothed one of the most engaging smiles she had ever seen all over his face. A double dimple. *Wow.*

'Lucie, what are your plans for the day?'

She mentally groaned at the thought of all those people crawling over the yacht, dismantling the party paraphernalia, wanting to ask her questions, getting into her space. She really ought to be there—she really oughtn't to have left. But she had and—damn it all—it had been so worth it.

'And the weekend?'

Well, that was easy—she would be fielding calls from her mother. There would be, *Where the hell have you been?* and then, *Who the hell were you with?* and undoubtedly, *Have I taught you nothing?* Then some sort of symbolic wringing of the hands, and after about ten seconds it would be all about Lady Viv again.

Only if she let it, she reminded herself. She'd had a lovely evening, and the last thing she was going to do was let her mother spoil it by dissecting it. There were some things at least that she could keep private.

'Only, if you've no particular plans I'd like you to come up to New York with me.'

He was moving about in that easy Hollywood way he had, as if the cameras were rolling, the director was in his chair and she was the starlet waiting to speak her lines. She narrowed her eyes.

'New York?'

He nodded.

'My mother is due to collect an award at the Woman of the Year Awards next weekend. There has been a lot of speculation in the press about it—I don't know if you keep up with all that stuff? Anyway, we've all got to put on a show for Eleanor, and I need to take a date. Princess, I can't think of anyone who would slip into the role better than you.'

She turned. She faced him. She could see herself in the mirror, with last night smeared all over her. And he'd just asked her out on a date? To an awards ceremony? With the rest of the Hermida family and the whole world watching?

'It's very flattering, but I don't know if that is such a great idea.'

'Why wouldn't it be a great idea?'

Lucie tried not to look at her reflection. 'Well, it would be public, I assume? If the press are all over it before it's actually happened, they're going to be even more interested when it does.'

She thought she heard him draw in a breath.

'And the problem with it being public is…?'

Cameras. Photographers. Lady Vivienne Bond, she thought, wincing.

'It's just not my thing. You know that.'

'I know that I'd like you to come with me.'

'But there must be tons of girls who could go with you. Girls who would actually *enjoy* getting all dressed

up in—' she held out the skirts of the satin dress '—
one of these.'

He laughed. 'It's not exactly torture, is it?'

She scowled, saw that blasted reflection again. 'Look,
it's not my thing. And my mother would—'

'Ah, that's it, isn't it? Your mother would…?'

He held her gaze—worse, he *probed* her gaze. She
felt as if he were looking right inside her mind. She
glanced away.

'What would your mother do, Lucie? Disapprove?
Are the aristocracy only supposed to date other aristo-
crats? Is that it?' He took a step towards her, laughed.
'Am I too low-rent for you, Princess?'

'Oh, stop it! You know I was only kidding.'

'Were you? Look, I don't give a damn what your
mother or anyone else thinks—I need a date for this
event, that's all. Someone who—*gets* it.'

'Gets what?'

'That it's just a date. A no-strings-attached, short-
term, all-you-can-eat buffet, and then—goodbye.'

'Sounds…filling.'

He laughed. 'You see—you get it. Plus, you know
what cutlery to use. I don't need to worry that you'll use
your fish knife to spread butter on your napkin, or any
other crime of the century like that.'

'It's not exactly a hanging offence.'

'Well, not to me and you—but to someone like my
mother it's on a par with genocide. *"There are certain
standards, Dante, and you know what they are…"'*

The low, slow tones he used to mimic Eleanor Hermida made her instantly compare them to Lady Viv's
shrill staccato.

'And, for all I normally don't give a damn about

melon forks and steak knives, this is her special day, and it would be *very* nice…' his cheeks slid into two slight furrows and his eyes twinkled endearingly '…if you would come along and show us all how it's done. It's not you who'll be in the spotlight. It's my mother. You'll just be there to make up the numbers.'

'Gosh, you make it sound so tempting.'

'Plus you get to seriously annoy your mother. Put another bit of emotional distance between you.'

'We're as emotionally distant as the two poles as it is. But I like your logic.'

'So we have a deal?'

'Let me go over this again. I come as your date on an all-inclusive, no-strings weekend and then we never meet again? And I do this because it will annoy my mother? It sounds childish.'

'It sounds perfect. It demonstrates much more effectively than words that you are your own boss. That you make your own choices and are answerable to yourself. And it has the advantage of being very public. There's no mistaking your intention.'

'And the no-strings bit?'

He looked at her sharply. 'That is non-negotiable.'

'Absolutely! As long as we're both clear.'

It was all very well to use a weekend with Dante to drive a long overdue wedge between herself and her mother. But there was no way she wanted to end up like her. Worrying over a playboy. Good grief, no!

'Crystal,' he said.

She stood in last night's rags, with last night's make-up gone and her hair flat and fallen. But this time when she looked at herself in the mirror she saw tomorrow's woman. Something had happened overnight. Whatever her motivation—and she wasn't *entirely* blind to the fact that of all the men in all the world she'd chosen the handsomest one to spend her first ever night with, and she wasn't *entirely* deaf to the little alarm bell that had rung at 'no strings'—she had taken a major step down a brand-new path. And she had liked it.

'So I come to New York…? What are the rest of the details?'

'We fly first to the Hamptons. There's a business deal I'm considering there. I've been putting it off, but I need to make a decision before I head to Dubai.'

He spoke quietly, gravely, and she saw then that there was more—much more—to him than a polo-playing playboy.

'Yes. We'll go there, hang out for a couple of days, see some friends, and I'll get this tied up. Then New York. With the family. But that's it. No, *Wouldn't it be nice if…?*—none of that. It's these few days and then we split.'

As if she needed any clearer explanation, he lifted his arms and pointed with each finger in the opposite direction.

'Look, I'm perfectly clear on that—you don't need to worry. And, sorry if this comes as a shock, I have no intention whatsoever of pursuing a romance with you. You're really not my type.'

'Pardon me?'

Lucie couldn't stifle a smirk.

'What? Hasn't anyone ever told you that before? You look as if I've just delivered the news that you've got two heads. Sorry, Dante, but you're not my type. It's that simple.'

He swiftly gathered himself together again, but there was no mistaking that it looked as if this was the first time in his life he'd ever been told *Thanks, but no thanks* by a woman. It certainly wouldn't do him any harm.

'What's not "your type" about what we just did? I don't recall you telling me that you'd had better.'

'I don't recall telling you that I'd had *anything*! There was no one before to compare you to.'

He was now pulling on jeans, fastening buttons, looking as if he had not a care in the world more than what shade of T-shirt he might choose. But she could taste a lick of tension in the air and see the edge of strain across his brow.

'Sorry—that came out all wrong. What I mean is— what I *mean* is that I've been surrounded by playboys my whole life. My own father practically invented the word! I've seen at very close range the devastation that they bring. So, lovely as you are, the last thing on this earth I want to be is anywhere near you after this weekend.'

Grey T-shirt selected and pulled down over his perfect golden torso, hair flicked effortlessly back into place and beautiful one-dimple smile slipped on, Dante faced her.

'Well, I'm glad we've got that cleared up. I'd hate to think that those screaming orgasms you had were such a disappointment.'

Lucie smiled through the flush of shame that she felt creep warmly over her chest and neck. Would she ever be able to think again of those moments without feeling a stab, a shadow, an echo of how he'd made her feel? But there was no way she was letting him get away with thinking he held all the cards.

'Ditto,' she said tartly. 'You seemed to be having a reasonable time yourself.'

At that he laughed. A proper laugh. His eyes sparkled and she hit the two-dimple jackpot.

'You're a match for me, Princess. That's for sure. More than a match.'

'And for the last time...' she began.

'You're not a princess,' he said. 'I know. And I'll drop it. Promise. So, we'll go to the Hamptons? Then on to New York? We'll dress up and go out and honour my mother. And we'll tell your mother via the world's press that her days of using you as therapist and whipping post are done. Deal?'

'Deal,' she said, smiling.

And all the while that tinkling little bell rang in her ears with a warning not to smile too broadly, or feel too happy, or fall too deeply. Because there was no one waiting to help her over these hurdles. There never had been. And wishes didn't come true.

CHAPTER SIX

How many Lear Jets had she flown in? Lucie wondered fleetingly as she crossed the tiny strip of Tarmac and prepared to board yet another.

The whole effort involved in being 'Party Aristocracy' as opposed to 'Dullard Aristocracy', as Lady Viv called her country cousins, seemed far too much like hard work. Apart from all the planning, the packing and the travelling, the whole angst around who would be waiting with their phone to snap a photo or record a video or—God forfend—lip-read, was just too hideous to contemplate.

Her father didn't give a damn, of course. He had been photographed and filmed and reported so many times that he'd become a bit of a caricature of himself, and was always being hunted by the press for some exploit or other. And her mother's method of second-guessing the second-guessers was simply exhausting! Why on earth either of them still felt the need to parade themselves across the world was beyond her.

Yet here she was—in jersey, sneakers, cashmere and sunglasses, a huge leather bag on her arm and a coterie of matching luggage being loaded onto the plane before her. So much for gorging on ice-cream and taking a sledgehammer to her bathroom scales. She felt a million miles apart from that girl already, she realised as she reached out for the little rail on the portable steps.

A million miles in terms of feeling like a 'woman' and of feeling in control. Had she *really* once sought comfort in clothes with elasticated waists and vats of calorific carbohydrates? Was she *honestly* the type of person who felt it vain and undignified to care if her hair was sitting nicely or if she looked her best before she greeted the world each day?

When exactly had she been transformed? she wondered. It had been so many weeks' work, and somewhere along the path she had become—what? A woman who took pride in herself? A woman who realised that although she might never be one of the petite slender blondes so beloved of the world, as Lady Viv was, she had a good mind and a healthy body and was simply being obstinate and churlish not to make best use of them?

Dante's hand touched the small of her back and the warring sensations of pleasure and anxiety sprang up, as they had every five minutes since he'd picked her up at her father's villa.

He was becoming even more tactile, she thought, pulling away without acknowledging him and climbing the short flight of steps. She really wasn't used to anyone touching her. It had simply never happened as a child, as a teenager, as an adult. She'd never sought out hugs or soothing little arm-rubs—and she didn't intend to start now. Not once did she remember climbing onto her mother's lap. And certainly no one had been there to comfort her at boarding school—apart from one awful night in the sanatorium, delirious with fever when she'd fallen into the hefty bosom of Nurse.

She could still remember the racking sobs, the sensation of her wet face on soaked cotton, of rocking and rubbing and finally the agony subsiding. But only that once. And it was a memory so painful that she never, ever aired it.

No, there hadn't been a lot of touch in her childhood. Nor a lot of love.

Even *making* love had had its challenges. Of course she'd seen enough of life to know what to expect, but it was almost a miracle that she'd rolled past the incredible urge to cut and run when he'd attempted to kiss between her legs! She couldn't explain to him why that had been so utterly unbearable. Hadn't the words in her own mind to know where to start. All she knew was that she most definitely was not and never would be able to relax enough to endure *that*.

Holding hands, nestling under an arm, exchanging starry-eyed glances…? She might just be able to pull that off this weekend. But it wasn't who she was, and she had no desire for it to be.

Cold fish? Yes. She'd been bred that way.

She walked into the cabin and settled herself into a cream leather bucket seat.

'Would you like anything, Lucie?' Dante asked, nodding to the crew, who waited at the side offering saccharine-sweet smiles as well as crystal glasses and ice and bottles galore.

'No, thank you,' she said, noting the slight edge of tension that had crept between them—or rather crept over *her* since he'd picked her up.

'Everything all right?' he asked, raising an amused eyebrow.

Of course this would be home from home for him. Making small talk after a one-night stand must be as easy as pie. She eyed him surreptitiously from under the veil of hair that cloaked her face now that she wore it down, rather in the perpetual ponytails of her youth. He was easily, breezily moving about the cabin, magnetically drawing all eyes with his innately elegant gait. Even the cabin staff in their silk blouses and tailored skirts looked like some Hollywood chorus line, gazing adoringly at the lead actor before adding their four-part harmonies.

Her mother would never have allowed that, she thought. All the staff at the castle were over the age of fifty and as broad as they were tall. And for the first time in her life Lucie really understood why. She was *jealous*—just like her mother.

'Of course.' She smiled sweetly.

She'd be damned if she would let it show.

Her coy look was rewarded by his taking her hand and leaning forward and whispering close to her ear.

'I can't wait to get you back into a bikini. Only this time there'll be no escape. You follow?'

She followed. Like a hot-heeled crab, lust scuttled over her skin as she imagined the moment when they would be alone again under a bright blue sky.

'Why don't we go and lie down right now? I'd be more than happy to get some rest if you would.'

Lucie's mind reacted with lightning speed—much more quickly than her libido.

'Not yet!' She laughed, her hand flying to her hair as she nervously checked and smoothed. 'No,' she said again, laughing as she clawed back her composure. 'Let's keep it…special.'

Dante stayed, hands braced on the armrests either side of her, bent low, his warm breath skimming her ear. She could see the honey-skinned cleft at the base of his throat and the smooth expanse of muscle that ran all the way to his navel. The faint scent of lemon and sandalwood wound around her, and the whole experience tugged her under as sure as any riptide. Lord, but resisting him took all her effort. He was supreme.

'Oh, it will be special, Princess. You can be sure of that.'

Lucie squirmed.

Wouldn't it be wonderful just to relax into this as if she were stepping into a warm bath? Suddenly the urge to scrub away all the hang-ups she had was overpowering. How many more times was she going to get a chance like this?

She raised her eyes up to his steady, twinkling gaze.

'I have absolutely no doubt.'

He grinned. *Wow.*

'Keep your hands where I can see them, mister!' she said, in a fake American accent.

'Won't be a problem,' he said.

He dipped his head and kissed her very, very carefully. His lips were warm and firm and smooth and wonderful. He didn't move a muscle—only his lips. She felt herself let go, just a tiny bit, slipping down a little in the seat, letting her head fall back and her lips rise up. He continued. His tongue slipped in on the soft sigh she breathed out and he lifted his hands from the chair to her jaw. Then slowly, never stopping his sensual oral caress, he lifted her up.

They stood aligned. Bodies pressed against one another. His hands cupped her face and her mouth was supplicant under his. She didn't want to stop this. She *couldn't* stop this.

His body and her body and her mouth and his mouth were all she knew. Her hands found his chest, the smooth cotton of his shirt over hard, strong muscle. She slid them round, feeling the layer of muscle beside his ribs, then on to his back. She felt the deep indentations of his backbone, the welt of muscle on either side, all the way down to the base of his spine and—oh, her hands fell even lower as she palmed his very fabulous buttocks.

Suddenly her hands were stopped, grabbed by the wrists.

'Keep your hands where I can see 'em, Princess.' He smiled as he kissed the corner of her mouth, her cheek, her ear. She squirmed out of reach and he moved back to her mouth.

There was nothing she wanted to do more than continue to feel those kisses, to rub her aching nipples against his hard body. He held her wrists in a strong grip, bringing his body into even closer contact with hers, so the long, hard ridge of his erection was imprinted on her stomach.

'Dante...' she sighed.

'I'll keep it special—I promise. Let's go.'

In one swift move he spun her round so she was marching ahead of him towards a door at the back of the cabin. She was supremely aware of the swollen lips between her legs, rubbing and throbbing with every step, but she welcomed it. Welcomed it as much as the firm pressure round each wrist and the knowledge that he was right behind her, helping her, pushing her out of this repressed fortress she'd built.

They got to the door and he reached past her to open it. Neat, elegant, compact—the room was exactly as it should be—but she had no time for detail. Behind her the strong, safe presence of Dante pushed on. The door closed.

She faced the bed, heard the door click and felt his hands on her shoulders. She gave a tiny jump—she couldn't help herself.

'Hey…'

He stepped closer—she could feel his warmth, his strength. She could sink back and lose herself in it. Couldn't she? It would be so lovely… But she'd stopped and thought for too long, let her brain take over, and all that mental chatter had started up again.

He can't really find you that attractive—you're nothing special…nothing like those other girls.

She felt his hands slide around her, skim her ribs, cup her breasts, flick over her nipples.

She flinched. Her hands jumped to his arms as he stepped forward.

'Sensitive? Perfect,' he whispered, and he stepped right up and welded himself to her back.

And then there was nowhere to go, nothing to think or do except just to *be*. His fingers trailed sinful little circles over her skin and the blaze of lust returned, burning up all the worries in her head. There was nothing but that feeling, those daring fingers circling and extending the pleasure, sensing her anticipation. It was going to hurt any second now. Building and aching and soothing and gorgeous. Relentless. And of course it wouldn't hurt—it was too perfect.

Her hands lay on his forearms, as limp as the folds of silk that skirted the bed. Her head flopped back and her breath was stolen away on a whisper of pleasure.

He stepped in to extinguish the final layer of air between them and she felt him. Hard and pressing. She wanted that feeling all over again. She wanted that sense of oblivion that only he could deliver. She wanted to lie in his arms as a naked offering. She wanted to be worshipped and to worship. And she didn't care that her thighs were pale and wobbly or that her tummy stuck out. She could let go—she could...she *really* could.

'You're amazing, Lucie,' he said, sliding his hand—finally!—under the layer of waterfall cashmere, under the thick cotton shirt to the fine silk of her bra. His fingers tugged the cups down and rubbed mercilessly at nipples she was sure were going to combust with the unstinting pleasure.

She had no will to argue. He could say what he wanted as long as he never stopped.

'Amazing...but far too overdressed.'

He spun her round, unhooked her bra, and groaned his own pleasure as her breasts fell heavily into his hands.

'You *kill* me,' he said, lifting her layers and peeling them up over her head. 'I try—I really try to take things easy. And slow. But one look at you and—see the state you've got me in again?'

He glanced down, indicating the huge bulge in his jeans.

The chill of the air-conditioned cabin prickled her bare skin. She stared at him and he laughed, lifting her hand and putting it right on him.

'Wow!' she said, laughing back and relishing the sensation of hot, hard flesh pushing against soft denim for release.

'Yes, *wow*,' he said, his tone changing. Becoming low, with an unmistakable curl of command. 'But first I want to see you on that bed.'

He reached his hands forward and followed them immediately with his mouth, latching on to a darkly pink distended nipple and tugging with his tongue.

She called out her pleasure, so intense was the glorious feeling, and felt herself fall back onto the bed. His hands were at the waistband of her leggings. She kicked off her sneakers. He tugged. Pulled the dark jersey down and with them her panties, exposing the dark golden curls at her apex.

His head bent and instantly she scissored away, her legs jerking as she rolled onto her side.

'No, please don't do that! I really *wouldn't* like it, you know.'

'Honey, there's not a woman alive who doesn't like it. And I want to do it for you.'

He grabbed her hip with one hand and tugged her free of her garments.

In a heartbeat she was naked on the bed and on her back. Her legs were still open as she scuttled to get some distance. How on earth could he want to put his mouth *there*? She wasn't built for that kind of attention. It was horrifying—she would never subject anyone to that.

But even as those chattering hateful voices loomed louder again in her mind he was tearing off his clothes and kicking off his shoes and lying beside her, his smooth golden skin so warm beside her own cloudy pale flesh. And that huge, thick thrust of his manhood— She reached out instinctively.

'Not yet—not until you've let me do what I want to you.'

'Dante, please—please don't do that.'

He slid over her, braced himself and looked down as she stared up anxiously into his face. She drew her knees up and knotted them under his body.

But he merely laughed and lay down beside her, hooked his elbow and settled his head into his hand, all the while looking at her with a faint one-dimple smile.

'You're a puzzle…but a very beautiful one.'

And he trailed a finger from her chin downwards, firm and fatally lighting up a path between her breasts and down further, slowing at her abdomen. She lay still as a corpse, loving the pleasure he gave her and hating her own stupid reactions. Here she was, about to join the mile-high club, and she was still trying to talk herself out of it.

'Lucie?'

She glanced up into that face. God, but he was outrageously handsome. He lifted his finger and hooked her chin, holding her face tilted while he flicked on another dimple.

'Are you listening to me?'

He tugged her chin, forcing her to nod. She giggled. He grinned.

'Repeat after me: *I am a beautiful woman and I will let my lover take pleasure in my beauty.*'

'I am a— Oh, heavens, Dante, don't be so ridiculous. I'm not saying that.'

'What part of it?'

He leaned up over her now, looming like a Greek god gazing at his mortal plaything.

'The stuff that's full of BS, baby!' she said, in her fake American accent, desperately trying to make light of this and squirming away even as he lowered himself onto her, pinning her to the bed.

His erection jabbed at her and he laughed again, positioning himself between her legs. Instantly she relaxed, hooked her legs around his back and urged him in.

'You're such a little tease, Princess—but there's no main course until we've had the starters.'

He dipped and kissed her. Gentle, sensual and slow. She felt herself sink back further into the bed.

'You're so kissable. Beautiful,' he said, sliding his tongue and tangling it with hers.

She moaned, relishing the sensation of his lips moulding to hers. His hand skimmed her thigh, her waist, cupped her breast and stroked.

'Your body is all-woman... Lucie, your *curves*—you should love these lush, lovely curves.'

He kissed her nipple and began to move further down her body, but tension surged again.

'No, please—'

He returned to her mouth, but slid his hand down, gripped her hip and eased onto his side, lying alongside her, his lips and tongue licking and lapping and loving her mouth. This was perfect—this was what she wanted. If only he would stay like this.

And then his expert fingers touched her throbbing little bud and she jumped.

He smothered her moans with his mouth. 'Relax, let me do this for you.'

And even if she'd wanted to there was no way she could have stopped it. She needed it. *Desperately.*

On and on he kissed her, and gently rubbed exactly where she needed to be rubbed. Moans filled the room. *Her* voice. Louder and louder. She wondered absently if anyone could hear her, and her mind flooded with images of the chorus line cabin girls.

And then the incredible peak she was climbing vanished, and all there was was this room, this bed, this man. And then all her worries began to pop up again, choking her pleasure, allowing self-consciousness to seep back in.

'Hey, Lucie...'

As if he knew, he pulled her back, kissed her more deeply, filled her head with just one feeling—making love. And she was back on the track, on the peak, surmounting all the chatter and the faces and the anxiety.

'Now, Lucie. Come for me. *Now.*'

His voice was filled with authority, and his fingers crazily, expertly tuned her like an instrument. Her body was unable to resist and her mind cleared—she felt herself sail over the edge. And she screamed, released. His fingers still worked on her and she craved and yearned and flew with the joy of it.

'Sweetheart, that was beautiful. You *beautiful* girl.'

He hugged her close and rocked them together for moments long and lovely. Slowly she settled back into her body, easing into his gentle hold. She could easily be held like this. For ever.

Her eyes flew open and she pushed him away, wondering if she'd said that out loud! Good grief, she was all over the place. *For ever?* There was no 'for ever' about this! This was most definitely 'for now'. She was the newly sexually confident lover of a man with a reputation as long as her arm. She wasn't going to fall for him, for heaven's sake! She wasn't *that* stupid.

But she needn't have worried. Even as she pushed out of his hold he was moving her round, and in one sure move he had eased himself right where he wanted to be. Lucie was bruised, she was tender, and she knew having his huge thrusting penis inside her was going to make her even more so, but all the voices were silenced. Her body was in control and it was clear and unequivocal. She *would* have him, and she would have him *now*.

So much pleasure—*so* much! Her mind cleared. There was nothing she could possibly do other than make love to this man. Her body was just her body, and all it could do was receive him.

'Oh, Dante,' she heard herself say, and her arms threaded around his back, sealing him closer to her, absorbing the swell and roll of muscle as he pushed himself in and out. Suddenly he was building to his own climax and, just knowing that, she tumbled again too.

He lay on her, panting, and she held him close, closed her eyes, squeezed every last moment, every gorgeous sensation. Her hand cupped the back of his head, felt sweat on his neck, and she smiled at that.

'I think you're getting the hang of things,' he said, suddenly lifting himself off and away.

He moved into the bathroom and closed the door without a backward glance.

Lucie opened her eyes, stared at the shadows that danced on the cabin's low ceiling. She heard the jet's harsh thrum and felt the steadily slowing beat of her heart. Under her the world was falling away, the oceans and islands thousands of feet below vanishing into a blue haze. And before her the sky was cloudless and clear and vast.

Dante had emboldened her. She'd lived more in the past two days than she'd done in the past two decades. But there were no illusions. None. The ink was barely dry on their contract and already she was seeing warning signs in the small print. Had she been more than a little naïve to think that she would be able to come out of it the same way she went in?

Probably. But being a cold fish had never been *this* much fun.

CHAPTER SEVEN

NEWS TRAVELLED FAST. A quiet couple of days in his house in East Hampton? Well, that was never going to happen. There were a dozen messages on his private line when he got to the house, as well as the usual assault of unsolicited texts offering all sorts of business. And all sorts of fun. It was as if they could sniff him coming in on the air before the helicopter even landed.

There was a time when he'd shied away from the tractor beam of adoration that followed him around the polo circuit—particularly since Rocco had taken himself off the field. But now he was cool with it. They were just looking for a leader—someone to follow, someone to idolise. All nonsense, but who was he to disabuse anyone of their dreams?

So when the polo club's land here had been parcelled up and sold off, and the diehards had wanted a replacement, he'd known he was in for another flood of offers he couldn't refuse. They saw him as a polo blue-blood—which, despite Her Ladyship's view, he was…like it or not. Yes, it seemed everyone saw him as some kind of elite.

Except her.

He chuckled to himself as he walked across the tennis court. It was too hot for tennis. Or rather *she* was too hot for tennis. His plans for Lady Lucie ran to something needing far fewer clothes.

Normally he'd have called Marco as soon as he'd fixed his schedule. Marco had become even more of a brother than Rocco—he was a local Montauk boy, born and bred, and in the long hot summers of his late youth they'd roamed the coasts and forests together. It had always been a wrench, leaving here to go back to Argentina. And school. Even after school there had been times when he'd nearly packed it all in and come up here to live permanently—but he hadn't wanted to involve anyone else in his mess. It had been *his* creation and *his* responsibility.

He was glad now that he'd handled the whole thing himself. He'd despise himself even more if anyone knew—especially someone like Marco, who'd been pretty much a constant for the last fifteen years and had been through his own tough times…way tougher than Dante's.

He'd be a bit more than bemused when he learned that Dante had finally arrived, with a woman in tow, and hadn't contacted him. He bent to pick up a lone tennis ball from the ash and lobbed it over the net, aiming for the fencepost beyond. Bullseye! He might have lost some of his mind, but at least he hadn't lost his vision.

This just never happened. East Hampton boys ran together and played together. They played tennis and surfed and rode and chased girls. It was what they always did. And Dante liked being one of the boys very much.

But here he was, in his very private home, with his soon to be very public mistress. And when he'd landed not only had he turned his phone to silent, he'd tossed it into a drawer and pretty much checked out of society for two days.

Two days left. Call him competitive, but he was determined to melt every last drop of his ice maiden before they hit Fifth Avenue and the next gruelling part of his schedule. A man with more sense would have walked away as soon as he'd recognised that uneasy, queasy feeling in his gut—a feeling he'd last felt fifteen years ago, just before life had hit the buffers—but the thought of walking away from Lucie Bond was like a hungry man walking away from an all-day diner. Why *would* he?

He was barely thirty. He had years before he had to get all down and dirty with analysts and accountants. Who wanted that kind of life? He loved to play polo. He loved his women. He had so much more fun to have before he needed to have daily massages to get the knots out of his neck—didn't he?

His decision to get involved in the polo club's real estate drama had been inevitable. He had felt the change in the wind, had tasted the sobering flavours of real business brewing in some corporate cauldron that he was being drawn closer and closer to. But that didn't mean he had to hang up his dancing shoes completely. Not yet, anyway.

He'd nearly completed his daily circuit—one of his little habits when he was here. Just checking it was all still there, with nothing that needed his immediate attention. He had staff—of course he did. But no one knew these grounds as he did. His parents had long since moved on and bought a much smaller property over on Bridgehampton, but this old place was in his blood.

Which made it all the more interesting that he had permitted himself to share it with Lucie.

He skirted the formal topiary garden that his mother had had planted. He couldn't recall her ever spending any time in it when it had been finished, but that was pretty much the way with Eleanor. 'Next' was her mantra. She had her projects, and occasionally they involved the family, but more often than not they didn't.

He wasn't sore about it—he'd long since accepted that having a high-achieving mother wasn't the same as having a stay-at-home mother. And her life was *her* choice, nobody else's. Good for her—he was proud of her. And he'd be clapping harder than anyone when she walked up and took that award on Saturday night.

He walked up the side of the lap pool and around the side of the east wing as the late-afternoon sun beat down through a couple of cheerful clouds. A few more minutes and he'd be clear of the shelter of the trees and would be able to hear the ever-satisfying sound of breakers crashing. And find Lucie.

He'd left her sitting on a lounger under a huge umbrella with a cup of tea and a phone. She was going to call her mother and start to put down some long-overdue boundaries.

He cornered the house and stepped down onto the wide pebbled path, still screened by a high flank of hedging—and there she was.

He stopped.

It was just like the moment when he'd first seen her.

She was standing on the edge of the terrace that wrapped around the house. The loungers, parasols, tables and chairs in all shapes and forms were behind her. Her head was high and her chin was proud. She stood staring out over the bay like a queen surveying her fleet. The wind whipped at her hair and she lifted a hand to hold it back from her face.

And in that moment he was struck—just as he'd been that first time. She was *regal*. In every sense of the word. She commanded respect and it gnawed at a part of him to think that others might not treat her well. And worst of all herself.

She had a depth and quality that he'd rarely come across. But she was so hung up on what people thought and couldn't see that it didn't matter a damn. Well, everyone had their crosses to bear—she'd figure herself out in time.

'Hey, Lucie!' He started his ambling again. There was no rush. They had days yet. It was the Hamptons…they were on a holiday—life was cool.

She turned slowly and, one hand held up to her eyes, shielding her gaze from the sun, let a smile spread across her face.

'Hey,' he said again as he restarted on his path towards her. 'How's it going? Did you get through to her? I mean, did you get your *message* through to her?'

She looked away and her smile faded as if someone had sucked the warmth from summer—just at the mention of her mother, that stupid, selfish woman. But she gathered herself—it was almost palpable. She looked strained, and then her smile was back in place.

For a heartbeat he hoped it was he who'd put it there. But, no, there was no mileage in those kinds of thoughts. He never allowed himself dumb daydreams like that. Because that was all it would be—one short, sugary dream, ending in decay.

Celine di Rosso had shown him the pain of love—and loss. And he would happily leave that to one side, thank you very much. He wasn't going to say it would never happen. It might in another couple of decades. Maybe. If he needed a wife to partner him at tedious dinner parties or on turgid cruises. Someone to tell him to trim his eyebrows or cut back on the beers.

You're not my type.

Thank God she felt the same way. He grinned, watching her pick her way down from the terrace to the tree-lined path to join him. Here she came—the woman who'd crushed his ego. But being told he didn't cut it for her had been the best news he could imagine. It guaranteed him a fantastic week of fun and sex and good company, with none of the usual 'relationship' dread. No speech. No guilt gift. Nothing but a mutually agreeable, time-limited private party.

Perfect. Absolutely *perfect*.

'Hello,' she said, pausing at the top of the steps and looking at him in that faintly bemused way.

'Hello, Princess,' he said back.

And before she could scowl he hopped up the three steps, grabbed her and kissed her. *Hard.*

She squealed and laughed. She pushed at him. Pathetically. And then she let herself go, the way she always did, and melted into him on a sigh. Another jagged clump of ice gone.

'So...' he said, pulling back and watching as her eyes slowly opened. All the little flecks of moss-green were surrounded by a darker ring of olive. There were smoky smudges under her lids, and the full swollen pout of her lips, unadorned with any make-up, tasted like a woman should taste. 'So you called your mother?'

She stepped back, and again her head began to dip.

He hooked her chin. Lifted it up and eyed her carefully. 'And…? How did it go?'

She tossed her head, pushed her shoulders back and stuck out her chin. He wondered again how many times she'd practised that particular little time-buying routine. In the face of questions about herself or anyone close to her she shut down, became imperial.

'All fine, yes. Everything is fine at home—well, as fine as it ever is. So,' she said breezily, 'did you get in touch with your friend? Are you *really* going to drag me out of this wonderful lair and into the spotlight?'

They took the steps to the beach together, flanked by the sun-splashed high white walls of the house and the curve of lawn that had seen more than its fair share of brotherly tussles and fights over the years.

'You'll bloom in the spotlight.'

'I *hate* the spotlight,' she said, rolling her eyes. 'You saw that—you saw what I'm like.'

'It'll only be a few friends.' He laughed. 'Nothing major. No grand prizes to call. You won't need to throw yourself overboard. Consider it a dress rehearsal for the awards ceremony.'

Lucie slowed. 'I suppose you're right. I won't be quite as bad as I was at the auction—big crowds are definitely the worst. But I'm still a Shrinking Violet. I *hate* being the centre of any attention—whatsoever.'

'I get it,' he said. 'I think… But haven't you had training or counselling or something to get you past this? Surely part of the package of being a member of the aristocracy is getting out there, meeting people?'

'Yes, of course, for some. But I've never had to do much of it. My mother normally takes care of that side of things. I hang back. One might even say I've been encouraged to—which suits me fine. I've tried hypnosis, and I've tried therapy, but the only thing that really works for me is deep breathing. And that's only if I'm in small groups. Public speaking? Forget it. I've *never* got over that.'

She smiled round at him, fleetingly.

Dante shot her a glance, a smile, a squeeze.

'You'll be great tonight—no speeches. In fact you'll be lucky to get a word in edgeways,' he said, thinking of the crowd that would be gathering at Betty's.

They'd be intrigued that he'd brought anyone at all, and the fact that she was a member of the British aristocracy—however minor—would be an added attraction. But they *knew* him. They knew better than to read anything into it.

There seemed to be no end of bars and restaurants in East Hampton. Grills, seafood, Italian, fusion. Chic, contemporary, bright, moody. All perfectly hideous, as far as Lucie could tell. With every passing minute in the car her appetite had decreased in direct proportion to their proximity to their destination.

Dante's friend—or rather Dante's *best* friend—Marco, was hosting a 'little get-together' at Betty's Kitchen—an old, established restaurant in an old, established clapboard house.

The things she now knew about Betty's Kitchen!

Dante had loved to go there as a child. Marco's cousin was the owner and it was incredibly well-patronised. The waiting list for a table for 'unknowns' stretched for months. And apparently the chowder was unmatched in the whole of The Hamptons.

Lucie was quite sure all of that was true, but she had

very little desire to find out for herself. And the thought of a 'little get-together' with almost a dozen new faces was something that made even the word 'chowder' stick in her throat like an unswallowed mouthful of whale blubber.

Dante sat beside her, one hand on the wheel, one hand on her thigh. As if at any moment she might leap from the car.

She looked down at his fingers, searching for some sign of imperfection in this crucifyingly perfect man. Truly, there was nothing. His fingers were long but strong, with flat, smooth nails. His hands were broad, with an appropriate scattering of bronzed hair starting at the outside edge and leading to his wrist. Veins stood out proudly, healthily. His grip was heavy and sure.

She sighed, thinking of the things he had done, the things he could do with those hands. Soothing her, pleasuring her, but most of all imbuing her with such a sense of calm and peace when he held her own hand in his.

As they'd walked hand in hand back from the shore to the house earlier, each holding their shoes in their free hand, she'd felt such a strange, such a beautiful feeling.

Why? She couldn't say. As beaches went it was lovely. But she'd been on better. As summer days went it was nice. Warm, slightly breezy and fresh. But for some reason the whole thing—the slide of water on her wet feet, their race up from the water's edge to dry off, the worm casts and gull cries and the steady, rhythmic motion of the lapping water, the ebb and flow of life—had struck her in that moment.

Such a beautiful moment. Such a treasured memory. She'd known that even as it had faded. Even as they'd stepped away from the soft swell of each broken wave...

even as their feet had splashed in the little pools left behind in the ridged sand. As Dante had held her hand and they'd walked silently away from the air that had been filled with her happy cries and his deep laughter mere minutes earlier.

He had turned just as she had, and they'd shared a smile. Just that. A single smile.

Lucie's throat closed and her eyes smarted for a moment at the thought. How strange that a beautiful memory could reduce her to tears. She quickly lifted her head, stared out at the passing scenery, blanked her mind and breathed from her diaphragm. In and out and all would be well. The last thing she needed to be was weepy about silly things like walks on the beach! Not when she had all these other things swimming about in her head.

Her mother, for one thing. Well, she couldn't be faulted for trying! And using a new angle this time. Gone was the, *Don't you dare!* approach, and in its place was, *Have your heard the rumours?*

Apparently Dante was the worst womaniser on the planet. He had never had a girlfriend for longer than three months. He was always in the coolest nightclubs, with the coolest people. With men who were just like him and girls who drank only champagne and ate only with their eyes. Oh, and finally—his adopted brother was a thug with a terrible past and no breeding whatsoever.

Lucie had shut her up at that point. She'd been able to hear the shrill desperation, the need for control, but she absolutely would not listen to her mother passing judgement on people she'd never even met.

People like Dante, whose hand now gently squeezed her thigh. She turned her head to look at him just as he gave her a sun-bright wink. And her heart nearly stopped beating in her chest.

'What is it?' she almost snapped at him. It really was unhelpful that he was just so heart-stoppingly handsome.

'Hey, don't go getting all icy on me now, Princess. You've been sweet all evening and we're almost there.'

He pressed another squeeze to her leg and rubbed it. Then lifted his hand and placed it back on the steering wheel as he began to turn the car into a car park lot. Lucie looked around at the dozen or so cars lined up on either side of the picket fence and the sign with curlicue letters picked out in red, reading 'Betty's Kitchen'.

'Well, here we are. And it looks like Marco's here already.' Dante nodded to a gleaming motorbike parked right at the front of the steps. 'Sounds like he's here already too,' he said, as a chorus of laughter erupted and carried all the way out to the car park.

Lucie's fingers fumbled on the seatbelt clasp, but in seconds Dante had opened her door, unclipped her and helped her up from the low bucket seat.

He slid her a smile and cocked his head as she smoothed her skirt and tried to tug it down an inch or so past the wobbly flesh above her knees.

'What are you doing that for? You've got fantastic legs,' he said, stilling her and giving her a bemused look. 'Come on.'

He took her hand and on they walked—five steps up and a short stroll past red-shuttered windows that opened onto a white deck offering glimpses of intimate tables and elegant bodies. The quiet, convivial buzz of conversation and clinks of glassware and tableware melted into the early-evening air.

'There he is!'

A girl's voice—American west coast, and positively brimming with confidence. Lucie felt her stomach lurch. The glossy black doors, pinned back with brass latches, were right in front of her now and there was nowhere else to go but forward.

Lucie's feet faltered.

'Dante—*baby!*'

In the gloom of the restaurant she could make out a polished floor, tables covered in white linen with fresh bowls of flowers, candles and glasses all catching the light, and there at the back one single long table. Her eyes landed there, on the dark-haired man who sat at the centre with a broad smile and a hand raised. And the sleek-limbed lovelies who sat all around him, each dress shorter than the next.

She steeled herself. It was just a restaurant…they were just people. No one was going to die and there was every chance she would have a nice time.

She found her breath and followed it for a moment.

From the corner of her eye she could see a man in black trousers and shirt approach them. He smiled broadly and gestured them inside.

'How lovely to see you, Dante. It's been too long. And you've brought a friend…'

Lucie felt herself being gently shoved forward.

'You're with me. You're beautiful. You're going to have a great time.'

Words whispered close to her ear, but instead of shivering she absorbed them.

'Gino, hey—thanks!' Dante strode past her but clasped her hand as he moved and tugged her along in his wake. 'This is my friend Lady Lucinda Bond. Though I reckon she'll let you call her Lucie.'

Smooth and sure, he slid his arm around her waist and kept them both moving inside, shaking the maître d's hand as he went and steering them through the room to the table at the back.

In a haze of air the slimmest, sleekest limbs and the shiniest, longest hair she had ever seen appeared—all swarming and air-kissing around Dante, with wide, perfect smiles and sooty-rimmed eyes. One after the other they paid homage and then slowly sat down, folding their limbs like retractable weapons and lifting glasses to their lips.

'And you must be Lucie!' The swarthy dark-eyed man who was clearly holding court beamed. He stood. A few faces turned at the noise of his chair scraping on the floor. He began to walk round the table and she could feel a bristle of energy.

'This must be and is Lady Lucinda Bond of Strathdee. Play nice, now, Marco.'

Suddenly she felt like a package at some silly show-and-tell event. She wasn't going to let herself down!

She tossed her hair back and lifted her chin. Thrust out her hand. 'Your reputation precedes you, Marco. Though one rather hopes it's undeserved.'

For a moment there was complete silence. And then she heard Dante's unmistakable chuckle. And the high-pitched titter of girls. Everybody seemed to be staring from her to Marco and back again.

'Well, I never thought I'd see you lost for words, man.'

He slapped his friend on the back, moved past him and pulled out a chair for Lucie. She sat down with a curt thank you and looked round the table. Marco took his place and everything started up again. Champagne glasses were lifted to lips and bottles of beer were clinked together.

Lucie's heart pounded in her ears. What on earth had prompted her to say that? She'd tried to be funny but it just hadn't worked. Why was she so gauche? Why couldn't she just relax when she met people? It was either a full-blown panic attack or...just an attack! She'd give anything to be able to smile and speak and act like a normal human being. And she had very little time before she'd have to go through it all over again. It had seemed such a good idea when he had suggested it, but now that the awards were mere days away, thqt mental chatter was really starting up.

'I'll take that one for the team, buddy. As long as you take ten minutes out of your...*ahem*...very busy private life to get this deal finally moving.'

A shadow passed over Dante's face. Swiftly, almost imperceptibly. But then he was back. He nodded. 'I read over the reports. And I guess I'm going to have to make the move some day.'

'Is that a yes?'

'It is,' said Dante, with a grin breaking right over his face.

Marco beamed. 'You'll never regret it. And the community here will never forget it. Honestly, I can't tell you how proud I am. This is massive Dante. *Huge.* Not only the investment, but the fact that you're prepared to make Little Hauk your base. I can't tell you what that means to me professionally. And personally.'

Dante nodded slowly. He looked directly at Lucie, those blue lasers finding their target easily.

Marco was still droning on. 'Well, that's part one of the master plan in place. All you need now is the picket fence and the beautiful wife and you'll be home free.' He laughed. 'More champagne anyone?'

And the words circled the air, causing all sorts of images to flare and then float.

Dante settled down? Married?

'I don't think you need any more to drink, buddy. My master plan has no space for your drunken hallucinations. Not any time in *this* millennium, that's for sure.'

A pause hung over the table like a thick cloud of smog.

'Aw, come on—we all know it's only a matter of time before you're down on one knee, begging some poor woman to marry you. God help her.'

The air crackled with laughter at Marco's comeback. Lucie touched her hair, fingered her earring, tugged her skirt down. She lifted her napkin and spread it out on her lap. The menu, in an old leather cover, stood lopsided, leaning on an ice bucket. She picked it up, pressed it flat onto the white plate before her.

Set Menu for Dinner... Starters... Entrees... Specials of the House.

She flicked the laminated pages and read the words, determined to erase the ones she had just heard spoken out loud. Even though she'd said she didn't want anything from him after this week, she suddenly realised that it hurt to know that she would never be a part of Dante's master plan.

CHAPTER EIGHT

'THE PLAN IS that we'll pass Sag Harbour Marina, fly along the Long Island Gold Coast, take a little tourist tour of Manhattan and land after about forty minutes. In time for lunch. How does that sound?'

Lucie clicked her belt closed, touched her headphones and nodded with a smile to Dante.

'Yeah? Okay?'

She made a thumbs-up sign and turned to look out at the landscape that was disappearing below her into a Toytown model of waterways, hedges, pools and matchbox mansions.

She'd only been there three days and at one thousand feet in the air above it already felt wistful for the place. Again she wondered at herself. She'd been in fabulous locations all over the world. Palaces, yachts, secluded villas tucked away on their own private islands. From her earliest memories she'd been away for weekends here and there, dragged about to parties and holidays in luxury locations that most people couldn't even dream of. Even her own idyllic Petit Pierre—her heaven on earth, the home that she normally pined for from the moment she left it until she arrived back, where she discarded her worries and woes and wrapped herself up in a warm, wonderful world—didn't feel quite so amazing as this stretch of island dotted with green, blue and brown.

She could dwell on that, let the mental chatter increase to deafening proportions, or she could simply let herself be swept along in the next few hours of what Dante had promised would be 'interesting' times.

She stole a glance at him, piloting the helicopter, making it look like the easiest thing on earth. He did that with most things, of course. It was something in the way he held himself—his shoulders were always low, never tensed, never hunched. Or was it the way he moved—as if every part of him was tuned and oiled, supple and strong? The way he held her eyes when he spoke. Or listened. The way he held her hand.

Held her hand.

Who would have thought that jumpy, jittery Lucie could stand to have someone hold her hand? Now, *that* was a miracle itself. But there were more miracles to come—he had promised her.

She knew exactly what he was referring to. And he had been incredibly patient with her. But there was only so far she could allow her intimacy with him to go. No matter how gentle, how tender, how sensitive he'd been, she still couldn't relax enough to allow him full access to her body.

'All in good time—no need to get anxious,' he'd said. And she'd said it was hardly worth bothering about.

But she knew and he knew that it was just one more in a long series of hang-ups that were holding her back. When those voices started their chattering in her head, their deafening anxious phrases going on and on, bringing her further and further down, she knew she was slipping back.

And when she felt that finger under her chin, lifting it up, and saw those eyes beaming into hers—well, that was all very well. He had a vested interest in keeping the party going. But when Dante went back to his life, his season in Dubai, and then moved back to Little Hauk to start up this new polo foundation—well, where would Lucie be? Tagging turtles. Dodging phone calls. Hiding.

'Okay?' he asked again, his voice resonating through the headphones, making her jump.

'Yes.' She smiled back as he slipped her a conspiratorial wink.

'See that place down there—?' He pointed to a huge sprawling series of buildings, a pool half-empty and green with moss, hard-baked brown earth and grass that hurt. Of course it had its own jetty, as all these huge places had—Little Hauk included. She looked round at Dante questioningly.

'That was Marco's family's place. Until his father gambled away every last cent and his mother upped and offed.'

Lucie looked back at the enormous rambling estate, sitting in the dust, surrounded by immaculate properties to the left, to the right and behind it, and the ocean in front. To think the swarthy, happy guy who'd held court with Dante, good-naturedly sparring with him, had been brought up there. It was easily the biggest landmass of prime real estate she had ever seen. They must have been immensely rich, even by her standards.

But he had no side. No airs. No graces. Just like Dante.

'Big, isn't it?' said the muffled voice in her ears. 'Just goes to show that there's nothing you can rely on in this world but yourself. Marco learned that the hard way. It's his dream to buy it back—to clear the family name. And I don't think it will be too long either.'

Lucie nodded at that. She'd learned last night that Marco had built up several local businesses, and that it had been his sheer willpower that had resulted in their dream of the polo foundation. And now he and Dante would be partners he was probably well on the way to making his dream come true.

What was *Lucie's* dream? What was *she* going to do to bring honour on her family? Could her family and her home be taken away? It had never even occurred to her that she might be anything other than Lady Lucinda Bond of Strathdee. It was like air and earth—the granite of the castle and the waters of Petit Pierre. It was unconscionable that the day might come when everything that defined her would go.

As mansion upon mansion passed beneath them in a blur she suddenly felt a sense of panic. What if it *did* all go? What if one day the privilege and the money vanished? If her father's title became no more than a piece of paper, with no power, pomp or even circumstance. What if she had nowhere to hide any more?

Baseball fields, an airport and then the towers of Manhattan appeared. She barely noticed them, so caught up was she in the thoughts rampaging through her mind.

She'd never once considered being anything other than Lady Lucinda Bond, and one day Duchess of Strathdee. And had never really been remotely grateful for it either. She'd spent such an age privately bemoaning the fact that she had two decadent, indolent parents and hadn't once appreciated the fact that were it not for them she wouldn't have so much as a bean to spend.

The castle in Scotland, the villa, the yacht, the annual income... None of that she had earned herself.

Her father's choices and her mother's choices were what they were. She shouldn't worry about them—she should be out there following her own dream. Tagging turtles, dodging phone calls and hiding? They weren't her dreams—they were holding tasks. Things to do to kill time.

She looked at Dante. He *never* bemoaned his mother. He never spoke about any of his family in anything other than glowing tones.

She could read between the lines, of course—when he described all his mother's achievements she got the sense of a woman who spent more time fixing other people's problems than attending to her own family. There were only so many hours in the day, and if she was spending them with other people's children who was spending time with hers?

But he was silently, resolutely loyal. No cracks showed in that family. And, though Lucie had never breathed a word of her own views about her parents to anyone other than Dante, the world could see by her actions that she wanted nothing to do with any of them.

It was time she grew up, stopped feeling sorry for herself and began to appreciate the gifts life had given her instead of taking it for granted and whining all the time.

'Central Park Reservoir,' said the voice in her ears, and she looked out across the vista of flat and jagged roofed towers in every shade of brown and beige, like a meadow filled with stumpy corncobs. And there sat the park, sunk down like some huge mossy stepping stone, with the flat blue puddle of the reservoir in the middle. 'Almost there.'

Dante tipped up his visor and winked and Lucie beamed right back. He had gone out on a limb, inviting her to this awards dinner. She knew that now—she could tell how important it was to him, despite how easily he played it down. He wouldn't want to upset anyone—least of all his mother—and there was no way that Lucie was going to get all needy on him. There would be no panic attacks, no blubbing, no fainting. Nothing but head up, chest out and onwards. She wouldn't be anything other than the perfect guest.

'One hour and we'll be sitting down to lunch in one of Manhattan's finest. And twelve hours after that we'll be through with this and we can both get back to our lives.'

He winked again, but this time the smile that Lucie returned was fixed. It was painted. It was fake.

'Bet you can't wait,' he said, widening his grin. Then he tipped down his visor and turned back to the job in hand.

Dante felt like a heel.

He gripped the collective lever and gave the helicopter another burst of speed as she banked to the left. The truth was that he couldn't wait for this whole thing to be over. It was getting under his skin like a third degree burn, and he was beginning to feel that he might need more than a cold compress to get through it.

He'd known as soon as Marco had made that stupid comment about picket fences and pretty wives that something had clicked in her head. He could have cheerfully reached across and strangled him, punched him, thrown him into the bay as shark bait.

His fingers gripped the control as he straightened up and settled himself down. He had less than twenty minutes before they came face to face with the formidable force of nature that was his mother. And then the toughest part of the gig—coming right up.

He should have thought this through a whole lot better. He should have seen it coming. Hell, a blind idiot would have seen it coming. Lucie was perfect for him. That was what his mother was going to conclude after about—oh, a nanosecond in her company. And even if he sent her an affidavit right now, got a restraining order, or even a gag, she would still manipulate the conversation round to suit her way of thinking.

Yes, she wanted her son married off. It was untidy otherwise. He was like a rope lying about that somebody could trip themselves up on.

Yes, he had to be married—but not just to anybody! Oh, no, someone with class, with pedigree. Someone beautiful, intelligent, witty and warm. Yes, Lucie was absolutely perfect for him. And for that reason she had to be told in no uncertain terms that their hot week in the Hamptons was a one-time, never to be repeated *ever* event.

He snatched a quick glance at her but she was sitting immobile, staring out at the scenery. He so badly wanted to be wrong about the whole 'picket fence' thing, but he knew in his heart of hearts how she'd looked when she'd heard those words. He'd seen it so many times before. That flare of an imagined future. Some crazy vision of them together that was just never going to happen. He'd spelled it out in words of one syllable…

So—he pressed his foot to the floor to turn—there would be today, then tonight, and then the final love scene. And then the wobbly lip while suitcases were packed and off they went.

Pity. She was as close to perfect as anyone had ever been.

But nobody was. *Nobody*. And didn't the fact that she had all those little hang-ups already just go to prove that she would be capable of descending to the depths, the way Celine had? Celine—who had once been a normal girl, who'd held down a job, got a car, an apartment.

To his teenage eyes she'd seemed the most sophisticated woman imaginable. Beautiful, sexy, clever, and in control of all those boys with their raging hormones. They'd practically drooled over her. Of course in retrospect he could see that by knowing that above all others *he* was her choice he'd been feeding some sort of hole in his ego. Perhaps...

But all that had been before the red rages, the wild moods, the threats. Before she'd started trying to close down the rest of his life.

Just as he'd woken up to the fact that he was a fifteen-year-old boy in a relationship more straitjacketed than any marriage, she'd decided she couldn't live without him.

Oh, no. He was never, *ever* going to go through that again. Lies. Manipulation. Guilt. Pain. Dark, dark days. Women were either fickle, governed by their emotions, or they were machines like his mother. And he didn't want any of those in his life.

So, much as he liked Lucie—and he did...he liked her a lot—he was never getting burned again.

With a start, Dante looked up. The helicopter had landed on the roof of the hotel—auto-piloted by him from somewhere out on the Hudson, it would seem.

Lucie was unclipping her belt and sticking her head-phones in the pouch. The day was clear and the timing was—perfect. They had time for a quick change and then would come the start of the onslaught. But he'd be kind. He'd be chivalrous and attentive. He'd make his mother proud and he'd make sure Lucie had a fantastic time to remember him by.

'Okay?' he asked as the doors closed on the elevator and started to drop them down to their floor.

'Dante, I'm not sure if you're aware, but that's the fourth time you've asked me that since we landed.'

He surveyed her carefully.

'And, yes, thank you very much—I am okay.'

'That's good. I'll remember that. You don't like to be asked if you're okay too often.'

'Why bother remembering? We'll be on two different continents shortly. I really don't think you need to store up any silly facts. You can be sure that *I* won't.'

She turned and stared at the coppery panels at the front of the elevator that reflected their blurred outlines. The LED display showed the floor numbers falling. And although she'd only uttered a few words Dante felt as if he'd just taken a hit to the back of the head. Interesting…

CHAPTER NINE

IF REAL ESTATE and polo failed as careers he should take up fortune-telling. Because—really—every single thing that he had predicted had come true.

His mother was *beyond* taken with Lucie. It was as if she'd prayed to the gods for a prospective daughter-in-law and, hey, one had dropped right out of the sky and into the Presidential Suite at The Park—complete with beauty, money, class and enough social graces to see her through every white tie, black tie and smart-but-casual function that could ever be dreamed up.

She had *no* idea—none—about the other stuff. Lucie's hang-ups about her body, about crowds, her hiding from the world in the middle of nowhere. The fact that she had a dysfunctional family just like almost every other person he knew. If she *did* know about it—or even suspect it—she was choosing in her own very particular way to ignore it.

And there was no way he was going to start dishing the dirt. Every single thing Lucie had told him had been in confidence. She had opened up more than he could ever have imagined—*should* ever have imagined. And that was great—but it also cast a shadow.

Trust, confidence, sharing secrets… It didn't scream

no-strings weekend the way he'd intended. If it had been confined to trusting him with her body—which she had, becoming increasingly confident in telling him what she wanted—then, yes, she'd done that. But there was still room for more. If only he could get her away from his mother for long enough.

Eleanor had barely passed the time of day with him, but she was all over Lucie. And Lucie was being 'such a darling' back. They had 'so much in common' he'd heard—easily five times in five hours.

It was a car crash. A pile-up of all his worst dreams.

He'd never made the cut to be one of his mother's 'projects' when he'd been growing up. And his younger, needier self had at times resented the fact that she'd been there for everyone else except him. But he'd grown up fast. Too fast. And the last thing he'd wanted since Celine was any kind of simpering interference in his life. Especially from his mother—and she had happily obliged by training her lasers elsewhere.

So what she thought she was doing by monopolising Lucie through lunch and during their stroll round Central Park was anybody's guess. Except *he'd* guessed it in the first five minutes, and it wasn't cool. If she didn't let up he was going to have to take her to one side and talk to her. Firmly.

He badly wanted to have some one-on-one time with Lucie. Whenever she came out of that damn shower. They had two hours until showtime. Two hours that he'd made clear were off-limits to any member of the family who might drop by their suite and hope for a lovely cup of English tea and a chat about the Queen. Or whatever.

He emptied the pockets in his jeans of phone and wallet and put his shades down on the bedside table at his side of the bed. *His* side of the bed. What did that even mean? *Every* side of the bed was his side.

'Hey, Princess,' he said, going up to the en-suite bathroom door. He rapped and pushed the handle. Locked? What was going down with her, exactly?

He lifted his hand to knock more loudly on the door just as it swung open. A puff of steam and a freshly scrubbed beauty emerged. Scowling.

'Hey, gorgeous,' he said, walking towards her to grab a kiss.

'Handsome,' she said, giving him a smile and her cheek for his kiss as she passed on into the room.

'I know you're planning to get ready, but there's something I need to discuss with you,' he said, catching her by the waist and pulling her round to face him. 'There's a crisis in the hotel and they need our help.'

She was smiling at him. She *loved* these little games they played.

'I didn't hear about any crisis. Are you quite sure you've not got the wrong end of the stick?'

He winked. 'It's a laundry crisis. They need their towels back. *Now.*'

She squealed and tried to move out of his grasp, but he was fast and strong and totally determined.

'I'm reporting you to the management!' she cried, giggling and writhing and then sighing as she allowed herself to be held, allowed him to unknot her towel. Allowed him to unwrap her and slide his hands all over that warm, damp, glorious flesh.

'You drive me crazy,' he said, pulling her close against him, sliding her lush, beautiful body against his. He pulled the towel off her head, ran his hands through her hair and held her head, tugged her even closer. 'God, you're lovely. *Lovely.*'

He found her mouth, and just that meeting of her lips on his lips had him straining so hard again. It was like a frenzy. He couldn't get enough of her. He still hadn't had her in all the ways he wanted. He'd taken his time, gone at her pace, but now he was crazy with need. He wanted *all* of her.

'Come on, baby,' he said, filling his hands with her breasts, filling his mouth with her nipple, laving it over and over, tugging and sucking. Kneading and loving. Walking her back to the bed.

Her hands dropped to his head, holding him there at her breasts, and her moans filled the room. She was as crazy for him as he was for her.

She said his name, over and over. She moaned and cried out. And he knew she was ripe for him—ready for every last bit of pleasure he could give her. It was time. Her last taboo.

He laid her down on the bed, pink and damp, those rosy-tipped breasts so prominent, so erotic, so purely, perfectly lovely.

He stood over her.

'Touch yourself, Lucie.'

She was flat on the bed. She was writhing, lost in her own pleasure. She was ready.

'Now.'

Her eyes flew open but she did as he said. She lifted her hand and laid it between her legs. And he watched as she began to slide her fingers over her bud.

'That's it, sweetheart. That's it.'

He lay down beside her on the bed as she closed her eyes and turned her head away.

'Baby…you beautiful girl.'

Gently he cupped her jaw and turned her to face him. Her eyes were glazed. He kissed her lips, kissed down between her breasts. He palmed her full, swollen flesh and pulled a nipple into his mouth. She moaned.

He shifted position and began to trail kisses down over her stomach. He waited—expecting to feel her jerk away, expecting the freeze. But still she touched and moaned, and he could not wait any more to know her in that most intimate way.

'Sweetheart…' he breathed as he slipped right down until his lips were level with her mound. 'Let me kiss you.'

He paused, and she paused—just for that tiny moment.

'*All* of you, Lucie. All of you is beautiful. Nothing should be hidden away. I love you—all of you.'

He screwed his eyes shut and bit down on a curse. He couldn't believe what he'd just said. But he had. Just said it. *Damn.*

But he'd deal with the fallout later, if there was any, because there was no way back now. She was easily the most lovely girl he'd ever known. And she was going to let him do what he should have been able to do from that first night. It was crazy that she'd needed all that nurturing and cosseting and coaxing to get her to this point. But here she was, trusting him as no one had ever trusted him before. God, it was beautiful.

He dipped his head. He kissed her most private part. He licked. She *was* beautiful.

He growled his praise and settled himself between her legs, gripping her hips and holding her just where he wanted, where she needed him. She didn't move, didn't jerk, didn't slide away or beg him to stop.

And then he found her and lapped her. Over and over. Revelling in the knowledge that *he'd* been the one to arouse her, to make her so wet, so swollen, so ready to burst into orgasm right there in his mouth.

She felt it coming, knew it was coming, and as the chatter in her head started up she would not have it. Would not let her silly head deny her this beautiful pleasure.

The warm, wet caress of his tongue, the sight of his head in that most erotic position, pouring his pleasure into her, the touch of his lips and the steadily building crescendo finally almost peaking—and then the break, the wonderful release.

She screamed. She heard his name rush from her lips. She gripped the sheets as his tongue pulsed again and again and again until the pleasure almost became pain and she finally begged him to stop.

He climbed up beside her and held her then in his arms. She was molten. She was replete. She was happier than she could ever have imagined. She had conquered one of her biggest hang-ups and stifled the voices that dominated her head and her life. Dante had done more for her than he would ever know.

As they lay back on the bed, he still fully dressed and she naked, wrapped in his arms, she listened to the far-off noise of the street. The bustle and buzz of New York—life in all its wonderful forms. The day was rolling on, just as it had when they had strolled around the park only an hour earlier, but it was changed for ever now.

He had given her that gift. But more than that—*so* much more than that—he had told her that he loved her. In his own way, not in a conventional way, but she knew. This wonderful man who played everything so cool, who'd never had a girlfriend for longer than five minutes, who spent his life travelling, avoiding commitment—he'd recognised that they had something special. And she had too—of course she had. She'd never had the courage to think it, never mind say it until now. But he was braver than she—he'd said it. And the only thing they could do now was move forward. Together.

But first she had to show him what he'd done for her. She had to make love to him now. She felt as if her whole life had suddenly become clear as crystal. She slid round and raised herself up above him, straddled him and began to unfasten his buttons. He'd been looking away, but now turned to face her. And he looked strangely grave, like a fallen angel.

'Dante...' She cupped his face and kissed him. She poured all her love and thanks into her kiss. 'That was so lovely. I'm sorry I was so silly, and I'm so grateful you cared enough not to give up on me. I love every part of you too.'

She bent forward to kiss him again, but he shifted, and instead of letting her lips land on his he tucked her under his arm.

'Hey...glad you enjoyed it. Knew you would.'

She was sandwiched against his chest, with her head pinned down, listening to the slow beat of his heart. She pushed herself up.

'So that's one I owe you,' she said, getting back to unbuttoning him.

'You owe me nothing, Princess.'

He twisted out of her reach, swung his legs round and sat on the edge of the bed, facing the window. Lucie kneeled up, placed her hands on his shoulders and bent forward to kiss his cheek. She slid her hands down between the open panels of his shirt and over the fabulous muscles of his chest. She nuzzled against his neck, absorbing his scent, scenting herself.

'Hey, look at the time!' he said, grabbing her lightly, embracing her softly. Then he stood, set her back and ruffled her still-damp hair. 'I'd better hit the shower.'

Lucie sank down on her heels and watched a flutter of tiny dust diamonds sparkle in the wake of his movement. A flood of warm afternoon sun bathed the whole room in golden honey tones that softened the heavy lacquered wood. She had stated when they'd checked in that she found the furniture dark and old-fashioned. Dante had smiled, in that way he did, and said that as long as the bed was firm he didn't have a problem with any of it.

She couldn't care less about any of that now. She barely noticed anything other than the space he'd left and the creeping chill that seeped across her bare skin.

What had just happened? Why had he turned away? Refused her? Rejected her. He had used the 'L' word— he *had*! She wasn't hearing things. And then he had *rejected* her. After saying what he'd said. After making her body sing and her heart burst.

She felt hot, fat tears of self-pity spring into her eyes and wiped them furiously with her hand. This did not make sense!

She stepped onto the carpeted floor, dragging a sheet round her shoulders, and walked to the windows. To the right was the spread of another huge brownstone building, windows in a grim grid above dreary awnings and the spikes of bare flagpoles. Below a red carpet seeped like a pool of blood to the street. To the left a sliver of darkening sky showed above the jutting edifices of a thousand faceless blocks, and in between people were swarming like ants and cars and trucks were screaming their impatience.

How could the world have tilted so awfully in those moments?

The world? *Her* world—which had been on a head-on collision course with confidence and happiness—had now been sent flying off in another direction completely. Was she really going to let herself sink back into the miserable world she'd once inhabited? Was she going to stay in hiding for ever?

So he had rejected her? Well, maybe she had read it wrong. Or maybe she should care less about what other people thought and did and more about what she was going to do next. Because in her talk with Dante's mother she had learned so much about how she could put something back into the world. She had made a start with the CCC, but there were a million charities she could patronise. And she didn't need Lady Viv to come anywhere near any of them. She was more than capable of working behind the scenes herself. And, while she wasn't exactly ready to jump up onto any podium, she did feel a lot more confident that one day she would. One day soon.

But first she had to tackle this. Head-on. She'd never had any problem confronting him before—why on earth would she start now? She paced to the door of the en-suite bathroom. She could hear the shower faintly. Before she rattled the door she should think this through. Perhaps. But her hand and her brain weren't working in tandem and she shoved it open.

The pile of clothes on the floor, the steam on every flat surface, the scent of that lemon soap he used... Her heart swelled and her throat squeezed. *Dante.*

'Hey,' he said as he tilted his face up and let the running water clear it of foam. Then he wiped his cheeks and lifted more soap. He rubbed his big hand over his big chest and under his big arm. 'Everything okay?'

As if she'd wakened from a coma, she suddenly came to.

'No, it's damned well *not* okay! And you know that perfectly well.'

He continued to soap his body—down his abdomen and further. Her eyes dropped to his penis. It was still semi-hard and stuck out. Totally uninhibited, he stroked it as he covered it in soap and let the water rush off. He turned to the side, replaced the soap in its dish, and continued to rinse his body clean.

'Is that right?' he said, shrugging slightly and putting his head back under the jet of water.

'I thought you'd made me angry that first time, when you put your paws all over me on your boat. And then when you strolled onto my father's yacht as if I should be grateful for you sharing your air with me. But to do what you just did to me is unforgivable!'

'You orgasmed in my mouth. People in Queens heard you. And *that's* unforgivable?'

Lucie stepped forward, sliding on the wet tiles and the sheet that was bunched about her feet. She stumbled and fell slightly towards him. In a flash he spun round and reached out to help her gain her balance, but all she wanted to do was drum her hands on his chest and his arms and make him feel some of the pain she was feeling.

He held her wrists. Looked right into her face. Droplets of water coursed down his brow, his nose and his chin. He blinked his eyes clear and stared and stared.

His face was fixed with a look that said absolutely nothing. *Nothing.* His blue eyes might have been made from stone for all the life they contained. She stared from one to the other and back again. Nothing.

'You know what I'm talking about,' she said.

'I know that you're a mature woman who walked into this with her eyes open.'

She twisted her face away as the tears burned their way forward.

'Walked into this? I still don't even know what *this* is! You say one thing and then you say another. What am I supposed to think?'

She tugged her arms down, trying to get out of his grasp. 'Let me go! I mean it—I don't even want to look at you.'

'Calm down, Lucie.'

His voice was dense, and as dark as the wooden furniture in the bedroom. There was no light, no life in his eyes. The more he shut down, the more she wanted to start a fire under him.

'What's *wrong* with you? Why on earth are you behaving like this?'

'You need to calm down. Do your breathing. You'll be fine.'

'Stop patronising me! Who do you think you are? You *caused* this! I was breathing perfectly normally until you weirded out on me.'

She jerked her hands more purposefully this time and he let her go. He faced her—water still coursing down his right shoulder. Droplets had gathered in his eyelashes and fell from his nose and chin. He stood like a cliff behind a waterfall. Powerful, elusive, utterly inaccessible. And *still* she wanted him.

'Dante...' she said, stepping forward, wrapping her arms around him, the way she had a hundred times in the past few days.

He didn't stop her, but he was rigid like rock. She pulled back from the warm, wet, firm body. From the care and caressing he had given her these past few days. She withdrew from the heat and the light, the joy. Her world tilted again and she reached out to grab the wall, to keep herself from falling through space.

'You told me you loved me.'

He flinched—a tiny movement but she saw it. His mouth opened and then he closed it again, dropped his head to one side. He reached behind him to turn off the shower. Grabbed a towel from the rail and passed one to her.

'I'm sorry. Heat of the moment. Didn't mean anything.'

He started to dry himself in that thoroughly male way that he had. Rubbing and patting and dragging the towel this way and that. She felt as if he was rubbing himself clear of every trace of her.

'Come on, Lucie. We got carried away. We were having a great time. We've had a great time, you and me. We don't need any drama. And we've only got hours left until we need to get on our planes. Why get heavy now? Hmm?'

He wrapped the towel around his hips and stepped forward, encircled her with his arms.

'We're going to a party! We're gonna have a good time!' he said, his grin sliding back into place.

He lifted the towel she held limply in her hand and patted her shoulders dry where they had been splashed.

She stood for a moment, passive. Then she grabbed the towel and tied it around her body.

'Princess? Hey, let's finish up on a high. A few more hours and I promise you will have an amazing time. I'll make sure of it.'

Her world was still at a tilt. She could let it slide even further on its back. Or she could spin it back on its axis, all by herself.

'You don't need to make sure of anything, Dante. I'm more than capable of sorting out my own "good time".'

He nodded. Beamed a brittle bright smile. 'That's more like it,' he said.

She stared at him, more and more incredulous with each passing second.

'For the record, the only reason I'm hanging on is because I made a commitment. I said I would do this and I stand by my word. I'm not some fake commitment-phobe, scared to put my money where my mouth is. I don't pretend to be someone I'm not, stifling my feelings and then lying about it.'

She couldn't quite believe that the words had been in her head, never mind that they had left her mouth. Her hand flew there, as if to slam the gate after the horse had bolted.

He had walked out of the bathroom. The door was open and his footsteps left a wet imprint on the carpet. A few droplets that had escaped his thorough towel-drying still clung like glass beads to his shoulders and in the spikes of his hair. Frozen in a shaft of late-afternoon sun, there was a haze of dust all around them, and the sense of a storm brewing was so profound she stood waiting.

'I told you to calm down, Lucie. And I meant it.'

'Calm down? What the hell are you talking about? I

don't have any *reason* to calm down. What the hell does my calming down have to do with anything?'

'You don't know what you're saying. I don't respond well to emotional blackmail, and I'm not going to be around to pick up the pieces.'

'Pieces? There are *pieces*? I just called you out. *You're* the one with the problem! You're a commitment-phobe and you're trying to turn this into something that's about *me*.' She grabbed a robe from the hook in the bathroom and shoved her arms in, tying it so tightly it hurt.

Dante moved through the room, still at that slow and steady pace, but poised as a boxer. She could feel the waves of tension. But she couldn't seem to stop herself.

'Are you still going to deny it, Dante? To me? Or— what's worse—to yourself. This has nothing to do with me going to pieces. When have you ever been close to anything that's fallen to pieces? You don't hang around long enough to see the sun set! You rock up and ship out! I'll bet you barely stay long enough to learn their names!'

'That's enough!'

He turned. A quarter-turn, but it was swift and it made her halt. And go quiet.

'You think I should learn *names*? There's only one name in my head. As if it's carved into my skull. And until I rub it out there will be no one else. Do you hear me, Lucie? Not you. Not anyone else. I don't want to be responsible for anyone else again. *Ever.*'

Lucie stood, her hand on the robe's soft towelling belt, her fingers slipping over the knot she had tied, unable to loosen it.

'You've no idea about my past—what I went through.'

'What you went through…? Poor Dante. Did someone hurt you?' She stepped forward. 'You think you're the only one who's ever been hurt? I've been around hurt. I propped up my mother after my father left her. I saw her pain. And she got through it. So it doesn't add up that you're going to lock down your emotions and check out of life because of a little bit of hurt.'

She tugged and tugged at the stupid belt and eventually it came loose. She glanced to the side, where the dress she was planning to wear to the awards dinner was hanging like some ghoulish spectre, observing them. Dante moved to his bag, pulled out underwear, shook off the towel and started to get dressed.

He had his back to her. She knew he was listening, but it was as if he was putting more and more distance between them. As if he had rubbed her off his skin in the shower and was now rubbing her out of his mind.

'Why can't you answer me? Why can't you tell me even one single thing about this—this woman? Help me understand why you're acting like this?'

'You're really not going to give up, are you?'

'Not if it's going to help me understand what's going on in your head, Dante. Not if there's a chance that this weekend might have a different outcome.'

'There's only one outcome, Lucie. And it hasn't changed since I drew up the terms on my yacht.'

'Is that all love is to you, Dante? A business deal?'

'You really want to know what love is to me? The last woman I loved took her own life. Because I wouldn't do what she wanted me to do. Is *that* a big enough detail for you? Does that help? Will you leave it alone now?'

CHAPTER TEN

LIKE A SEA of giant white polka dots, tables extended into the farthest corners of the hotel's grand ballroom. A wall of silver curtains encircled them, and to the front, accessed by a short sweep of steps on either side, was the imposing empty stage. A single spotlight splashed harsh yellow light down onto a solitary lectern, from which poked a long, thin microphone, and a vast screen articulated clearly that this was indeed the Twenty-fifth Annual Woman of the Year Awards.

As guests in silks and satins, jewel-bright, and in black and white took their seats, waiters hovered and then swept round them, brandishing bottles and laying out plates with a flourish. Glasses seemed to be permanently fizzing and popping, and the buzz of conversation tinkled higher and louder with each passing minute.

The heavy leaden twist of Lucie's stomach had not eased in the two hours since Dante had uttered his declaration about his first love and then silently finished dressing. She had known that her overwhelming instinct—to go to him, hold him, comfort him—would be completely rejected. Instead they'd both skirted each other in some choreographed dance, as if it was a thousand years and the vast dry sands of the Sahara that lay between them rather than an opalescent wool carpet and a half-hour deadline.

She'd watched from the corners of her eyes, aching for him, but he hadn't acknowledged her pleas and within moments had been dressed, and back in the easy, lazy zone he commanded so well.

With a curt, 'Back in ten,' he'd left her sitting at the dressing table, a clutter of products in front of her. *Miracle* this and *Illusion* that. She'd picked up one of the tiny tubes and bottles, refusing to believe that what they had shared had been an illusion. She'd travelled so far from the person she'd been that no matter what happened she would always treasure this time. But it was painful to think that for Dante it had been just another few days…

She'd shuddered. She wasn't judging. He'd clearly been through hell. And to live with the pain of feeling responsible for someone else's decision to end their life was unimaginable. She had seen her mother in agonies of despair, had brought her handkerchiefs in her childish way, trying to make her feel better, but this was something entirely different. No wonder Dante wanted nothing to do with love.

He'd returned, wordlessly, as she'd clipped her earrings into place. She'd glanced at him in the mirror but that rocky edifice had still been intact. If she had known what to say it might have helped, but she hadn't, and they had noiselessly finished getting ready and then joined his family—straight from the arctic silence of their room to the warm, excited hubbub of aperitifs and air-kisses.

Lucie glanced across the table to where Dante now sat, his body tilted slightly to the side, engaged in conversation with his sister-in-law, Frankie. He was at his most handsome, in black tails, white bow tie and sharp-collared shirt. His golden skin and dark blond hair were utterly arresting. He stopped her heart—it was that simple.

Inwardly stifling the pain of another stab of hurt at how their time together was trickling to its close, Lucie allowed her glass to be refilled and stole another glance across the table, watching as he nodded slowly, occasionally allowing a dimple to form, as he reacted to Frankie's ebullient delivery of some story or other involving polo ponies and a great deal of hand gestures.

Frankie looked so radiantly, contentedly happy. Her skin glowed with the hormones of the early pregnancy she and Rocco had announced when she'd beamingly refused the first of the glasses of champagne that had been passed around. Rocco had put his arms around her, laid his chin on her head and squeezed his eyes shut as if he couldn't give enough thanks to God for her very existence.

At that moment Lucie had glanced at Dante. He had looked cast in stone, immobile, but had only stayed like that for mere seconds before he'd slipped on the full-power, two-dimpled smile and twinkling eyes charm mask. He'd slapped his brother's back affectionately, shaken his hand, embraced Frankie gently and convinced the whole gathering that he'd never heard happier news.

Only Lucie knew differently.

She could see past the golden glow, the sunburst smiles and the azure-blue eyes, and with every passing moment it was clearer and clearer to her that Dante simply wasn't able to form *any* kind of relationship that would lead to commitment—never mind a wedding or children.

So her mother had been right after all. Playboy. Heart-breaker. Just like her father. A boy in a man's body. Never wanting to grow up, never wanting to take on responsibility. Wanting a lifetime of playing the field.

Right on cue a striking-looking brunette appeared behind him. She placed her hands over his eyes and leaned in close. 'Surprise!' she whispered in a sultry voice, and as he turned to see who it was she twisted herself *and* her full cleavage almost into his face.

'Lana! How lovely to see you.' Dante composed himself and stood up. He kissed each proffered cheek, holding her at a distance that was *just* acceptable.

'Mind if borrow your date?' the brunette threw at Lucie as she slid her arm through Dante's, without waiting for a reply, and walked with him to another table.

'Subtle, huh?' said a voice at her side. Frankie. 'You get used to it. In time. I spent the first six months ready to claw their eyes out, you know?'

Lucie dragged her gaze back from where Dante was being pawed and stroked to the quirky smiling face of Dante's sister-in-law.

'Every time I was taken to a function like this I'd ask Rocco for a pre-match report—you know, to prepare for former lovers launching themselves at him. And then I'd stick to him the whole night, scanning the joint and making it obvious he was with me and me alone.'

'Sounds like a lot of work,' said Lucie, her eyes darting back to where Dante was now meeting and greeting the rest of the table.

'Oh, it was, yes. I stopped as soon as I realised that Rocco might be the most handsome man in the world, as far as I was concerned, but he was also the most loyal. He could see past every one of those offers he was getting. What's a roll in the hay compared to a lifetime of happiness? As soon as I accepted that I stopped trying to beat everyone off with a stick.'

'Yes, well, perhaps there's more than just hair colour that separates the brothers,' said Lucie, rather archly. 'Sorry,' she added, when Frankie's elfin features knitted into a frown. 'It's not that I don't applaud your efforts. But I'm just passing through.'

'Dante's worth the effort. *More* than worth it. Everything good in life is. You get back what you put in. I'm not saying it's about being on your guard—I'm saying it's about understanding one another...accepting one another.'

Lucie nodded. She smiled. 'And *I'm* saying that the first step is accepting yourself. I've just turned that corner. And he helped me to do that.'

'I can imagine.' Frankie sat back in her chair. Her hands fell to her tiny bump. 'He's a good man,' she said. 'The best.'

Lucie looked across at him. At the man she loved. *She loved.* The man who would not admit that he loved her back.

Time was running out for her to do anything. Another few hours here, for the ceremony itself, then dancing, and then—that was it. Curtains closed. Back to their room and then goodbye.

A rumble of anticipation went around the room, signalling that the awards were about to be announced. Dante excused himself and came back to their table.

The house lights and stage lights dimmed until only the glow from hundreds of flickering candles lit the cavernous space. Suddenly an uplifting overture boomed through the speakers and the Master of Ceremonies walked out onto the stage. The huge screen started to show images of the ballroom, focusing in on various tables and various dignitaries and celebrities. Whoops and applause followed when the camera hit upon someone of particular interest to the crowd.

There was no doubt that the women here were massively important figures in their worlds, be it literature, fashion, art, medicine, acting, science, business, community or politics.

A voice boomed out that these pictures were being beamed live around the world, and then there on the giant screen was their table. The voice, which it soon became apparent belonged to a roving reporter, told the ballroom—and presumably the world—that here was Eleanor Hermida and her family. They heard that she was due to be honoured shortly and that her wonderful family were here to share her joy. And wasn't that Lady Vivienne Bond's daughter there with them?

Lucie's heart leaped into her mouth. Of course she'd known there would be cameras, that it was a live broadcast. But nothing intrusive—nothing that involved any attention on *her*. That wasn't part of the deal! She was here as a date, as an icon of her own free will that her mother could observe from wherever she was on the planet. Free will that declared her independence.

The last thing—the *very* last thing—she wanted the world or her mother to see was her fumbling for words or breath. Thankfully the camera zoomed off to another table. She sat back in her seat and expelled a huge lungful of air through clenched teeth. She *had* to get this under control. It was a dinner—nothing else. She was a guest at a dinner, just as hundreds of others were.

'Everything all right?' Dante leaned across.

For the first time since they'd entered the ballroom his gaze snapped straight onto hers, and in that second a thousand things fell into place. Whatever he was looking for in this world, a simpering, vacuous woman wasn't it.

Lucie straightened her spine, tugged her shoulders back, raised her chin and thanked God and her mother's incessant moaning for at least this default face-saving movement.

'Of course,' she chimed. 'Isn't it wonderful? I feel honoured to be here. All these worthy women, doing such worthwhile things for their causes.'

The swell of applause caused both of them to turn back to face the podium. The moment had come to honour Eleanor. A reverent hush spread round the room. A montage of pictures of some of the projects she had supported began to roll on the screen and a quick summary of her achievements sounded out.

The lights dimmed further, apart from the single yellow spot that illuminated her, and the room was imbued with humbled silence. The Master of Ceremonies relayed tales of her years of work, the money she'd raised, the lives she'd touched. And then, in a poignant tribute, a young man who'd benefited took to the stage to deliver a speech and present the lifetime award.

Eleanor sat completely composed.

Well, that's where he gets it, thought Lucie. Not a flicker of emotion other than a smile more enigmatic than the Mona Lisa's. Not a hint or a suggestion that anything other than supreme self-possession ran through her veins, like liquid steel through iron pipes.

She looked at Dante and Rocco. Nothing. Complete control. Frankie was weeping, but that could be explained by her hormones—and anyway she was a Hermida only by marriage. But as Lucie looked around she saw other people similarly moved. She saw handkerchiefs pressed to eyes, heads shaking in disbelief. This woman was exceptional. Her achievements unsurpassed. But she and her sons looked as if they were listening to a travel report.

Even when Eleanor took to the podium herself, to deliver her acceptance speech, in which she paid homage to the patience of her family, their masks remained intact—Rocco's dark stare and Dante's golden gaze. Immovable. Solid. Set.

What hope did she have of piercing his impenetrable shield? He had no wish, no desire to let anyone chip through the rock to see what happiness there might be underneath. He was made of something other than flesh and blood. He had given her so much—had helped her past her own terrors, made her at home in her own skin—yet he wasn't prepared to step out from the golden shield he hid behind—his mask.

Eleanor returned to the table. Her boys kissed her courteously and saw her seated. Frankie beamed and Lucie watched, spellbound. The understated grace was mesmeric, the filial attention hypnotic. The only thing missing was any genuine warmth. And the lack of that, as far as Lucie was concerned, was the most emotional aspect of all.

A standing ovation marked the end of the awards and the start of the dancing. People left their tables and started milling around, and Lucie felt her anxiety surge. She had convinced herself that she would be able to deal with strangers with Dante by her side, but now…? After all the emotion of earlier…? Now she'd rather just slope off to the bathroom and wait it out. No one would really notice if she took a very long time to powder her nose.

She lifted her clutch and started to make her way through the people. The music had changed and a deep, heavy bass was drawing people onto the floor. She noticed Rocco and Frankie, clasped in a slow dance, but though she looked all around there was no sign of Dante. The floor continued to fill. Her need to get some air continued to build. She could see the archway that led to the restrooms and she put her head down.

And there in her way was a tall, blond, handsome figure in full white tie. Dante—with his back to her.

And then he turned. Draped around him was the slim brunette. Her backless dress was scooped so low that Lucie could almost see the cheeks of her bottom—but not quite, because Dante's hands were resting there. And as they swayed to the music the brunette tipped back her head and laughed.

Lucie looked to see the flash of white teeth, the burst of flame-blue eyes, the shock of blond hair. Two proud dimples.

They swayed to the music, the brunette pressing herself close as they moved. He spoke…she laughed again…and Lucie saw exactly what Frankie had meant. This was it for him. This was how he lived. This was what women did to him. All the time. Just as with her father, they threw themselves at him. It was his version of love.

He'd had his fingers burned with love in his youth and had learned that it was much easier to play the super-shallow, super-smooth playboy. Just as her mother had said.

Frankie could say all she wanted about him being

worth the fight, but what price lay ahead? Couldn't he even see out the end of this evening before he defaulted back to Dante the Lothario?

Anger bloomed inside her.

She put her head down and pushed past them.

She saw feet, heard voices, the pulsing bass of the music and the high, happy calls of people celebrating. The archway was close, and she brushed past a waiter pushing a trolley piled high with rows and towers of chalky-coloured *petits-fours*.

'Lucie.'

It was his voice. Deep and commanding. She ignored it.

'Hey, what do you think you're doing?'

The waiter stopped his trolley as she felt her arm pulled back and heard Dante's voice hissing in her ear.

She spun round to face him. 'Get your hands off me! Don't ever touch me again!' she hissed.

He grabbed her by the hand and put his arm around her so quickly that in seconds he had steered her down a harshly lit, plushly carpeted corridor. Her heels sank and snagged as she walked. And then he stopped, turned and twisted her round.

'Get off!' she spat, tugging out of his grip.

'Do not speak to me like that.'

'Like what? You deserve it.'

'For what? Dancing?'

'I couldn't give a damn if you dance with an entire troupe of naked go-go dancers—but not tonight! Not when you invited me here as your partner. Even though you've spent the past five hours making it perfectly clear to me *and* everyone else that that's the last thing I am!'

'It was only a dance. I *know* her. She's an old friend, for God's sake.'

'It looked to me as if you'd like to get to know her a whole lot better. Your hands were all over her backside. Is that it, Dante? Have you spent too long with just one woman? Did it all get a bit stale after—what?—five days? Are you reminding yourself what its like to have your pick? Just to reassure yourself that your commitment phobia is absolutely the right thing to have?'

For a moment it was as if a torch had been lit behind his eyes. For a moment she saw through the glare to the man. Anger. Passion. His eyes were like bright blue flames. Fire inside. And then as quickly it was doused.

'I was having a dance with an old friend. And you made a fool of yourself.'

'Yes, I did, didn't I? By agreeing to this stupid charade. But there's no point crying about it. We've only got a few hours left, and then we can chalk this one up to a very bad experience.'

'You don't mean that. We had a great time.'

'*Had* a great time. *Had.* Until you turned out to be a deluded liar. Now, get out of my way.'

She pushed past him. The corridor stretched ahead. Candelabra stuck out like wizened brass claws, grasping into the empty air. Ugly oil paintings of pastoral scenes in hugely ornate frames studded each wall. A little girl in a wide skirted dress with a satin bandeau ran past her, chased by another, laughing and screaming.

'Lucie!'

'Go to hell,' she said to the stagnant breeze.

Too angry for tears, she kept her head high and her chest out. She passed by the bathrooms. Too late now to hide out. She made her mind up to go on. The hateful crowd and the throbbing music were drawing her like some hideous harpies, luring her to the rocks.

The ballroom itself was thronged with people, slowed by the seven-course dinner and made noisy by wine. She paused for a second, to locate Eleanor and the others. She had to say her goodbyes. It was the least she could do. And then she could simply leave. It would be that easy. Leave and grieve and get on with her life.

'Lady Lucinda—how lovely to see you here in New York. And with the Woman of the Year Lifetime Achievement recipient herself! May we ask how you are connected?'

Lucie stared into the overly made up face of a reporter who had materialised from thin air. She could see thick lines of kohl eyeliner drawn around each slightly wrinkled eye, every mascaraed spike of her eyelashes, the slight smudge of her lipstick where it had bled past her mouth. She saw the scratchy black head of the microphone that had been thrust under her nose and the camera that sat on some man's shoulder.

'I...I...'

She stepped back, suddenly aware of the aeons of time and space that were opening up all around her as the woman waited for her to finish the sentence. She could sense a wave of movement as people close by turned their heads to watch, and she tried again to speak. But the voices had started in her head. Chattering on in their infernal way, telling her that she wouldn't be able to answer, that she would let her mother down and her father down. And now, to add to it all, Eleanor Hermida, who radiated such composure, would know that silly, ungainly Lucinda Bond couldn't even answer a simple question.

Her legs began to shake and her heart raced, and a sickening black fog suddenly began to fall all around her. The sea of people became a yawning pit of faces, greedy for her failure. She felt vomit rise.

And then she felt him.

Dante's arm was upon her shoulders and he pulled her to his side. He held her cold, clammy hand in his, and then there was his voice in her ear, telling her to breathe. She did. She breathed. And she felt him nuzzle the side of her face, felt his lips on her cheek.

Fear trumped anger—but love trumped fear.

She let him.

'Well, that answers one question!' said the reporter as she beamed a smile right into the camera. 'I guess you're here to give respect to Eleanor Hermida? You've heard for yourself of her many accomplishments this evening. What do you want to add for the people back home?'

Lucie lifted her chin and smiled. Those spiky mascaraed eyes were still blinking at her, but the reporter's face was beaming in an expectant smile. She felt the air pass through her nose, her throat. In and out slowly. She felt her mouth opening. She looked into the square black box of the camera.

'She's a wonderful woman,' she said.

It wasn't exactly the Declaration of Independence, but for Lucie it was the speech of her life.

The reporter nodded enthusiastically and then whooped off with her crew to another group. Lucie stood, stunned. Her heart pounded in her ears and her cheeks burned like firebrands. The mental chatter started up again in her head, but this time it was cheering her on. She had done it. She had actually overcome the sickness and formed a sentence in front of strangers. In front of the world. She had found her voice.

She turned to look at Dante. He had helped her. He had given her that little push of confidence, shown that bit of faith—all she needed—but she had done it herself.

But no amount of well-timed pecks on the cheek could erase what he had done to her this evening.

'Thanks,' she said. And turned to walk away.

'Lucie, wait,' he said. 'I owe you an apology.'

She stopped in her tracks, waited until he came level with her.

'We owe each other nothing. Remember?'

CHAPTER ELEVEN

THE COPPER-PLATED ELEVATOR moved at a sedate pace. Lucie stared at their silent shimmery reflections. The doors opened into their suite, lit lamps glowed. Lucie walked in ahead of him—ten steps across parquet, three steps down on silk-carpeted stairs. She longed to rip the heeled shoes from her feet and hurl them in the bin, to get out of the dress, the underwired bra and the Brazilian thong and throw open the window and launch them into the night air. She longed to be free of this whole experience.

'I hope your mother enjoyed her evening,' she said instead. 'Despite your glacial mood.'

'It was a sham, and you know it. The whole thing. End to end.' He walked on through the lounge, unfastened his cufflinks—one then the other—his words as wooden as the floor.

'So now it's your mother's fault you're in this awful mood?'

He sat on the bed heavily, as if he really was made of rock. Shoes came off, tie was flipped open, pulled off and cast aside. Shirt swiftly unbuttoned. He stood then. Faced her. Peeled it off. And there he was in all his pure male form, and her eyes burned with the image.

'My relationship with my mother is not up for discussion.'

'Perhaps not. But your relationship with me is.'

He almost flinched when she said the word 'relationship'. His eyes squeezed shut, just for a second, but there was no mistaking it.

'I owe you an apology and I meant it. I should never have asked you to do this. It was naïve of me to think that you and I could pull this off without someone reading more into it than there is.'

'"Someone" meaning me?'

'I thought I was clear, Lucie. I tried to be clear that this was only a short-term affair. I said at the start that there would be no happy-ever-after.'

'Yes, you were honest. At the start. But things changed, Dante. I know they did. For both of us.'

He looked at her, but there was no light, no life in his eyes—as if there was no audience to play to any more. She'd never seen him like this. Never seen him so closed down. The contrast between *her* Dante and this was unbearable. She couldn't comprehend it.

'What are you going to say next, Dante? That none of those things happened? That you didn't say you loved me? Of all the things I pegged you for, being a liar wasn't one of them!'

He stared at her. And she saw it again—she'd penetrated his mask. His eyes were lit up and his mouth was a thin, angry line.

'Good try, Princess. But it isn't going to work. I learned a long time ago not to take the bait.'

'Why do you think everything is a game? I'm not baiting you! I've had it now. All I want is to understand *why* you did what you did. Why you spent all that time…'

Her voice trailed off as she furiously bit down on the giant sob that had risen like a fist into her throat.

'Why you spent all that time loving me. Because that's what you did, Dante. You made love to me.'

He unfastened the strap of his watch—his grandfather's watch. The one he'd been wearing when he'd hauled her onto his speedboat. The minute they'd got to the Hamptons he'd had it picked up and repaired. For a moment she recalled the joy in his face when he'd got it back—real joy.

He slid it off and cradled it in his hand, then walked to the bedside table and laid it down gently, lovingly. And in that single motion she saw a flicker of something—something worth saving. Something worth all the effort in the world.

She paced towards him, arms out, imploring.

'Maybe if you explained what happened? Maybe if you opened up about it?'

'Opened up about *what*? I'm not the guy you want me to be. That's it.'

'You know what I'm talking about, Dante. You're capable of love but you've made up your mind that you don't want it because of whatever it was that happened all those years ago.'

'Whatever it was? I was a fifteen-year-old, having a love affair with a woman twice my age. If you could call it that. Miss di Rosso. She was supposed to teach us *science*.' He scoffed woodenly at the word. 'Taught me plenty of other stuff. Is that what you want to hear? Are you shocked, Lucie?'

He looked right at her now.

'You in all your first-time innocence.'

'I'm not so innocent now. Why don't you let me in? I could help, Dante—I'm sure I could.'

But he just shook his head, as if she was a memory herself—a fading figment of his imagination.

'Celine di Rosso...' He lifted his grandfather's watch. 'I would have done anything for her. Anything she wanted. I stole this watch.' He lifted it up, showed it to her from across the room. 'From my own grandfather. She wanted nice things, good times. She thought I had money. Of my own. I stole this to sell it, to pay for us to have sordid sex in a sordid motel out of town.'

Lucie watched, mesmerised. His face shifted from glazed and expressionless to anger, revulsion.

'I pawned my grandfather's watch so that I could take that woman to a sleazy dump and have sex with her because that was what she wanted. And what Celine wanted, Celine got. Every time.'

'But she was your *teacher*, Dante. You weren't old enough to know what was going on—she was abusing you!'

He made a face, replaced the watch on the bedside table and stared down at it.

'And I let her. We all have choices. I was old enough to know what I was getting myself into. I just wasn't smart enough to know how to get myself back out.'

'But surely she was terrified that someone would find out? Surely she saw it was going to end in disaster?'

'Terrified? She wasn't afraid of anything. She was a manipulative, crazy bitch. She wanted control—in everything. Where we went. When. What we did. What gifts she was to get. And when I started to wake up— when I began to call time on her demands—that's when things started to get really heavy.'

He looked round the room, as if seeking some sort of distraction.

'Anyway, you don't want to know this stuff. It's all in the past.'

'But it's haunting your present.'

A jug of water stood on a sideboard between two lamps. Four crystal tumblers and a small silver ice bucket. A tiny bowl of sliced fresh lemon. She followed his gaze as he walked over and began to pour himself a glass of water. Carefully he picked up the tongs, opened the ice bucket and dropped in three cubes. He swilled the glass, stared at it.

'It's all in the past,' he said again, his voice hollow.

'That woman did you a disservice, Dante. She was in a position of trust and she abused that trust. And now you have a terrible view of all women because of that. She was unstable.'

He swallowed the water, drained the glass, placed it on the table.

'She blew my mind—and then she blew her own. Called me on the phone while she did it. I heard the gun. I was on my way to see her at the boathouse where we would meet. I was going to tell her it was over. She beat me to it.'

Lucie felt her hand fly to her mouth. 'Oh, my God. I'm so sorry.'

'That's when I really learned the meaning of the phrase "emotional blackmail". It doesn't get more emotional than that.'

He picked up the glass and tipped the ice cubes into his mouth, crunched them.

'I don't know what to say.'

'There's nothing to say. It happened. Life moves on.'

'But not yours. Your life is stuck. Normal people don't act like that. She seduced a boy half her age and then—then killed herself. It's possible you have such a jaded view of women because you went through all that.'

'Don't psychoanalyse me, Lucie. I've spent years going over what happened—I don't need your ten-second therapy.'

Hot sharp tears sprang to her eyes. He walked back over to the bedside, oblivious.

'I'm not psychoanalysing you. I'm only trying to understand you.'

He pulled his phone from his pocket and stood staring at it, each broad groove and cleft of muscle and bone in his chest and shoulders in light and shade from the lamps. Lucie could feel her fists bunching in the watery satin of her dress, could feel the world she'd thought she'd found slipping away as the ravine between them yawned into a gaping gorge. Soon there would be no way back.

'What time do you want to go to the airport? I don't think joining the family for breakfast is the best idea.'

She had to try one more time.

'Dante—you did more for me than anyone has ever done. You helped me—you *rescued* me! You showed me things and *mended* me and…'

Tears oozed from her eyes. She wiped them furiously.

'You told me loved me, Dante.'

Her voice closed over those last words—words that were her lifeline. She had thrown it out and all she could do now was watch to see if he would catch it.

Still and silent he stood. As perfect a figure of a man as it was possible to imagine. But only so much of him was flesh and blood. He was a man whose heart was stone.

She felt the tracks of her tears as they streaked down her face. She felt the painful lump form in her throat. She tried to swallow as the entire room slipped into a series of glazed shapes. She longed for him to come to her, to hold her, cradle her.

'I'm sorry, Lucie. It should never have happened.'

He walked into the bathroom.

And closed the door.

In the silence of the room candles flickered skittishly, mockingly doubled in each mirror's glare. Each flame a tiny glassy yellow flicker, dancing in the dim light.

There was the dull sound of the shower… The deadened hubbub of the never sleeping streets… The sounds of life starting up again…

She had done what she could. She had truly tried to make him see. But he was locked in his own glass coffin, frozen in time, living a life with the guarantee of never being hurt again. Because how could he be hurt if he kept his heart buried away?

He would have his fun—he would have his parties and his women. And in time when she heard his name she might remember him fondly. But right now she had to put as much distance and time between them as she could. She had to get herself away from the sight of him, the scent of him, the *sense* of him.

She couldn't see that body one more time and know she would never feel those arms around her, never lay her face against his smooth firm chest… Never hear her name from his lips…the way he rolled the 'L'…the way he smiled when he said 'Princess'…

To know that those moments of wakening together,

when he'd gather her into his arms, press himself into her back, slip inside her...to know that it would never happen again.

Tears coursed freely down her face. She saw nothing but images of Dante. Facing her open-mouthed on his speedboat, mocking her as he stood between the turtle posters, beaming with two dimples and lifting her, spinning her in the air at Little Hauk. Walking along the beach.

Huge, silent sobs racked her body as the shower continued to flow.

She wiped her hands across her eyes, her nose and cheeks. She gathered up her bag and her passport. Her phone.

She looked around to see the debris of their day, but it was too painful now. She couldn't bear to see their shared things, his things she'd never see again.

She crossed the opalescent carpet, moved up the three steps and onto the landing. Back across the parquet floor. She pressed the button and waited for the copper-tinted elevator.

Two steps in, she turned. The doors closed. Her own image, alone, was the reflection now.

In the suite the bathroom door opened. Steam bled into the empty space.

CHAPTER TWELVE

IT WAS HARD to be sure when he'd begun to feel anything again. Hard to know when the mist had cleared enough for him to see that what other people were telling him. That he'd changed. That he'd lost his 'sparkle'—whatever that was. That he'd become harder, fiercer, angrier.

All of that was true. He made no apology for any of it. The alternative didn't bear thinking about—give in, give up, let the team down? Let Marco down? He needed a series of wins in Dubai to make him rock-solid as a commodity. He was going all out for every investment opportunity available. He knew that the Hermanos Hermida brand was his now. And just because his heart had been ripped out of his body, it didn't mean that he should inflict that pain on anyone else.

There was always a bright side. Always. In the middle of utter blackness he knew there was. He couldn't see it. Had no idea when he *would* see it. But it was a certainty that it would come.

'This time will pass,' his grandfather had used to say. Even on the day when he'd called him to his study and asked what had happened to his watch. Even when Dante had silently refused to tell him why he had pawned it—

not in fear, but in dread of how ashamed he would make the old man feel.

It hadn't worked, though. He had given him the money to get the watch back. Money that Dante had paid back by working every hour that God sent— labouring in the city, far enough away so that no one knew who he was.

The timing had been perfect. Just when he'd needed something to bury himself in, had needed to work until his muscles ached, using his body heaving hard materials and risking his own life on high-rise building sites because that was what he deserved. Celine had died. And he had slipped back into his adolescent world, realising that he was just another privileged pupil in one of her classes.

He'd spent days waiting for the police to come. Days until he'd given up and gone to them himself. They told him to 'run along'. He knew his grandfather had had a hand in it. But it had never been mentioned. Not a whisper, not a look, not an embrace. There had been nothing to suggest that anyone had any idea that Miss di Rosso had been any more to Dante than the teacher who'd once taught him.

This time will pass. And it had. Days had bled into weeks, into months and years. Until it had taken an actual *doppelgänger* to make him remember her at all.

This time... This pain... The days had bled as his heart had bled. But there was no let-up, no sign of a clot forming, let alone a scar. No sign that this time would ever pass. The bright side was that he could still put one foot in front of the other. That he could still ride a horse and fire a ball past three players. That he could raise money and invest money and had put the Little

Hauk Polo Foundation on the map. And he had. He had cleaned up. He was on fire. He was 'the man to watch'. 'Unstoppable'.

Everyone's hero.

He stepped out from the club house now. As was his routine. It was all about routines now. The little things that were part of his day—to make sure that the wheels of his life kept turning. Like running on the beach—the beach she'd declared her favourite. Like eating at the breakfast table and ignoring the image of her that sprang to mind and would choke him if he let it. Because she was everywhere. In everything.

What a fool! *What a fool.* He'd thought it was Lucie who had fallen hard! He'd been worried that she had cast her dream net wide and tried to ensnare him in a life of picket fences and *Hi, honey, I'm home.* He'd been so busy worrying about her projections that he'd never noticed for a second that he'd fallen deeply in love himself. He'd been so determined to make sure she'd take a different fork in the road that he hadn't seen the edge of the cliff and had run right off it himself.

'Hey! Handsome!'

He turned at the sound of Marco's voice. Even those words pierced through his heart for a moment, as if he'd just stepped out of the bathroom at The Park and into the sickening vacuum that his life had become since that moment he'd found her gone.

'S'up?' he called back, slowing his pace to let his buddy catch up.

His buddy with whom he'd shared everything—apart from any discussion about Celine. And now Lucie.

'I'm heading to Betty's. Wanna come?'

'No, thanks. I've got a ton of stuff to do here tonight.'

They walked along in the early-evening sunshine, strides matching, shadows lengthening before them.

'Ah, yeah, of course. Those blades of grass won't count themselves.'

Dante paused, turned to look at Marco, who had continued to walk on.

'What's that supposed to mean?'

Marco shrugged, looked back at him.

'Well, it's the sort of out-of-character irrelevant nonsense you seem to be dedicating your life to. Instead of moving on, forgetting about her. There are loads of fish in that sea,' he said, casting his arm out in a wide sweep. 'Come on, you're not trying to tell me she's "the one"?'

Dante stared at him, trying to follow what he was saying.

'I mean, yeah, she was pretty—but not amazing. And she had a good body... Okay, she had a great body—and that rack—but she wasn't—'

Dante didn't know what had happened until it happened, and he saw his best friend staring at him with dazed eyes, clutching the side of his face where he'd just taken a punch. Blue and purple bloomed under his hand and a trickle of blood escaped from the corner of his mouth. Dante's fist ached, and he looked at the red mark that now formed there.

'Hell, there's nothing much wrong with your uppercut, is there?'

'What did you say that for? What are you trying to say about her? You aren't fit to breathe the same air as her, you piece of crap.'

'Well, that makes two of us,' Marco said through lips that seemed to be swelling. 'Because you're as much fun as a hot date with death. She'll have moved on by now anyway. Why would she hang around waiting on a loser like you if she's that great?'

Dante swung again, but this time Marco blocked him. They struggled together, pushing against one another, heels kicking up the dust of the day. The ponies moved warily closer, then edged away.

'You got me once but you won't get me again,' Marco hissed. 'Why don't you take all that energy and redirect it to getting her back. Give us all a break. God knows we need it—we've been looking at your moping face for months now. You're putting me off my chowder and the damn horses off their game.'

Dante gave him a final shove and fell back against the fence. His friend's comments had taken the wind from him and he stepped to the side, leaned his two hands against the warm, smooth wood and hung his head.

'It's that obvious?'

'Of *course* it's obvious! From the moment you took her to Betty's we could all see that you were perfect for one another. But you and your crazy rules about women—you never gave it a chance.'

Dante stared across the fields. He had created this place in six months flat. Training ground, stables, clubhouse and gym. He had worked round the clock and poured every last ounce of energy into making it perfect. He had shut himself off from everything, making this the excuse, when all the while he'd known—and clearly so did everyone else—that he was hiding out, licking his wounds.

Well, no more.

'Hey, where are you going?' Marco's voice trailed into his back.

'To get back in the game. To get on with my life. To get my woman.'

'I'd get yourself some kevlar first, buddy. Or a suit of armour. I don't think she's going to just roll over for you.'

Dante dusted his hands together. He stared out across the yard. The sun was fiery and sinking fast. There were about a million chores to be done before he hit the sack. But all of it could wait. There was nothing more important than this.

'This really is the most spectacular view of the bay,' said Lady Vivienne, lowering her tiny white binoculars, squinting at the scene and then raising them again. 'What a lot of fabulous yachts. One could quite easily stay here all day and not become bored.'

Lucie replaced her cup in its saucer, where it rested on her knee. She looked to where her mother was pointing, registering that there were indeed a lot more gleaming white yachts in the bay than even an hour ago.

'Do you think they're all here for Simon's wedding?'

A swell of something close to nausea threatened to burst into her throat, but Lucie was well prepared now, and immediately wiggled her toes and tuned in her attention. It was remarkable just how easily she was able to control those impulses now. They still happened— they probably always would—but the dedicated sessions she'd had with a psychologist meant she was much more in control now. Thank heavens.

'I think there's every chance, Mother. You have invited nearly everyone in possession of a yacht, after all.'

'Not *everyone*,' her mother replied archly. 'Your father, for one. And that awful—'

'That's enough!' said Lucie sharply, before her mother could say another word. She placed the cup and saucer on the breakfast table and stood up, slowly and deliberately dusting the crumbs from her linen dress. She had only been sitting on the balcony of this Majorcan cliffside hotel with her mother for an hour, and already it was as crumpled and stretched as her nerves.

Her mother gave a little sniff and turned back to the bay. 'I must say you're incredibly short-tempered these days, Lucinda. I don't think all that conservation nonsense is doing you any good at all.'

Lucie gripped the railing a little more tightly than necessary and stared out across the immaculate view of the Mediterranean. The water was flat as sheet glass. The sun was halfway up in a cloudless sky. The air was light and bright. It was a beautiful day for her brother to be married, and nothing—not even her mother's fractious moods—was going to ruin it.

'We've been through this twice already, but I don't mind saying it all over again—just so we're clear.'

She turned, leaned back on the railing and waited until her mother had lowered her glass of orange juice.

'My decisions are none of your business. My job at the CCC, my choice of friends, the colour of my nail varnish—none of those or anything else is up for discussion.'

Lady Vivienne sniffed a little more and raised her glass to her lips.

'Is that quite clear, Mother?'

'You've no need to be quite so brutal about it.'

'Yes, I do. And until you stop interfering *brutal* is exactly what to expect.'

'I won't say another word,' said her mother, raising

her eyebrows and tottering over on ridiculously high heels to join her.

'Let's not spoil Simon's day, hmm? God knows he's had a lot of growing up to do these past months,' said Lucie. 'Surely we can hold it together for him for one day?'

'Well, he should have thought of that before the Brigadier caught him with his daughter and we ended up footing the bill for this wedding. But I agree. You're right. As always.'

'The last thing he needs is any more worry or upset.'

Hadn't there been enough of that? she thought. Just as she'd been about to drag herself from her burrow in Petit Pierre she'd had to field another barrage of calls from her mother about this. But she'd crossed the Rubicon by then. And no amount of whining from the other side of the Atlantic would have made her budge. Her mother had to learn to step back and let Simon sort out his own mess. Which he had. Admirably!

They both turned to stare out at the bay, which was lined with criss-crosses of berthed yachts near the shore, and further out to where two huge vessels had now dropped anchor.

'Oh, I say! I'm sure I recognise that one,' said Lady Viv, lifting the binoculars to her eyes and straining forward. 'What's that flag? Blue and white. Isn't that the Argentine flag? And the name. The *Sea Devil*...'

'What? What did you say? Give me those!'

Lucie's stomach whirled. She grabbed the binoculars from her mother. Pushed them against her eyes and tried desperately to see those beloved words amongst all the sparkling white fibreglass of the yacht.

'Is that his? That polo player? Is *that* whose boat it is?'

Lucie's stomach continued to churn and her heart began to race. She scanned the yacht. There were people on it. Male, female, uniformed, casual... Walking up and down the decks, cleaning, prepping, lounging... But none of them was him. There was no sign of the tall, strong, handsome man of her heart and her dreams. Where could he be? Below? In that beautiful bedroom? Staring out at the bay? How awful if he was here with a new girlfriend. She couldn't stand it. After all she had been through, simply hearing his name was too much most days. Thinking of him with anyone else was a place she wasn't ready to travel to.

'Yes, it's the *Sea Devil*. It's Dante's yacht,' she whispered, hardly believing her eyes, hardly aware she had just said his name. 'But he's not there. I can't see him.'

'That's because he's here, Princess.'

She dropped the binoculars. She spun around. She took two paces. He stood framed in the French doors, beside the table scattered with crockery, glasses and food where they'd just breakfasted.

He was wearing a white shirt and a wary smile.

He looked at her with those eyes that startled her with their intensity in that face that winded her with its male beauty.

'Who is this, Lucie?'

Lady Viv, like a wisp of smoke, appeared at her side.

'My name is Dante Salvatore Vidal Hermida. I apologise for the interruption, but I'm here to speak to Lucie.'

His eyes never left hers.

'Did you know about this, Lucie?'

'Excuse us, Mother.'

They waited, immobile, until the clicking of heels faded and the French doors were firmly closed.

'I didn't contact you.'

She swallowed, her mind running over all the possibilities.

'I know.'

'I got lost, Lucie. I've been lost. For years.'

She gazed into his earnest face, so familiar, yet so new.

'I'm sorry. For what I did. For how I treated you. I have so much to say to you.'

She nodded. A huge swell, a tidal wave of emotion, suddenly bloomed from her heart, choking her. Her eyes burned and her throat opened on a single sob. How long had she held herself together, waiting for this moment? She clutched her arms around her body, hugging herself tightly in case part of her flew away.

'My angel. I love you. Can you forgive me?'

He walked towards her, then stopped a pace away. His face was grave, his cheeks hollow, his eyes sincere. He held his arms at his sides, palms open, as if he was offering his heart in the only way he could. And she knew she could take it or leave it. That knowledge alone unleashed her last ounce of control.

'I don't know, Dante. You hurt me more than anyone has ever hurt me. You denied me. You denied *us*.'

His eyes clenched shut at that. A shadow of pain crossed his face.

'I know. And I've lived with that since the moment you left. It will live with me for ever—unless you give me another chance.'

She looked at him—her protector, her defender, her healer. The man to whom she'd given herself—on every level. But he was damaged. He was cold. Her heart had been trampled once. Letting him back into her life was so, so risky. She couldn't have more of those times—she had barely survived this one.

She glanced away from his penetrating gaze to the railing and the bay beyond. Wedding guests were arriving—there and in the town. Preparations would already be underway here in the hotel.

'My brother is getting married today,' she said simply. 'I woke up this morning hoping that I might feel some happiness, some joy when I watched him with his bride.' She shook her head. 'Of all the people to be married— but it does seem to be the right thing…for both of them.'

'I want to marry *you*, Lucie. I want all of you—only you. No one else.'

She smiled as her throat closed over another sob. She couldn't answer. It was too huge. It was too soon.

'Did you sail here?' was all she said.

He swallowed, looked away. 'No. Flew. But the *Sea Devil* wasn't far, and I told the crew to get her here by today.'

There was a noise from inside—the muffled sound of something falling on the tiled floor—Dante glanced behind him.

'How has it been with your mother? Did you get stuff sorted?'

She nodded. 'Dante…' She clasped her hands in an entreaty. 'I waited for this moment. Months. I prayed that you would come. Or call. Or text. Anything. And you were completely silent. You knew how I felt. Yet you offered me not a single crumb of comfort.'

'I will apologise until my dying day for hurting you. But I didn't know how I felt—how to feel, even. I was so determined to get back to the life I knew—and to build the foundation with Marco—I couldn't let myself go there. I didn't know I even *could* go there. I've never felt like this—it's like a sickness, Lucie, not having you in my life.'

In the village square a clock sounded the half-hour. Lucie looked past Dante's shoulder. Shapes and shadows moved behind the glass. She should be getting ready now, her mother, but no doubt she was hovering indoors, behind a twitching curtain.

'Dante, my brother is about to get married. My mother is having kittens in there…'

'I don't give a damn about any of them. I only care about *us*!' he thundered.

'No, you only give a damn about *you*!' she thundered back. 'Did you care when I was pleading with you in New York? When I literally begged you to give us a chance? *No*. But you turn up here now, ready to lay out the cloths of heaven at my feet. Back then you wouldn't even give me the lint from your pocket.'

His eyes widened in surprise.

'Did you *really* think after what you did that you would click your fingers and I'd come running? Do you understand what you did to me?'

She stepped forward now, her anger stoked.

'You built me up. You gave me confidence to be myself—with you, and with other people. You actually made me believe in myself, and believe that I had something valuable to offer. That I was more than just Lady Vivienne's awkward daughter.'

'And you *are*,' he said quietly. 'Way more. You're a wonderful woman. You're everything to me. I'm only sorry it took me this long to say these words to you.'

'You built me up and then you threw me down. You treated me worse than my mother ever did. Because she's oblivious. But you *knew* what you were doing. And as long as you got out without anything sticking that was all that mattered.'

He closed his eyes, screwed them up, and though it hurt her to see it, she'd had to say it—had to tell him straight.

'I'll spend the rest of my life making it up to you,' he said.

And when she looked again into those eyes the blue blazed with an honesty, an integrity that she felt deep within. There was no mask. There was no façade. There was nothing but the living, breathing truth and goodness and beauty of this man.

As if a rock had rolled away from her path, as if the day had suddenly brightened with colours she had never seen, as if her whole life had fallen into place, she realised that her future was right here in this moment—ripe and ready for her to make a choice.

'And how do you propose to do that?' she said, unable to disguise the softening in her voice.

He smiled, and a tiny hint of a single dimple appeared. 'Are you leading the witness with that question?'

She smiled too, trying to hold her emotions inside as joy began a sing-song chorus from within.

'Would you object if I was?'

His smile deepened. His eyes crinkled. She saw two dimples. He stepped closer. And then he kneeled before her.

Lucie's hand flew to her chest as she gasped.

'Princess—Lucie. Love of my life. Will you marry me? Will you promise never to leave me? Will you let me love you and cherish you for ever? Because I will.'

Her head began to nod, her eyes began to stream, and

the words she had never dared imagine she would say sang from her lips.

'I will. Oh, yes, I will.'

He stood, scooped her into his arms. He kissed her long and hard, and with every fibre of her being she kissed him back, loved him back.

Her eyes found his, her body melted into his, and her world righted itself on its axis.

'Your mother should be told. Before we go to this wedding.'

'She should, yes. Shall we...?'

With one final kiss he scooped her under his arm and turned them around. Their outline was one form against the beautiful clear day. And above them the hot, bright summer sun spilled light across the bay.

* * * * *

If you enjoyed this first part of Bella Frances's
CLAIMED BY A BILLIONAIRE *duet,*
look out for the second instalment

THE ITALIAN'S VENGEFUL SEDUCTION
Available May 2017!

MILLS & BOON®
MODERN™

POWER, PASSION AND IRRESISTIBLE TEMPTATION

MILLS & BOON®

EXCLUSIVE EXTRACT

Persuading plain Jane to marry him was easy
enough – but Shiekh Zayed Al Zawba hadn't
bargained on the irresistible curves hidden under
her clothes, or that she is deliciously untouched.
When Jane begins to tempt him beyond his
wildest dreams, leaving their marriage
unconsummated becomes impossible…

Read on for a sneak preview of
THE SHEIKH'S BOUGHT WIFE

It was difficult to be *distant* when your body seemed to
have developed a stubborn will of its own. When she found
herself wanting to push her aching breasts against Zayed's
powerful chest as he caught her in his arms for the traditional first dance between bride and groom. As it was, she
could barely think straight and wasn't it the most infuriating
thing in the world that he immediately seemed to pick up
on that?

'You seem to be having trouble breathing, dear wife,'
he murmured as he moved her to the center of the marble
dance floor.

'The dress is very tight.'

'I'd noticed.' He twirled her around, holding her back
a little. 'It looks very well on you.'

She forced a tight smile but she didn't relax. 'Thank you.'

'Or maybe it is the excitement of having me this close
to you which is making you pant like a little kitten?'

'You're *annoying* me, rather than exciting me. And I do
wish you'd stop trying to get underneath my skin.'

'Don't you like people getting underneath your skin, Jane?'

'No,' she said honestly. 'I don't.'

'Why not?'

She met the blaze of his ebony eyes and suppressed a shiver. 'Does everything have to have a reason?'

'In my experience, yes.' There was a pause. 'Has a man hurt you in the past?'

This was her chance to tell him yes—even though the very idea that someone had got that close to her was laughable.

Zayed had already guessed she might be a virgin, but that didn't even come close to her shameful lack of experience.

Trying to ignore the way his groin was brushing against her as he edged her closer, she glanced up at him, her cheeks burning. 'I refuse to answer that on the grounds that I might incriminate myself. Tell me instead, do you always insist on interrogating women when you're dancing with them?'

'No. I don't,' he said simply. 'But then I've never had a bride before and I've never danced with a woman who was so determined not to give anything of herself away.'

'And that's the only reason you want to know,' she said quietly. 'Because you like a challenge.'

'All men like a challenge, Jane.' His black eyes gleamed. 'Haven't you learned that by now?'

She didn't answer—because how was she qualified to answer any questions about what men did or didn't like?

Don't miss
THE SHEIKH'S BOUGHT WIFE
By Sharon Kendrick

Available May 2017
www.millsandboon.co.uk